THE COMPLETE
VOORKAMER STORIES

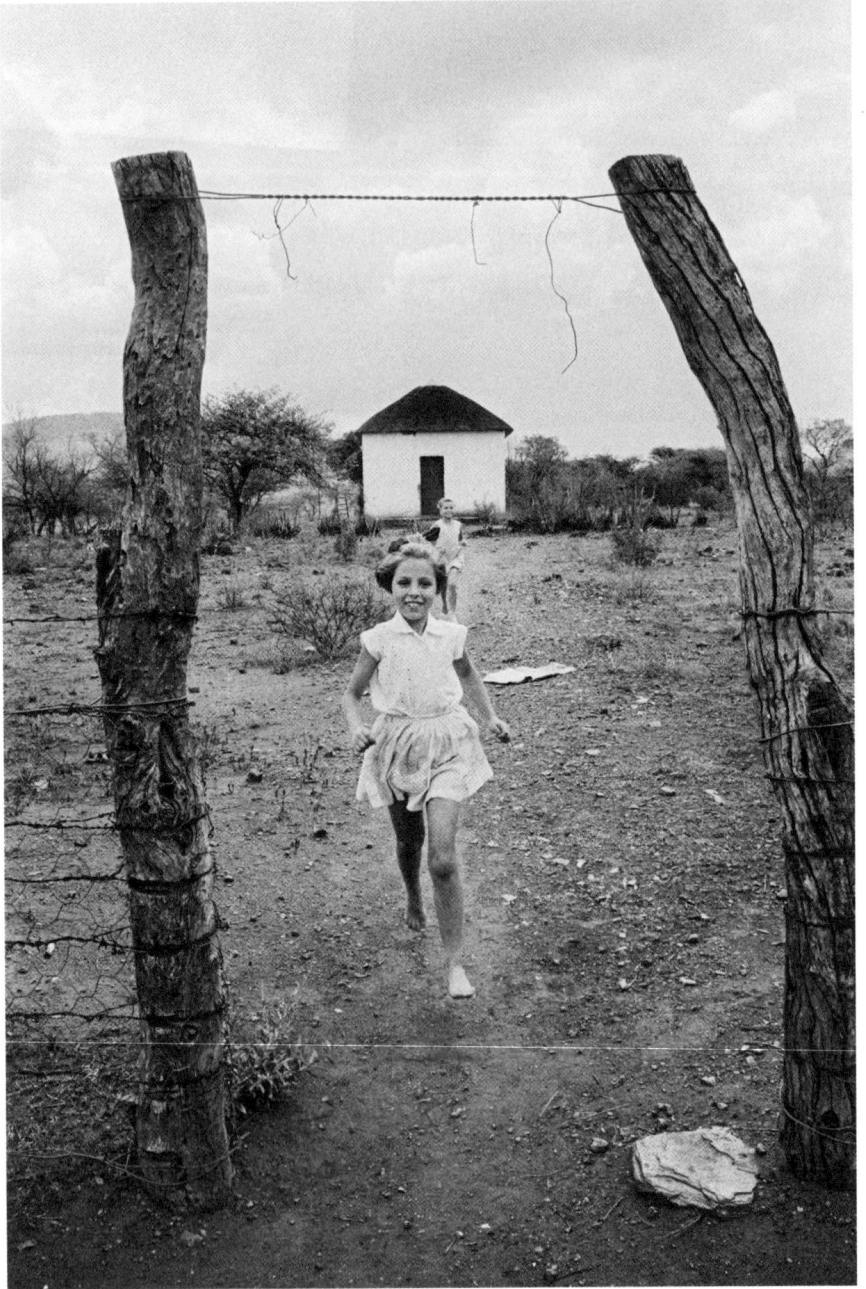

HERMAN CHARLES BOSMAN

THE COMPLETE VOORKAMER STORIES

Edited by

Craig MacKenzie

With a Bushveld Portfolio by

David Goldblatt

HUMAN & ROUSSEAU

Cape Town Pretoria

Acknowledgments: This volume draws substantially on
the Anniversary Edition of Bosman's works that Stephen Gray and I
undertook between 1997 and 2005, the centenary year of Bosman's birth.
My grateful thanks are extended to my co-editor, both for his assistance with
the Voorkamer collections I edited for the Anniversary Edition and, more particularly,
for advice here. I wish also to record my thanks to David Goldblatt for so
graciously giving up his time to pore over his bushveld
collection with me. – C. M.

First published in this form in 2011 by Human & Rousseau,
an imprint of NB Publishers,
40 Heerengracht, Cape Town, 8001
Cover image and photographs in the
text © David Goldblatt 2011
Cover photograph by David Goldblatt:
*The remains of Jurie Prinsloo's post office and voorkamer,
between Nietverdiend and Abjaterskop at the side of the
"Government road" to Bechuanaland (Botswana). 1964*
Frontispiece photograph by David Goldblatt:
*The barn in which Herman Charles Bosman and John
Callaghan taught school. The Haasbroek farm,
Heimweeberg, Nietverdiend. 1964*
Cover design and typography by Chérie Collins
Set in 10.5 on 12.75 pt Palatino
Printed and bound by Interpak Books, Pietermaritzburg

ISBN   978-0-7981-5298-3
Epub   978-0-9781-5595-3

Contents

Preface 9

I

THE BUDGET 19
A BEKKERSDAL MARATHON 25
PSYCHO-ANALYSIS 30
SECRET AGENT 36
BULL-CALF 41
LOCAL COLOUR 46
GHOST TROUBLE 51
OOM TOBIE'S SICKNESS 57

II

NEWS STORY 65
SCHOOL CONCERT 70
RAILWAY DEPUTATION 79
WHITE ANT 83
PIET SIENER 88
POTCHEFSTROOM WILLOW 92
SEA-COLONELS ALL 96

III

IDLE TALK 103
BIRTH CERTIFICATE 108
PLAY WITHIN A PLAY 113

SPRINGTIME IN MARICO   117
THE COFFEE THAT TASTED LIKE TAR   121
STARS IN THEIR COURSES   125
GREEN-EYED MONSTER   130
CASUAL CONVERSATION   135
THE CALL OF THE ROAD   139
LATH AND PLASTER   143
DO PROFESSORS SMOKE DAGGA?   147
ART CRITICISM   151

IV

PART OF A STORY   157
HOME FROM FINISHING-SCHOOL   162
SINGULAR EVENTS   167
YOUNG MAN IN LOVE   172
DREAMS OF RAIN   177
ILL-INFORMED CRITICISM   182
TOYS IN THE SHOP WINDOW   187
. . . AT THIS TIME OF YEAR   193
NEW-YEAR GLAD RAGS   199

V

GO-SLOW STRIKE   207
BLACK MAGIC   212
LAUGH, CLOWN, LAUGH   218
ANXIOUS TO HEAR   224
DAY OF WRATH   231
LANGUAGE OF FLOWERS   237
DIVINITY STUDENT   244
SLEEPY AFTERNOON   249
ALARM CLOCK   255
CIRCUMSTANTIAL EVIDENCE   261
LITERARY GIANTS   267
ALCOHOLIC REMORSE   273

VI

THE TERROR OF THE MOLOPO 281
BORDER BAD MAN 287
KITH AND KIN 293
ROLLED GOLD 299
HOME TOWN 304
MONUMENT TO A HERO 309
COFFIN IN THE LOFT 314
DETECTIVE STORY 319
WONDER WOMAN OF WINDHOEK 324
THE RECLUSE 329
THE UGLY TALE OF A PRETTY WIDOW 335
EAVESDROPPER 341
FAILING SIGHT 347

VII

SIXES AND SEVENS 355
MENTAL TROUBLE 360
MAN TO MAN 365
FEAT OF MEMORY 371
EASY CIRCUMSTANCES 376
WEATHER PROPHET 382
LOST CITY 388
MOTHER-IN-LAW 394
FIVE-POUND NOTES 400
FORBIDDEN COUNTRY 406
AT EASE ON THE DUNG HEAP 412

VIII

NO SPOON-FEEDING 421
BEKKERSDAL CENTENARY 427
DYING RACE 433
IN THE OLD DAYS 439
NEIGHBOURLY 445
MARICO MAN 450
HOMECOMING 456

PREFACE

In April 1950, just eighteen months before his death, Herman Charles Bosman embarked on one of his most ambitious projects: a series of 2 000-word stories written to a weekly deadline for Johannesburg's *The Forum*. It is testimony to his manic creative drive that he was able to produce eighty of these pieces in all, over a period of eighteen months without a single break, until his sudden death from cardiac arrest in October 1951.

In Die Voorkamer

The Forum, April 15, 1950

THE BUDGET

By HERMAN CHARLES BOSMAN

WE were sitting in Jurie Steyn's voorkamer at Drogevlei, waiting for the Government lorry from Bekkersdal, that brought us our letters and empty milk-cans. Jurie Steyn's voorkamer had served as the Drogevlei post office for some years, and Jurie Steyn was postmaster. His complaint was that the post office didn't pay. It didn't pay him, he said, to be called away from his lands every time somebody came in for a penny stamp.

This is the first of a series of humorous sketches—in Die Voorkamer — by the well-known South African writer, Herman Charles Bosman. Mr. Bosman's personae are a set of Bushveld neighbours who foregather in a voorkamer which doubles as local post office.

MEANWHILE, Oupa Sarel Bekker, who was one of the oldest inhabitants of the Marico and had known Bekkersdal before it was even a properly measured-out farm, started taking part in the conversation. But because Oupa Bekker was slightly deaf, and a bit queer in the head through advancing years, he thought we were saying that Jurie Steyn had been running along the main road, carrying a letter in a cleft stick. Accordingly, Oupa Bekker warned Jurie Steyn to be careful of mambas. The kloof was full of brown mambas at that time of year, Oupa Bekker said.

The series was clearly intended to provide a comic counterpoint to the more sober political commentary and opinion-pieces that constituted the staple of *The Forum*, and it is typical of Bosman that he chose to locate his "forum" in a narrow, backveld setting. In the bushveld meeting-place of Jurie Steyn's voorkamer, also the Drogevlei post office, local farmers gather under the pretext of waiting for the Government lorry bearing their letters and empty milk-cans from Bekkersdal.

The "Government lorry" at Frik Loubser's place near Nietverdiend. December 1964

Usually prompted by At Naudé, they offer their weekly Marico perspective on topical subjects. The pattern of the pieces is typically a desultory, meandering conversation sparked off by an item of news (a marathon dancing competition, atomic testing, the appointment of General Douglas MacArthur to the supreme command in South Korea, a race classification mix-up), an event in the district (the return of a pretty girl from finishing-school in the Cape, the annual school concert, a stranger arriving on the Government lorry), or a perennial topic (ghosts, white ants, bank managers). Various voices, almost entirely in direct or reported speech, take up the thread of chat, usually turning it in a different direction and often having fun needling or duping one of the present company.

The pieces are more accurately described as "conversation pieces" or "sketches" rather than "short stories" in that they are often less formal and seldom have a strong narrative line. Like Bosman's famous Oom Schalk Lourens stories, however, the Voorkamer pieces are firmly rooted in the medium of the spoken word. The sequence can in fact be seen to be a further development of Bosman's preoccupation with oral narrative modes, his fascination with *telling* stories. This time, in the place of a single storyteller figure through whom the entire narrative is filtered, we have a set of speakers – the habitués of Jurie Steyn's voorkamer.

Apart from Jurie Steyn himself, puffed up with his new role as postmaster, we usually encounter Gysbert van Tonder, cattle-smuggler and hostile neighbour of Jurie's; Chris Welman, the Dopper from the Eastern Cape who prides himself on his singing abilities, and who was once a "white labourer" digging foundations in Johannesburg; At Naudé, avid radio-listener and the chief purveyor of news; young "Meneer" Vermaak, the earnest schoolmaster who is remorselessly baited by the others; Johnny Coen, the most romantically inclined of the backveld rustics; and Oupa Sarel Bekker, their elder statesman, who bears a distinct resemblance to Schalk Lourens. Conveying all of this to the reader is an anonymous narrator, memorably described by Gillian Siebert as "a transparent minutes secretary of the eternal, inconclusive voorkamer debates" (*New Nation*, June, 1972).

These Marico denizens are situated a generation after Oom Schalk Lourens and his Boer War comrades in the 1920s. The unbounded liberties of frontier life have gradually been fenced in by outside agencies – legislating bodies in Pretoria, border police patrols, the Land Bank. The ox-wagon and mule-cart of Oom Schalk's day have been supplanted by the Government lorry that runs between Bekkersdal and Groblersdal, delivering visitors and gossip from the outside world into the heart of the Marico.

Bekkersdal, we learn near the end of the sequence, is named after Oupa Bekker's grandfather; both it and Groblersdal have been relocated by Bosman to the Dwarsberg and are not to be confused with the present-day places. Jurie Steyn's post office, however, is modelled on the one run by Jurie Prinsloo on the Nietverdiend–Abjaterskop road, photographed by David Goldblatt in a ruined state in 1964 (featured on the cover of this book).

At Naudé's "wireless" also brings the outside world to the reluctant farmers' doorstep, and, resist though they might (indeed, they cussedly

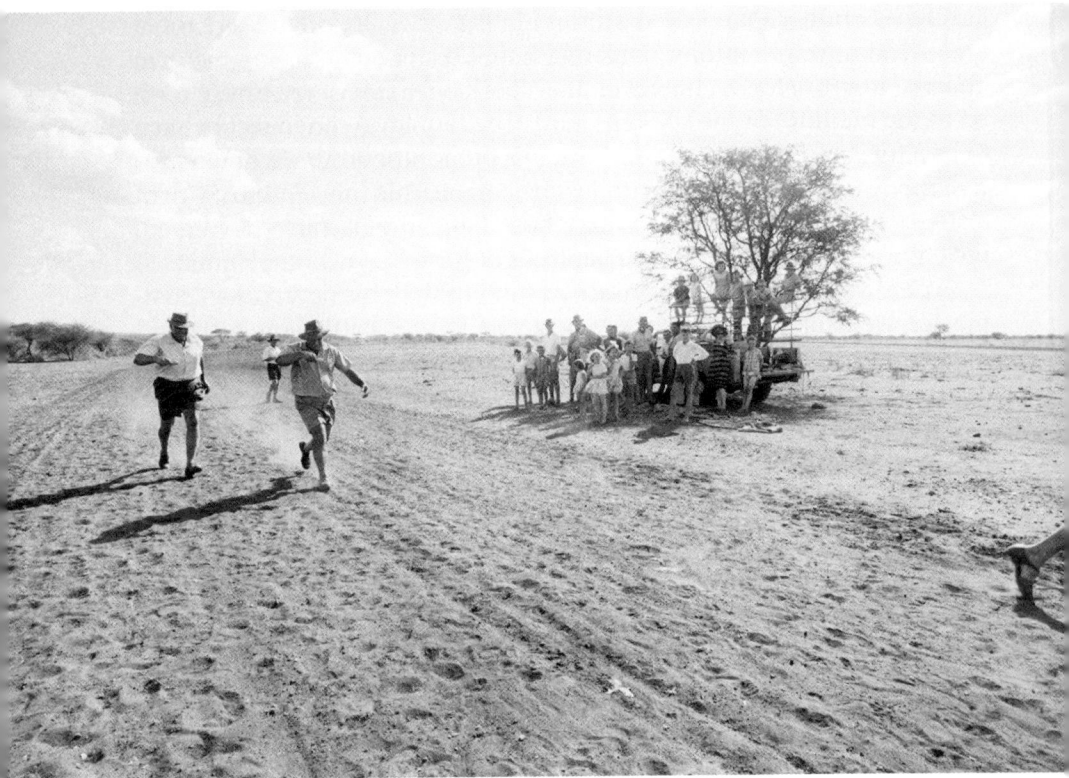

Egg and spoon race of the Dwarsberg Boerevereniging's Boeresport, in the seventh year of drought. 31 December 1965

ignore At Naudé's recycled bulletins), their world, with all the glamour of the open veld life, is steadily and irrevocably being encroached upon. Where the "rooinek" in *Mafeking Road* came with a laden ox-wagon and the desire to settle, people pass in and out of this world on a regular basis; there are even seasonal tourists. The lure of the big cities is proving irresistible: Johnny Coen pines for a Marico lass who has gone to the bad in Johannesburg; Chris Welman's son, Tobie, has spent some years at a reform school there; their representative in Pretoria visits them only at election time . . . This is becoming a forgotten world, containing people increasingly marginalised by developments elsewhere. Impoverished and abandoned, but obstinately resisting the inevitable, these farmers gather to pit their homely wisdom against all innovations. Indeed, a great deal of the humour of the pieces lies in the way these wiseacres attempt to fit such novelties into their limited frames of reference.

Oom Schalk's romantic world may be fading away, but now we have Oupa Bekker to recall that era for us with his stories about how news was conveyed "in the old days", how the freebooting republics of Goshen (which they pronounce Goosen), Stellaland and Ohrigstad (of which he was apparently Finance Minister) were run, and what the Transvaal was like in the days when Potchefstroom was its capital. Where Schalk Lourens had oracular status in this society, however, Oupa Bekker is more of a deaf and doddery museum-piece. Like Schalk, he can still catch his listeners out with a twist in the narrative, but whereas Schalk had a ready circle agape for the unexpected, Oupa Bekker's interlocutors resist his increasingly demented tales of "die ou dae", and head him off on more than one occasion.

These farmers are disillusioned and disgruntled, and they no longer want to hear Oupa Bekker's tales of better times. Their alienation from the soil is particularly evident in "Local Colour", in which a writer coming to the district for local lore and folk-wisdom leaves dismayed at the farmers' unrelenting literalness and lack of interest in the hazy wonders of nature. The story humorously registers their deracination: there is no romance left, it seems, just a harsh, grinding struggle for survival. Bosman's self-irony is present in this story as well, in the figure of the writer looking for the kind of rural romance about which only leisured city-dwellers have illusions. It is also present in the portraits of the young schoolmasters Charlie Rossouw and Vermaak, sent out, as Bosman himself once was, to educate the rustics – and receiving an education from them instead.

Oupa Bekker and At Naudé are rivals for the attention of the voorkamer audience, as they represent two different, and opposed, worldviews. Perversely, Bosman often has Oupa Bekker winning this battle. Unlike At Naudé, Oupa Bekker still heeds Schalk Lourens's dicta concerning the telling of a tale: how fast to go, when to mention certain details and what to leave out. At Naudé's news is like the modern world itself that threatens this isolated region: fragmented, diverse and discordant, it brings little solace to the marginalised men in the voorkamer and they often wilfully misunderstand At Naudé as a form of retribution. Scornfully pushing aside his information about "stone-

Tant Nellie Haasbroek and her grandson. Tant Nellie was Bosman's landlady. Heimwee-berg. 1964

throwings in Johannesburg locations and about how many new kinds of bombs the Russians had got", they are more interested in whether it "was true that the ouderling at Pilanesberg really forgot himself in the way that Jurie Steyn's wife had heard about from a kraal Mtosa at the kitchen door . . . Now, there was news for you" ("News Story").

Bosman situates Jurie Steyn's voorkamer at the boundary between the old and the new. This is suggested by the room itself: it is simultaneously an old-world waiting room, where guests are served coffee while passing the time of day in leisurely loquacity, and an actual post office, rather poorly equipped but nevertheless the sorting-house of information and communication. Jurie Steyn may loyally hang his stamps to dry on the wall when the leaky roof lets in the rain, and he may take great pride in his brass scales and new wire-netting, but once modern developments reach the Marico in earnest, he too will be superseded. The institution of Jurie Steyn's post office is on the brink of passing away, and with it the last vestiges of its old-world charm.

This volume is intended to capture some of this charm, with Bosman's classic Voorkamer stories presented here in their entirety and original sequence, enhanced by David Goldblatt's 1960s Marico portraits, which have been used as visual lead-ins to the various story-clusters.

The closing item here, "Homecoming" (which, appropriately, deals with the return of a disillusioned Marico native to his home district), was also the last piece Bosman wrote. Uncannily, as if the writer were attempting a trickster's last twist, it appeared on the Friday just after his death. The concluding piece to this volume thus contains Bosman's last contribution to the literary culture of a country he loved deeply and captured with such enduring vitality. It represents his final homecoming.

Craig MacKenzie
Johannesburg, 2011

I

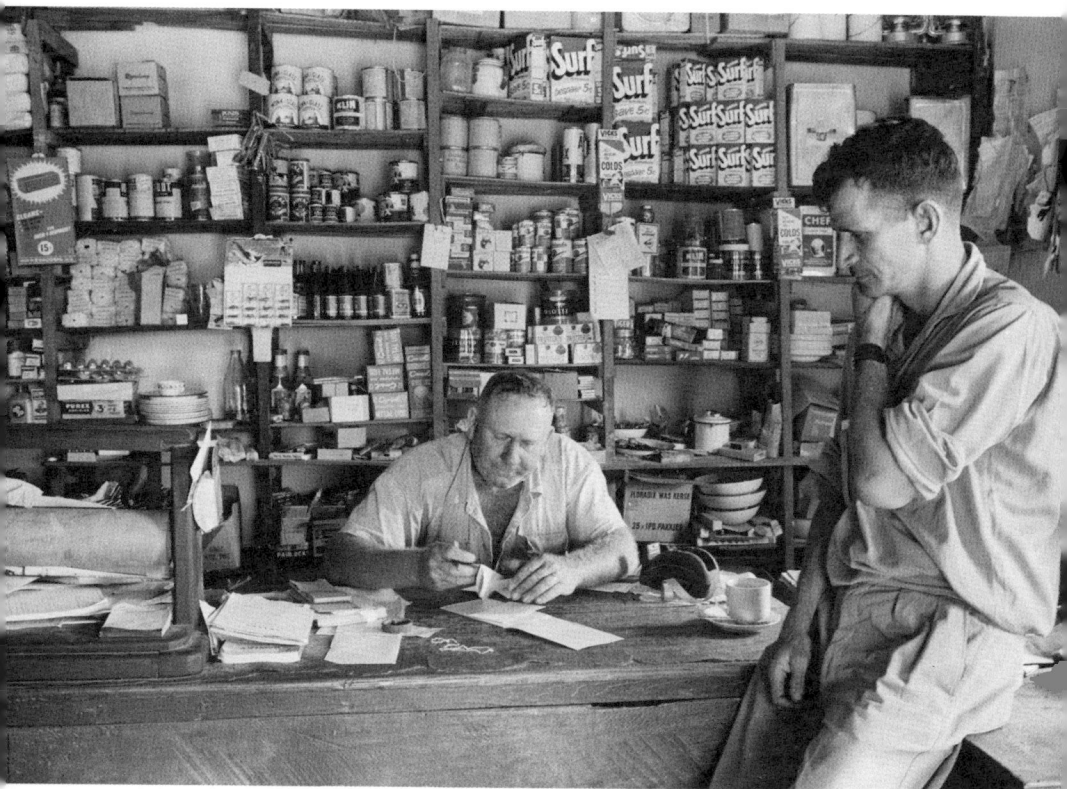

Frik Loubser (behind the counter of his shop and post office) and the driver of the "Government lorry". Near Nietverdiend. December 1964

THE BUDGET

We were sitting in Jurie Steyn's voorkamer at Drogevlei, waiting for the Government lorry from Bekkersdal, which brought us our letters and empty milk-cans. Jurie Steyn's voorkamer had served as the Drogevlei post office for some years, and Jurie Steyn was postmaster. His complaint was that the post office didn't pay. It didn't pay him, he said, to be called away from his lands every time somebody came in for a penny stamp. What was more, Gysbert van Tonder could walk right into his voorkamer whenever he liked, and without knocking. Gysbert was Jurie Steyn's neighbour, and Jurie had naturally not been on friendly terms with him since the time Gysbert van Tonder got a justice of the peace and a land-surveyor and a policeman riding a skimmel horse to explain to Jurie Steyn on what side of the vlei the boundary fence ran.

What gave Jurie Steyn some measure of satisfaction, he said, was the fact that his post office couldn't pay the Government, either.

"Maybe it will pay better now," At Naudé said. "Now that you can charge more for the stamps, I mean."

At Naudé had a wireless, and was therefore always first with the news. Moreover, At Naudé made that remark with a slight sneer.

Now, Jurie Steyn is funny in that way. He doesn't mind what he himself says about his post office. But he doesn't care much for the ill-informed kind of comment that he sometimes gets from people who don't know how exacting a postmaster's duties are. I can still remember some of the things Jurie Steyn said to a stranger who dropped in one day for a half-crown postal order, when Jurie had been busy with the cream separator. The stranger spoke of the buttermilk smudges on the postal order, which made the ink run in a blue blotch when he tried to fill it in. It was then that Jurie Steyn asked the stranger if he thought Marico buttermilk wasn't good enough for him, and what he thought he could get for half a crown. Jurie Steyn also started coming from behind the counter, so that he could explain better to the stranger what a man could get in the Bushveld for considerably less than half a crown. Unfortunately, the stranger couldn't wait to hear. He said that he had left his engine running when he came into the post office.

From that it would appear that he was not such a complete stranger to the ways of the Groot Marico.

With regard to At Naudé's remark now, however, we could see that Jurie Steyn would have preferred to let it pass. He took out a thick book with black covers and started ticking off lists with a pencil in an important sort of a way. But all the time we could sense the bitterness against At Naudé that was welling up inside him. When the pencil-point broke, Jurie Steyn couldn't stand it anymore.

"Anyway, At," he said, "even twopence a half-ounce is cheaper than getting a Mchopi runner to carry a letter in a long stick with a cleft in the end. But, of course, you wouldn't understand about things like progress."

Jurie Steyn shouldn't have said that. Immediately three or four of us wanted to start talking at the same time.

"Cheaper, maybe," Johnny Coen said, "but not better, or quicker – or – or – *cleaner* –" Johnny Coen almost choked with laughter. He thought he was being very clever.

Meanwhile, Chris Welman was trying to tell a story we had heard from him often before about a letter that was posted at Christmas time in Volksrust and arrived at its destination, Magoeba's Kloof, twenty-eight years later, and on Dingaan's Day.

"If a native runner took twenty-eight years to get from Volksrust to Magoeba's Kloof," Chris Welman said, "we would have known that he didn't run much. He must at least have stopped once or twice at huts along the way for kaffir beer."

Meanwhile, Oupa Sarel Bekker, who was one of the oldest inhabitants of the Marico and had known Bekkersdal before it was even a properly measured-out farm, started taking part in the conversation. But because Oupa Bekker was slightly deaf, and a bit queer in the head through advancing years, he thought we were saying that Jurie Steyn had been running along the main road, carrying a letter in a cleft stick. Accordingly, Oupa Bekker warned Jurie Steyn to be careful of mambas. The kloof was full of brown mambas at that time of year, Oupa Bekker said.

"All the same, in the days of the Republics you would not get a white man doing a thing like that," Oupa Bekker went on, shaking his head. "Not even in the Republic of Goosen. And not even after the Republic of Goosen's Minister of Finance had lost all the State revenues in an unfortunate game of poker that he had been invited to take part in at the Mafeking Hotel. And there was quite a big surplus, too, that year, which the Minister of Finance kept tucked away in an inside pocket right through the poker game, and which he could still remember having had on him when he went into the bar. Although he could never remember what happened to that surplus afterwards. The Minister of Finance never went back to Goosen, of course. He stayed on in Mafeking. When I saw him again he was offering to help carry people's luggage from the Zeederberg coach station to the hotel."

Oupa Bekker was getting ready to say a lot more, when Jurie Steyn interrupted him, demanding to know what all that had got to do with his post office.

"I said that even when things were very bad in the old days, you would still never see a white postmaster running in the sun with a letter in a cleft stick," Oupa Bekker explained, adding, "like a Mchopi."

Jurie Steyn's wife did not want any unpleasantness. So she came and sat on the riempies bench next to Oupa Bekker and made it clear to him, in a friendly sort of way, what the discussion was all about.

"You see, Oupa," Jurie Steyn's wife said finally, after a pause for breath, "that's just what we have been *saying*. We've been saying that in the old days, before they had proper post offices, people used to send letters with Mchopi runners."

"But that's what I've been saying also," Oupa Bekker persisted. "I say, why doesn't Jurie rather go in his mule-cart?"

Jurie Steyn's wife gave it up after that. Especially when Jurie Steyn himself walked over to where Oupa Bekker was sitting.

"You know, Oupa," Jurie said, talking very quietly, "you have been an ouderling for many years, and we all respect you in the Groot Marico. We also respect your grey hairs. But you must not lose that respect through – through talking about things that you don't understand."

Oupa Bekker tightened his grip on his tamboetie-wood walking-stick.

"Now if you had spoken to me like that in the Republican days, Jurie Steyn," the old man said, in a cracked voice. "In the Republic of Stellaland, for instance –"

"You and your republics, Oupa," Jurie Steyn said, giving up the argument and turning back to the counter. "Goosen, Stellaland, Lydenburg – I suppose you were also in the Ohrigstad Republic?"

Oupa Bekker sat up very stiffly on the riempies bench, then.

"In the Ohrigstad Republic," he declared, and in his eyes there gleamed for a moment a light as from a great past, "in the Republic of Ohrigstad I had the honour to be the Minister of Finance."

"Honour," Jurie Steyn repeated, sarcastically, but yet not speaking loud enough for Oupa Bekker to hear. "I wonder how *he* lost the money in the State's skatkis. Playing snakes and ladders, I suppose."

All the same, there were those of us who were much interested in Oupa Bekker's statement. Johnny Coen moved his chair closer to Oupa Bekker, then. Even though Ohrigstad had been only a small republic, and hadn't lasted very long, still there was something about the sound of the words "Minister of Finance" that could not but awaken in us a sense of awe.

"I hope you deposited the State revenues in the Reserve Bank, in a proper manner," At Naudé said, winking at us, but impressed all the same.

"There was no Reserve Bank in those days," Oupa Bekker said, "or any other kind of banks either, in the Republic of Ohrigstad. No, I just kept the national treasury in a stocking under my mattress. It was the safest place, of course."

Johnny Coen put the next question.

"What was the most difficult part of being Finance Minister, Oupa?" he asked. "I suppose it was making the budget balance?"

"Money was the hardest thing," Oupa Bekker said, sighing.

"It still is," Chris Welman interjected. "You don't need to have been a Finance Minister, either, to know that."

"But, of course, it wasn't as bad as today," Oupa Bekker went on. "Being Minister of Finance, I mean. For instance, we didn't need to worry about finding money for education, because there just wasn't any, of course."

Jurie Steyn coughed in a significant kind of way, then, but Oupa Bekker ignored him.

"I don't think," he went on, "that we would have stood for education in the Ohrigstad Republic. We knew we were better off without it. And then there was no need to spend money on railways and harbours, because there weren't any, either. Or hospitals. We lived a healthy life in those days, except maybe for lions. And if you died from a lion, there wasn't much of you left over that could be *taken* to a hospital. Of course, we had to spend a good bit of money on defence, in those days. Gunpowder and lead, and oil to make the springs of our Ou-Sannas work more smoothly. You see, we were expecting trouble any day from Paul Kruger and the Doppers. But it was hard for me to know how to work out a popular budget, especially as there were only seventeen income-tax payers in the whole of the Republic. I thought of imposing a tax on the President's state coach, even. I found that that suggestion was very popular with the income-tax paying group. But you have no idea how much it annoyed the President.

"I imposed all sorts of taxes afterwards, which nobody would have to pay. These taxes didn't bring in much in the way of money, of course. But they were very popular, all the same. And I can still remember how popular my budget was, the year I put a very heavy tax on opium. I had heard somewhere about an opium tax. Naturally, of course, I did not expect this tax to bring in a penny. But I knew how glad the burghers of the Ohrigstad Republic would be, each one of them, to think that there was a tax that they escaped. In the end I had to repeal the tax on opium, however. That was when one of our seventeen income-tax payers threatened to emigrate to the Cape. This income-tax payer had a yellowish complexion and sloping eyes, and ran the only laundry in the Ohrigstad Republic."

Oupa Bekker was still talking about the measures he introduced to counteract inflation in the early days of the Republic of Ohrigstad, when the lorry from Bekkersdal arrived in a cloud of dust. The next few minutes were taken up with a hurried sorting of letters and packages, all of which proceeded to the background noises of clanking milk-cans. Oupa Bekker left when the lorry arrived, since he was expecting neither correspondence nor a milk-can. The lorry-driver and his assistant seated themselves on the riempies bench which the old man had vacated. Jurie Steyn's wife brought them in coffee.

"You know," Jurie Steyn said to Chris Welman, in between putting sealing wax on a letter he was getting ready for the mailbag. "I often wonder what is going to happen to Oupa Bekker – such an old man and all, and still such a liar. All that Finance Minister rubbish of his. How they ever appointed him an ouderling in the church, I don't know. For one thing, I mean, he couldn't have been *born*, at the time of the Ohrigstad Republic." Jurie reflected for a few moments. "Or could he?"

"I don't know," Chris Welman answered truthfully.

A little later the lorry-driver and his assistant departed. We heard them putting water in the radiator. Some time afterwards we heard them starting up the engine, noisily, the driver swearing quite a lot to himself.

It was when the lorry had already started to move off that Jurie Steyn remembered about the registered letter on which he had put the seals. He grabbed up the letter and was over the counter in a single bound.

Chris Welman and I followed him to the door. We watched Jurie Steyn for a considerable distance, streaking along in the sun behind the lorry and shouting and waving the letter in front of him, and jumping over thorn-bushes.

"Just like a Mchopi runner," I heard Chris Welman say.

A Bekkersdal Marathon

At Naudé, who had a wireless set, came into Jurie Steyn's voor-kamer, where we were sitting waiting for the railway lorry from Bekkersdal, and gave us the latest news. He said that the newest thing in Europe was that young people there were going in for non-stop dancing. It was called marathon dancing, At Naudé told us, and those young people were trying to break the record for who could remain on their feet longest, dancing.

We listened for a while to what At Naudé had to say, and then we suddenly remembered a marathon event that had taken place in the little dorp of Bekkersdal – almost in our midst, you could say. What was more, there were quite a number of us sitting in Jurie Steyn's post office who had actually taken part in that non-stop affair, and without know-ing that we were breaking records, and without expecting any sort of a prize for it, either.

We discussed that affair at considerable length and from all angles, and we were still talking about it when the lorry came. And we agreed that it had been in several respects an unusual occurrence. We also agreed that it was questionable if we could have carried off things so successfully that day, if it had not been for Billy Robertse.

You see, our organist at Bekkersdal was Billy Robertse. He had once been a sailor and had come to the Bushveld some years before, travelling on foot. His belongings, fastened in a red handkerchief, were slung over his shoulder on a stick. Billy Robertse was journeying in that fashion for the sake of his health. He suffered from an unfortunate complaint for which he had at regular intervals to drink something out of a black bottle that he always carried handy in his jacket pocket.

Billy Robertse would even keep that bottle beside him in the or-ganist's gallery in case of a sudden attack. And if the hymn the predi-kant gave out had many verses, you could be sure that about halfway through Billy Robertse would bring the bottle up to his mouth, leaning sideways towards what was in it. And he would put several extra twirls into the second part of the hymn.

When he first applied for the position of organist in the Bekkersdal church, Billy Robertse told the meeting of deacons that he had learnt to play the organ in a cathedral in Northern Europe. Several deacons felt, then, that they could not favour his application. They said that the cathedral sounded too Papist, the way Billy Robertse described it, with a dome 300 feet high and with marble apostles. But it was lucky for Billy Robertse that he was able to mention, at the following combined meeting of elders and deacons, that he had also played the piano in a South American dance hall, of which the manager was a Presbyterian. He asked the meeting to overlook his unfortunate past, saying that he had had a hard life, and anybody could make mistakes. In any case, he had never cared much for the Romish atmosphere of the cathedral, he said, and had been happier in the dance hall.

In the end, Billy Robertse got the appointment. But in his sermons for several Sundays after that the predikant, Dominee Welthagen, spoke very strongly against the evils of dance halls. He described those places of awful sin in such burning words that at least one young man went to see Billy Robertse, privately, with a view to taking lessons in playing the piano.

But Billy Robertse was a good musician. And he took a deep interest in his work. And he said that when he sat down on the organist's stool behind the pulpit, and his fingers were flying over the keyboards, and he was pulling out the stops, and his feet were pressing down the notes that sent the deep bass tones through the pipes – then he felt that he could play all day, he said.

I don't suppose he guessed that he would one day be put to the test, however.

It all happened through Dominee Welthagen one Sunday morning going into a trance in the pulpit. And we did not realise that he was in a trance. It was an illness that overtook him in a strange and sudden fashion.

At each service the predikant, after reading a passage from the Bible, would lean forward with his hand on the pulpit rail and give out the number of the hymn we had to sing. For years his manner of conducting the service had been exactly the same. He would say, for instance: "We will now sing Psalm 82, verses 1 to 4." Then he would allow his head to sink forward onto his chest and he would remain rigid, as though in prayer, until the last notes of the hymn died away in the church.

Now, on that particular morning, just after he had announced the number of the psalm, without mentioning what verses, Dominee Welthagen again took a firm grip on the pulpit rail and allowed his head to sink forward onto his breast. We did not realise that he had fallen into a trance of a peculiar character that kept his body standing upright while his mind was a blank. We learnt that only later.

In the meantime, while the organ was playing the opening bars, we began to realise that Dominee Welthagen had not indicated how many verses we had to sing. But he would discover his mistake, we thought, after we had been singing for a few minutes.

All the same, one or two of the younger members of the congregation did titter, slightly, when they took up their hymn-books. For Dominee Welthagen had given out Psalm 119. And everybody knows that Psalm 119 has 176 verses.

This was a church service that will never be forgotten in Bekkersdal.

We sang the first verse and then the second and then the third. When we got to about the sixth verse and the minister still gave no sign that it would be the last, we assumed that he wished us to sing the first eight verses. For, if you open your hymn-book, you'll see that Psalm 119 is divided into sets of eight verses, each ending with the word "Pouse."

We ended the last notes of verse eight with more than an ordinary number of turns and twirls, confident that at any moment Dominee Welthagen would raise his head and let us know that we could sing "Amen."

It was when the organ started up very slowly and solemnly with the music for verse nine that a real feeling of disquiet overcame the congregation. But, of course, we gave no sign of what went on in our minds. We held Dominee Welthagen in too much veneration.

Nevertheless, I would rather not say too much about our feelings, when verse followed verse and Pouse succeeded Pouse, and still Dominee Welthagen made no sign that we had sung long enough, or that there was anything unusual in what he was demanding of us.

After they had recovered from their first surprise, the members of the church council conducted themselves in a most exemplary manner. Elders and deacons tiptoed up and down the aisles, whispering words of reassurance to such members of the congregation, men as well as women, who gave signs of wanting to panic.

At one stage it looked as though we were going to have trouble from the organist. That was when Billy Robertse, at the end of the 34th verse, held up his black bottle and signalled quietly to the elders to indicate that his medicine was finished. At the end of the 35th verse he made signals of a less quiet character, and again at the end of the 36th verse. That was when Elder Landsman tiptoed out of the church and went round to the konsistorie, where the Nagmaal wine was kept. When Elder Landsman came back into the church he had a long black bottle half hidden under his manel. He took the bottle up to the organist's gallery, still walking on tiptoe.

At verse 61 there was almost a breakdown. That was when a message came from the back of the organ, where Koster Claassen and the assistant verger, whose task it was to turn the handle that kept the organ supplied with wind, were in a state near to exhaustion. So it was Deacon Cronjé's turn to go tiptoeing out of the church. Deacon Cronjé was head-warder at the local gaol. When he came back it was with three burly native convicts in striped jerseys, who also went through the church on tiptoe. They arrived just in time to take over the handle from Koster Claassen and the assistant verger.

At verse 98 the organist again started making signals about his medicine. Once more Elder Landsman went round to the konsistorie. This time he was accompanied by another elder and a deacon, and they stayed away somewhat longer than the time when Elder Landsman had gone on his own. On their return the deacon bumped into a small hymn-book table at the back of the church. Perhaps it was because the deacon was a fat, red-faced man, and not used to tiptoeing.

At verse 124 the organist signalled again, and the same three members of the church council filed out to the konsistorie, the deacon walking in front this time.

It was about then that the pastor of the Full Gospel Apostolic Faith Church, about whom Dominee Welthagen had in the past used almost as strong language as about the Pope, came up to the front gate of the church to see what was afoot. He lived near our church and, having heard the same hymn tune being played over and over for about eight hours, he was a very amazed man. Then he saw the door of the konsistorie open, and two elders and a deacon coming out, walking on tiptoe – they having apparently forgotten that they were not in church, then. When the pastor saw one of the elders hiding a black bottle under his manel, a look of understanding came over his features. The pastor walked off, shaking his head.

At verse 152 the organist signalled again. This time Elder Landsman and the other elder went out alone. The deacon stayed behind on the deacon's bench, apparently in deep thought. The organist signalled again, for the last time, at verse 169. So you can imagine how many visits the two elders made to the konsistorie altogether.

The last verse came, and the last line of the last verse. This time it had to be "Amen." Nothing could stop it. I would rather not describe the state that the congregation was in. And by then the three native convicts, red stripes and all, were, in the Bakhatla tongue, threatening mutiny. "Aa-m-e-e-n" came from what sounded like less than a score of voices, hoarse with singing.

The organ music ceased.

Maybe it was the sudden silence that at last brought Dominee Welthagen out of his long trance. He raised his head and looked slowly about him. His gaze travelled over his congregation and then, looking at the windows, he saw that it was night. We understood right away what was going on in Dominee Welthagen's mind. He thought he had just come into the pulpit, and that this was the beginning of the evening service. We realised that, during all the time we had been singing, the predikant had been in a state of unconsciousness.

Once again Dominee Welthagen took a firm grip of the pulpit rail. His head again started drooping forward onto his breast. But before he went into a trance for the second time, he gave out the hymn for the evening service. "We will," Dominee Welthagen announced, "sing Psalm 119."

Psycho-analysis

"Koos Nienaber got a letter from his daughter, Minnie, last week," Jurie Steyn announced to several of us sitting in his voorkamer that served as the Drogevlei post office. "It's two years now that she has been working in an office in Johannesburg. You wouldn't think it. Two years . . ."

"What was in the letter?" At Naudé asked, coming to the point.

"Well," Jurie Steyn began, "Minnie says that . . ."

Jurie Steyn was quick to sense our amusement.

"If that's how you carry on," he announced, "I won't tell you anything. I know what you are all thinking, laughing in that silly way. Well, just let one of you try and be postmaster, like me, in between milking and ploughing and getting the wrong statements from the creamery and the pigs rooting up the sweet-potatoes – not to talk about the calving season, even – and then see how much time you'll have left over for steaming open and reading other people's letters."

Johnny Coen, who was young and was more than a little interested in Minnie Nienaber, hastened to set Jurie Steyn's mind at rest.

"You know, we make the same sort of joke about every postmaster in the Bushveld," Johnny Coen said. "We don't mean anything by it. It's a very old joke. Now, if we were living in Johannesburg, like Minnie Nienaber, we might perhaps be able to think out some newer sort of things to say –"

"What we would say," At Naudé interrupted – At Naudé always being up-to-date, since he has a wireless and reads a newspaper every week – "What we would say is that you sublet your post office as a hideout for the Jeppe gang."

Naturally, we did not know what the Jeppe gang was. At Naudé took quite a long time to explain. When he had finished, Oupa Bekker, who is the oldest inhabitant of the Marico Bushveld, said that there seemed to him to be something spirited about the Jeppe gang, which reminded him a lot of his own youth in the Pilanesberg area of the Waterberg District. Oupa Bekker said that he had several times, lately, thought of visiting his youngest grand-daughter in Johannesburg. Maybe they could teach him a few things in Johannesburg, he said. And maybe, also, he could teach *them* a thing or two.

But all this talk was getting us away from Minnie Nienaber's letter. And once again it was Johnny Coen that brought the subject round to Jurie Steyn's first remark.

"It must be that Koos Nienaber told you what was in his daughter's letter," Johnny Coen said. "Koos Nienaber must have come round here and told you. Otherwise you would never have known, I mean. You couldn't *possibly* have known."

That was what had happened, Jurie Steyn acknowledged. He went on to say that he was grateful to Johnny Coen for not harbouring those unworthy suspicions against him that were sometimes entertained by people living in the Groot Marico who did not have Johnny Coen's advantages of education and worldly experience. We knew that he just said that to flatter Johnny Coen, who had once been a railway shunter at Ottoshoop.

Thereupon Jurie Steyn acquainted us in detail with the contents of Minnie Nienaber's letter, as retailed to him by her father, Koos Nienaber.

"Koos said that Minnie has been," Jurie Steyn said, "has been – well, just a minute – oh, yes, here it is – I got old Koos Nienaber to write it down for me – she's been psycho – psycho-analysed. Here it is, written down and all – 'sielsontleding'."

I won't deny that we were all much impressed. It was something that we had never heard of before. Jurie Steyn saw the effect his statement had made on us.

"Yes," he repeated, sure of himself – and more sure of the word, too, now –"yes, in the gold-mining city of Johannesburg, Minnie Nienaber got psycho-analysed."

After a few moments of silence, Gysbert van Tonder made himself heard. Gysbert often spoke out of his turn, that way.

"Well, it's not the first time a thing like that happened to a girl living in Johannesburg on her own," Gysbert said. "One thing, the door of her parents' home will always remain open for her. But I am surprised at old Koos Nienaber mentioning it to you. He's usually so proud."

I noticed that Johnny Coen looked crestfallen for a moment, until Jurie Steyn made haste to explain that it didn't mean that at all.

According to what Koos Nienaber told him – Jurie Steyn said – it had become fashionable in Johannesburg for people to go and be attended to by a new sort of doctor, who didn't worry about how sick your body was, but saw to it that he got your mind right. This kind of doctor could straighten out anything that was wrong with your *mind*, Jurie Steyn explained. And you didn't have to be sick, even, to go along and get yourself treated by a doctor like that. It was a very fashionable thing to do, Jurie Steyn added.

Johnny Coen looked relieved.

"According to what Koos Nienaber told me," Jurie Steyn said, "this new kind of doctor doesn't test your heart anymore, by listening through that rubber tube thing. Instead, he just asks you what you dreamt last night. And then he works it all out with a dream-book. But it's not just an ordinary dream-book that says if you dreamt last night of a herd of cattle it means that there is a grave peril ahead for some person that you haven't met yet . . ."

"Well, I dreamt a couple of nights ago that I was driving a lot of Afrikander cattle across the Bechuanaland Protectorate border," Fritz Pretorius said. "Just like I have often done, on a night when there isn't much of a moon. Only, what was funny about my dream was that I dreamt I was smuggling cattle *into* the Protectorate, instead of out of it. Can you imagine a Marico farmer doing a foolish thing like that? I suppose this dream means I am going mad, or something."

After At Naudé had said how surprised he was that Fritz Pretorius should have to be told in a dream what everybody knew about him in any case – and after Fritz Pretorius's invitation to At Naudé to come and repeat that remark outside the post office had come to nothing – Jurie Steyn went on to explain further about what that new kind of treatment was that Minnie Nienaber was receiving from a new kind of doctor in Johannesburg, and that she had no need for.

"It's not the ordinary kind of dream-book, like that Napoleon dreambook on which my wife set so much store before we got married," Jurie Steyn continued, "but it's a dream-book written by professors. Minnie has been getting all sorts of fears, lately. Just silly sorts of fears, her father says. Nothing to worry about. I suppose anybody from the Groot Marico who has stayed in Johannesburg as long as Minnie Nienaber has done would get frightened in the same way. Only, what puzzles me is that it took her so long to start getting frightened . . ."

"Maybe she has also begun to listen in to the wireless, like At Naudé," Chris Welman said. "Maybe she has also started hearing things about the Jeppe gang. It's queer that she wasn't frightened like that, when she first went there. But I could have told her that Johannesburg was no place for a young girl. Why, you should have seen the Angus bull they awarded the Challenge Trophy to, the year I went down to the Agricultural Show with my Shorthorns. And they even tried to chase my fat cow, Vleisfontein III, out of the showgrounds. They said they thought it was some animal that had strayed in from across the railway line."

Thereupon At Naudé told us about a Rand Agricultural Show that *he* had attended. That was the year in which his Afrikander bull Doornboom IV, which he had fed on lucerne and turnips throughout the winter, was awarded the silver medal. An agricultural magazine even took a photograph of himself and of Doornboom IV, At Naudé said. But unfortunately, through some mistake that the printer made, the wrong words were printed under At Naudé's photograph. Instead of being called "Proud Owner", At Naudé was called "Silver Medal Pedigree Bull." He complained to the magazine about it, afterwards, At Naudé said, but the editor just wrote back to say that none of his readers had noticed anything wrong.

"That just shows you," At Naudé said to us – and even though it had happened a long time ago, he still sounded quite indignant – "and they couldn't possibly have thought that I looked like Doornboom IV, because that was the year I shaved off my moustache."

What annoyed him most of all, At Naudé added, was that it stated under his photograph that he had been fed on lucerne and turnips for the whole winter.

"It's very funny," Jurie Steyn said, just then, "but all this talk of yours fits in with what Minnie Nienaber said in her letter. That was the reason why, in the end, she decided to go along and get herself psycho-analysed. I mean, there was nothing wrong with her, of course. They say you have got to have nothing wrong with you, before you can get psycho-analysed. This new kind of doctor can't do anything for you if there is something the matter with you –"

"I don't know of any doctor that can do anything for you when there is something the matter with you," Oupa Bekker interrupted. "The last time I went to see a doctor was during the rinderpest. The doctor said I must wear a piece of leopard skin behind my left ear. That would keep the rinderpest away from my oxen, he said, and it would at the same time cure me of my rheumatism. The doctor only said that after he had thrown the bones for the second time. The first time he threw the bones the doctor said –"

But by that time we were all laughing very loudly. We didn't mean *that* kind of a doctor, we said to Oupa Bekker. We did not mean a Mshangaan witch-doctor. We meant a white doctor, who had been to a university, and all that.

Oupa Bekker was silent for a few moments.

"Perhaps you are right," he said at last. "Because all my cattle died of the rinderpest. Mind you, I have never had rheumatism since that time. Perhaps all that that witch-doctor *could* cure was rheumatism. From what Jurie Steyn tells us, I can see he was just old-fashioned. It seems that a doctor is of no use today, unless he can cure nothing at all. But I still say I don't think much of that doctor that threw the bones upward of fifty years ago. For I was more concerned about my cattle's rinderpest than about my own ailment. All the same, if you want a cure for rheumatism – there it is. A piece of leopard skin tied behind your left ear. The skin from just an ordinary piece of leopard."

With all this talk, it was quite a while before Jurie Steyn could get a word in. But what he had to say, then, was quite interesting.

"You don't seem to realise it," Jurie Steyn said, "but you have been talking all this while about Minnie Nienaber's symptoms. The reason why she went to get herself psycho-analysed, I mean. It was about those awful dreams she has been having of late. Chris Welman has mentioned his prize cow that got chased out of the Rand Show, and At Naudé has told us about his silver-medal bull, and Oupa Bekker has reminded us of the old days, when this part of the Marico was all leopard country. Well, that was Minnie Nienaber's trouble. That was why she went to that new kind of doctor. She had the most awful dreams – Koos Nienaber tells me. She dreamt of being ordered to leave places – night clubs, and so on, Koos Nienaber says. And she also used to dream regularly of being chased by wild bulls. And of being chased by Natal Indians with long sugar-cane knives. And latterly she had nightmares almost every night, through dreaming that she was being chased by a leopard. That was why, in the end, she went to have herself psycho-analysed."

We discussed Minnie Nienaber's troubles at some length. And we ended up by saying that we would like to know where the Afrikaner people would be today, if our women could run to a new sort of doctor, every time they dreamt of being chased by a wild animal. If Louis Trichardt's wife dreamt that she was being chased by a rhinoceros, we said, then she would jolly well have to escape from that rhinoceros in her dream. She would not be able to come to her husband with her dream-troubles next day, seeing that he already had so many Voortrekker problems on his mind.

Indeed, the whole discussion would have ended in quite a sensible and commonplace sort of fashion, were it not for the strange way in which Johnny Coen reacted.

"You know, Oupa Bekker," Johnny Coen said, "you spoke about going to Johannesburg. Well, you can come with me, if you like. I know you aren't really going to join the Jeppe gang. But I am going to look for Minnie Nienaber. Dreams and all that – I know it's just a lot of nonsense. But I feel somehow – I *know* that Minnie needs me."

SECRET AGENT

The stranger who arrived on the Government lorry from Bekkers-dal told us that his name was Losper. He was having a look round that part of the Marico, he said, and he did not expect to stay more than a few days. He was dressed in city clothes and carried a leather briefcase. But because he did not wear pointed black shoes and did not say how sad it was that Flip Prinsloo should have died so suddenly at the age of sixty-eight, of snakebite, we knew that he was not a life insurance agent. Furthermore, because he did not once seek to steer the conversation round to the sinful practices of some people who offered a man a quite substantial bribe when he was just carrying out his duty, we also knew that the stranger was not a plain-clothes man who had been sent round to investigate the increase in cattle-smuggling over the Conventie-lyn. Quite a number of us breathed more easily, then.

Nevertheless, we were naturally intrigued to know what Meneer Losper had come there for. But with the exception of Gysbert van Tonder – who did not have much manners since the time he had accompanied a couple of Americans on safari to the lower reaches of the Limpopo – we were all too polite to ask a man straight out what his business was, and then explain to him how he could do it better.

That trip with the two Americans influenced Gysbert van Tonder's mind, all right. For he came back talking very loudly. And he bought a waistcoat at the Indian store especially so that he could carry a cigar in it. And he spoke of himself as Gysbert O. van Tonder. And he once also slapped Dominee Welthagen on the back to express his appreciation of the Nagmaal sermon Dominee Welthagen had delivered on the Holy Patriarchs and the Prophets.

When Gysbert van Tonder came back from that journey, we understood how right the Voortrekker, Hendrik Potgieter, had been over a hundred years ago, when he said that the parts around the lower end of the Limpopo were no fit place for a white man.

We asked Gysbert van Tonder how that part of the country affected the two Americans. And he said he did not think it affected them *much*. But it was a queer sort of area, all round, Gysbert explained. And there was a lot of that back-slapping business, too. He said he could still remember how one of the Americans slapped Chief Umfutusu on the back and how Chief Umfutusu, in his turn, slapped the American on the ear with a clay pot full of greenish drink that the chief was holding in his hand at the time.

The American was very pleased about it, Gysbert van Tonder said, and he devoted a lot of space to it in his diary. The American classed Chief Umfutusu's action as among the less understood tribal customs that had to do with welcoming distinguished white travellers. Later on, when Gysbert van Tonder and the Americans came to a Mshangaan village that was having some trouble with hut tax, the American who kept the diary was able to write a lot more about what he called an obscure African ritual that that tribe observed in welcoming a superior order of stranger. For that whole Mshangaan village, men, women and children, had rushed out and pelted Gysbert and the two Americans with wet cow-dung.

In his diary the American compared this incident with the ceremonial greeting that a tribe of Bavendas once accorded the explorer Stanley, when they threw him backwards into a dam – to show respect, as Stanley explained, afterwards.

Well anyway, here was this stranger, Losper, a middle-aged man with a suitcase, sitting in the post office and asking Jurie Steyn if he could put him up in a spare room for a few days, while he had a look round.

"I'll pay the same rates as I paid in the boarding-house in Zeerust," Meneer Losper said. "Not that I think you might overcharge me, of course, but I am only allowed a fixed sum by the department for accommodation and travelling expenses."

"Look here, Neef Losper," Jurie Steyn said, "you didn't tell me your first name, so I can only call you Neef Losper –"

"My first name is Org," the stranger said.

"Well, then, Neef Org," Jurie Steyn went on. "From the way you talk I can see that you are unacquainted with the customs of the Groot Marico. In the first place, I am a postmaster and a farmer. I don't know which is the worst job, what with money orders and the blue-tongue. I have got to put axle-grease on my mule-cart and sealing wax on the mailbag. And sometimes I get mixed up. Any man in my position would. One day I'll paste a revenue stamp on my off-mule and I'll brand a half-moon and a bar on the Bekkersdal mailbag. Then there will be trouble. There will be trouble with my off-mule, I mean. The post office won't notice any difference. But my off-mule is funny, that way. He'll pull the mule-cart, all right. But then everything has got to be the way *he* wants it. He won't have people laughing at him because he's got a revenue stamp stuck on his behind. I sometimes think that my off-mule *knows* that a shilling revenue stamp is what you put on a piece of paper after you've told a justice of the peace a lot of lies –"

"Not lies," Gysbert van Tonder interjected.

"A lot of lies," Jurie Steyn went on, "about another man's cattle straying into a person's lucerne lands while that person was taking his sick child to Zeerust –"

Gysbert van Tonder, who was Jurie Steyn's neighbour, half rose out of his riempies chair, then, and made some sneering remarks about Jurie Steyn and his off-mule. He said he never had much time for either of them. And he said he would not like to describe the way his lucerne lands looked after Jurie Steyn's cattle had finished straying over them. He said he would not like to use that expression, because there was a stranger present.

Meneer Losper seemed interested, then, and sat well forward to listen. And it looked as though Gysbert van Tonder would have said the words, too. Only, At Naudé, who has a wireless to which he listens in regularly, put a stop to the argument. He said that this was a respectable voorkamer, with family portraits on the wall.

"And there's Jurie Steyn's wife in the kitchen, too," At Naudé said. "You can't use the same sort of language here as in the Volksraad, where there are all men."

Actually, Jurie Steyn's wife had gone out of the kitchen, about then. Ever since that young schoolmaster with the black hair parted in the middle had come to Bekkersdal, Jurie Steyn's wife had taken a good deal of interest in education matters. Consequently, when the stranger, Org Losper, said he was from the department, Jurie Steyn's wife thought right away – judging from his shifty appearance – that he might be a school inspector. And so sent a message to the young schoolmaster to warn him in time, so that he could put away the saws and hammers that he used for the private fretwork that he did in front of the class while the children were writing compositions.

In the meantime, Jurie Steyn was getting to the point.

"So you can't expect me to be running a boarding-house as well as everything else, Neef Org," he was saying. "But all the same, you are welcome to stay. And you can stay as long as you like. Only, you must not offer again to pay. If you had known more about these parts, you would also have known that the Groot Marico has got a very fine reputation for hospitality. When you come and stay with a man he gets insulted if you offer him money. But I shall be glad to invite you into my home as a member of my own family."

Then Org Losper said that that was exactly what he didn't want, anymore. And he was firm about it, too.

"When you're a member of the family, you can't say no to anything," he explained. "In the Pilanesberg I tore my best trousers on the wire. I was helping, as a member of the family, to round up the donkeys for the watercart. At Nietverdiend a Large White bit a piece out of my second-best trousers and my leg. That was when I was a member of the family and was helping to carry buckets of swill to the pig troughs. The farmer said the Large White was just being playful that day. Well, maybe the Large White thought I was also a member of the family – *his* family, I mean. At Abjaterskop I nearly fell into a disused mineshaft on a farm there. Then I was a member of the family, assisting to throw a dead bull down the shaft. The bull had died of anthrax and I was helping to pull him by one haunch and I was walking backwards and when I jumped away from the opening of the mineshaft it was almost too late.

"I can also tell you what happened to me in the Dwarsberge when I was also a member of the family. And also about what happened when I was a member of the family at Derdepoort. I did not know that that family was having a misunderstanding with the family next door about water rights. And it was when I was opening a water furrow with a shovel that a load of buckshot went through my hat. As a member of the family, I was standing ankle-deep in the mud at the time, and so I couldn't run very fast. So you see, when I say I would rather pay, it is not that I am ignorant of the very fine tradition that the Marico has for the friendly and bountiful entertainment that it accords the stranger. But I do not wish to presume further on your kindness. If I have much more Bushveld hospitality I might never see my wife and children again. It's all very well being a member of somebody else's family. But I have a duty to my *own* family. I want to get back to them alive."

Johnny Coen remarked that next time Gysbert van Tonder had an American tourist on his hands, he need not take him to the Limpopo, but could just show him around the Marico farms.

It was then that Gysbert van Tonder asked Org Losper straight out what his business was. And, to our surprise, the stranger was very frank about it.

"It is a new job that has been made for me by the Department of Defence," Org Losper said. "There wasn't that post before. You see, I worked very hard at the last elections, getting people's names taken off the electoral roll. You have no idea how many names I got taken off. I even got some of our candidate's supporters crossed off. But you know how it is, we all make mistakes. It is a very secret post. It is a top Defence secret. I am under oath not to disclose anything about it. But I am free to tell you that I am making certain investigations on behalf of the Department of Defence. I am trying to find out *whether something has been seen here*. But, of course, the post has been made for me, if you understand what I mean."

We said we understood, all right. And we also knew that, since he was under oath about it, the nature of Org Losper's investigations in the Groot Marico would leak out sooner or later.

As it happened, we found out within the next couple of days. A Mahalapi who worked for Adriaan Geel told us. And then we realised how difficult Org Losper's work was. And we no longer envied him his Government job – even though it had been especially created for him.

If you know the Mtosas, you'll understand why Org Losper's job was so hard. For instance, there was only one member of the whole Mtosa tribe who had ever had any close contact with white men. And he had unfortunately grown up among Trekboers, whose last piece of crockery that they had brought with them from the Cape had got broken almost a generation earlier.

We felt that the Department of Defence could have made an easier job for Org Losper than to send him round asking those questions of the Mtosas, they who did not even know what ordinary kitchen saucers were, leave alone flying ones.

BULL-CALF

The Government lorry from Bekkersdal was late. Jurie Steyn had several times come from behind his post office counter and had stood at the front door, gazing in the direction of the poort.

"How am I going to get through the milking?" he asked in an aggrieved tone, cupping a hand over his eyes some more and staring across the kameeldorings. "I've had these mailbags ready and everything since early this morning – before the cattle went out of the kraal, even."

Johnny Coen looked at the untidy bundles on the counter and his lip curled.

"Next time you make up the mailbags in the kraal, you should perhaps wait until the cattle have gone out," Johnny Coen said. "Then they wouldn't walk over the mailbags . . . Or was it pigs?"

To our surprise, Jurie Steyn did not take offence.

"I really do believe, sometimes," he replied, thoughtfully, "that it would be better if I did go and do my post office work in the stable. I get no peace here, in the voorkamer. It is that Duusman. He's been chewing the mailbags again. It's a habit I despise in him. But that's the worst of rearing a bull-calf by hand. I've sometimes thought I'll just *give* Duusman the voorkamer and I'll move into the stable. That's at least one place that Duusman never goes into, anyway. He won't be seen in a stable – not him. He's much too stuck-up."

Gysbert van Tonder said that that showed you how intelligent a handraised bull-calf like Duusman could be. To be able to tell the difference between Jurie Steyn's voorkamer and a stable. Many a human being would hardly know the difference, even. Not at first glance, that was, Gysbert explained.

Now, although he was always saying things to Duusman's detriment, Jurie Steyn was secretly very proud of his hansbul, and he really

41

thought that Duusman was different from any other bull-calf in the Marico that had been brought up by hand. And so Jurie Steyn felt not a little flattered at Gysbert van Tonder's remark.

"I won't say Duusman hasn't got brains," Jurie Steyn acknowledged, modestly, "if only he'll use them in the right way."

We could not help feeling that, with those words, Jurie Steyn would like us to think that he himself had brains – just because he had brought Duusman up by hand.

In the meantime, Oupa Bekker had been nodding his head up and down.

"It's all very well rearing a calf or a goat or a sheep by hand," he announced, "but you mustn't also *educate* him. The moment a bull-calf gets educated above his station in life, he's got no more respect for you. He doesn't seem to understand that, just because you're older than he is, you must know more."

"I wouldn't say that's always the case, Oupa," Johnny Coen said. "I mean, it's not just only age. There are also other things that broaden the mind – like travel, say."

We knew, of course, that Johnny Coen was referring to the time he was working on the railways at Ottoshoop.

"Well, I wouldn't object if Duusman took it into his head to travel a bit," Jurie Steyn asserted. "It would do him good. He'll soon find out that it's not every hand-raised bull-calf that has got as good a home as he has. And he's so inconsiderate. After he's been loafing about the vlei all morning, Duusman will never think of wiping the clay from between his hooves before he comes walking into the voorkamer for his dish of kaboe-mealies. That's a hand-raised bull-calf all over. But it's my wife that spoilt him, of course. I knew right from the start that no good could come from her feeding him in the voorkamer. 'Give Duusman his lunch in the kitchen, Truitjie,' I used to say to my wife from the very beginning. 'Then, later on, when he's more grown up, he'll be used to coming round to the back door for his meals. If Duusman gets into the habit of walking in at the front door he'll start having ideas about himself before he's much older. You watch if I'm not right.' But she wouldn't listen to me. Now you see what's happening. I'm only looking forward to the day when Duusman will have grown so wide and fat that he won't be able to come in through the door of the voorkamer anymore."

That was the moment when Oupa Bekker giggled. It was a disturbing sort of sound. Oupa Bekker was, after all, somebody aged and respected. Except when he said silly things – such as when he said that he could make quite a good living even if mealies were only ten shillings a bag, never mind the new price of twenty-four shillings. Then we knew that he was just aged.

And the way Oupa Bekker giggled now was not pleasant. Even At Naudé looked unhappy. And At Naudé had a wireless set and had heard some queer noises coming over it in his time – and not merely as a result of his not having been properly tuned in, by any means. There was the time, for instance, when he invited several of us to come and listen in to what he informed us was an opera being broadcast, and right through, at intervals, At Naudé said, "Yes, I know what you kêrels think. You think it's the atmospherics."

"What I want to say is," Oupa Bekker remarked, after his laughter had set over into coughing and Chris Welman had slapped – some of us thought punched – the old man vigorously on the back, "if you think that will be the end of your trouble with a bull-calf that you've reared by hand –"

Oupa Bekker gave signs of wanting to laugh again. But he stopped himself in time. That was when he saw Chris Welman, with a determined look in his eye, making a move to get out of his chair for the second time.

Oupa Bekker pulled himself together, then.

Before that, I had noticed a strained look on Chris Welman's face. He did not seem to be himself, somehow. Chris Welman seemed to be taking it much too seriously, this nonsense that was being talked about Jurie Steyn's bull-calf.

"You say your wife has spoilt Duusman, Jurie?" Oupa Bekker asked.

"Completely," Jurie Steyn admitted.

Oupa Bekker looked thoughtful.

"But you don't think," he asked, "that you might also perhaps have had a hand in spoiling him? Think carefully, now."

"Well," Jurie said, somewhat reluctantly, "a little, maybe."

That seemed to be the sum of what Oupa Bekker wanted to know. In any case, he said nothing more. That made us all feel uncomfortable. It was a good deal worse than when he giggled in that annoying old-man sort of way, that was not much different from an old woman's giggle. But now he remained silent. And you couldn't go and thump an old man on his back just for keeping quiet. At least, in public you couldn't. Not when people were looking.

"Duusman chew?" Oupa Bekker asked.

"Chew – how do you mean, chew?" Jurie Steyn repeated. We could see he was hedging.

"Tobacco," Oupa Bekker insisted, firmly.

"Well," Jurie Steyn said, "he does come in every morning for a plug of Piet Retief rolled tobacco. It started as a joke, of course. But, all right, if you put it that way, Duusman does chew. But he spits most of it out again. I started him off on the habit. It seemed funny to me, the idea of a bull-calf chewing. But he's got into the habit, now. It seemed funny at the time, if you understand what I mean. But now, well, I think Duusman will burst the doorframe down if he doesn't get his chew every morning –"

"And you blame it on your wife," Oupa Bekker said. And he started laughing again. And even when his laughter went up into very high notes he did not bother to look round to see how Chris Welman was taking it.

It was almost as though Oupa Bekker knew that Chris Welman would not slam him on the back again, even if Oupa Bekker's laughter ended in his coughing his head off.

"You yourself can't stop chewing tobacco, no matter how hard you try – can you, now?" Oupa Bekker remarked to Jurie. "I know I can't. And all I've got left are a few top teeth that aren't near as good as yours or Duusman's."

When Jurie Steyn did not answer, Oupa Bekker said that he should send Duusman to the butcher's shop. But he did not think that Duusman would make even good butcher's meat, Oupa Bekker added.

Well, we all knew, of course, that if you had once reared a bull-calf by hand, you could never send him to the butcher's shop, even if the land company were foreclosing on you.

It was a relief to us all when the lorry arrived in dust and noise and with milk-cans and circulars from shopkeepers.

But we should have felt more surprised, somehow, when, along with the driver and his assistant, there also alighted from the lorry young Tobie, Chris Welman's son, who had gone to Johannesburg and whom we had not seen for several years.

Tobie Welman was slim and good-looking, and he walked with a light step, and his black hair was slicked back from his forehead, and a cigarette dangled from his lip.

And when Chris Welman walked out to meet Tobie, as though he had been expecting him, we wondered why he had not told us that his son was coming back. We would, after all, not have said anything about Tobie Welman having been in reform school.

Duusman forced his way into the voorkamer, about then, lowing. "Moo," Duusman said.

Local Colour

We were talking about the book-writing man, Gabriel Penzhorn, who was in the Marico on a visit, wearing a white helmet above his spectacles and with a notebook and a fountain pen below his spectacles. He had come to the Marico to get local colour and atmosphere, he said, for his new South African novel. What was wrong with his last novel, it would seem, was that it did not have enough local colour and atmosphere in it.

So we told Penzhorn that the best place for him to get atmosphere in these parts was in that kloof other side Lobatse, where that gas came out from. Only last term the schoolteacher had taken the children there, and he had explained to them about the wonders of Nature. We said to Gabriel Penzhorn that there was atmosphere for him, all right. In fact, the schoolmaster had told the children that there was a whole gaseous envelope of it. Penzhorn could even collect some of it in a glass jar, with a piece of rubber tubing on it, like the schoolmaster had done.

And as for local colour, well, we said, there was that stretch of blue bush on this side of Abjaterskop, which we called the bloubos. It wasn't really blue, we said, but it only looked blue. All the same, it was the best piece of blue bush we had seen anywhere in the Northern Transvaal. The schoolmaster had brought a piece of that home with him also, we explained.

Gabriel Penzhorn made it clear, however, that that stretch of blue bush was not the sort of local colour he wanted at all. Nor was he much interested in the kind of atmosphere that he could go and collect in a bottle with a piece of rubber tubing, just from other side Lobatse.

From that we could see that Gabriel Penzhorn was particular. We did not blame him for it, of course. We realised that if it was things that a writer had to put into a book, then only the best could be good enough. Nevertheless, since most of us had been born in the Marico, and we took pride in our district, we could not help feeling just a little hurt.

"As far as I can see," Johnny Coen said to us one day in Jurie Steyn's post office, "what this book-writing man wants is not atmosphere, but stinks. Perhaps that's the sort of books he writes. I wonder. Have they got pictures in, does anybody know?"

But nobody knew.

"Well, if it's stinks that Penzhorn wants," Johnny Coen proceeded, "just let him go and stand on the siding at Ottoshoop when they open a truck of Bird Island guano. Phew! He won't even need a glass jar to collect that sort of atmosphere in. He can just hold his white helmet in his hand and let a few whiffs of guano atmosphere *float* into it. But if he puts a white helmetful of that kind of atmosphere into his next book, I think the police will have something to say."

Oupa Bekker looked reflective. At first we thought that he hadn't been following much of our conversation, since it was intellectual, having to do with books. We knew that Oupa Bekker had led more of an open-air sort of life, having lived in the Transvaal in the old days, when the Transvaal did not set much store on book learning. But to our surprise we found that Oupa Bekker could take part in a talk about culture as well as any of us. What was more, he did not give himself any airs on account of his having this accomplishment, either.

"Stinks?" Oupa Bekker enquired. "Stinks? Well, let me tell you. There never have been any stinks like the kind we had when we were running that tannery on the Molopo River in the rainy season, in the old days. We thought that the water of the Molopo that the flour-mill on the erf next to us didn't use for their water-wheel would be all right for us with our tannery. We didn't need running water. Just ordinary standing water was good enough for us. And when I say standing water, I mean standing. You have got no idea how it stood. And we didn't tan just plain ox-hides and sheepskins, but every kind of skin we could get. Tanning was our business, you understand. We tanned lion and zebra skins along with the elephant and rhinoceros hides. After a while the man who owned the flour-mill couldn't stand it any longer. So *he* moved higher up the river. And if I tell you that he was a Bulgarian and he couldn't stand it, that will possibly give you an idea of what that tannery smelt like. Then, one day, a farmer came from the Dwarsberge . . . Yes, they are still the same Dwarsberge, and they haven't changed much with the years. Only, to-day I can't see as far from the top of the Dwarsberge as I could when

I was young. And they look different, also, somehow, with that little whitewashed house no longer in the poort, and with Lettie Gouws no longer standing at the front gate, in an apron with blue squares."

Oupa Bekker paused and sighed. But it was quite a light sigh, that was not so much regret for the past as a tribute to the sweetness of vanished youth.

"Anyway," Oupa Bekker continued, "this farmer from the Dwarsberge brought us a wagon-load of polecat skins. You can imagine what that stink was like. Even before we started tanning them, I mean. Above the smell of the tannery we could smell that load of muishond when the wagon was still fording the drift at Steekgrasvlei. Bill Knoetze – that was my partner – and I felt that this was going slightly too far, even though we were in the tanning business. At first we tried to laugh it off, in the way that we have in the Marico. We tried to pretend to the farmer from the Dwarsberge when he came into the office that we thought it was *he* that stank like that. And we asked him if he couldn't do something about it. Like getting himself buried, say. But the farmer said no, it wasn't him. It was just his wagon. He made that statement after he had held out his hand for us to shake and Bill Knoetze, before taking the farmer's hand, had play-acted that he was going to faint. And it wasn't just all play-acting either. How he knew that there was something about his wagon, the farmer said, that was peculiar, was through his having passed mule-carts along the road. And he noticed that the mules shied.

"All the same, that was how we came to give up the first tanning business that had ever been set up along the Molopo. Bill Knoetze left after that wagon-load of polecat skins had been in the tanning fluid for about a fortnight. I left a week later. But just before that the Chief of the Mahalapis had come from T'lakieng to find out if we had koedoe leather that he wanted for veldskoens. And when he walked with us through the tannery the Chief of the Mahalapis sniffed the breeze several times, as though trying to make up his mind about something. In the end, the Chief said it would appear to him as though we had a flower garden somewhere near. And he asked could he take a bunch of asters back to his kraal with him for his youngest wife, who had been to mission school and liked such things. It was too dry at T'lakieng for geraniums, the Chief said."

Oupa Bekker was still talking when Gabriel Penzhorn walked into Jurie Steyn's voorkamer. He intended taking the lorry back to civilisation, Penzhorn explained to us. His stay in the Marico had been quite interesting, he said. He didn't say it with enthusiasm, however. And he added that he had not been able to write as many things in his notebook as he had hoped to.

"They all say the same thing," Gabriel Penzhorn proceeded. "I no sooner tell a farmer or his wife that I am a novelist and that I am looking for material to put into my next book, than he or she tells me – sometimes both of them together tell me – about the kind of book that they would write if *they* only had time; or if only they remembered to order some ink, next time they went to the Indian store at Ramoutsa."

He consulted his notes in a dispirited sort of way.

"Yes," Penzhorn went on, "the Indian store at Ramoutsa. Most of the farmers use also another word, I've noticed, in place of Indian. Now, what can one do with material like that? What I want to know are things about the veld. About the ways of the bush and the way the farmers think here . . . I've come to the conclusion that they don't think here."

At Naudé pulled Penzhorn up sharp, then. And he asked him, what with the white ants and galblaas, if he thought a farmer ever got time to think. And he asked him, with the controlled price of mealies 24s. a bag, instead of 24s 9d., as we had all expected, what he thought the Marico farmer had left to think *with?* By that time Fritz Pretorius was telling us, with a wild sort of laugh, about the last cheque he got from the creamery, and Hans van Tonder was saying things about those contour walls that the Agriculture Department man had suggested to stop soil erosion.

"The Agriculture Department man looks like a contour wall himself," Hans van Tonder said, "with those sticking up eyebrows."

Meanwhile, Jurie Steyn was stating, not in any spirit of bitterness, but just as a fact, the exact difference that the new increase in railway tariffs meant to the price of seven-and-a-half-inch piping.

Gabriel Penzhorn closed his notebook.

"I don't mean that sort of talk," he said. "Buying and selling. The low language of barter and the market-place. I can get that sort of talk from any produce merchant in Newtown. Or from any stockbroker I care to drop in on. But I don't care to. What I came here for was –"

That was the moment when Jurie Steyn's wife, having overheard part of our conversation, flounced in from the kitchen.

"And what about eggs?" she demanded. "If I showed you what I pay for bone-meal then you *would* have something to write in your little notebook. Why should there be all that difference between the retail price of eggs and the price I get? I tell you it's the middlem –"

"Veld lore," Gabriel Penzhorn interrupted, sounding quite savage, now. "That's what I came here for. But I can see you don't know what it is, or anything about it. I want to know about things like the red sky in the morning is the shepherd's warning. Morgen rood, plomp in die sloot. I want to know about how you can tell from the yellowing grass on the edge of a veld footpath that it is going to be an early winter. I want to know about when the tinktinkies fly low over the dam is it going to be a heavy downpour or a slow motreën. I want to know when the wren-warbler –"

"I know if the tinktinkies fly low over my dam, the next thing they'll be doing is sitting high up eating my cling-peaches in the orchard," At Naudé said. "And if that canning factory at Welgevonden ever thinks I'm going to deal with them again . . ."

In the meantime, Jurie Steyn's wife was talking about the time she changed her Leghorns from mealies and skim milk to a standard ration. They went into a six-month moult, Jurie Steyn's wife said.

When the lorry from Groblersdal arrived Hans van Tonder was feeling in his pockets to show us an account he had got only the other day for cement. And Gabriel Penzhorn, in a voice that was almost pathetic, was saying something, over and over again, about the red sky at night.

The driver told us afterwards that on the way back in the lorry Gabriel Penzhorn made a certain remark to him. If we did not know otherwise, we might perhaps have thought that Gabriel Penzhorn had overheard some of the earlier part of our conversation in the voorkamer that morning.

"The Marico," Gabriel Penzhorn said to the lorry-driver, "stinks."

GHOST TROUBLE

They were having ghost trouble again in the Spelonksdrift area, Chris Welman said to us when we were sitting in Jurie Steyn's post office. The worst kind of ghost trouble, Chris Welman added.

We could guess what that meant.

Everybody knew, of course, that Spelonksdrift was swarming with ghosts, any time after midnight. The ghosts came out of the caves in the Dwarsberge nearby. During the day it was quite all right. Then even the most difficult spectres would go and lie down in the hollowed-out places at the foot of the koppie and try and get some rest. But after dark they would make their way to the drift, dragging chains and carrying on generally. That much we all knew. I mean, there was not even a Mtosa cattle-herd so ignorant as willingly to venture near the drift after nightfall.

When it came to having to do with ghosts, a Mtosa could be almost as educated as a white man.

Again, with regard to ghosts, we still remember the time when the new schoolteacher, Charlie Rossouw, who was fresh from college, taught the Standard Five class, in the history lesson, about the Great Trek. He was talking about the Voortrekker leader, Lodewyk Loggenberg, and about the route his party took, and about the *Dagboek* that Lodewyk Loggenberg kept. The young schoolteacher said that he did not want his class to think of history as just names of persons that they had to remember, but that the Voortrekkers belonged to their own nation, and were people like their own fathers, say, or – if that was too unpleasant a thought – perhaps like their uncles. Or maybe even like the second cousins of their aunts' half-sisters by marriage. That young schoolteacher was very thorough in his way.

Then, drawing on the blackboard with a piece of chalk, Charlie Rossouw explained to the class that Lodewyk Loggenberg had passed through the Groot Marico with his wagons. "Perhaps the trek passed right in front of where this schoolhouse is today," the teacher said. "Maybe Lodewyk Loggenberg's long line of wagons, with voorryers and agterryers and with the Staats Bybel in the bok and with copper moulds from which to make candles six at a time after you fixed the wick in the middle, properly (I mean, you know the difference now between a form candle and a water candle: we did that last week) – maybe these Voortrekkers passed along right here, and the tracks that their wagon-wheels made over the veld were the beginning of what we today call the Government Road. Think of that. I wonder what Lodewyk Loggenberg wrote in his *Dagboek* when he went along this way towards Spelonksdrift? What he thought of this part of the country, I mean. That grand old Patriarch. Does anybody know what a Patriarch is?"

Practically every child in his Standard Five class put up his or her hand, then. No, they did not know what a Patriarch was. But they did know what Lodewyk Loggenberg wrote in his *Dagboek* about Spelonksdrift. And they told the schoolmaster. And the schoolmaster, because he was young and fresh from college, laughed in a lighthearted manner at the answers the pupils gave him. It was all the same answer, really. And it was only after Faans Grobler, who was chairman of our school committee, had spoken earnestly to Charlie Rossouw about how serious a thing it was to laugh at a Standard Five pupil when he gave the right answer, that Charlie Rossouw went to Zeerust on a push bicycle over a weekend. Charlie Rossouw spent several hours in the public library at Zeerust. When he came back he was a changed man.

After that, he put in even more time than he had done in the Zeerust library in explaining to Standard Five – which was the top class – that he had not known, until then, that that particular passage about the haunted character of the Spelonksdrift appeared in Lodewyk Loggenberg's *Dagboek*. He had never been taught that at university, Charlie Rossouw said. But it was clear enough, now, of course. He had read it in print. It gave him an insight into Lodewyk Loggenberg's mind that he did not have before, he acknowledged. But then, while he was at the teachers' college, he was not able to go into all those details about South African history. He had to study subjects like blackboard work and cardboard modelling and the theory of education and the depth of the Indian Ocean and the Scholastic Philosophers, including Archbishop Anselm and Thomas Aquinas and Peter Lombard and Duns Scotus. And there was also Albertus Magnus, Charlie Rossouw said. So he should not be blamed for not knowing *everything* Lodewyk Loggenberg wrote in his *Dagboek*. He had been so busy, night after night, trying to make out what Duns Scotus was trying to get at. But now that he had himself gone into the world a bit, the schoolmaster said, it seemed to him that there was quite a lot in common between Duns Scotus and Lodewyk Loggenberg. In his opinion, they would both of them have got pretty high marks for cardboard modelling.

Francina Smit, who was in Standard Five, and who was good at arithmetic, said afterwards that Charlie Rossouw made that remark with what she could only describe as a sneer.

All the same, Charlie Rossouw said to his class, even though it was true that Lodewyk Loggenberg *had* written those things about Spelonksdrift in his *Dagboek*, it would be best if the class kept quiet about it when the inspector came. He was sure that the school inspector would misunderstand an answer like that. He did not believe that the school inspector knew Lodewyk Loggenberg's *Dagboek* very well. He even went so far as to doubt whether the school inspector knew much about Thomas Aquinas.

A little later, when Charlie Rossouw was sacked from the Education Department, we in the Groot Marico were pleased about it. There was just something about Charlie Rossouw that made us feel that he was getting too big for his boots. The next thing he would be telling his class was that the earth turns around the sun. Whereas you've only got to lie in the tamboekie grass on Abjaterskop towards evening and *watch*, and you'll see for yourself it isn't so. All those astronomers and people like that – where would they be if they once lay on Abjaterskop in the setting sun, and shredded a plug of roll-tobacco with a pocket knife, in the setting sun, and looked about them, and thought a little? Put an astronomer on top of Abjaterskop, in the setting sun, and with a plug of roll-tobacco, and lying in the tamboekie grass, and where would he *be*?

Anyway, even though we who were sitting in Jurie Steyn's voorkamer that also served as the Drogevlei post office were not astronomers, or anywhere near, we were nevertheless much impressed by Chris Welman's statement that they were having ghost trouble at Spelonksdrift. When it came to seeing a ghost you didn't need to be an astronomer and to have a telescope: a ghost was something that you could actually see best just with the naked eye.

Now, if the spirits of the dead were content to haunt only the drift after nightfall, then no harm would come to any human being. No human being was ever *there* after nightfall. It was when a pale apparition took to the road, and wandered through the poort to have a look round, that unfortunate incidents occurred.

If you were travelling along the Government Road at night and you saw a person walking – or riding on horseback, even – and you saw the moon shining through that person, then you would know, of course, that you had met a ghost. If there was no moon, then you would see the stars shining through the ghost. Or you might even see a withaak tree or a piece of road showing through the ghost.

Gysbert van Tonder once encountered an elderly ghost, riding a mule, right in the middle of the poort. And Gysbert van Tonder held long converse with the ghost, whom he took to be an elderly farmer that had come back from a dance at Nietverdiend – coming back so late because he was elderly. It was when Gysbert van Tonder recognised the mule that the elderly farmer was sitting on as old Koffiebek, that had belonged to his grandfather and that had died many years before of grass-belly, that Gysbert van Tonder grew to have doubts. What made him suspicious, Gysbert van Tonder said, was that he had never in his life seen Koffiebek standing so still, with a man on his back, talking. During the whole conversation Koffiebek did not once try to bite a chunk out of his rider's leg. In the same moment Gysbert van Tonder realised that it was because there wasn't much of his rider for Koffiebek *to* bite.

"What made it all so queer," Gysbert van Tonder said, "was that I had been talking to the elderly farmer on the mule about a new comet that there was in the sky, then. And I had asked him if he thought it meant the end of the world, and he said he hoped not, because there were several things that he wanted to do still. And it didn't strike me that, all the time we were talking about the comet, the old farmer was sitting between me and the comet, and I was seeing the comet through the middle of his left lung. I could see his right lung, too, the way it swelled out when he breathed."

It was getting late, not only in Jurie Steyn's post office, but everywhere in the Marico, and the lorry from Bekkersdal had not yet arrived with our letters and milk-cans. They must be having trouble along the road, we said to each other.

And because of the line of conversation that Chris Welman had started we were glad when Jurie Steyn, on his return from the milking shed, lit the paraffin lamp in the voorkamer before it was properly dark.

Oupa Bekker had been very quiet, most of the evening. Several times he had looked out into the gathering dusk, shaking his head at it. But after Jurie Steyn had lit the oil-lamp, Oupa Bekker cheered up a good deal. Then he started telling us about the time when he encountered a ghost near Spelonksdrift, in the old days.

"I had lost my way in the dark," Oupa Bekker declared, "and so I thought that that stretch of water was just an ordinary crossing over the Molopo River. I had no idea that it was Spelonksdrift. So I pulled up at the edge of the stream to let my horse drink. Mind you, I should have known that it was Spelonksdrift just through my horse not having been at all thirsty. Indeed, afterwards it struck me that I had never before seen a horse with so little taste for water. All he did was to look slowly about him and shiver."

At Naudé asked Jurie Steyn's wife to turn the paraffin lamp up a bit higher, just about then. He said he was thinking of the lorry-driver. The lorry-driver would be able to see the light in Jurie Steyn's voorkamer from a long way off, if the lamp was turned up properly, At Naudé explained. It was queer how several of us, at that moment, started feeling concern for the lorry-driver. We all seemed to remember, at once, that he was a married man with five children. Jurie Steyn's wife did not have to turn much on the screw to make the lamp burn brighter. We men did it all for her. But then, of course, we Marico men are chivalrous that way.

In the meantime, Oupa Bekker had been drooling on in his old-man way of talking, with the result that when we were back in our seats again we found that we had missed the in-between part of his story. All we heard was the end part. We heard about his dispute with the ghost, which had ended in the ghost letting him have it across the chops with the back of his hand.

"So I went next day to see Dr Angus Stuart," Oupa Bekker continued. "In those days he was the only doctor between here and Rysmierbult. I didn't tell him anything about what had happened at Spelonksdrift. I just showed him my face, with those red marks on it . . . And do you know what? After he had had a good look at those marks through a magnifying glass, the doctor said that they could have been caused only by a ghost hitting me over the jaw with the back of a blue-flame hand."

That story started Johnny Coen off telling us about the time he was walking through the poort one night, with Dawie Ferreira who had once been a policeman at Newclare. And while he and Dawie Ferreira were walking through the poort, a Bechuana through whom they could see the Milky Way shining came up to them. In addition to having the Milky Way visible through his spine, the Bechuana was also carrying his head under his arm. But Dawie Ferreira, because he was a former policeman, knew how to deal with that Bechuana, Johnny Coen said. He promptly asked him where his pass was for being on a public road at that time of night. You couldn't see the Bechuana for dust after that, Johnny Coen said. In fact, the dust that the Bechuana with his head under his arm raised on the Government Road of the Marico seemed to become part of, and to reach beyond, the Milky Way that shone through his milt and was also a road.

The lorry from Bekkersdal arrived very late. The driver looked perturbed.

"We had big-end trouble at Spelonksdrift," the lorry-driver said, "and an old farmer riding a mule came up and gave me a lot of sauce. He acted as though he was a ghost, or something. As though I'd take notice of that sort of nonsense. *I saw through him, all right.* Then he sloshed me one across the jaw. When I tried to land him one back he was gone."

The lorry-driver had marks on his cheek that could have been caused by a back-hander from an elderly farmer riding a mule.

OOM TOBIE'S SICKNESS

From the way he was muffled to the chin in a khaki overcoat and his wife's scarf in the heat of the day, we knew why Tobias Schutte was sitting on the riempies bench in Jurie Steyn's voorkamer. We knew that Tobias Schutte was going by lorry to Bekkersdal to get some more medical treatment. There was nobody in the Groot Marico who suffered as regularly and acutely from maladies – imaginary or otherwise – as did Tobias Schutte. For that reason he was known as "Iepekonders Oom Tobie" from this side of the Pilanesberg right to the Kalahari: a good way into the Kalahari, sometimes – the exact distance depending on how far the Klipkop Bushmen had to go into the desert to find msumas.

"You look to be in a pretty bad way again, Oom Tobie," Chris Welman said in a tone that Oom Tobie accepted as implying sympathy. Nobody else in the voorkamer took it up that way, however. To the rest of us, Chris Welman's remark was just a plain sneer. "What's it this time, Oom Tobie," he went on, "the miltsiek or St. Vitus's dance? But you got it while you were working, I'll bet."

"Just before I started working, to be exact," Oom Tobie replied. "I was just getting ready to plant in the first pole for the new cattle camp when the sickness overtook me. Of a sudden I came all over queer. So I just had to leave the whole job to the Cape Coloured man, Pieterse, and the Bechuanas. The planting of the poles, the wiring, chasing away meerkats – I had to leave it all to them. They are at it now. I don't know what I'd do without Pieterse. I must give him an old pair of trousers again, one of these days. I've got a pair that are quite good still, except that they are worn out in the seat. It's queer how all my trousers get worn out like that, in the seat. The clothes you get today aren't what they used to be. I buy a new pair of trousers to wear when I go out on the lands, and before I know where I am they're frayed all thin, at the seat . . ."

57

"Was Pieterse – I mean, did Pieterse not look very surprised, sort of, at your being taken ill so suddenly, Oom Tobie?" Jurie Steyn asked, doing his best to keep a straight face.

"Well, no," Oom Tobie replied in all honesty. "When he helped me back onto the stoep from the place where we were going to put up the fence, Pieterse said he had felt for quite some days that I had this illness coming on. It wasn't so much anything he could see about me as what he *felt*, he said. And he could remember the exact time, too, when he first had that feeling. It was the afternoon when the poles and the rolls of barbed wire came from Ramoutsa. He didn't himself feel too good, either, that afternoon, he said. It was as though there was something unhealthy in the air. He's an extraordinary fellow, Pieterse. But that's because he's Cape Coloured, I suppose. I wouldn't be surprised if he's some part of him Slams, too. You know these Malays . . ."

Chris Welman asked Oom Tobie what he thought his illness was, this time. "Well, I know it can't be the horse-sickness," Oom Tobie said, "because I had the horse-sickness last year. And when you've had the horse-sickness once you don't get it again. You're salted."

The new schoolteacher, Vermaak, who wasn't long out of college, and whom Jurie Steyn's wife seemed to think a lot of, on account of his education, then said that it was the first time he had ever heard of a human being getting horse-sickness.

Several of us, speaking at the same time, told the schoolteacher that there were lots of things he had never heard of, and that a white man getting horse-sickness was what he now had an opportunity of getting instructed about. We told him that if he remained in the Groot Marico longer, and observed a little, he would no doubt learn things that would surprise him, yet.

The schoolmaster said that that had already happened to him. Just from looking around, he said.

"What I have got this time, now, is, I think, the blue-tongue," Oom Tobie continued. "Mind you, I used to think that only sheep get the blue-tongue. When there is rain after a long drought – that is the worst time for the blue-tongue. And you know the dry spell was pretty long, here in the district, before these rains started. So I think it must be blue-tongue."

Gysbert van Tonder asked Oom Tobie to put his tongue out, so we could see. We all pretended to take a lot of interest in Oom Tobie's tongue, then. It was, of course, quite an ordinary-looking sort of tongue, perhaps somewhat on the thick side and with tobacco-juice stains in the cracks. Oom Tobie first protruded his tongue out straight in front of his face as far as it would go – a by no means inconsiderable distance. Then he let his tongue hang down on his chin, for a bit.

Oom Tobie was engaged in lifting his tongue up again, in the direction of his eyebrows, so that we could see the underneath part of it, when Jurie Steyn's wife came into the voorkamer from the kitchen. From her remarks, then, it was clear that she had not heard any of our previous conversation.

"I am ashamed of you, Oom Tobie," Jurie Steyn's wife announced, speaking very severely. "Sticking out your tongue at Mr Vermaak like that."

The schoolmaster was sharing the riempies bench with Oom Tobie.

Oom Tobie started to explain what it was all about. But because he forgot, in the excitement of the moment, to put his tongue back again, first, all he could utter was a sequence of somewhat peculiar noises.

"If you disagree with Mr Vermaak on any subject," Jurie Steyn's wife went on, "then you can at least discuss the matter with him in a respectable sort of way. To stick out your tongue at a man, and to wobble it, is no way to carry on a discussion, Oom Tobie. I can only hope that Mr Vermaak does not think *everybody* in the Bushveld is so unrefined."

By that time Oom Tobie had found his tongue again, however, in quite a literal way. And in a few simple sentences he was able to acquaint Jurie Steyn's wife with the facts of the situation. Oom Tobie might have made those sentences even simpler, perhaps. Only he happened, out of the corner of his eye, to catch a glimpse of Jurie Steyn behind the counter. And Oom Tobie was sick enough on account of the blue-tongue. He did not want to become still more of an invalid as a result of a misunderstanding with Jurie Steyn, who was known for his strength and ill-temper.

"But if it's the blue-tongue in sheep that I've got," Oom Tobie proceeded, hastily, "then it won't show first in my tongue, so much. You see it first in the limp sort of way my wool hangs. It was the same with the horse-sickness. The first sign of it was a feeling of stiffness just behind the fetlock. It was several days before I started getting the snuffles –"

Gysbert van Tonder interrupted Oom Tobie at that point.

"Tell us, Oom Tobie . . ." Gysbert van Tonder began, and as he spoke his glance travelled in the direction of young Vermaak, the schoolteacher. We guessed what was going on in Gysbert van Tonder's mind. We felt the same way about it, too. You see, in the Marico we might perhaps laugh at Oom Tobie, and invent a nickname for him, and we didn't mind if the Klipkop tribe of Bushmen in the Kalahari also spoke of him by that nickname. Those things we could understand. But even when we laughed at Oom Tobie, we also had a respect for him. And we didn't like the idea that a stranger straight from university, like young Vermaak, wearing city clothes and all, should not give Oom Tobie his due. For that matter, the Klipkop Bushmen still gave Oom Tobie his due. And *they* did not wear city clothes. Not by a long chalk the Klipkop Bushmen didn't.

And what we were genuinely proud of Oom Tobie about was the fact that he had had more wild and domestic animal diseases than any man you could come across anywhere in Africa. At catch-weights and with no holds barred, we could put him, in his own line, against any sick man from Woodstock Beach to the Zambezi. And while we could laugh at him as much as we wanted, we did not like strangers to.

Consequently, when Gysbert van Tonder turned to Oom Tobie with a determined expression on his face, we knew what Gysbert was going to say. He was going to ask Oom Tobie, salted with horse-sickness and all, *really* to show his paces.

"Tell us," Gysbert van Tonder said, getting up from his chair and folding his arms across his chest. "Tell us, Oom Tobie, about the time you had *snake*-sickness."

Thus encouraged, Oom Tobie told us, and with an elaborate amount of detail.

"But I wouldn't like to have to go through all that again," he ended up.

"All the time I was suffering from snake disease I felt so *low*, if you understand what I mean. With my backside right on the ground, as it were."

Chris Welman coughed, then.

For Jurie Steyn's wife was still present, and it seemed as though Oom Tobie was perhaps getting a bit coarse. To our surprise, however, Jurie Steyn himself said that it was quite in order. When you were talking about snakes, it was only natural that you should talk about them as they were, he said. It would be ungodly to pretend that a snake was different from what we all knew a snake to be.

He spoke with a warmth that made us all feel uncomfortable.

"For that matter," Jurie Steyn added, with a sort of careful deliberation, "there is more than just one kind of snake right here in the Marico. There are *lots* of kinds."

I noticed that the young schoolteacher looked down, when Jurie spoke like that. I also noticed that shortly afterwards Jurie Steyn's wife went back to the kitchen.

We were glad when Oom Tobie started talking about his illness again. It seemed to remove quite a lot of strain.

"Maybe it isn't the blue-tongue," Oom Tobie said, "because I felt it coming on even before the time that Pieterse spoke to me about it. I felt it after I had bought that barbed wire at the store at Ramoutsa. So I think maybe it's something I ate. I ate two bananas. They gave me those two bananas as a bonsella for all the wire I bought."

Shortly afterwards the Government lorry came. And I still remember what At Naudé, who reads the newspapers, said when Oom Tobie, all buttoned up in his coat and scarf, and with a cushion under his arm, climbed aboard the lorry.

"Oom Tobie looks like he's a Member of Parliament," At Naudé said, "fixed up for an all-night sitting."

Nevertheless, we were not too happy when, next time the lorry came, the driver told us what the doctor at Bekkersdal had told him was wrong with Oom Tobie. For it was a human disease, this time. And it would almost appear as though the Cape Coloured man, Pieterse, really was to some extent Slams. Moreover, we ourselves had been in somewhat close contact with Oom Tobie, and so we did not feel too comfortable about it.

It looked as though Oom Tobie had landed a winner, all right, and it was not impossible that the bonsella bananas had played a part in it.

All the same, it's queer how frightened everybody gets when you hear the word smallpox.

II

Onlookers at the New Year's eve dance of the Mamba
Klub of the Dwarsberg Boerevereniging's Boeresport.
31 December 1965

News Story

"The way the world is today," At Naudé said, shaking his head, "I don't know what is going to happen."

From that it was clear that At Naudé had been hearing news over the wireless again that made him fear for the future of the country. We did not exactly sit up, then. We in the Dwarsberge knew that it was the wireless that made At Naudé that way. And he could tremble as much as he liked for the country's future or his own. There was never any change, either, in the kind of news he would bring us. Every time it was about stonethrowings in Johannesburg locations and about how many new kinds of bombs the Russians had got, and about how many people had gone to gaol for telling the Russians about still other kinds of bombs they could make. Although it did not look as though the Russians *needed* to be educated much in that line.

And we could never really understand why At Naudé listened at all. We hardly ever listened to *him*, for that matter. We would rather hear from Gysbert van Tonder if it was true that the ouderling at Pilanesberg really forgot himself in the way that Jurie Steyn's wife had heard about from a kraal Mtosa at the kitchen door. The Mtosa had come by to buy halfpenny stamps to stick on his forehead for the yearly Ndlolo dance. Now, there was news for you. About the ouderling, I mean. And even to hear that the Ndlolo dance was being held soon again was at least something. And if it should turn out that what was being said about the Pilanesberg ouderling was not true, well, then, the same thing applied to a lot of what At Naudé heard over the wireless also.

"I don't know what is going to happen," At Naudé repeated, "the way the world is today. I just heard over the wireless –"

"That's how the news we got in the old days was better," Oupa Bekker said. "I mean in the real old days, when there was no wireless, and there was not the telegraph, either. The news you got then you could do something with. And you didn't have to go to the post office and get it from the newspaper. The post office is the curse of the Transvaal . . ."

Jurie Steyn said that Oupa Bekker was quite right, there. He himself would never have taken on the job of postmaster at Drogevlei if he had as much as guessed that there were four separate forms that he would have to fill in, each of them different, just for a simple five-shilling money order. It was so much brainier and neater, Jurie Steyn said, for people who wanted to send five shillings somewhere, if they would just wrap up a couple of half-crowns in a thick wad of brown paper and then post them in the ordinary way, like a letter. That was what the new red pillar-box in front of his door was *for*, Jurie Steyn explained. The authorities had gone to the expense of that red pillar-box in order to help the public. And yet you still found people coming in for postal orders and money orders. The other day a man even came in and asked could he telegraph some money, somewhere.

"I gave that man a piece of brown paper and showed him the pillarbox," Jurie Steyn said. "It seemed, until then, that he did not know what kind of progress we had been making here. I therefore asked him if I could show him some more ways in regard to how advanced the Groot Marico was getting. But he said, no, the indications I had already given him were plenty."

Jurie Steyn said that he thought it was handsome of the man to have spoken up for the Marico like that, seeing that he was quite a newcomer to these parts.

Because we never knew how long Jurie Steyn would be when once he got on the subject of his work, we were glad when Johnny Coen asked Oupa Bekker to explain some more to us about how they got news in the old days. We were all pleased, that is, except At Naudé, who had again tried to get in a remark but had got no further than to say that if we knew something we would all shiver in our veldskoens.

"How did we get news?" Oupa Bekker said, replying to another question of Johnny Coen's. "Well, you would be standing in the lands, say, and then one of the Bechuanas would point to a small cloud of dust in the poort, and you would walk across to the big tree by the dam, where the road bends, and the traveller would come past there, with two vos horses in front of his Cape-cart, and he would get off from the cart and shake hands and say he was Du Plessis. And you would say you were Bekker, and he would say, afterwards, that he couldn't stay the night on your farm, because he had to get to Tsalala's Kop. Well, there was *news*. You could talk about it for days. For weeks even. You have got no idea how often my wife and I discussed it. And we knew everything that there was to know about the man. We knew his name was Du Plessis."

At Naudé said, then, that he did not think much of that sort of news. People must have been a bit *simpel* in the head, in those old times that Oupa Bekker was talking about, if they thought anything about that sort of news. Why, if you compared it with what the radio announcer said, only yesterday . . .

Jurie Steyn's wife came in from the kitchen at that moment. There was a light of excitement in her eyes. And when she spoke it was to none of us in particular.

"It has just occurred to me," Jurie Steyn's wife said, "that is, if it's *true* what they are saying about the Pilanesberg ouderling, of course. Well, it has just struck me that, when he forgot himself in the way they say – provided that he *did* forget himself like that, mind you – well, perhaps the ouderling didn't know that anybody was looking."

That was a possibility that had not so far occurred to us, and we discussed it at some length. In between our talk At Naudé was blurting out something about the rays from a still newer kind of bomb that would kill you right in the middle of the veld and through fifty feet of concrete. So we said, of course, that the best thing to do would be to keep a pretty safe distance away from concrete, with those sort of rays about, if concrete was as dangerous as all that.

We were in no mood for foolishness. Oupa Bekker took this as an encouragement for him to go on.

"Or another day," Oupa Bekker continued, "you would again be standing in your lands, say, or sitting, even, if there was a long day of ploughing ahead, and you did not want to tire yourself out unnecessarily. You would be sitting on a stone in the shade of a tree, say, and you would think to yourself how lazy those Bechuanas look, going backwards and forwards, backwards and forwards, with the plough and the oxen, and you would get quite sleepy, say, thinking to yourself how lazy those Bechuanas are. If it wasn't for the oxen to keep them going, they wouldn't do any work at all, you might perhaps think.

"And then, without your in the least expecting it, you would again have news. And the news would find a stone for himself and come along and sit down right next to you. It would be the new veldkornet, say. And why nobody saw any dust in the poort, that time, was because the veldkornet didn't come along the road. And you would make a joke with him and say: 'I suppose that's why they call you a *veld*kornet, because you don't travel along the road, but you come by the *veld*langes.' And the veldkornet would laugh and ask you a few questions, and he would tell you that they had good rains at Derdepoort . . . Well, there was something that I could tell my wife over and over again, for weeks. It was news. For weeks I had that to think about. The visit of the veldkornet. In the old days it was real news."

We could see, from the way At Naudé was fidgeting in his chair, that he guessed we were just egging the old man on to talk in order to scoff at all the important European news that At Naudé regularly retailed to us, and that we were getting tired of.

After a while At Naudé could no longer contain himself.

"This second-childhood drivel that Oupa Bekker is talking," At Naudé announced, not looking at anybody in particular, but saying it to all of us, in the way Jurie Steyn's wife had spoken when she came out of the kitchen. "Well, I would actually sooner listen to scandal about the Pilanesberg ouderling. There is at least some sort of meaning to it. I am not being unfriendly to Oupa Bekker, of course. I know it's just that he's old. But it's also quite clear to me that he doesn't know what news *is*, at all."

Jurie Steyn said that it was at least as sensible as a man lying on the veld under fifty feet of concrete because of some rays. If a man were to lie under fifty feet of concrete he wouldn't be able to breathe, leave alone anything else.

In the meantime, Johnny Coen had been asking Oupa Bekker to tell us some more.

"On another day, say," Oupa Bekker went on, "you would not be in your lands at all, but you would be sitting on your front stoep, drinking coffee, say. And the Cape-cart with the two vos horses in front would be coming down the road again, but in the opposite direction, going *towards* the poort, this time. And you would not see much of Du Plessis's face, because his hat would be pulled over his eyes. And the veldkornet would be sitting on the Cape-cart next to him, say."

Oupa Bekker paused. He paused for quite a while, too, holding a lighted match cupped over his pipe as though he was out on the veld where there was wind, and puffing vigorously.

"And my wife and I would go on talking about it for years afterwards, say," Oupa Bekker went on. "For years after Du Plessis was hanged, I mean."

School Concert

The preparations for the annual school concert were in full swing.
In the Marico these school concerts were held in the second part of June, when the nights were pleasantly cool. It was too hot, in December, for recitations and singing and reading the Joernaal that carried playful references to the activities and idiosyncrasies of individual members of the Dwarsberg population. On a midsummer's night, in a little school building crowded to the doors with children and adults and with more adults leaning in through the windows and keeping out the air, the songs and the recitations sounded limp, somehow. Moreover, the personal references in the Joernaal did not sound quite as playful, then, as they were intended to be.

The institution of the Joernaal dated back to the time of the first Hollander schoolmaster in the Groot Marico. The Joernaal was a very popular feature of school concerts in Limburg, where he came from, the Hollander schoolmaster explained. For weeks beforehand the schoolmaster, assisted by some of the pupils in the upper class, would write down, in the funniest way they knew, odds and ends of things about people living in the neighbourhood. Why, they just about killed themselves laughing, while they were writing those things down in a classroom in old Limburg, the Hollander schoolmaster said, and then, at the concert, one of the pupils would read it all out. Oh, it was a real scream. You wouldn't mention people's names, of course, the Hollander schoolmaster went on to say. They would just *hint* at who they were. It was all done in a subtle sort of way, naturally, but it was also clear enough so that you couldn't possibly miss the allusion. And you knew straight away who was *meant*.

That was what the first Hollander schoolmaster in the Marico explained, oh, long ago, before the reading, at a school concert, of the first Joernaal.

Today, in the Dwarsberge, they still talk about that concert.

It would appear, somehow, that in drawing up the Joernaal, the Hollander schoolmaster had not been quite subtle enough. Or, maybe, what they would split their sides laughing at in Limburg would raise quite different sorts of emotions north of the railway line to Ottoshoop. That's the way it is with humour, of course. Anyway, while the head pupil was reading out the Joernaal – stuttering a bit now and again because he could sense what that silence on the part of a Bushveld audience meant – the Hollander schoolmaster had tears streaming down his cheeks, the way his laughter was convulsing him. Seated on the platform next to the pupil who was reading, the schoolmaster would reach into his pocket every so often for his handkerchief to wipe his eyes with. That made the audience freeze into a yet greater stillness.

A farmer's wife said afterwards that she felt she could just choke, then.

"If what was in that Joernaal were *jokes*, now," Koos Kirstein – who had been a prominent cattle-smuggler in his day – said, "well, I can laugh at a joke with the best of them. I read the page of jokes at the back of the *Kerkbode* regularly every month. But can anybody see anything to titter at in asking where I got the money from to buy that harmonium that my daughter plays hymns on? That came in the Joernaal."

Koos Kirstein asked that question of a church elder a few days after the school concert, and the elder said, no, there was nothing funny in it. Everybody in the Marico *knew* where Koos Kirstein got his money from, the elder said.

"And saying I am so well in with the police," Koos Kirstein continued. "Saying in the Joernaal that a policeman on border patrol went and hid behind my harmonium when a special plain-clothes inspector from Pretoria walked into my voorkamer unexpectedly. Why, the schoolmaster just about doubled up laughing, when that bit was being read out."

Anyway, the reading of that first Joernaal at a Marico school concert never reached a proper end. When the proceedings terminated the head pupil still had a considerable number of unread foolscap sheets in his hand. And he was stuttering more than ever. For he had just finished the part about the Indian store at Ramoutsa refusing to give Giel Oosthuizen any more credit until he paid off something on last year's account.

Before that he had read out something about a crateful of muscovy ducks at the Zeerust market that Faans Lemmer had loaded onto his own wagon by mistake, and that he afterwards, still making the same error, unloaded into his own chicken pen – not noticing at the time the difference between the muscovy ducks and his own Australorps, as he afterwards explained to the market master.

The head pupil had also read out something about why Frikkie Snyman's grandfather had to stay behind in the tent on the kerkplein when the rest of the family went to the Nagmaal. It wasn't the rheumatics that kept Frikkie Snyman's grandfather away from the Communion service, the Joernaal said, but he stayed behind in the tent because he didn't have an extra pair of laced-up shop boots. It was when Frikkie Snyman's wife, Hanna, knelt in church at the end of a pew and her long skirt that had all flowers on came up over one ankle – the Joernaal said that you realised how Frikkie Snyman's grandfather was sitting barefooted in the tent on the kerkplein.

That was about as far as the head pupil got with the reading of the Joernaal . . . And to this day they can still show you, in an old Marico schoolroom, the burnt corner of a blackboard from where the lamp fell on it when the audience turned the platform upside down on the Hollander schoolmaster. Nothing happened to the head pupil, however. He sensed what was coming and got away, in time, into the rafters. Unlike most head pupils, he had a quick mind.

All that happened very long ago, of course, as we were saying to each other in Jurie Steyn's post office. Today, the Marico was very different, we said to one another. Those old farmers didn't have the advantages that we enjoyed today, we said. There was no Afrikander Cattle Breeders' Society in those days, or even the Dwarsberge Hog Breeders' Society, and you would never see a front garden with irises in it – or a front garden at all, for that matter. And you couldn't order clothes from Johannesburg, just filling in your measurements, so that all your wife had to do was . . .

But it was when Jurie Steyn's wife explained what she had to do to the last serge suit that Jurie Steyn ordered by post, just giving his size, that we saw that this example that we mentioned did not perhaps reflect progress in the Marico in its best light.

From the way Jurie Steyn's wife spoke, it would seem that the easiest part of the alterations she had to make was cutting off the trouser turn-ups and inserting the material in the neck part of the jacket. "And then the suit still hung on Jurie like a sack," she concluded.

But Gysbert van Tonder said that she must not blame the Johannesburg store for it too much. There was something about the way Jurie Steyn was *built*, Gysbert van Tonder said. And we could not help noticing a certain nasty undertone in his voice, then, when he said that.

Johnny Coen smoothed the matter over very quickly, however. He had also had difficulties, ordering suits by post, he said. But he found it helped the Johannesburg store a lot if you sent a full-length photograph of yourself along with the order. They always returned the photograph. No, Johnny Coen said in reply to a question from At Naudé, he didn't know why that Johannesburg store sent the photographs back so promptly, under registered cover and all. And then, when he saw that At Naudé was laughing, Johnny Coen said that that firm could, perhaps, if it wanted to, keep all those photographs and frame them. But, all the same, he added, it would help the shop a lot if, next time Jurie Steyn ordered a suit by post, he also put in a full-length photograph of himself.

But all this talk was getting us away from what we had been saying about how more broad-minded the Groot Marico had become since the old days, due to progress. It was then that Koos Nienaber brought us back to what we were discussing.

"Where our forefathers in the Marico were different from the way we are today," Koos Nienaber said, "is because they hadn't learnt to laugh at themselves, yet. They took themselves much too seriously. Although they had to, I suppose, since it was all going to be put into history books. Or at least as much of it as could be put into history books. But we today are different. We wouldn't carry on in an undignified manner if, at the next concert, there should be something in the Joernaal to show up our little human weaknesses. We would laugh, I mean. Take Jurie Steyn and his serge suit, now. Well, we've got a sense of humour, today. I mean, Jurie Steyn would be the first to laugh at how funny he looks in that serge suit –"

"How do you mean I look funny in my new suit?" Jurie Steyn demanded.

At Naudé came in between the two of them, then, and made it clear to Jurie Steyn that Koos Nienaber had been saying those things merely by way of argument, and to prove his point. Koos Nienaber didn't mean that Jurie Steyn actually *looked* funny in his new suit, At Naudé explained.

"If he doesn't mean it, what does he want to say it for?" Jurie Steyn said, sounding only half convinced. "And, anyway, Koos Nienaber needn't talk. When he came round with the collection plate at the last Nagmaal, and he was wearing his new manel, I thought Koos Nienaber was an ourang-outang."

Nevertheless, we all acknowledged at the end that we were looking forward to the school concert. And there should be quite a lot of fun in having the Joernaal, we said. Seeing how today we had a sense of humour.

It was not only schoolchildren and their parents that came to attend the concert in that little school building of which the middle partition had been taken away to make it into one hall. For instance, there was Hendrik Prinsloo, who had come all the way from Vleispoort by Cape-cart, and had not meant to attend the concert at all, since he was on his way to Zeerust and was just passing that way, when some of the parents persuaded him, for the sake of his horses, to outspan under the thorn-trees on the school grounds by the side of the Government Road.

It was observed that Hendrik Prinsloo had a red face and that he mistook one of the swingle-bars for the step when he alighted from the Cape-cart. So – after they had looked to see what was under the seat of the Cape-cart – several of the farmers present counselled Hendrik Prinsloo to rest awhile by the roadside, seeing it was already getting on towards evening. They also sent a native over to At Naudé's house for glasses, instructing him to be as quick as he liked. And if At Naudé didn't have glasses, cups would do, one of the farmers added, thoughtfully. By the look of things it was going to be a good children's concert, they said.

Meanwhile the schoolroom was filling up quite nicely. There had been some talk, during the past few days, that a scientist from the Agricultural Research Institute, who was known to be in the neighbourhood, would distribute the school prizes at the concert and also give a little lecture on his favourite subject, which was correct winter grazing. Even that rumour did not keep people away, however. They had the good sense to guess that it was only a rumour, anyhow. Afterwards it was found out that it had been started by Chris Welman, because the schoolmaster had turned down Chris Welman's offer to sing "Boereseun", with actions, at the concert.

There was loud applause when young Vermaak, the schoolmaster, came onto the platform. His black hair was neatly parted in the middle and his city suit of blue serge looked very smart in the lamplight. You could hardly notice those darker patches on the jacket to which Jurie Steyn's wife drew attention, when she said that you could see where Alida van Niekerk had again been trying to clean the schoolmaster's suit with paraffin. Vermaak was boarding at the Van Niekerks', and Alida was their eldest daughter.

The schoolmaster said he was glad to see that there was such a considerable crowd there, tonight, including quite a number of fathers, whom he knew personally, who were looking in at the windows. There were still a few vacant seats for them inside, he said, if they would care to come in. But Gysbert van Tonder, speaking on behalf of those fathers, said no, they did not mind being self-sacrificing in that way. It was not right that the schoolroom should be cluttered up with a lot of fat, healthy men, over whose heads the smaller children would not be able to see properly. There was also a neighbour of theirs, from Vleispoort, Hendrik Prinsloo, who was resting a little. And they wanted to keep an eye on his Cape-cart, which was standing there all by itself in the dark. If the schoolmaster looked out of that nearest window he would be able to see that lonely Cape-cart, Gysbert van Tonder said.

Young Vermaak, who didn't know what was going on, seemed touched at this display of solicitude for a neighbour by just simple-hearted Bushveld farmers. Several of the wives of those farmers sniffed, however.

Three little boys carrying little riding whips and wearing little red jackets came onto the platform and the schoolmaster explained that they would sing a hunting song called "Jan Pohl", which had been translated from English by the great Afrikaans poet, Van Blerk Willemse. Everybody agreed that the translation was a far superior cultural work to the original, the schoolmaster said. In fact you wouldn't recognise that it was the same song, even, if it wasn't for the tune. But that would also be put right shortly, the schoolmaster added. The celebrated Afrikaans composer, Frik Dinkelman, was going to get to work on it.

At Naudé said to the other fathers standing at the window that that man in the song, Jan Pohl, must be a bit queer in the head. "Wearing a red jacket and with a riding whip and a bugle to go and shoot a ribbok in the rante," At Naudé said.

Another father pointed out that that Jan Pohl didn't even have such a thing as a native walking along in front, through the tamboekie grass, where there was always a likelihood of mambas.

The next item on the programme was a group of boys and girls, in pairs, pirouetting about the platform to the music of "Pollie, Ons Gaan Pêrel Toe". Since many of the parents were Doppers, the schoolmaster took the trouble first to explain that what the children were doing wasn't really *dancing* at all. They were stepping about, quickly, sort of, in couples, kind of, to the measure of a polka in a manner of speaking. It was Volkspele, and had the approval of the Synod, the schoolmaster said. All the same, a few of the more earnest members of the audience kept their eyes down on the floor, while that was going on. They also refrained, in a quite stern manner, from beating time to the music with their feet.

For that reason it came as something of a relief when, at the end of the Volkspele, a number of children with wide blue collars trooped onto the stage. They were going to sing "Die Vaal se Bootman". It was really a Russian song, the schoolmaster explained. But the way the great Afrikaans poet Van Blerk Willemse had handled it, you wouldn't think it, at all. Maybe why it was such an outstanding translation, the schoolmaster said, was because Van Blerk Willemse didn't know any Russian, and didn't want to, either.

The song was a great success. The audience was still humming "Yo-ho-yo" to themselves a good way into the next item on the programme.

Meanwhile, the fathers outside the school building had deserted their places by the windows and had drifted in the direction of the Cape-cart to make sure that everything was still in order there. And they sat down on the ground as close as they could get to the Cape-cart, to make sure that things stayed in order. One of the fathers, still singing "Yo-ho-yo" even went and sat right on top of Hendrik Prinsloo's face, without noticing anything wrong. Hendrik Prinsloo didn't notice anything, either, at first, but when he did he made such a fuss, shouting "Elephants" and such-like, that At Naudé, who had remained at the schoolroom window, came running up to the Cape-cart, fearing the worst.

"Is that all?" At Naudé asked, when it was explained to him what had happened. "From the way Hendrik Prinsloo was carrying on, I thought some clumsy ——" he used a strong word, "some clumsy ——" had kicked over the jar."

In the meantime Hendrik Prinsloo had risen to a half-sitting posture, with his hand up to his face. "Feel here, kêrels," he said. "The middle part of my face has suddenly gone all flat, and my jaw is all sideways. Just feel here."

The farmers around the Cape-cart were fortunately able – in between singing "Yo-ho-yo" – to set Hendrik Prinsloo's mind at rest. He was worrying about nothing at all, they assured him. His face had always been that way.

Nevertheless, Hendrik Prinsloo did not appear to be as grateful as he should have been for that explanation. He said quite a lot of things that we felt did not fit in with a school concert.

"The schoolmaster says the Joernaal is going to be read out shortly," At Naudé announced. "Well, I hope there is going to be nothing in it like the sort of things Hendrik Prinsloo is saying now. All the same, I wonder what there is going to be in the Joernaal – you know what I mean – funny stories about people we all know."

Gysbert van Tonder started telling us about a Joernaal he had once heard read out at a Nagelspruit school concert. A deputation of farmers saw the schoolmaster onto the Government lorry immediately afterwards, Gysbert van Tonder said. The schoolmaster's clothes and books they sent after him, carriage forward, next day.

"I wonder, though," At Naudé said, "will young Vermaak mention in the Joernaal about himself and – and – you know who I mean – that *will* be a laugh."

As it turned out, however, there was no mention of that in the Joernaal. Nor was there any reference, direct or indirect, to anybody else in the Marico, either. In compiling the Joernaal, all that the schoolmaster had done was to cut a whole lot of jokes out of back numbers of magazines and to include also some funny stories that had been popular in the Marico for many years, and for generations, even. And because there was nothing that you enjoy as much as hearing an old joke for the hundredth time, the Joernaal got the audience into a state of uproarious good humour.

It was all so *jolly* that Jurie Steyn's wife did not even say anything sarcastic when Alida van Niekerk went and picked up the schoolmaster's programme, that had dropped onto the floor, for him.

The concert in the schoolroom went on until quite late, and everybody said how successful it was. The concert at the Cape-cart, which nearly all the fathers joined in, afterwards, was perhaps even more successful, and lasted a good deal longer. And Chris Welman did get his chance, there, to sing "Boereseun", with actions.

And when Hendrik Prinsloo drove off eventually, in his Cape-cart, into the night, there was handshaking all round, and they cheered him, and everybody asked him to be sure and come round again to the next school concert, also.

Next day there was only the locked door of the old school building to show that it was the end of term.

And at the side of a footpath that a solitary child walked along to and from school lay fragments of a torn-up quarterly report.

Railway Deputation

Because it was nearing the end of the Volksraad session, it was decided that a deputation of Dwarsberg farmers would go and call on the member when he got back to Pretoria. Over the generations it had developed into an institution – a deputation of farmers going to see the Volksraad member about a railway line through the Bushveld.

The promise of a railway line was an essential part of any election speech delivered north of Sephton's Nek. A candidate would no more contemplate leaving that promise out of his speech than he would think of omitting the joke about the Cape Coloured man who went to sleep in the graveyard. For a candidate not to mention the railway line through the Bushveld would be just as much of a shock to his constituents as if the candidate had forgotten to ask an ouderling to open the meeting with prayer.

But we never seemed to *get* that railway line, somehow.

"What's the good of a deputation, anyway?" Jurie Steyn asked. "When you think of what happened to the last deputation, I mean. Or take the deputation before that, when I was one of the delegates. Well, I'll say this much for our Volksraad member – he did take us to the bioscope, because we were strangers to Pretoria. And he spoke up for us, too, when a girl with yellow hair sitting in a glass compartment asked how far from the front we wanted to be. And our Volksraad member said not too near the front, because it was a film with shooting in it, and he didn't want anything to happen to us, seeing how we were his constituents."

Jurie Steyn said that the girl with yellow hair and a military-looking man in a red-and-gold uniform who opened the door for them – because they were friends of the Volksraad member, no doubt – laughed a good deal.

"I must say that our Volksraad member is very considerate that

79

way," Jurie Steyn added. "It made us feel at home in the city, straight off, having that pretty girl and that high army man so friendly and everything. When we came out of the bioscope and they saw us again, the two of them started laughing right from the beginning, almost. That made us feel as though we *belonged*, if you understand what I mean."

Then Gysbert van Tonder told us about the time when he was a member of a railway-line deputation in Pretoria. And he said the same thing about how thoughtful the Volksraad member was in regard to giving the delegates pleasure.

"He took us to the merry-go-round," Gysbert van Tonder said. "To right in front of the merry-go-round, as far as his motor-car could go. And he told the man who collected the tickets that we were friends of his from the platteland and that the man must keep a look out to see that Oom Kasper Geel's beard didn't get tangled in the machinery that made the horses turn round and round. So everything was very friendly, straight away. You've got to admit that our Volksraad member has got a touch for that sort of thing. The man that our Volksraad member spoke to about us nearly fell off the merry-go-round himself, laughing."

We all said that we knew, of course, that a delegation that we sent from the Bushveld to Pretoria about the railway line could always be sure of a good time. Our Volksraad member never minded how much trouble he put himself to in the way of introducing the delegation to the best people, and providing the delegation with the classiest entertainments that the big city offered, and making the delegation feel really at *home* through the things he said about the delegation to persons standing around. Like the time he bought the delegates a packet of bananas and a tin of fish and he showed them where they could go and eat it.

"He went with us right up to the building," Gysbert van Tonder, who was one of the delegates on that occasion also, said. "In fact, he took us right in at the front door. There were koedoe and gemsbok and tsessebe horns all round the walls, just like in my voorkamer. But big – you've got no idea how big. And grand – all along the walls were glass cases and stuffed giraffes and medals with gold and brass flower-pots and things. It was the finest dining room you could ever imagine. And our Volksraad member told the owner of the place that we were from his constituency and that he must look after us and that, above all, he mustn't keep us there. The owner, who was dressed all in blue, with a blue cap, laughed a lot, then, and so we were all as at home, there, as you please, and he showed us what staircase we had to go up by."

Gysbert van Tonder said that all they found to sit on, upstairs, was a tamboetie riempiesbank with a piece of string in front of it, that they had to unfasten, first. It was a comfortable enough riempiesbank, Gysbert said, but a bit on the old-fashioned side, he thought. On the left was a statue in white stone of a young woman without much clothes on who was bending forward with her arms folded, because of the cold. On the right was a stuffed hippopotamus.

Gysbert van Tonder said that the delegation felt that the Volksraad member had that time done them really proud – using his influence to provide them with elegant surroundings in which to eat their bananas and tinned fish, which they opened with a pocket knife.

But there was some sort of unfortunate misunderstanding about it afterwards, Gysbert van Tonder added. That was when another man wearing a blue suit and a blue cap came up and spoke to them. This man looked older than the owner and he was shorter and fatter. They took him to be the owner's father-in-law. And he spoke about the banana peels lying on the floor and about their sitting calm as you like on a historical riempiesbank that hadn't been in use for over a hundred and fifty years. But mostly the owner's father-in-law spoke about the fish oil that had got splashed on the behind part of the young woman without clothes on when the pocket knife slipped that the delegates had opened the tin with.

"And although we said to the owner's father-in-law that we were railway-line delegates from the Dwarsberge, it didn't seem to make much difference," Gysbert van Tonder finished up. "He said we weren't on the railway line now. I must say that I did feel afterwards that what the Volksraad member arranged for our happiness and comfort that time was a bit *too* stylish."

And Jurie Steyn said that after all that we still didn't get a railway line, or anywhere near. All that happened, he remembered, was that the Government arranged for the weekly lorry through the Bushveld from Bekkersdal to be given a new coat of light-green paint.

Then Oupa Bekker started telling us about the first railway-line deputation from the Dwarsberge that ever went to Pretoria. He was a member of that deputation.

"The railway engine was quite different from what it's like today, of course," Oupa Bekker said. "It had a long thin chimney curving up from in front of it, I remember. And above the wheels it was all open and you could see right into the works and things. In the same way, I suppose, a Bushveld railway delegation in those days would have looked a lot different from the kind of deputation that will be going to Pretoria again at the end of the Volksraad session next month."

But he said that with the years the principle of the thing hadn't changed so you would notice.

"We had written to our Volksraad member to say we were coming, and what it was about," Oupa Bekker continued. "And when he received us he was most sympathetic. He received us in his hotel room and he had a bottle of brandy sent up and he said it had to be the best, because only that was good enough for us. He said that in his opinion steam had come to stay and he showed us a lot of coloured pictures of engines that he had cut out of children's papers. And he asked us would we rather have a condensing or a low-pressure engine.

"Afterwards a man with black side-whiskers and wearing a stiff collar came into the hotel room and the Volksraad member told us that he was a civil engineer and could help us a lot. The civil engineer started talking to us straight away about how important it was that we should have the right kind of printing on our railway timetables. We could see from that what a fine, full sort of mind the civil engineer had – a brain that took in everything. He also spoke about the kind of buns that we would sell in the station tea-rooms.

"Later on, with the brandy and the talk, the civil engineer got really friendly, and started calling us by our first names, and all. We saw then that, in spite of his full mind, there was a playful side to him, also. Indeed, after a while, the civil engineer got so playful that he brought out three little thimbles and a pea, that he had found in one of his pockets. And, just to sort of pass the time, he asked us to guess under which thimble the pea was hidden."

Oupa Bekker sighed.

"All the same," he remarked, "that Volksraad member was a real gentleman. There are not many like him today. When he saw us back to the coach station he was apologising all the way because the civil engineer had cleaned us out."

WHITE ANT

Jurie Steyn was rubbing vigorously along the side of his counter with a rag soaked in paraffin. He was also saying things which, afterwards, in calmer moments, he would no doubt regret. When his wife came into the voorkamer with a tin of Cooper's dip, Jurie Steyn stopped using that sort of language and contented himself with observations of a general nature about the hardships of life in the Marico.

"All the same, they are very wonderful creatures, those little white ants," the schoolmaster remarked. "Among the books I brought here into the Marico, to read in my spare time, is a book called *The Life of the White Ant*. Actually, of course, the white ant is not a true ant at all. The right name for the white ant is isoptera –"

Jurie Steyn had another, and shorter, name for the white ant right on the tip of his tongue. And he started saying it, too. Only, he remembered his wife's presence, in time, and so he changed the word to something else.

"This isn't the first time the white ants got in behind your counter," At Naudé announced. "The last lot of stamps you sold me had little holes eaten all round the edges."

"That's just perforations," Jurie Steyn replied. "All postage stamps are that way. Next time you have got a postage stamp in your hand, just look at it carefully, and you'll see. There's a law about it, or something. In the department we talk of those little holes as perforations. It is what makes it possible for us, in the department, to tear stamps off easily, without having to use a scissors. Of course, it's not everybody that knows that."

At Naudé looked as much hurt as surprised.

"You mustn't think I am *so* ignorant, Jurie," he said severely. "Mind you, I am not saying that, perhaps, when this post office was first opened, and you were still new to affairs, and you couldn't be expected to *know* about perforations and things, coming to this job raw, from behind the plough – I'm not saying that you mightn't have cut the stamps loose with a scissors or a No. 3 pruning shears, even. At the start, mind you. And nobody would have blamed you for it, either. I mean, nobody ever has blamed you. We've all, in fact, admired the way you took to this work. I spoke to Gysbert van Tonder about it, too, more than once. Indeed, we both admired you. We spoke about how you stood behind that counter, with kraal manure in your hair, and all, just like you were Postmaster-General. Bold as brass, we said, too."

The subtle flattery in At Naudé's speech served to mollify Jurie Steyn. "You said all that about me?" he asked. "You did?"

"Yes," At Naudé proceeded smoothly. "And we also admired the neat way you learnt to handle the post office rubber stamp, Gysbert and I. We said you held onto it like it was a branding iron. And we noticed how you would whistle, too, just before bringing the rubber stamp down on a parcel, and how you would step aside afterwards, quickly, just as though you half expected the parcel to jump up and poke you in the short ribs. To tell you the truth, Jurie, we were *proud* of you."

Jurie Steyn was visibly touched. And so he said that he admitted he had been a bit arrogant in the way he had spoken to At Naudé about the perforations. The white ants had got amongst his postage stamps, Jurie Steyn acknowledged – once. But what they ate you could hardly notice, he said. They just chewed a little around the edges.

But Gysbert van Tonder said that, all the same, that was enough. His youngest daughter was a member of the Sunshine Children's Club of the church magazine in Cape Town, Gysbert said. And his youngest daughter wrote to Aunt Susann, who was the woman editor, to say that it was her birthday. And when Aunt Susann mentioned his youngest daughter's birthday in the Sunshine Club corner of the church magazine, Aunt Susann wrote that she was a little girl staying in the lonely African wilds. *Gramadoelas* was the word that Aunt Susann used, Gysbert van Tonder said. And all just because Aunt Susann had noticed the way that part of the springbok on the stamp on his youngest daughter's letter had been eaten off by white ants, Gysbert van Tonder said.

He added that his daughter had lost all interest in the Sunshine Children's Club, since then. It sounded so uncivilised, the way Aunt Susann wrote about her.

"As though we're living in a grass hut and a string of crocodiles around

84

it, with their teeth showing," Gysbert van Tonder said. "As though it's all still konsessie farms and we haven't made improvements. And it's no use trying to explain to her, either, that she must just feel sorry for Aunt Susann for not knowing any better. You can't explain things like that to a child."

Nevertheless, while we all sympathised with Gysbert van Tonder, we had to concede that it was not in any way Jurie Steyn's fault. We had all had experience of white ants, and we knew that, mostly, when you came along with the paraffin and Cooper's dip, it was too late. By the time you saw those little tunnels, which the white ants made by sticking grains of sand together with spit, all the damage had already been done.

The schoolmaster started talking some more about his book dealing with the life of the white ant, then, and he said that it was well known that the termite was the greatest plague of tropic lands. Several of us were able to help the schoolmaster right. As Chris Welman made it clear to him, the Marico was not in the tropics at all. The tropics were quite a long way up. The tropics started beyond Mochudi, even. A land-surveyor had established that much for us, a few years ago, on a coloured map. It was loose talk about wilds and gramadoelas and tropics that gave the Marico a bad name, we said. Like with that Aunt Susann of the Sunshine Children's Club. Maybe we did have white ants here – lots of them, too – but we certainly weren't in the tropics, like some countries we knew, and that we could mention, also, if we wanted to. Maybe what had happened was that the white ants had come down here *from* the tropics, we said. From way down beyond Mochudi and other side Frik Bonthuys's farm, even. *There* was tropics for you, now, we said to the schoolmaster. Why, he should just see Frik Bonthuys's shirt. Frik Bonthuys wore his shirt outside of his trousers, and the back part of it hung down almost onto the ground.

The schoolmaster said that he thought we were being perhaps just a little too sensitive about this sort of thing. He was interested himself in the white ant, he explained, mainly from the scientific point of view. The white ant belonged to the insect world, that was very highly civilised, he said. All the insect world didn't have was haemoglobin. The insect had the same blood in his veins as a white man, the schoolmaster said, except for haemoglobin.

Gysbert van Tonder said that whatever that thing was, it was enough.

Gysbert said it quite hastily, too. He said that when once you started making allowances for the white ant, that way, the next thing the white ant would want would be to vote. And *he* wouldn't go into a polling booth alongside of an ant, to vote, Gysbert van Tonder said, even if that ant *was* white.

This conversation was getting us out of our depths. The talk had taken a wrong turning, but we couldn't make out where, exactly. Consequently, we were all pleased when Oupa Bekker spoke, and made things seem sensible again.

"The worst place I ever knew for white ants, in the old days," Oupa Bekker said, "was along the Molopo, just below where it joins the Crocodile River. *There* was white ants for you. I was a transport rider in those days, when all the transport was still by ox-wagon. My partner was Jan Theron. We called him Jan Mankie because of his wooden leg, a back wheel of the ox-wagon having gone over his knee-cap one day when he had been drinking mampoer. Anyway, we had camped out beside the Molopo. And next morning, when we inspanned, Jan Mankie was saying how gay and *light* he felt. He couldn't understand it. He even started thinking that it must be the drink again, that was this time affecting him in quite a new way. We didn't know, of course, that it was because the white ants had hollowed out all of his wooden leg while he had lain asleep.

"And what was still more queer was that the wagon, when he inspanned it, also seemed surprisingly light. It didn't strike us what the reason for that was, either, just then. Maybe we were not in a guessing frame of mind, that morning. But when our trek got through the Paradys Poort, into a stiff wind that was blowing across the vlakte, it all became very clear to us. For the sudden cloud of dust that went up was not just dust from the road. Our wagon and its load of planed Oregon pine were carried away in the finest kind of powder you can imagine, and all our oxen were left pulling was the trek-chain. And Jan Mankie Theron was standing on one leg. His other trouser leg, that was of a greyish-coloured moleskin, was flapping empty in the wind."

Thus, Oupa Bekker's factual account of a straightforward Marico incident of long ago, presenting the ways and characteristics of the termite in a positive light, restored us to a sense of current realities.

"But what are you supposed to do about white ants, anyway?" Johnny Coen asked after a while. "Cooper's dip helps, of course. But there should be a more permanent way of getting rid of them, I'd imagine."

It was then that we all turned to the schoolmaster, again. What did it say in that book of his about the white ant, we asked him.

Well, there was a chapter in his book on the destruction of termites, the schoolmaster said. At least, there had been a chapter. It was the last chapter in the book. But he had unfortunately left the book lying on his desk in the schoolroom over one weekend. And when he had got back on Monday morning there was a little tunnel running up his desk. And the pages dealing with how to exterminate the white ant had been eaten away.

PIET SIENER

Jurie Steyn jerked his thumb over his shoulder at the square crate in the corner of the voorkamer. "That is for Piet Siener," he announced. "Funny he hasn't come to fetch it. Maybe he doesn't know it has arrived."

We realised that this was a joke of Jurie Steyn's, of course. As though there was anything Piet Siener, living away at the back of Kalkbult, didn't know . . .

I mean, that was why we called him Piet Siener. He not only knew everything that happened, but he also knew it before it happened. Some of his more fervent admirers in the Groot Marico even went so far as to say that Piet Siener also knew about things that didn't happen at all.

So when Jurie Steyn said that maybe Piet Siener didn't *know* that that square box had come for him on the Government lorry, and was waiting to be fetched – well, we understood right away that Jurie Steyn was being playful.

"Piet Siener doesn't go about much these days," Gysbert van Tonder said. "There's nearly always somebody at his house, wanting to know from him about the future. They say he gets it out of the ground. That's why you always see him walking about his farm with his eyes down, like that. It's a great gift, knowing everything, the way he does. And he won't take money for telling you what you want to know. All he'll take is just a little present, perhaps."

Then Johnny Coen told us about the last time he went to Kalkbult about something he was keen on getting enlightenment on.

"I came across Piet Siener on his lands," Johnny Coen said. "He was walking about with his eyes cast down, just like Gysbert said. Piet Siener was walking over uneven ground to try out a new pair of shop boots that his last visitor had made him a little present of."

But Piet Siener was actually looking more at his feet than at the ground, Johnny Coen added. It seemed that it was a pair of somewhat tight shop boots.

"And what did Piet Siener say?" At Naudé asked. "Did he tell you when Minnie Nienaber would be coming back from Johannesburg?"

Johnny Coen looked mildly surprised.

"Well, I did, as a matter of fact, mention something along those lines to Piet Siener," he said. "I'm sure I don't know how you guessed, though. You don't seem too bad yourself at being a seer."

But Gysbert van Tonder said that there was nobody in the Groot Marico north of Sephton's Nek who wouldn't have been able to guess, just immediately, what it was that Johnny Coen would want to go and see Piet Siener about.

"And, of course, Piet Siener guessed it, too," Johnny Coen explained. "But in his case, naturally, he didn't guess it so much as that he *divined* it. It gave me quite a turn, too, the way he was standing there on the veld with his black beard flowing in the wind and his eyes fixed on his feet divining, because all I said to him was that I had come to see him about a girl, and he asked me her name. And I said Minnie Nienaber. And he said, oh, that must be the daughter of Koos Nienaber. And I said, yes. And he asked me wasn't she in Johannesburg, or something. He asked it just like that, with his eyes down and seeming as though his gaze would pierce right into the middle of the earth, if it wasn't that his feet were in the way."

And we all admitted then that Piet Siener did indeed have very great gifts. And he was so very modest about it, too, we said. It was almost because it was so easy for him to be a seer that he didn't value it. And so we were not surprised when Johnny Coen told us that when he offered Piet Siener his watch and chain, he wouldn't take it.

"Piet Siener was quite cross about it, too," Johnny Coen proceeded. "He said that what he had told me was nothing – just nothing at all. And he said he already had over two dozen watches and chains, and what he would do with any more he just didn't know. I felt that was one of the few things that Piet Siener really *didn't* know. And he said that if I had no more use for my new guitar with the picture of gold angels on it, and if I was determined to give him a little present . . ."

So we said that that was Piet Siener all over. He would never accept from you anything that you thought something *of*. If you did give him a present, then it had to be something that you were finished with.

"Like the time I went to see Piet Siener about a cure for my wife's asthma," Gysbert van Tonder said. "It was just after I had bought that mealie-planter with the green wheels. I did not say anything to Piet Siener about my wife's asthma. There was no need for me to. In fact, before I could tell him what I had come about, he told me something quite different. That's how great a seer he is. He said he could see a most awful disaster hanging over my head. No, he wouldn't tell me what that disaster was, because if he *did* tell me it would turn my hair grey overnight, having that size of calamity hanging over my head. It was more than flesh and blood could stand.

"But there was still time to turn that misfortune aside from me onto someone else. So I asked him would he turn it aside onto the market master in Zeerust, and I wouldn't care how much of a disaster it was then, I said. And Piet Siener said all right. And he said that if I had to give him a little present, well, if I had perhaps thought of throwing away my mealie-planter with the green wheels, then I mustn't do any such thing. *He* would take it, he said."

After that Jurie Steyn told us about the last time Piet Siener came to his post office, and about how there was in the post bag for Jurie Steyn a new kind of hair clipper he had ordered from Johannesburg, having seen a picture of it in the *Kerkbode*. "I told Piet Siener what was in the parcel," Jurie continued. "And do you know what, before I had unwrapped it, even, Piet Siener said I mustn't throw it away on the rubbish heap, or give it to the first Bechuana I saw."

"Well, can you beat that?" At Naudé asked, and in his tone there was real admiration.

It was while we were still talking about how wonderful he was that Piet Siener himself came into the post office. He walked with a quick step, his black beard flapping. You could see he was excited.

Then he walked straight up to the counter and said to Jurie Steyn: "There's something come for me in a small packing case. It was sent free on rail."

We nudged each other when we heard that. We felt that there was just nothing you could keep from the seer.

"I got the rail note yesterday," Piet Siener said, producing a piece of paper from his pocket. "Weight 98 lb., it says on the consignment. I'll take it with me."

Jurie Steyn pointed to the crate in the corner.

90

"I could have guessed as much," Piet Siener said when he lifted the crate and then turned it round. "Look, it says 'This side up, with care.' Instead of that you've got it standing on its end. I could have guessed that would happen."

"You mean you could have *divined* it," At Naudé said. But we didn't laugh. The moment seemed too solemn, somehow.

Jurie Steyn apologised and said there was no doubt something very precious inside. And we realised that Jurie spoke those words as though he meant them. It wasn't the way he usually apologised to people in his post office, that made you feel sorry you had brought the matter up at all.

Piet Siener said that it was all right, then. But he said that what was inside that crate was something of such importance that you couldn't be careful enough with it. He had ordered it from America, he said. And it was the latest invention in electro-biology and some kind of rays that he hadn't quite got the hang of yet, but that he was still studying the pamphlet. By means of that instrument you could tell if there was gold or diamonds under the ground.

"You can stand it on a tripod anywhere you like," Piet Siener explained. "And it will tell you what minerals there are in the crust of the earth under your feet up to a depth of two miles. Think of that – two miles."

We did think of it, after Piet Siener had gone out with the crate. And we said he couldn't be much of a siener if he didn't know what was two miles under the ground without having to look through an electric instrument that he had to order from America. And we thought nothing of his gift anymore.

He could throw his seer's mantle away on the rubbish heap, now, for all we cared. Or he could make a present of it to the first down-and-out Bechuana passing along the road.

POTCHEFSTROOM WILLOW

"The trouble," At Naudé said, "about getting the latest war news over the wireless, is that Klaas Smit and his Boeremusiek orchestra start up right away after it, playing 'Die Nooi van Potchefstroom'. Now, it isn't that I don't like that song –"

So we said that it wasn't as though we didn't like it, either. Gysbert van Tonder began to hum the tune. Johnny Coen joined in, singing the words softly – "Vertel my neef, vertel my oom, Is hierdie die pad na Potchefstroom?" In a little while we were all singing. Not very loudly, of course. For Jurie Steyn was conscious of the fact that his post office was a public place, and he frowned on any sort of out of the way behaviour in it. We still remembered the manner in which Jurie Steyn spoke to Chris Welman the time Chris was mending a pair of his wife's veldskoens in the post office, using the corner of the counter as a last.

"I can't object to your sitting in my post office, waiting for the Government lorry," Jurie Steyn said, "as long as you're white. You're entitled to sit here. You're also entitled to drink the coffee that my wife is soft-hearted enough to bring round to you on a tray. I'm sure I don't know why she does it. I was in the post office in Johannesburg, once, and I didn't see anybody coming around *there*, with cups of coffee on a tray. If you wanted coffee in the Johannesburg post office you would have to go round to the kitchen door for it, I suppose. And I feel that's what my wife should do, also. But she doesn't. All right – she's soft-hearted. But I won't let any man come and mend boots on my post office counter and right next to the official brass scales, too, I won't. If I allow that, the next thing a man will do is he'll come in here and sit down on my rusbank and read a book. We all know my voorkamer is a public place, but I will not let anybody take liberties in it."

For that reason we did not raise our voices very much when we sang "Die Nooi van Potchefstroom". But it was a catchy song, and Jurie

Steyn joined in a little, too, afterwards. Not that he let himself go in any way, of course. He sang in a reserved and dignified fashion, that made you feel he would yet go far. You felt that even the Postmaster-General in Pretoria, on the occasion of a member of the public coming to him to complain about a registered letter that had got lost, say – well, even the Postmaster-General would not have been able to sit back in his chair and sing "Die Nooi van Potchefstroom" in as elevated a manner as what Jurie Steyn was doing at that very moment.

Before the singing had quite died down, Oupa Bekker was saying that he knew Potchefstroom when he was still a child. It was in the very old days, Oupa Bekker said, and the far side foundations of the church on Kerkplein had not sunk nearly as deep as they had done today. He said he remembered the first time that there was a split in the Church. It was between the Doppers and the Hervormdes, he said. And it was quite a serious split. And because he was young, then, he thought it had to do with the way the brickwork on the wall nearest the street had to be constantly plastered up, from top to bottom, the more the foundations sank.

"I remember showing my father that piece of church wall," Oupa Bekker continued, "and I asked my father if the Doppers had done it. And my father said, well, he had never thought about it like that, until then. But all the same, he wouldn't be surprised if it was so. Not that anybody would ever *see* the Doppers kneeling down there on the sidewalk, loosening the bricks with a crowbar, my father added. The Doppers were too cunning for that. Whatever they did was under the cover of darkness."

At Naudé started talking again about the news of the war in Korea, that he had heard over the wireless. But because so much had been spoken in between, he had to explain right from the beginning again.

"It's the way the war news gets *crowded* by Klaas Smit and his orchestra," At Naudé said. "You're listening to what the announcer is making clear about what part of that country General MacArthur is fighting in now – and it's hard to follow all that, because it seems to me that sometimes General MacArthur himself is not too clear as to what part of the country he is in – and then, suddenly, while you're still listening, up strikes Klaas Smit's orchestra with 'Die Nooi van Potchefstroom'. It makes it all very difficult, you know. They don't give that General MacArthur a chance at all. 'Die Nooi van Potchefstroom' seems to be crowding him even worse than the Communists are doing – and that seems to be bad enough, the Lord knows."

This time we did not start singing again. We had, after all, taken the song to the end, and even if it wasn't for Jurie Steyn's feelings we ourselves knew enough about the right way of conducting ourselves in a post office. You can't go and sing the same song in a post office twice, just as though it's the quarterly meeting of the Mealie Control Board. We were glad, therefore, when Oupa Bekker started talking once more.

"This song, now," Oupa Bekker was saying, "well, as you know, I remember the early days of Potchefstroom. The very early days, that is. But I would never have imagined that some day a poet would come along and make up a song about the place. Potchefstroom was the first capital of the Transvaal, of course. Long before Pretoria was thought of, even. And there's an old willow tree in Potchefstroom that must have measured I don't know how many feet around the trunk where it goes into the ground. It measured that much only a little while ago, I mean. I am talking about the last time I was in Potchefstroom. But I never imagined anybody would ever write a poem about the town. It seemed such a hard name to make verses about. But I suppose it's a lot different today. People are so much more clever, I expect."

Johnny Coen, who had worked on the railways at Ottoshoop and knew a good deal about culture, assured Oupa Bekker that that was indeed the case. For a poet that wanted to write poetry today, Johnny Coen said, there was no word that would put him off. In fact, the harder the word, the better the poet would like it. Not that he knew anything about poetry himself, Johnny Coen acknowledged, but he had been round the world a bit, and he kept his eyes open, and he had seen a thing or two.

"If you saw the way they concreted up the buffers for the shunting engine on the goods line," Johnny Coen said, "then you would know what I am talking about. It was five-eighths steel reinforcements right through. After that, for a poet to make up a poem with the name of Potchefstroom in it, why, man, if you saw how they built up that extra platform in all box sections, you'll understand how it is that people have got the brains today to deal with problems that were a bit beyond them, no doubt, in Oupa Bekker's time."

Oupa Bekker nodded his head several times. He would have gone on nodding it a good deal longer, maybe, if it wasn't that Jurie Steyn's wife came in just about then with the coffee. Consequently, Oupa Bekker had to sit up properly and stir the sugar round in his cup.

"I heard that song you were singing, just now," Jurie Steyn's wife remarked to all of us. "I thought it was – well, I *liked* it. I didn't catch the words, quite."

Nobody answered. We knew that it was school holidays, of course. And we knew that young Vermaak, the schoolmaster, had gone to his parents in Potchefstroom for the holidays. Because we knew that Potchefstroom was young Vermaak's home town, we kept silent. There was no telling what Jurie Steyn's reactions would be.

Oupa Bekker went on talking, however.

"All the same, I would like to know how many feet around the trunk of that willow tree it is today," Oupa Bekker said. "And they won't chop it down either. That willow tree is right on the edge of the graveyard. You can almost say that it's *inside* the graveyard. And so they won't chop it down. But what beats me is to think that somebody could actually write a song about Potchefstroom. I would never have thought it possible."

Oupa Bekker's sigh seemed to come from far away.

From somewhere a good deal further away than the rusbank he was sitting on. We understood then why that Potchefstroom willow tree meant so much to him.

And the result was that when Gysbert van Tonder started up the chorus of that song again we all found ourselves joining in – no matter what Jurie Steyn might say about it. "En in my droom," we sang, "is die vaalhaar nooi by die wilgerboom."

Sea-colonels All

The passenger on the motor-lorry from Bekkersdal that afternoon was Japie Maasdyk, Oom 'Rooi' Maasdyk's son. We knew that Japie would be coming back to his parents' farm in the Dwarsberge on leave. We were somewhat disappointed that he came back dressed in a sports jacket and grey flannel trousers.

"We were looking forward to your return," Jurie Steyn said, "all rigged out in the blue sea-army suit that we thought you would be wearing at that college for sea-soldiers."

Japie said that if Jurie meant his naval uniform, well, it was in his luggage all neatly folded up.

"You know," At Naudé said, "I've been reading in the papers that they are going to call the different ranks in the South African Navy by a lot of new names. Has it reached to you boys in the training ship yet, Japie? I believe they are going to call the man that is in charge of your ship a sea-colonel, or something. Have you heard of it at all?"

So Japie said that he couldn't call to mind that particular name. But there were lots of other names that the young sea-cadets called the captain of the training ship. Not loud enough for him to hear, of course. He couldn't remember if sea-colonel was one of them, Japie said. But one name he could recall was son of a sea-cook.

"Anyway, they're making quite a lot of jokes about it in the papers," At Naudé went on. "But I can't see anything funny about it. I mean, if a man is a sea-colonel, what else could you call him, really?"

Young Japie Maasdyk was just opening his mouth to say the word, when Chris Welman signalled to him to be careful not to use bad language, at the same time pointing in the direction of the kitchen, where Jurie Steyn's wife was. From the quick way in which Japie picked up the signal, we could see that he had learnt a thing or two during the time he was at the naval college.

Gysbert van Tonder started telling us about a sea-soldier that he met, once, in Zeerust. And so he knew the sort, Gysbert van Tonder said. Only, of course, he didn't want young Japie Maasdyk to think that he intended any personal reflection on himself. Thereupon Japie Maasdyk said Good Lord, no.

"Why, to come back here and listen to all of you talking," Japie said, "it's almost as though I've never been away. You were talking exactly the same things when I left. And I feel just as though I have missed nothing in between. Nothing worthwhile, that is."

We said that it was most friendly of Japie Maasdyk to talk like that. It was good to think that his having been on the high seas, and all, hadn't changed him from the little Bushveld boy with a freckled face and sore toes that we had seen growing up in front of us, we said. At Naudé was even able to remember the time when the new ouderling went to call at the Maasdyk farmhouse. And the only member of the family that the ouderling found at home was little Japie.

"And you stood under a camel-thorn tree, talking to the ouderling," At Naudé went on, laughing so much that the tears ran down his cheeks. "And you stood on one foot. On your left foot. You stood with your right foot resting on your left knee. Every little Bushveld boy stands that way when he's shy. And because the ouderling had much wisdom, he knew what you meant when you said that your parents weren't at home. The ouderling knew that your mother was in the kitchen and that your father had run away into the bush to hide. Like we all do in these parts when we see a stranger driving up to the front door. Ha, ha, ha."

We all laughed at that, of course. And it seemed as though Japie Maasdyk was gratified to think that we felt that he was still one of us, and that the time he had spent aboard the training ship had not changed him in any way. From the way he kept his eyes fixed straight on the floor in front of him, the while his face turned red as a beetroot, we could see just how gratified Japie Maasdyk was.

Gysbert van Tonder went on with his story about the sailor he encountered in Zeerust. And although we knew that in the story he wasn't making even an indirect sort of reference to Japie Maasdyk – since he had given us his personal assurance on that point – nevertheless, as Gysbert went on talking, more than one of us sitting in that voorkamer on that afternoon found his thoughts going, in spite of himself, to that little hand trunk in which Japie Maasdyk's blue uniform was all neatly parcelled up.

"That sea-trooper now," Gysbert van Tonder was saying, "well, I know the *sort* of man. He was swaying from side to side as he walked along that Zeerust pavement. And when he went into the bar he missed the first step. It would seem, from what he told me, that at sea all ship-soldiers walk like that. And when I saw what he had to drink – and it was before midday, too – I understood why. He tried to explain to me, of course, that the reason he walked that way was because the submarine he was employed on was so unsteady on its keel. All the same, it gave me a pretty good idea why that submarine was so unsteady. If the other underwater infantrymen were like him, I mean. He told me that he hadn't found his land-legs yet."

When Gysbert van Tonder spoke about land-legs, it gave Jurie Steyn an idea. In that way, Jurie Steyn was enabled to say a few words derived from his personal knowledge of the lore of the seafarer.

Jurie Steyn dealt with the answer that our Volksraad member had given a questioner at a meeting some years ago. The questioner had asked our Volksraad member if it wasn't a waste of money, and all that, keeping up a South African Navy, with the sea so far away. And with the Molopo River having been dry for the past four years because of the drought, the questioner added.

"The Volksraad member spoke very beautiful things, then," Jurie Steyn said. "He explained about how our forefathers that came over with Jan van Riebeeck were all ship-military men. They were common sea-soldiers who, with their trusty sea-pots filled with common boiling lead, kept the Spaniards at arm's length for eighty years. Arm's length did not, perhaps, amount to very much, our Volksraad member said, but eighty years did count for something, and we all cheered."

Chris Welman said "Hear, hear," then, and several of us clapped. We knew that Jurie Steyn had allowed his name to go forward as a candidate for the next school committee elections, and from the way he spoke now, it seemed that he was likely to get in. A strong stand in the war against Spain was still a better bet than parallel-medium education.

"I remember that our Volksraad member said that the call of the sea was in our blood," Jurie Steyn continued. "He said that, when he first got elected, and he got a free pass to Cape Town, and he alighted from the train at the docks, by mistake, and he saw all that blue water for the first time in his life – he said how very moved he was. He said that he wanted to climb up to the top of one of those cranes, there, and empty a sea-pot full of boiling lead – or whatever was in that sea-pot – onto any-body passing within throwing distance and speaking out of his turn. That had been a hard-fought election, our Volksraad member said, just like the war against Spain had also been hard-fought, and his Sea Beg-gar blood was up."

It was after we had cheered Jurie Steyn for the second time that we realised how strange a thing it was to be a politician. For Jurie Steyn, who had never been to sea, received all our applause, while young Japie Maasdyk, with his blue uniform no doubt getting more and more crumpled in the hand baggage, the longer Jurie Steyn spoke, got no kind of recognition at all as a ship-private, in spite of the fact that he had been trained for the work. Whereas, if we had been told that in addition to being postmaster for the area Jurie Steyn had also been appointed sea-colonel for the whole of the Dwarsberge we would not have been at all surprised. There was something about Jurie Steyn that made you *think*, somehow, of a sea-colonel.

Oupa Bekker tried to say something, just about then. But we shut him up, the moment he sought to raise a skinny hand. We wouldn't stand for him stopping one of three, with his long grey beard and glittering eye. In the Dwarsberge there was no room for an ancient sea-private talking about an albatross. Quite rightly, we did not wish to hear about a sadder and a wiser man rising the morrow morn.

Shortly afterwards, Jurie Steyn's wife brought in coffee. When she went out of the voorkamer again, with an empty tray, she gave one look over her shoulder at Japie Maasdyk. There really was something about a sailor, we felt then.

But it was when, there being no other form of transport at that late hour, Jurie Steyn lent Japie Maasdyk his horse, that we realised how much Japie had indeed learnt at that naval college. From the awkward way he sat on that horse you could see that they had truly made Japie Maasdyk a sea-burgher.

III

Oom At Geel, Cape rebel, soldier, farmer and the man who sold Bosman the rifle with which he later killed his stepbrother, Nietverdiend. 1964

IDLE TALK

"You know," Jurie Steyn said, right out of nothing, sort of – since we weren't talking of his voorkamer at all, at that moment, but of the best way of crating a pig that you are sending to the market – "there is something about my post office. I can't quite explain it, but I have noticed that each time there is a small gathering of farmers here, waiting for the lorry, well, quite a lot of sense seems to be talked here, somehow. You know what I mean – sense."

Gysbert van Tonder said, then, in a dignified kind of manner, that it wasn't clear to him why Jurie Steyn should give his voorkamer all the credit for it.

"If we were sitting out on the veld, under a camel-thorn tree, say," Gysbert van Tonder said, "and we were talking sensible things, as we always do, then there would be much reason and sound judgment in whatever we had to say. You haven't got to be in the konsistorie of the church in Zeerust in order to make a judicious remark. Indeed, Jurie, with all respect to your wife's cousin, who is a deacon, I actually think that some of the things I have heard said that have been least thoughtful, have been said *in* the Zeerust konsistorie."

Chris Welman said that, in talking that way, Gysbert van Tonder was being equally unfair. There was something about the way you felt when you were in the vestry, Chris Welman said, with the walls so clean and high and whitewashed, and with a couple of elders next to you that looked – well, if not *clean*, exactly, then at least high up and whitewashed. Anyway, you couldn't be yourself, then, quite, Chris Welman said.

Yes, he ended up very lamely.

Jurie Steyn felt called on, then, to come to the defence of his wife's cousin, Deacon Kirstein. For it wasn't a happy picture, somehow, that Chris Welman had left us with, of the deacons and elders meeting in the

Zeerust konsistorie before a church service. And with Deacon Kirstein perhaps looking more whitewashed than any of them.

"I can't understand Chris Welman talking that way," Jurie Steyn said, primly. "Because if Chris Welman's name ever had to be put forward, for a deacon, I am sure that nobody would talk against him and mention a truckload of Afrikander oxen that a –"

"That a *what*?" Gysbert van Tonder demanded, his voice sounding almost fierce.

"Oh, nothing, nothing," Jurie Steyn answered. "I don't know what you are suggesting, even, Gysbert. I was just trying to say that if Chris Welman's name, now, had to be put forward as deacon, well, there would be nothing against him, if you know what I mean. Chris Welman's name would be held in great respect."

Gysbert van Tonder was on the point of replying. But we realised that he pulled himself up short. Jurie Steyn had caught him, all right. For what Gysbert van Tonder *might* have said was that maybe there was nothing at all against Chris Welman as an honourable burgher and a regular churchgoer. But there was Chris Welman's son, Tobie . . .

It was almost as though Jurie Steyn had challenged Gysbert van Tonder to mention the name of Chris Welman's son. For then there would, indeed, have been trouble. In any case, Gysbert van Tonder sat silent for a few moments. And you could see that it was on the tip of his tongue to talk about Chris Welman's son, Tobie. And to say that Chris Welman might be a good churchgoer, and all that. But that Chris Welman's son, Tobie, was even more regular. Singing a lot of hymns and psalms every Sunday without fail, for almost three years, in the chapel of the reform school.

From his silence, it was clear that that was something Gysbert van Tonder dared not mention. So Gysbert van Tonder contented himself with explaining that whatever Jurie Steyn was hinting at, about the time the stationmaster refused to have those oxen trucked unless he knew who the owner was, well – Gysbert van Tonder said – a lot of people had already had occasion to complain about how officious that stationmaster was.

"What about the time our Volksraad member's brother-in-law himself went down to the station and spoke to the stationmaster very firmly?" Gysbert van Tonder went on. "And he asked the stationmaster if he thought that every farmer in the Groot Marico was a cattle thief.

He asked him that straight out, because he had brought witnesses with him. And the stationmaster said, no, but he knew that every Marico farmer was a cattle farmer, and he knew that any cattle farmer could make a mistake."

We all said, then, that that was quite a different thing. And we said that if you weren't there to see to it yourself, and you left it to a Bechuana herd-boy to go and have a lot of cattle railed to Johannesburg, why, mistakes were almost sure to happen, we said. Thereupon At Naudé started telling us about a mistake that one of his Bechuana herd-boys had made on a certain occasion, as a result of which six of Koos Nienaber's best trek-oxen got railed to Johannesburg along with some scrub animals that At Naudé was sending to the market.

"That was the time Koos Nienaber went to Johannesburg to have his old Mauser mended," At Naudé explained. "And it just happened that because he didn't know where to get off, Koos Nienaber was shunted onto a siding, somewhere, past Johannesburg station. And what should take place but that Koos Nienaber alighted from his second-class compartment just at the same time that his six trek-oxen should be walking out of a truck on the other side of the line. That caused quite a lot of trouble, of course. And before he got his six trek-oxen back, Koos Nienaber had to explain to a magistrate what he meant by loading all the five chambers of his Mauser on a railway platform, even though the bolt action and foresight of the Mauser were in need of repair. I believe the magistrate said that there were quite enough brawls and ugly scenes that had to do with gun-play taking place in Johannesburg every day, without a farmer having to come all the way from the Marico with a rusty Mauser to add to all that unpleasantness. Naturally, I gave my Bechuana herd-boy a good straight talking-to about it afterwards, for being so ignorant."

At Naudé paused, as though inviting one of us to say something. But we had none of us any comment to make. For we had long ago heard Koos Nienaber's side of the story. And from what he had told us, it would appear that all the fault did not lie with At Naudé's herd-boy. At Naudé seemed to fit a little into the story, himself.

"Anyway," At Naudé added – smiling in a twisted sort of way – "what Koos Nienaber was most sore about, in court, was that that Johannesburg magistrate spoke of his Mauser as a rusty old fowling-piece."

Koos Nienaber didn't object to the fowling-piece part of it, so much,

At Naudé said. Because he wasn't quite sure what a fowling-piece was. But it took him a long time to get over the idea of the magistrate saying that his Mauser was rusty.

There was an uncomfortable silence, once again. It was broken by young Johnny Coen. Often, in the past, when there had been some misunderstanding in Jurie Steyn's post office, Johnny Coen had said something to smooth matters over.

"Maybe it's like what it says in the Good Book," Johnny Coen remarked. "Perhaps it's to do with Mammon. Perhaps if we sought the Kingdom of Heaven more, then we wouldn't have such thoughtless things happening. Like a farmer sending some of his own neighbour's cattle to the market by mistake. It's a mistake that happens with every truck-load, almost. I was working at Ottoshoop siding, and I know. It used to give the stationmaster there grey hairs. Loading a lot of cattle into a truck and then not knowing how many would have to be unloaded again before the engine came to fetch that truck. And all the time it was through some mistake, of course. A mistake on the part of an ignorant Bechuana herd-boy."

It was then that some of us remembered the mistakes that the herd-boy of Deacon Kirstein had made, long ago, along those same lines. We felt not a little pained at having to mention those mistakes, considering the high regard in which we held Deacon Kirstein, who was Jurie Steyn's wife's cousin. We only made mention of it because of the circumstance that that mistake on the part of the deacon's herd-boy had gone on over a period of years, before it was detected. And maybe the mistake would never have been found out, either, if it wasn't that, along with a truck full of Deacon Kirstein's Large White pigs, there was also loaded a span of mules belonging to a near neighbour of Deacon Kirstein's.

And because he was already a deacon, we all felt very sorry for Deacon Kirstein, to think that his herd-boy should be so ignorant. And we winked at each other a good deal, too, in those days, one Marico farmer winking at another. And we said that it was just too bad that Deacon Kirstein should have so uneducated a herd-boy, who couldn't tell the difference between a Large White and a mule. And we would wink a lot more.

That was the line that the conversation suddenly took, in Jurie Steyn's voorkamer. We were just recalling the old days, we said to each other.

And we were enjoying this talk about the past. And we could see that Jurie Steyn was enjoying it also. And then Johnny Coen tried to spoil everything. Johnny Coen, without anybody asking him, began to talk about the Sermon on the Mount. And let any of us that was without sin, Johnny Coen added, cast the first stone.

Jurie Steyn summed it all up.

"Maybe a lot of sense gets talked here in my post office," Jurie Steyn said, "but a lot of ——, also."

Jurie Steyn said that word softly, because he didn't want his wife to hear.

Birth Certificate

It was when At Naudé told us what he had read in the newspaper about a man who had thought all his life that he was white, and had then discovered that he was coloured, that the story of Flippus Biljon was called to mind. I mean, we all knew the story of Flippus Biljon. But because it was still early afternoon we did not immediately make mention of Flippus. Instead, we discussed, at considerable length, other instances that were within our knowledge of people who had grown up as one sort of person and had discovered in later life that they were in actual fact quite a different sort of person.

Many of these stories that we recalled in Jurie Steyn's voorkamer as the shadows of the thorn-trees lengthened were based only on hearsay. It was the kind of story that you had heard, as a child, at your grandmother's knee. But your grandmother would never admit, of course, that she had heard that story at *her* grandmother's knee. Oh, no. She could remember very clearly how it all happened, just like it was yesterday. And she could tell you the name of the farm. And the name of the landdrost who was summoned to take note of the extraordinary occurrence, when it had to do with a more unusual sort of changeling, that is. And she would recall the solemn manner in which the landdrost took off his hat when he said that there were many things that were beyond human understanding.

Similarly now, in the voorkamer, when we recalled stories of white children that had been carried off by a Bushman or a baboon or a werewolf, even, and had been brought up in the wilds and without any proper religious instruction, then we also did not think it necessary to explain where we had first heard those stories. We spoke as though we had been actually present at some stage of the affair – more usually at the last scene, where the child, now grown to manhood and needing trousers and a pair of braces and a hat, gets restored to his parents and the magistrate after studying the birth certificate says that there are things in this world that baffle the human mind.

And while the shadows under the thorn-trees grew longer, the stories we told in Jurie Steyn's voorkamer grew, if not longer, then, at least, taller.

"But this isn't the point of what I have been trying to explain," At Naudé interrupted a story of Gysbert van Tonder's that was getting a bit confused in parts, through Gysbert van Tonder not being quite clear as to what a werewolf was. "When I read that bit in the newspaper I started wondering how must a man *feel*, after he has grown up with adopted parents and he discovers, quite late in life, through seeing his birth certificate for the first time, that he isn't white, after all. That is what I am trying to get at. Supposing Gysbert were to find out suddenly –"

At Naudé pulled himself up short. Maybe there were one or two things about a werewolf that Gysbert van Tonder wasn't too sure about, and he would allow himself to be corrected by Oupa Bekker on such points. But there were certain things he wouldn't stand for.

"All right," At Naudé said hastily, "I don't mean Gysbert van Tonder, specially. What I am trying to get at is, how would any one of us feel? How would any white man feel, if he has passed as white all his life, and he sees for the first time, from his birth certificate, that his grandfather was coloured? I mean, how would he *feel*? Think of that awful moment when he looks at the palms of his hands and he sees –"

"He can have that awful moment," Gysbert van Tonder said. "I've looked at the palm of my hand. It's a white man's palm. And my fingernails have also got proper half-moons."

At Naudé said he had never doubted that. No, there was no need for Gysbert van Tonder to come any closer and show him. He could see quite well enough just from where he was sitting. After Chris Welman had pulled Gysbert van Tonder back onto the rusbank by his jacket, counselling him not to do anything foolish, since At Naudé did not mean *him*, Oupa Bekker started talking about a white child in Schweizer-Reneke that had been stolen out of its cradle by a family of baboons.

"I haven't seen that cradle myself," Oupa Bekker acknowledged, modestly. "But I met many people who have. After the child had been stolen, neighbours from as far as the Orange River came to look at that cradle. And when they looked at it they admired the particular way that

Heilart Nortjé – that was the child's father – had set about making his household furniture, with glued klinkpenne in the joints, and all. But the real interest about the cradle was that it was empty, proving that the child had been stolen by baboons. I remember how one neighbour, who was not on very good terms with Heilart Nortjé, went about the district saying that it could only have *been* baboons.

"But it was many years before Heilart Nortjé and his wife saw their child again. By *saw*, I mean getting near enough to be able to talk to him and ask him how he was getting on. For he was always too quick, from the way the baboons had brought him up. At intervals Heilart Nortjé and his wife would see the tribe of baboons sitting on a rant, and their son, young Heilart, would be in the company of the baboons. And once, through his field-glasses, Heilart had been able to observe his son for quite a few moments. His son was then engaged in picking up a stone and laying hold of a scorpion that was underneath it. The speed with which his son pulled off the scorpion's sting and proceeded to eat up the rest of the scorpion whole filled the father's heart of Heilart Nortjé with a deep sense of pride.

"I remember how Heilart talked about it. 'Real intelligence,' Heilart announced with his chest stuck out. 'A real baboon couldn't have done it quicker or better. I called my wife, but she was a bit too late. All she could see was him looking as pleased as anything and scratching himself. And my wife and I held hands and we smiled at each other and we asked each other, where does he get it from?'

"But then there were times again when that tribe of baboons would leave the Schweizer-Reneke area and go deep into the Kalahari, and Heilart Nortjé and his wife would know nothing about what was happening to their son, except through reports from farmers near whose homesteads the baboons had passed. Those farmers had a lot to say about what happened to some of their sheep, not to talk of their mealies and watermelons. And Heilart would be very bitter about those farmers. Begrudging his son a few prickly-pears, he said.

"And it wasn't as though he hadn't made every effort to get his son back, Heilart said, so that he could go to catechism classes, since he was almost of age to be confirmed. He had set all sorts of traps for his son, Heilart said, and he had also thought of shooting the baboons, so that it would be easier, after that, to get his son back. But there was always the danger, firing into a pack like that, of his shooting his own son.

"The neighbour that I have spoken of before," Oupa Bekker continued, "who was not very well-disposed towards Heilart Nortjé, said that the real reason Heilart didn't shoot was because he didn't always know – actually *know* – which was his son and which was one of the more flatheaded kees-baboons."

It seemed that this was going to be a very long story. Several of us started getting restive . . . So Johnny Coen asked Oupa Bekker, in a polite sort of way, to tell us how it all ended.

"Well, Heilart Nortjé caught his son, afterwards," Oupa Bekker said. "But I am not sure if Heilart was altogether pleased about it. His son was so hard to tame. And then the way he caught him. It was the simplest sort of baboon trap of all . . . Yes, *that* one. A calabash with a hole in it just big enough for you to put your hand in, empty, but that you can't get your hand out of again when you're clutching a fistful of mealies that was put at the bottom of the calabash. Heilart Nortjé never got over that, really. He felt it was a very shameful thing that had happened to him. The thought that his son, in whom he had taken so much pride, should have allowed himself to be caught in the simplest form of monkey-trap."

When Oupa Bekker paused, Jurie Steyn said that it was indeed a sad story, and was, no doubt, perfectly true. There was just a certain tone in Jurie Steyn's voice that made Oupa Bekker continue.

"True in every particular," Oupa Bekker declared, nodding his head a good number of times. "The landdrost came over to see about it, too. They sent for the landdrost so that he could make a report about it. I was there, that afternoon, in Heilart Nortjé's voorkamer, when the landdrost came. And there were a good number of other people, also. And Heilart Nortjé's son, half-tamed in some ways but still baboon-wild in others, was there also. The landdrost studied the birth certificate very carefully. Then the landdrost said that what he had just been present at surpassed ordinary human understanding. And the landdrost took off his hat in a very solemn fashion.

"We all felt very embarrassed when Heilart Nortjé's son grabbed the hat out of the landdrost's hand and started biting pieces out of the crown."

When Oupa Bekker said those words it seemed to us like the end of a story. Consequently, we were disappointed when At Naudé started making further mention of that piece of news he had read in the daily paper. So there was nothing else for it but that we had to talk about Flippus Biljon. For Flippus Biljon's case was just the opposite of the case of the man that At Naudé's newspaper wrote about.

Because he had been adopted by a coloured family, Flippus Biljon had always regarded himself as a coloured man. And then one day, quite by accident, Flippus Biljon saw his birth certificate. And from that birth certificate it was clear that Flippus Biljon was as white as you or I. You can imagine how Flippus Biljon must have felt about it. Especially after he had gone to see the magistrate at Bekkersdal, and the magistrate, after studying the birth certificate, confirmed the fact that Flippus Biljon was a white man.

"Thank you, baas," Flippus Biljon said. "Thank you very much, *my basie.*"

Play within a Play

"But what did Jacques le Français want to put a thing like that on *for*?" Gysbert van Tonder asked.

In those words he conveyed something of what we all felt about the latest play with which the famous Afrikaans actor, Jacques le Français, was touring the platteland. A good number of us had gone over to Bekkersdal to attend the play. But – as always happens in such cases – those who hadn't actually seen the play knew just as much about it as those who had. More, even, sometimes.

"What I can't understand is how the kerkraad allowed Jacques le Français to hire the church hall for a show like that," Chris Welman said. "Especially when you think that the church hall is little more than a stone's throw from the church itself."

Naturally, Jurie Steyn could not let that statement pass. Criticism of the church council implied also a certain measure of fault-finding with Deacon Kirstein, who was a first cousin of Jurie's wife.

"You can hardly call it a stone's throw," Jurie Steyn declared. "After all, the plein is on two morgen of ground and the church hall is at the furthest end from the church itself. And there is also a row of bluegums in between. Tall, well-grown bluegums. No, you can hardly call all that a stone's throw, Chris."

So At Naudé said that what had no doubt happened was that Jacques le Français with his insinuating play-actor ways had got round the members of the kerkraad, somehow. With lies, as likely as not. Maybe he had told the deacons and elders that he was going to put on that play *Ander Man se Kind* again, which everybody approved of, seeing it was so instructive, the relentless way in which it showed up the sinful life led in the great city of Johannesburg and in which the girl in the play, Baba Haasbroek, got ensnared, because she was young and from the backveld, and didn't know any better.

"Although I don't know if that play did any good, really," At Naudé added, thoughtfully. "I mean, it was shortly after that that Drieka Basson of Enzelsberg left for Johannesburg, wasn't it? Perhaps the play *Ander Man se Kind* was a bit too – well – relentless."

Thereupon Johnny Coen took a hand in the conversation.

It seemed very long ago, the time Johnny Coen had gone to Johannesburg because of a girl that was alone there in that great city. And on his return to the Marico he had not spoken much of his visit, beyond mentioning that there were two men carved in stone holding up the doorway of a building near the station and that the pavements were so crowded that you could hardly walk on them. But for a good while after that he had looked more lonely in Jurie Steyn's voorkamer than any stranger could look in a great city.

"I don't know if you can say that that play of Jacques le Français's about the girl that went to Johannesburg really is so very instructive," Johnny Coen said. "There were certain things in it that are very true, of course. But there are also true things that could never go into one of Jacques le Français's plays – or into any play, I think."

Gysbert van Tonder started to laugh, then. It was a short sort of laugh.

"I remember what you said when you came back from Johannesburg, that time," Gysbert van Tonder said to Johnny Coen. "You said the pavements were so crowded that there was hardly room to walk. Well, in the play, *Ander Man se Kind*, it wasn't like that. The girl in the play, Baba Haasbroek, didn't seem to have trouble to walk about on the pavement, I mean, half the time, in the play, she was walking on the pavement. Or if she wasn't walking she was standing under a street-lamp."

It was then that At Naudé mentioned the girl in the new play that Jacques le Français had put on at Bekkersdal. Her name was Truida Ziemers. It was a made-up name, of course, At Naudé said. Just like Jacques le Français was a made-up name. His real name was Poggenpoel, or something. But how any Afrikaans writer could *write* a thing like that . . .

"It wasn't written by an Afrikaans dramatist," young Vermaak, the schoolteacher, explained. "It is a translation from –"

"To think that any Afrikaner should fall so low as to *translate* a thing like that, then," Gysbert van Tonder interrupted him. "And what's more, Jacques le Français or Jacobus Poggenpoel, or whatever his name is, is coloured. I could see he was coloured. No matter how he tried to make himself up, and all, to look white, it was a coloured man walking about there on the stage. How I didn't notice it in the play *Ander Man se Kind* I don't know. Maybe I sat too near the back, that time."

Young Vermaak did not know, of course, to what extent we were pulling his leg. He shook his head sadly. Then he started to explain, in a patient sort of way, that Jacques le Français was actually *playing* the role of a coloured man. He wasn't supposed to be white. It was an important part of the unfolding of the drama that Jacques le Français wasn't a white man. It told you all that in the title of the play, the schoolmaster said.

"What's he then, a Frenchman?" Jurie Steyn asked. "Why didn't they say so, straight out?"

Several of us said after that, each in turn, that there was something you couldn't understand, now. That a pretty girl like Truida Ziemers, with a blue flower in her hat, should fall in love with a coloured man, and even marry him. Because that was what happened in the play.

"And it wasn't as though she didn't know," Chris Welman remarked. "Meneer Vermaak has just told us that it says it in the title of the play, and all. Of course, I didn't see the play myself. I meant to go, but at the last moment one of my mules took sick. But I saw Truida Ziemers on the stage, once. And even now, as I am talking about her again, I can remember how pretty she was. And to think that she went and married a coloured man when all the time she *knew*. And it wasn't as though he could tell her that it was just sunburn, seeing that she could read it for herself on the posters. If the schoolmaster could read it, so could Truida."

Anyway, that was only to be expected, Gysbert van Tonder said. That Jacques le Français would murder Truida Ziemers in the end, he meant. After all, what else could you expect from a marriage like that? Maybe from that point of view the play could be taken as a warning to every respectable white girl in the country.

"But that isn't the *point* of the play," young Vermaak insisted, once more. "Actually it is a good play. And it is a play with real educational value. But not that kind of educational value. If I tell you that this play is a translation – and a pretty poor translation too: I wouldn't be surprised if Jacques le Français translated it himself – of the work of the great –"

This time the interruption came from Johnny Coen.

"It's all very well talking like they have been doing about a girl going wrong," Johnny Coen said. "But a great deal depends on circumstances. That is something I have learnt, now. Take the case now of a girl that . . ."

We all sat up to listen, then. And Gysbert van Tonder nudged Chris Welman in the ribs for coughing. We did not wish to miss a word.

"A girl that . . .?" At Naudé repeated in a tone of deep understanding, to encourage Johnny Coen to continue.

"Well, take a girl like that girl Baba Haasbroek in the play *Ander Man se Kind*," Johnny Coen said. Jurie Steyn groaned. We didn't want to hear all *that* over again.

"Well, anyway, if that girl *did* go wrong," Johnny Coen proceeded – pretty diffidently, now, as though he could sense our feelings of being balked – "then there might be reasons for it. Reasons that didn't come out in the play, maybe. And reasons that we sitting here in Jurie Steyn's voorkamer would perhaps not have the right to judge about, either."

Gysbert van Tonder started clearing his throat as though for another short laugh. But he seemed to change his mind halfway through.

"And in this last play, now," Johnny Coen added, "if Jacques le Français had really loved the girl, he wouldn't have been so jealous."

"Yes, it's a pity that Truida Ziemers got murdered in the end, like that," At Naudé remarked. "Her friends in the play should have seen what Jacques le Français was up to, and have put the police onto him, in time."

He said that with a wink, to draw young Vermaak, of course.

Thereupon the schoolmaster explained with much seriousness that such an ending would defeat the whole purpose of the drama. But by that time we had lost all interest in the subject. And when the Government lorry came soon afterwards and blew a lot of dust in at the door we made haste to collect our letters and milk-cans.

Consequently, nobody took much notice of what young Vermaak went on to tell us about the man who wrote the play. Not the man who translated it into Afrikaans but the man who wrote it in the first place. He was a writer who used to hold horses' heads in front of a theatre, the schoolmaster said, and when he died he left his second-best bed to his wife, or something.

SPRINGTIME IN MARICO

"It will soon be spring," Gysbert van Tonder observed, looking out of the door of Jurie Steyn's voorkamer to where the bush began.

"I don't know what spring is," Jurie Steyn replied, gruffly. "But if you mean that it's near the end of the winter, well, there I suppose you are right. You have not got such a thing as what you could call the springtime in the Groot Marico. All you get here is the end of the winter. Now, that's where the Cape is different."

We all knew that Jurie Steyn had been born in the Western Province and had lived there for the first years of his young manhood.

"The old Boland," Jurie Steyn went on, "there you do, indeed, have spring. I remember that at school in the Cape we learnt a recitation to say for the inspector, about 'viooltjies in die voorhuis.' That was in Standard Three. What recitation they learnt for the inspector the next year, I don't know. I wasn't there to find out. All the same, I expect I am better educated than most. If you don't count just book learning, I mean."

And so we all said, no, of course, we didn't count just such a thing as book learning, either. We knew that education – *real* education, that was – consisted in far more than what you learnt sitting at a school desk. In fact, there was not one of us in Jurie Steyn's voorkamer at that very moment that had had much book learning to speak of, we said. And yet look at us. Not that we gave ourselves *airs*, on that account, we said. It was just that we were privileged, perhaps.

Thereupon At Naudé turned to young Vermaak, the schoolmaster, and explained that we naturally did not mean him. We were all friends together, At Naudé made it clear to young Vermaak, and so young Vermaak must not get hold of the idea that we thought any the less of him, just on account of his having passed a couple of schoolteacher's exams, and so on.

"Oh, no," young Vermaak answered. "You mustn't misunderstand me, either. As a matter of fact – ha-ha – nobody has got more contempt for just book learning than what I have. No, I am one hundred percent in agreement with what Jurie Steyn has been saying."

Gysbert van Tonder looked somewhat surprised.

"You know," he said, "isn't that putting it rather high? One hundred percent, I mean. We all know, of course, that a schoolteacher doesn't get *much* of an education. We know that a schoolteacher doesn't go as high as a doctor or a lawyer, say. Or even as high as a foreman shunter and station accounts that you study through the correspondence college. But when you say you are one hundred percent ignorant – why, surely, you don't mean to say you're as ignorant as a na– ?"

Johnny Coen interrupted Gysbert van Tonder to say that he would be surprised if he knew how ignorant a schoolteacher was, really. It was in connection with that same matter of railway promotion examinations that Gysbert had just mentioned.

"It was when I was on the railways at Ottoshoop and I was studying electric unit working by correspondence," Johnny Coen said, "and I asked a schoolteacher about how the flanged wheels operate for points and crossings and the schoolteacher said he hadn't learnt so far. Another time I asked the teacher when do you have an overhead conductor and when do you electrify the line with a third rail, and the teacher said search him. Just like that, he said. Well, if that isn't plain ignorance, I'd like to know what *is*."

At Naudé nodded his head solemnly.

"That's just what I've been thinking, also," he said. "It's all very well for Meneer Vermaak here to say that he despises book learning – meaning that he hasn't got any book learning, I suppose – but then I don't see what right he has got to be educating our children. You can see that the education department don't care what sort of people they appoint these days. When I went to school you never heard a schoolteacher saying he had a contempt for education – meaning thereby that he hasn't got any."

So Jurie Steyn said that that was a scandal. What was worse, he said, was that a lot of people, including women, didn't know those things about schoolmasters, and had a silly sort of admiration for them, thinking they had book learning. Maybe they would think different about it if they knew that a schoolteacher was as ignorant as a –

"But all the same," At Naudé remarked, bringing us back to what we had started off discussing. "I do not think that Gysbert van Tonder is right. We are just about at the end of the winter. Jurie Steyn says it's not the beginning of the spring. I don't quite know what he means by that. But you haven't simply got to go and look at a mopane tree to know if the winter is nearly over. You can *feel* it. You can feel it in the wind, as much as anything else. Jurie Steyn had been talking about the Western Province, seeing that I was brought up at Rooigrond. But if you were to go to Rooigrond right now, I know just what you'll find. You'll find that it's the beginning of the springtime at Rooigrond. I know it, even though I haven't been there for years. There will be a soft wind blowing over the bult at Rooigrond, at this very moment. And under the peppercorn trees the yellow soil will be streaked with white dust. And if that isn't springtime in the Transvaal – in that part of the Transvaal – I should like to know what is."

Jurie Steyn shook his head.

"End of the winter," he announced, "that's all it is. End of the winter. Spring is something quite different. In the Boland I've known the spring. It's been a real springtime, and no nonsense. You can tell it, man. After the last loose showers have fallen, and the raindrops hang on the under part of the leaves, and a fresh smell hangs over the lands – over the wheatlands and over the watermelon lands. You've just got to breathe it in, and you know straight away that it's not just the end of winter, it isn't. You know clear in your heart that it is the *spring*."

If At Naudé was surprised at the way Jurie Steyn spoke, that was nothing compared with how surprised the rest of us were. It certainly was most peculiar to hear Jurie Steyn talking about the heart. You would almost be led to think, from that, that he had such a thing himself as a human heart. Only, of course, we knew better.

"It must be because you were young then, Jurie," Gysbert van Tonder said. "You know, it is when you were young that you were in the Boland, and so I suppose that the Cape has all sorts of memories for you, and so on. You have got more feeling for the spring when you are young than when you are – well – perhaps not quite so young."

Gysbert van Tonder framed that remark with a certain measure of diplomatic skill. And we understood why. Gysbert van Tonder was no chicken himself, for that matter.

"I think I understand what Gysbert means," At Naudé said, winking.

"Your youth is also like the springtime. When I was a young man – Lord, what wouldn't I give to be a young man again and to know what I know now. If I was young today, and I was so low as to be a bywoner on a farm, say, and I knew what I know now and the farmer came and said to me he didn't like the way I was slopping the pigs' swill all over the place instead of pouring it into the middle of the troughs – Lord, I'd turn that swill upside down over the farmer's head, trough and all. And when I was young I didn't know these things."

We didn't know whether At Naudé had started life as a bywoner. But we did know that today At Naudé did have a young bywoner working for him. And that young bywoner seemed quite content to walk about in broken trousers and with a battered khaki hat pulled down flat over his ears.

From all the wise things we were saying, it seemed as though we were just about as old as Oupa Bekker, the lot of us. Especially when Jurie Steyn went on to say that the only way he ever knew it was spring was by the dust.

"When the front door is open," Jurie Steyn said, "and a lot of dust blows into the voorkamer – red dust – then I know either that it's the Government lorry from Bekkersdal or the spring. What you *call* the spring, I mean."

But Johnny Coen said that he had that very day, on his way to Jurie Steyn's post office, seen a strange bird with long black legs by the spruit.

"I could see by his wings that that bird was very tired," Johnny Coen said. "I could see that he had come from far. And so I knew that spring was near at hand."

Shortly afterwards Jurie Steyn's wife came in from the kitchen, carrying a tray. She usually brought us our coffee at about that time. But we saw at once that Jurie Steyn's wife looked different. Only afterwards we realised that it was because of the blue ribbon that she had wreathed in her hair.

"Without any book learning," the young schoolteacher said with a laugh, as he helped himself to sugar, "I can tell that it's spring. How do you like that, Jurie? Yes, it's springtime in the Marico."

The Coffee that Tasted like Tar

"When the coffee tastes like tar," Jurie Steyn announced sombrely, after his wife had gone round with the tray, "then I know I have got influenza."

So At Naudé said that he himself was still all right, then, since the coffee tasted to him like what it really was – that was to say, like burnt mealies.

Gysbert van Tonder made haste to sympathise with Jurie Steyn. "I know that feeling, Jurie," Gysbert van Tonder said. "And that taste, too. I remember how very bad I had the influenza when I was staying at Derdepoort, that time. For days on end the coffee tasted like roast baobab roots. And so you can imagine how I felt, one day, when I saw the farmer I was staying with digging up baobab roots and roasting them for coffee."

Jurie Steyn looked at Gysbert van Tonder steadily for a few moments. But Gysbert went on stirring the spoon round in his cup, very calmly.

"I really don't know what you are trying to suggest with that story, Gysbert," Jurie said after a pause. "But my head feels too thick for me to try and work it out. It's the influenza, of course."

Jurie Steyn made that explanation rather quickly. You could see he wasn't in a mood to provide Gysbert van Tonder with an opening for any low innuendoes.

Speaking to Jurie Steyn for his own good, Gysbert van Tonder thereupon advised him to take things very easily, and not to let trifles upset him.

"Actually, you ought to be in bed, Jurie," Gysbert van Tonder went on in soothing tones. "You really do look terrible. We can all see you're not normal, you know."

Jurie Steyn admitted that he wasn't feeling himself. He made this acknowledgment several times. "With this influenza I am just not my-self," Jurie Steyn said, "and that's the truth."

Gysbert van Tonder said that he wouldn't like to go so far as to say that Jurie Steyn wasn't *himself*. That was a matter on which he would rather not offer an opinion, Gysbert continued. Maybe Jurie Steyn was himself, and maybe he wasn't. But what nobody could deny was that at that moment there was something very queer about Jurie Steyn. Like he was funny in the head, sort of, Gysbert van Tonder added. Winking at At Naudé, Gysbert van Tonder said that he was not prepared to say that it *wasn't* the influenza, of course –

"Oh, no," Jurie Steyn interrupted him hastily. "I know it's the influenza, all right. That you don't need to worry about. I felt it coming on for some time."

"A pretty long time, I should think," At Naudé said, taking his cue from Gysbert van Tonder and speaking in a voice that was full of kindliness. "Yes, I should say you must have been feeling it coming on for a longish time, Jurie."

It was clear that, influenza and all, Jurie Steyn was trapped. Leaning forward on his counter he looked from one to the other of us. All he saw was a row of Bushveld farmers sitting with straight faces.

"Well, they do say that the influenza is sort of – well, more severe this year," Jurie Steyn informed us, as though hoping that that word would explain a great deal. "That is no doubt the reason why I may of late have seemed to you somewhat – well, queer."

"Queerer than usual, even," Gysbert van Tonder said, trying hard not to choke. "That's what we've all been feeling about you for a little while, Jurie, that you have been queerer even than *usual*."

At Naudé coughed several times before he spoke. That alarmed us. For just one titter from At Naudé would set us all off laughing, and then Jurie Steyn would realise that it had all been a leg-pull. But At Naudé didn't let us down.

"It's how you look, Jurie," he said, still speaking in that unnaturally courteous sort of way, and taking trouble to say each word very clearly, "it's how you *look* more than how you act, even, that has made us – us farmers here on this side of the Dwarsberge – anyway, Jurie, old friend, you don't know how happy we all are to know that it is only the influenza. And you are quite right about saying that it is a very severe form of influenza, Jurie. Perhaps you don't even know how right you are, Jurie. Indeed – indeed, I hope you'll *never* know."

At Naudé did not say very much. But he did talk very distinctly. And at the end his voice grew quite hushed. He did it so well that even we, who knew what At Naudé was up to, began almost to believe that there was some sort of dark underneath meaning in that piece of nonsense that he had just seen fit to utter.

As for Jurie Steyn, the effect on him was most pronounced. The part of his face between his eyes and his ears turned a kind of greenish colour, and when we saw that he was standing with both hands pressed heavily on the counter, we knew that it was quite different from the old days, when he had stood like that to show that he was master in his own post office. He leant in that fashion on the counter now, for support. It was almost as though he realised that he wasn't getting any support from us.

After a while Jurie Steyn said something. And his voice was a good deal softer even than Gysbert van Tonder's or At Naudé's had been.

"I think," Jurie Steyn said, infirmly, "I think I'll go and have a bit of a lie down. My head *has* been funny lately, I know. But I am sure it is only the influenza. At least, I am almost sure."

Before we had quite realised what had happened, Jurie Steyn had left his place behind the counter and had gone out through the kitchen door, on his way to bed. On the threshold of the kitchen he had paused, however. "It *must* be the influenza," Jurie Steyn had said, as if to reassure both himself and us. "Because, you know, that coffee *did* taste like tar."

The moment Jurie had gone out we could permit ourselves to laugh. We didn't overdo it, naturally. After all, there was no point in making Jurie Steyn's wife suspicious. Or in laughing so loudly that Jurie would hear us in the bedroom.

"Anyway," Gysbert van Tonder said, after a little while, "it's not so very unhealthy that the coffee his wife makes for him should taste to Jurie Steyn like tar. It could taste a lot worse. It could taste like Cooper's dip, or like that weed-killer arsenic, for instance."

We did not laugh, this time, at Gysbert van Tonder's remark. There seemed to be too much in it that was near the truth. Maybe there wasn't actually any weed-killer arsenic in the words that Gysbert van Tonder spoke. But we wouldn't swear to it that in what he said there wasn't something very near to rat poison.

More than one of us took a sideways glance at young Vermaak, the schoolteacher, then. But he sat straight up on the riempies bench, with his dark hair slicked back, trying to look as unconcerned as you please.

"It's funny," Chris Welman said a little later, "that Jurie Steyn should have fallen for our little bit of fun in the way he did. I mean, we got him so easily. That's not quite like Jurie. Or is it?"

So we said, no, there quite clearly did seem to be something preying on his mind. Maybe it was the influenza, after all, Johnny Coen suggested.

We couldn't quite accept it that way, however. For that matter, we were, the majority of us, married men. And it suddenly appeared to us that what could happen to one man might just as likely as not befall another. And although we would always be willing to admit that there were certain peculiarities in Jurie Steyn's nature that made him unpopular with us, we nevertheless found ourselves looking at the young schoolmaster with a certain measure of disfavour. It seemed as though he could almost sense what we were thinking.

"Ah, well, Jurie will get over it," young Vermaak said. "We all do, I mean. The influenza isn't as serious as all that."

There seemed quite a lot of sense in the schoolmaster's statement, too. And also in the comment that At Naudé made.

"We all," At Naudé said, "we all get it sooner or later."

Afterwards it seemed to us that Oupa Bekker's remark was pretty profound, also.

"I don't quite follow what you are getting at," Oupa Bekker said. "As you know, I am a bit deaf. But all this talk of influenza, and so on . . . Well, all I can say is that Jurie Steyn was looking for it."

From then onwards the conversation took a somewhat desultory turn. And when the lorry arrived from Bekkersdal we started wondering as to whether we really had been so very clever, in the way we had pulled Jurie Steyn's leg. For while he was lying in bed at ease and snoring, no doubt, we were falling about all over the place, trying on our own to sort out our letters and milk-cans and parcels, and thoughts.

STARS IN THEIR COURSES

"It said over the wireless," At Naudé announced, "that the American astronomers are moving out of Johannesburg. They are taking the telescopes and things they have been studying the stars with, to Australia. There is too much smoke in Johannesburg for them to be able to see the stars properly."

He paused, as though inviting comment. But none of us had anything to say. We weren't interested in the Americans and their stars. Or in Australia, either, much.

"The American astronomers have been in Johannesburg for many years," At Naudé went on, wistfully, as though the impending removal of the astronomical research station was a matter of personal regret to him. "They have been here for years and now they are going, because of the smoke. It gets into their eyes just when they have *nearly* seen a new star in their telescopes, I suppose. Well, smoke is like that, of course. It gets into your eyes just at the wrong time."

What At Naudé said now was something that we could all understand. It was something of which we had all had experience. It was different from what he had been saying before about eyepieces and refracting telescopes, that he had heard of over the wireless, and that he had got all wrong, no doubt. Whereas getting smoke in your eyes at an inconvenient moment was something everybody in the Marico understood.

Immediately, Chris Welman started telling us about the time he was asked by Koos Nienaber, as a favour, to stand on a rant of the Dwarsberge from where he was able to see the Derdepoort police post very clearly. Koos Nienaber, it would seem, had private business with a chief near Ramoutsa, which had to do with bringing a somewhat large herd of cattle with long horns across the border.

"I could see the police post very well from there," Chris Welman said. "I was standing near a Mtosa hut. When the Mtosa woman lifted a petrol tin onto her head and went down in the direction of the spruit, for water, I moved over to an iron pot that a fire had been burning underneath all afternoon. All afternoon it had smelt to me like sheep's insides and kaboe-mealies. And when Koos Nienaber had asked me to do that small favour for him, of standing on the rant and watching if the two policemen just went on dealing out cards to each other and taking turns to drink out of a black bottle, Koos Nienaber had forgotten to give me something to take along that I could eat."

He could still see those two policemen quite distinctly, Chris Welman said, when he lifted the lid off the iron pot. He wasn't in the least worried about those two policemen, then. Actually, he admitted that he was, if anything, more concerned lest that Mtosa woman should suddenly come back to the hut, with the petrol tin on her head, having forgotten something. And it had to be at that moment, just when he was lifting the lid, that smoke from the fire crackling underneath the pot got into his eyes. It was the most awful kind of *stabbing* smoke that you could ever imagine, Chris Welman said. What the Mtosa woman had made that fire with, he just had no idea. Cow-dung and bitterbessie he knew. That was a kind of fuel that received some countenance, still, in the less frequented areas along the Molopo. And it made a kind of smoke which, if it got into your eyes, could blind you temporarily for up to at least quarter of an hour.

Chris Welman went on to say that he was also not unfamiliar with the effects of the smoke from the renosterbos, in view of the fact that he retained many childhood memories of a farm in the Eastern Province, where it was still quite usual to find a house with an old-fashioned abba-kitchen.

It was obvious that Chris Welman was beginning to yield to a gentle mood of reminiscence. The next thing he would be telling us some of the clever things that he was able to say at the age of four. Several of us pulled him up short, then.

"All right," Chris Welman proceeded, "I think I know how you feel. Well, to get back to that rant where I was standing on – well, I don't know what kind of fuel it was under that iron pot. What I will never forget is the moment when that smoke got into my eyes. It was a kind of smart that you couldn't rub out with the back of your sleeve or with the tail of your shirt pulled up, even. I don't think that even one of those white handkerchiefs that you see in the shop windows in Zeerust would have helped much. All I know is that when some of the pain started going, and I was able to see a little bit, again, I was lying under a mdubu tree, halfway down that rant. I had been running around in circles for I don't know how long. And it might give you some sort of an idea of the state I was in, if I tell you that I discovered, then, that I had been carrying that pot lid around with me all the time. I have often wondered if the Mtosa woman ever found that lid, lying there under the mdubu. And if she did, what she thought."

Chris Welman sighed deeply. Partly, we felt, that that sigh had its roots in a nostalgia for the past. His next words showed, however, that it was linked with a grimmer sort of reality.

"When I got back to the top of that rant," Chris Welman declared simply, "the two policemen weren't there at the post anymore. And Koos Nienaber had been fined so often before that this time the magistrate would not let him off with a fine. Koos Nienaber took it like a man, though, when the magistrate gave him six months."

More than one of us, sitting in Jurie Steyn's voorkamer, sighed, too, then. We also knew what it was to get smoke in your eyes, at the wrong moment. We also knew what it was to hold sudden and unexpected converse with a policeman on border patrol, the while you were nervously shifting a pair of wire-cutters from one hand to the other.

Gysbert van Tonder brought the discussion back to the subject of the stars.

"If the American astronomers are leaving South Africa because they can't stand our sort of smoke," Gysbert van Tonder declared, "well, I suppose there's nothing we can do about it. Maybe they haven't got smoke in America. I don't know, of course. But I didn't think that an astronomer, watching the stars at night through a telescope, would worry very much about smoke – or about cinders from looking out of a train window, either – getting into his eyes. I imagined that an astronomer would be above that sort of thing."

Young Vermaak, the schoolteacher, was able to put Gysbert van Tonder right then. In general, of course, we never had much respect for the schoolteacher, seeing that all he had was book learning and didn't know, for instance, a simple thing like that an ystervark won't roll himself up when he's tame.

"It isn't the smoke that gets into their eyes," the schoolteacher explained. "It's the smoke in the atmosphere that interferes with the observations and mathematical calculations that the astronomers have to make to get a knowledge of the movements of the heavenly bodies. There's Tycho Brahe and Galileo, for one thing, and there's Newton and the mass of the sun in tons. And there's Betelgeuse in the constellation of Orion and the circumference of the moon's orbit. The weight of a terrestrial pound on the moon is two-and-a-half ounces and the speed of Uranus round the sun is I forget how many hundred thousand miles a day – *hundred* thousand miles, mind you."

We looked at each other, then, with feelings of awe. We were not so much impressed with the actual *figures*, of course, that the schoolmaster quoted. We could listen to all that and not as much as turn a hair. Like when the schoolmaster spoke about the density of the sun, reckoning the earth as 1.25, we were not at all overwhelmed. We were only surprised that it was not a lot more. Or when the schoolmaster said that the period of the sun's rotation on its axis was twenty-five days and something – that didn't flatten us out in the least. It could be millions of years, for all we cared; millions *and* millions of years – that couldn't shake us. But what did give us pause for reflection was the thought that just in his brain – just inside his head that didn't seem very much different from any one of our heads – the young schoolmaster should have so much knowledge.

When the schoolmaster had gone on to speak about curved shapes and about the amount of heat and light received by the other planets being as follows, we were rendered pretty well speechless. Only Jurie Steyn was not taken out of his depth.

"It's like that book my wife used to study a great deal before we got married," Jurie Steyn said. "I have told you about it before. It's called Napoleon's dream-book. Well, that's a lot like what young Vermaak has been talking about now. At the back of the Napoleon dream-book it's got 'What the Stars Foretell' for every day of the year. It says that on Wednesday you must wear green, and on some other day you must write a letter to a relative that you haven't seen since I don't know when. The dream-book doesn't know, either, mostly. Anyway, I suppose that's why those American stargazers are leaving Johannesburg. It's something they saw in the stars, I expect."

Chris Welman said he wondered if what the American astronomers saw through their telescope said that the star of the American nation was going up, or if it was going down.

"Perhaps Jurie Steyn's wife can work it out from the dream-book," Gysbert van Tonder said.

GREEN-EYED MONSTER

It was again something At Naudé had read in the papers that started off the conversation in Jurie Steyn's voorkamer. At Naudé had read something about a man who, committing suicide, left behind somewhat detailed instructions for the ultimate disposition of his cremated ashes. We soon found that this was a subject that lent itself readily to discussion of a sprightly sort.

"Well, if ever I commit suicide," Chris Welman said, "I'll have my cremated ashes sent to the president of the Land Bank. Because, if I do commit suicide – and I've thought of it once or twice, lately – it will be his fault. The Land Bank seems to think that just because the price of wool has gone up, every farmer in the Groot Marico must be in a good way. Not that I envy the Eastern Province and Karoo sheep farmers, of course . . ."

So we all said that we of the Marico, who were cattle farmers, naturally did not begrudge the sheep farmers the big money they were making. They were welcome to their fat motor-cars and the parquet blocks on their floors. We were quite content to blacken our floors with just olieblaar, we said. We cattle farmers of the Marico simply did not believe in giving ourselves airs with long shiny pianos that took up half of the voorhuis. Although we acknowledged, of course, that our womenfolk felt quite different about such things. Not that we took much notice of our womenfolk, indeed, seeing that this was a man's world, but all the same, well, it wasn't that we *begrudged* those sheep farmers their good fortune. They were welcome to everything, we said, and *more*, even.

Nevertheless, there was something about those Cape sheep farmers, taken in conjunction with certain communications of a somewhat unreasonable nature that several of us Marico farmers had been receiving from the Land Bank lately, that – very well, let us be truthful about it – that *rankled*.

"Let the Land Bank come and try to breed sheep here in the Marico," Gysbert van Tonder said – in those few words summing up what we all felt – "let the Land Bank come along and try to shear a sheep after that sheep has been through a patch of wag-'n-bietjie bush . . ."

"Or a clump of haak-en-steek," Jurie Steyn said, with much feeling.

"Or young soetdorings," At Naudé added. "I'd like to know how many years a soetdoring takes to grow more than sheep-high. I've never tried to work it out. But, off-hand, I should say a lifetime. Not a sheep's lifetime but a human being's, I mean. Just let the Land Bank come and try it here for a little while, that's all. And I am not even talking about blue-tongue." (And we all said, no, of course not, we were not one of us even talking about blue-tongue.) "And then I would like to see the Land Bank go back to Pretoria. I'd like to see the Land Bank, then, that's all. Or, rather, I *wouldn't* like to see the Land Bank, then. With its ceiling coming all down, I mean. And with cracks in its plaster the size of a – the size of a –"

At Naudé paused. He wasn't able to think of something quite suitable to serve as a figure for conveying the size of the cracks in the Land Bank's facade.

Then Chris Welman started talking about how stupid a sheep was. A flock of sheep couldn't go anywhere at all unless they had a goat to lead them. And as for a goat . . . We spent quite a while in detailing sundry authentic anecdotes that had to do with a more unintelligent sort of goat that we had at various times come across.

But, all the same, we didn't envy the sheep farmers their prosperity, Gysbert van Tonder ended up by saying. And we all agreed with Gysbert van Tonder. The last thing in the world we wanted, we said, was to grow rich through just standing by the side of a stile and counting sheep jumping over it.

"Buying blue serge shop suits with wide, rolled lapels, and the pockets high up, and double-breasted," Johnny Coen said, a trifle wistfully.

"Or a trek-klavier," Gysbert van Tonder said, "with silver stars on the band that goes over your shoulders. Who wants a thing like *that* – just for counting sheep, that is?"

And so we all said again, just to make it quite clear, that we weren't in any way jealous of the sheep farmers. Jealous? Why, the whole idea was so ridiculous that we didn't have to discuss it, even.

"Counting a lot of sheep jumping over a stile," At Naudé said. "Why, that's not work at all. If I had to do that, I'd be asleep before I knew where I was. Fifteen, sixteen, eighteen, twenty-two – and two crept through underneath, that's twenty-four – twenty-five, twenty-seven – chase back that goat there – twenty-eight . . . and so on. I could do that lying right in bed, and I'd be asleep before I knew where I was. And that's what I've found about almost every sheep farmer I've come across. He's fast asleep. He's like in a dream. And he's more like in a dream than ever when he opens the letter from the Port Elizabeth market and he studies the size of the wool cheque he's got. He holds onto the cheque very tight with one hand and then pinches himself with the other, to make sure it's real. He still thinks he's dreaming and that he's back at that stile, there, saying, 'Chase that goat away'."

All this talk had carried us rather a long way from the subject we had started off by discussing, which was about the man who had committed suicide and had left instructions about what they had to do with his cremated ashes. It was only after Oupa Bekker had started off on a rambling account of the circumstances attendant on the suicide and subsequent cremation of his friend, Hans Potgieter, in the old days, that we were recalled to some sort of realisation of what was going on around us. The truth was that we had got into something of a dreamy state ourselves, in the course of which we were each of us imagining what we would do with a wool cheque – not that we envied the wool farmers in the least, of course.

We were able to catch up with Oupa Bekker's story quite easily, however. In the first place, Oupa Bekker had invested his recital of past events with a good deal of circumstantial detail. And, in the second place, the young schoolmaster, Vermaak, had pulled Oupa Bekker up several times for talking about "cremated ashes". According to the schoolmaster, it was enough to say just "ashes". The word "cremated", it would seem, meant no more than plain ashes. Moreover, the schoolmaster would make no concessions to the standpoint taken up by Oupa Bekker, which was to the effect that the words "cremated ashes" made his story *sound* much more impressive.

"If I've got to say just 'ashes', and not 'cremated ashes', it won't be anything like what I felt on my farm by the Molopo when the post-cart brought me that jam bottle with the screw-top and the letter from my friend, Hans Potgieter, who had hanged himself after he had been two years in Johannesburg," Oupa Bekker said. "I had been looking forward to my friend, Hans Potgieter, coming back to the Marico from Johannesburg in a new spider with green wheels and carrying a real leather portmanteau in his hand, and with a tie with stripes blowing over one shoulder, in the wind. Instead, I got just a bottle with a screw-top and a letter. From that it looked as if Hans Potgieter had not succeeded as well in the big city as he had hoped when he set out from alongside the Molopo."

Oupa Bekker paused, to allow his words to sink in. And they did deeper than he himself knew, maybe.

"It was quite a cheap sort of jam jar, too," Oupa Bekker added. "And in his letter my friend Hans Potgieter asked me to do him a last favour. It would appear that he had grown a trifle embittered during those two years of his stay in Johannesburg, and so he had asked me would I please give his crema – I mean – his ashes, to the devil. He trusted me enough, he said, to know that I would not fail him. He said I must hand over his ashes to Beelzebub himself."

The silence that followed was of some duration.

"Did Hans Potgieter say in his letter," Jurie Steyn asked – for, of course, Jurie Steyn could not let slip this opportunity of taking the young schoolteacher down a peg – "did he say 'his cremated ashes', or just 'his ashes'?"

Oupa Bekker flung a triumphant look at the schoolteacher. "'His *cremated* ashes'," Oupa Bekker announced.

"Well, of course, that was an awful one for me," Oupa Bekker went on. "There, alone by the Molopo. Perhaps you can imagine it. With nobody to talk to. And with Hans Potgieter's ashes in a kist in my bedroom. And the funny part of it is that I was all the time expecting Hans Potgieter to come back to the Marico. Wearing a stiff white collar and white cuffs on his sleeves, like I have said. And then, writing me such a letter. Well, it seemed to me, at times, that a man who could go and commit suicide belonged to the devil, in any case. He was the property of the devil, flesh and soul and bones and everything, even before they had cremated him and put his ashes in a jam pot. He already belonged to the devil, body and spirit, the moment he put that rope round his neck with his own hands. So there was no point in his asking me to hand just his cremated ashes over to the devil, when everything about him already belonged to the devil."

We understood Oupa Bekker's difficulty, of course. He must have been in a pretty awkward predicament, that time. And we said so.

"There were nights when I was afraid to go to bed," Oupa Bekker continued. "I would think of the jam jar in that kist, and I would think of what Hans Potgieter had asked me to do, in his last letter, and I would wonder where I could find Beelzebub, so that I could hand over Hans Potgieter's ashes to him. But the most awful feeling of everything was when it seemed to me that Hans Potgieter *was* the devil. And that where Beelzebub really was, was inside that screw-top bottle locked up in the kist in my bedroom."

Although the incident of Hans Potgieter's suicide and his strange request and the funeral urn and the last letter written by someone about to take his own life – although all those things belonged to the distant past, we could see that Oupa Bekker was still strongly moved when he thought about it. We urged him to continue. Not in words, but through saying nothing . . . which is at times the most strident sort of speech.

"But I worked it all out," Oupa Bekker said, after a while. "I found the answer, alone here in the Marico. Before any of you came here. I wanted to know where I could find the devil, so that I could give the devil Hans Potgieter's ashes. And I began to fear that Hans Potgieter was the devil, and that the devil was in that glass bottle with the screw-top. But because I was alone, I suppose it didn't take me as long as it would otherwise to find out that Hans Potgieter hadn't made a mistake about where to send his cremated ashes to.

"That jar is still there, in my kist. And I expect the devil is still – as I found out then – inside me. Or a good deal of him is, anyway."

CASUAL CONVERSATION

"It's again the season," Jurie Steyn announced, "when travellers with black spectacles and mosquito nets and white helmets swarm to these parts. Tourists, they call themselves."

He himself wouldn't go so far as to say *swarm* exactly, Chris Welman replied. It wasn't quite as bad as all that. Not that tourists might not become a bit of a nuisance, in time, Chris Welman added, if the authorities did not start exercising some sort of control.

But At Naudé said that that was just what those tourists would *like*, and what they could never get enough of. In fact, the surest way of having the whole of the Marico overrun with tourists, would be through making it hard for them to get here, At Naudé said.

There was that party of tourists of a couple of years back, At Naudé went on, that he came across on the other side of the Dwarsberge. It was his first tourists of the year. He spotted them through his field-glasses when he had gone onto a koppie to look for a strayed mule. And he couldn't see them too well, either, through all their mosquito netting.

"Anyway, I would have thought nothing more of it," At Naudé said. "I would just have gone back home, and I would have told my wife that I had seen my first tourists of the year, in the same way that, the week before, I had seen my first pair of yellow-tailed tinktinkies. They had grey spots on their bellies. That is, the tinktinkies had. I couldn't see the tourists as well as all *that*, of course, because of what I have told you about the mosquito nets. And they were making queer twittering sounds, and they were hopping. The tourists were, I mean. I wasn't near enough to the tinktinkies to make out what kind of sounds, if any, *they* were letting out."

He was just on the point of turning his field-glasses in the other direction, towards the kloof, At Naudé said, when something caught his attention. He had thought nothing of the way the tourists were jumping about and uttering strange cries, At Naudé explained, since he had grown to accept the fact that tourists were not quite human, so that nothing they did ever came as a surprise to you, much. Thereupon we all said no, of course, there was nothing in what a tourist did that could awaken any sort of real interest, anymore. Even the most ignorant kind of Kalahari Bushman had by that time come to recognise a tourist for what he was. And it was many years since even a Koranna from the reserve had last raised an eyebrow at a tourist's foolishness.

It was just because he was well bred, At Naudé went on to say, that he started to take the field-glasses away from his eyes and to turn the screw in the middle so that he could focus on the kloof instead. But what he observed at that moment was of so extraordinary a character that he had to polish his field-glasses on his shirt-sleeve to make sure that there wasn't a mistake, somewhere.

"It wasn't that I mistrusted those field-glasses," At Naudé said. "But it was just something I couldn't believe, somehow. I mean those field-glasses – why, my uncle, Stefaans Welgemoed, used them right through the Boer War. And that was why he was never caught and sent to St. Helena. Through those field-glasses you could see an Englishman with a red neck and a Lee-Metford quicker than through any telescope anywhere in the world, my Uncle Stefaans always used to say."

It was reasonable to expect from At Naudé a plainer statement about those tourists he had seen behind the Dwarsberge. We felt that we could not just leave them there all afternoon, jumping and making noises. So Chris Welman broached the subject, and with true Bushveld straightforwardness – which is perhaps not quite the same thing as the ordinary sort of candour. After all, where would you *be*, if wherever you go you just say straight out what you think or what you *mean*, even? After all, everybody in the Marico Bushveld prides himself on his bluff frankness of speech, and all that, but that doesn't imply that you've got to be a simpleton. Consequently, because he wanted to know more from At Naudé about those tourists, Chris Welman put the question to him in a way that At Naudé would understand. Chris Welman started talking some more about those field-glasses; and he said that we all knew that those field-glasses had been in the Naudé family for many generations; and that some very strange sights must on occasion have been presented to the view of the persons who had looked through those field-glasses down the years.

136

That was blunt talk, all right, if you liked. But then we knew that Chris Welman always was like that. No subterfuge about his words. No fancy frills. He was inquisitive about the antics of those tourists, and so he asked At Naudé about them straight out.

"Yes," At Naudé said, beginning to sound sentimental, almost, over those field-glasses. "Yes, some pretty funny sights, I should think, down the years. Maybe, the Huguenots landing, also. You know, French. Like old Pollyvoo at the Derdepoort mission station, jumping about and waving his arms, all the time. I suppose that's how the Huguenots looked, landing at the Cape . . . waving their arms and jumping and calling out pollyvoo to each other. Yes, it must have been very funny. I don't suppose they could talk a word of Afrikaans, either."

Young Vermaak, the schoolmaster, was able to help At Naudé right, then. He explained that the Huguenots were French communities of the seventeenth century and that why they came to the Cape had to do with Henry of Navarre and the Edict of Nantes. It also had quite a lot to do with the Massacre of Bartholomew's Eve, the schoolmaster said. That made the Huguenots decide to go and start the cultivation of the grapevine at the Cape. Although if it *hadn't* been for St. Bartholomew's, the schoolmaster said, there might possibly have been more passengers aboard that ship that docked at Table Bay. The schoolmaster also said that you could tell by his name that At Naudé was himself a descendant of the Huguenots. So At Naudé needn't talk.

The schoolmaster sighed a little also when he said that. It was as though he sorrowed at At Naudé's ignorance, and at At's presence in the voorkamer. It was almost as though the schoolmaster regretted the fact that the St. Bartholomew affair had not been better organised.

After that we discussed other groups – and individuals, also – that had been seen through At Naudé's field-glasses. Zulu impis, we said. And Piet Retief. And Napoleon, we said. And Dr Philip, the schoolmaster said.

"And Oupa Bekker," Jurie Steyn said, with a laugh. "More than once in the old days, somebody must have looked through those same field-glasses and seen Oupa Bekker come riding over the hill, with his long beard and all."

All this talk would have got us nowhere, if it wasn't for Johnny Coen.

"I know why you spoke like that about the Huguenots," Johnny Coen said to At Naudé. "About their jumping around and waving their arms. It's because you were thinking about those tourists behind the Dwarsberge. Forget all about your field-glasses. Why *were* those tourists acting in that way?"

But when At Naudé told us, it sounded so tame that we would rather not have heard the explanation. At Naudé reminded us that he had been out looking for his mule that had strayed. Well, it appeared that his mule had wandered down to the tourist camp. And because the tourists didn't know how a mule thinks they had tried to drive it away. As a result, the mule walked right up into their camp and started eating their mosquito netting as quick as he could get it down, which was quite a large number of square yards a minute. And why the tourists were making those twittering sounds was because they were barefooted and, in trying to chase the mule, they had landed in a patch of last season's dubbeltjie thorns.

"But why I said that it's no use making it hard for tourists if you want to keep them out of the Marico," At Naudé explained, "is this. After my mule had wandered off into the bush, there not being any more mosquito netting around for him to eat, as far as he could see, I talked to one of the tourists. And he said he had been an explorer in Tibet. And he said Tibet was averse to Western incursions. Just like that, he said it. And he was very happy about it. He had a very happy time there, he said, and he stole two prayer-wheels. Tibet was called the Forbidden Country, and so it was a pleasure for him to visit it, he said. And for that reason he was disappointed in the Marico."

What At Naudé told us, then, took a little while to sink in. There was a fairly long silence, during which we all thought pretty hard.

Jurie Steyn was the first to speak. And the words he spoke expressed all our feelings.

"Just let him wait a bit," Jurie Steyn said, *"that's all."*

THE CALL OF THE ROAD

The latest news that At Naudé had to communicate to us in Jurie Steyn's voorkamer was about the mayor of a highveld dorp who walked a long distance to Pretoria in order to interview a Minister about the housing shortage.

"It was as a protest," At Naudé explained, "that he set off on foot across the whole length of the Southern Transvaal, sleeping at night in the straw with a tramp who didn't have an overcoat, but only a bottle of vaaljapie wine."

Gysbert van Tonder said, then, that on a cold night, when you were sleeping in the straw, a bottle of vaaljapie could be of more use to you than an overcoat. As long as there was enough straw, Gysbert added. And enough vaaljapie.

At Naudé went on to say that the mayor had a hot flask of coffee, there in the straw, which the tramp did not wish to share with him. He never drank coffee, the tramp said.

Thereupon Johnny Coen said that he could just imagine what sort of a tramp that was – giving himself airs, and all the rest of it. He knew that sort of tramp, Johnny Coen said, since he had once been on the road himself. You came across some quite insufferable tramps, at times, Johnny Coen went on. He knew about them from his own experience – dating from the time when he himself had just suddenly felt full up to the neck with his job at the Ottoshoop siding, and had set off on foot along the road leading to the big cities of South Africa, having drawn his pay first.

"The kind of tramp that sneers at you because you forgot to tie pieces of newspaper to the bottom parts of your trousers before you left home," Johnny Coen declared, bitterly. "I know *that* sort. And I can imagine how that tramp in the straw must have sneered when the mayor pulled a hot flask of coffee out of his pocket. When the only proper pocket that the tramp had left had got its lining fastened with a safety pin, so that the bottle of vaaljapie wouldn't drop out before the tramp got into the straw. I suppose that tramp laughed outright. Right in the mayor's face, I should imagine. And yet what brought me back to Ottoshoop, after I had run away, was also no more than a hot flask. When I had set off down the road to the south, I had left my hot flask in the wood-and-iron lean-to that the Public Works Department had erected for us workmen next to the Ottoshoop siding. And the farther I went along the road from Ottoshoop, the more I missed the hot flask, that I used to take coffee in to work. And I was too *proud* to turn back for that hot flask, if you'll understand what I mean. But in the end I overcame my pride, and I went back. And so I know just how the highveld mayor must have felt, when the tramp in the straw regarded his hot flask as . . . well . . . You see, it's not what a tramp *says*, that's important. It's the way his lip curls, without his having to use any words."

Because Johnny Coen was young, we did not feel called upon to take much notice of anything he said. We were much more interested in Gysbert van Tonder's next remark.

"To tell you the truth," Gysbert said, "I am not surprised at that mayor just taking it into his head to pack his things and walk off. I have lived in more than one highveld dorp myself. And I know what sort of things go on there. That's why I don't blame that mayor in the least. Just think what it's like to wake up in the morning and to look at the sunrise, and there's no mdubu trees or withaaks or maroelas. There's just a piece of flat veld starting right at your kitchen door, and it has rained, and you've got to start ploughing. I can quite understand a person living on the highveld putting a piece of biltong and a spare shirt into a suitcase and walking away from there, then. I mean, isn't that how quite a few of us landed here, in the Marico? And without a spare shirt, either, in some cases – in some cases that I wouldn't like to mention here in this voorkamer, I mean."

Naturally, we each of us, after that, felt it was necessary to make it clear that when we arrived in the Marico it was with more than a spare shirt in our suitcases. It was funny, and all that, what Gysbert van Tonder had said, but we weren't tramps, exactly, when we came to the Marico the first time it was thrown open to white settlement. Still, it was a good joke Gysbert van Tonder had made, we said – ha, ha.

"Who has ever heard of a tramp coming into a place with a harmonium fastened onto the middle of his wagon, just above the bok, with ox-riems?" Jurie Steyn asked. "I don't say that the top notes of the harmonium vibrated as well as you would like, perhaps. But, of course, that was just because of the way that the wagon got bumped during the long journey through the Roggeveld. Still, I helped to civilise these parts with my harmonium, all right, I think."

In reply, Chris Welman said that it all depended, of course, on what you meant by civilised. He had had somewhat different thoughts himself, he confessed, on that Sunday morning when the strains of a hymn tune came floating over the vlaktes, for the first time.

"It wasn't only the top notes," Chris Welman explained. "But I could tell by the bottom notes, also, that the harmonium had trekked through some of the worst parts of the Roggeveld. I kept saying to myself that it was a pity you hadn't taken a bit of a detour."

"Well, I know that I didn't come to the Marico with just a shirt on my back," At Naudé said. "I had at least several shirts. And also my Nagmaal suit. And I have still got my Nagmaal suit. What's more, I can still wear it. I was already fat when I *came* to the Groot Marico. I didn't come to the Marico like a starved person that only starts getting fat after he has been here for some time. I *came* to the Marico fat."

After we had all explained that we were none of us tramps, or anywhere near like *some* people we knew – when we first came to live in the lowveld, it was by way of a relief when At Naudé made it clear that the mayor did not walk away from that highveld dorp because he had had enough of it, but to let the Minister know that there weren't enough houses to go round, in the dorp where he was.

So we said, couldn't he rather have gone by train?

"Or what's wrong with him writing a letter?" Jurie Steyn asked, the while his eye travelled the length of his counter, with the shiny brass scales and rubber stamps on it. "Or haven't they got a *reliable* post office there?"

But At Naudé said, no, the matter was too urgent. And when Jurie Steyn opened his mouth to say something, we all laughed.

That gave Johnny Coen his chance to tell us about the time when he himself took to the road.

"It was the Foreman," Johnny Coen said. "The Siding Foreman. Now, it doesn't matter how bad a Third Class Running Staff *Station* Foreman can get, he's nothing at all next to a *Siding* Foreman. And so, after I had been working at Ottoshoop quite a while I suddenly found I couldn't stand it any longer. The Siding Foreman had been a farmer at Rysmier-bult before he went to the railways, and, as you know, there's nobody can be as inhuman to you as your own *sort*."

That statement of Johnny Coen's awakened quite a lot of memories in the consciousness of each of us, and we all nodded our agreement. Indeed, the vigour with which Gysbert van Tonder inclined his head forward was so noticeable that Jurie Steyn, who was his neighbour, took it as a personal affront. We managed to stop the argument, however, before anything really unseemly happened.

"And so, when I saw that road there, winding away to the south, through the hills," Johnny Coen proceeded, "I just walked away, out of the lean-to. I didn't hand in my notice or say goodbye to the Siding Foreman, or anything. I saw only the open road, winding away amongst the hills, and I started walking. Since then, of course, I have learnt that it was wrong of me to have acted like that – running away because I found things were too hard, and being so unfriendly, as well. I am sure that the mayor that At Naudé spoke about didn't act like that. I am sure that the mayor at least went and said goodbye to the Siding Foreman, no matter what he might have thought of him privately."

Johnny Coen went on to relate to us the details of some of his adventures along the road. Mostly, his stories were of encounters with tramps, who, lying in a farmer's loft and wrapped around in the best straw, were so superior that they would hardly talk to him.

"But what brought me back, in the end, was my hot flask, that I had left behind in the lean-to," Johnny Coen said. "My hot flask had gold and green bands painted all round it, and I could picture the Siding Foreman drinking coffee out of it, and enjoying it. And wiping his beard, afterwards."

He slipped into the lean-to at an hour in the morning when he expected the Siding Foreman to be off duty.

"So you can imagine how surprised I was, when I turned round to see the Siding Foreman behind me," Johnny Coen added. "And he said he knew I would come back. He had once run away from a job, too, when he was my age. *And he could tell that I was a lot like he was*, and that I wasn't the tramp sort. And as he walked out the Siding Foreman said that I was half an hour late for work. And before I knew what I was doing, I was taking off my hat and jacket, there in the lean-to."

142

LATH AND PLASTER

They were going to do it right here, in South Africa, At Naudé declared, retailing to us what he had read in the newspapers.

It was called a sound-track, At Naudé said, meaning that part of a
film which makes the glug-glug noises when an ocean liner goes down
after having struck an iceberg, in a bioscope.

So we said that, while we did not know that it was called a sound-
track, we were all of us familiar with that part of a movie picture that
At Naudé was talking about. We were surprised that it had a name at
all, we said. It seemed to us too wild a thing to be actually *called* by a
name, we said.

We each of us then started remembering, from occasional visits to
the bioscope in Bekkersdal, various bits of sound-track, now that At
Naudé had given us the word for it.

"I remember about a white-haired clergyman," Chris Welman said.
"The clergyman wore a dark suit and a round collar right through the
film. It was a murder picture of course – I mean with a clergyman in
it – although at the beginning it looked as though it was going to be
a film just about sandbagging and forgery. But I'll never forget that
sound-track piece when the handcuffs clicked on his wrists and the
white-haired clergyman said, 'Y' got me, pal.' Of course, it turned out,
in the end, that he wasn't a real clergyman. Or his hair wasn't really
white – I forget which. But I thought then, that even one of our own
predikants – and I belong to the Dopper Church myself – could not
have done it so well."

In case we might perhaps misunderstand his words, Chris Welman
went out of his way to say that it wasn't as though he didn't give Dor-
ninee Welthagen every credit. And so we all said, no, of course not. We
all had a great respect for Dominee Welthagen, we said. And we knew
just what Dominee Welthagen *was*. And if Dominee Welthagen didn't

wear a round collar, he did wear a white tie and a black hat with a broad brim, we said.

Nevertheless, we felt, somehow, that if Dominee Welthagen *did* get into the kind of awkward situation that Chris Welman spoke about – well, we took leave to doubt as to whether Dominee Welthagen would have had enough sound-track experience to *know* that the game was up.

"If the clergyman had started arguing at that stage," Chris Welman said, "or if he had asked to have the handcuffs taken off, so that he could first read out a few verses from Chapter 3 of the Kolossense – why, it wouldn't have been the same thing. It would have spoilt the whole film. That is why I say that in some things, you must hand it to these sound-track ministers of religion. And I say it, even though I am a Dopper myself."

Thereupon Gysbert van Tonder stated that when he was a child growing into young manhood, he was the only kategisant in the confirmation class who could recite John Calvin's Formulier from the first word to the last without once having to draw breath. He acquired that skill through having practised swimming under water in the dam on his father's farm at Welverdiend, where there was Spanish reed and polgras, on the edge. And in an American film to do with the Church he had heard a young kategisant repeating those same words, Gysbert van Tonder said. Of course, he didn't understand the words so well, because it was in English. But he could see by the look of despair and general bewilderment on the face of that young fellow that it *must* be John Calvin's Formulier that he was reciting.

"And do you know what?" Gysbert van Tonder ended up. "He had to pause for breath *three* times. So I thought, well, they can't know much about religion in America. Either that, I thought, or else that young fellow had been studying for the catechism in a time of drought when no Spanish reeds grew on the edge of the dam on his father's farm. Maybe there wasn't any water in it, either."

Oupa Bekker coughed then. We all knew what that cough meant. We knew that Oupa Bekker was clearing his throat preparatory to embarking on a story of drought in the old days of the Marico, when the ground really *was* dry. It was fortunate for us that At Naudé was able to head Oupa Bekker off.

"Today, when you see an American film, the words the actors say and the noises they make are all in English, with the result that we can't understand it too well – the noises, especially. Anyway, I read in the newspaper that all that is going to be changed. There's a firm in South Africa is going to take those films and is going to translate the sound-tracks into Afrikaans. It's still going to be the same *film*, the people and the actions, and all that. Only, they are going to have Afrikaans actors and actresses to make the sound-track – you know, the speeches and the noises. You'll only hear these Afrikaans actors and actresses on the films. You won't see them."

Gysbert van Tonder said, straight away, that that was a very good thing. The fact that you wouldn't see them, he explained. And Chris Welman went on to say that it would be even better if you couldn't hear them, either. We did not take much notice of this remark of Chris Welman's, however, since we felt that there was a lot of jealousy in it.

We knew that Chris Welman prided himself on the way in which he could sing "Boereseun", with actions. And we also knew that Chris Welman felt that he had never received proper appreciation for it, except in the Bushveld. And he didn't count *that* sort of appreciation, Chris Welman always said. It was the applause of the wider world he wanted – even if there were a few overripe tomatoes thrown in with the wider world's applause. It didn't mean much to him, Chris Welman was in the habit of explaining, to know that a Marico audience would regularly clap its hands and stamp its feet and shout "Dagbreek toe!" and "Askoek!" every time he sang "Boereseun" with actions. And even when some of us said that, if he liked, we would bring along a packet of tomatoes and a lot of rotten eggs and a dead cat, too, if that would make him feel any better, next time he sang – it would even be a *pleasure*, we said – Chris Welman still made it clear that it wasn't quite the same thing.

"All the same, I am in favour of it," Jurie Steyn said, thoughtfully, "having these American films in Afrikaans, now."

"Why?" Oupa Bekker asked. We could sense that Oupa Bekker was in a nasty mood, because we wouldn't listen to his drought story.

"Well," Jurie Steyn said, "we'll now be able to understand everything they say in these American films."

"Why?" Oupa Bekker asked, again.

Yes, we could see that Oupa Bekker was just being difficult.

"Mind you, I don't say that these American films have always got a very good influence," Jurie Steyn went on, quickly, in case Oupa Bekker had any more questions to ask. "Especially where young people are concerned. I sometimes think that when *young* persons see an American film they may get inclined to form wrong opinions about what life is like, really. After all, if a girl smiles at you, sort of, in the moonlight, under a camel-thorn tree, when you are walking home from work and she is going to the stable for a bucket of milk to put into the stamped mealies for supper, say, well, it's downright silly to think it *means* anything. In any case what are you doing, walking home from work under a camel-thorn tree, when you should have stuck right to the Government Road, on your way home from work? There's a lot in these American films that is just foolish."

We knew that Jurie Steyn was addressing that remark to all of us who were sitting there, in his voorkamer, and not to just one person, in particular. Nevertheless, it was peculiar, the way several of us glanced swiftly in the direction of young Vermaak, the schoolteacher.

And we all agreed with Jurie Steyn. Indeed, we said, the American films gave one a distorted view of life. The American films had an unhealthy effect on the minds of South African youth, we said. The American films gave you the idea that all life was just that pale kind of moonlight that you see through the thorns of a camel-thorn tree on the other side of the Dwarsberge. Some of our young people had even begun to *talk*, we said, like the men and women actors talk in a film made in America.

Johnny Coen said that that was quite true. And he told us about the way he had parted, near Vleisfontein, from a Bushveld girl who didn't want him anymore. He was broken-hearted, Johnny Coen said, because that girl didn't care for him, and was going to marry a young man who would one day inherit his father's Karoo farm that had eight thousand morgen of sheep pasture.

"And although I meant every word I said, about how broken-hearted I was," Johnny Coen declared, "it was only afterwards that I realised I had actually been talking words to her that I had heard in these American films. Still, it didn't hurt any the less. 'I will say,' I said to her, 'I will away to Africa, there to seek peace for my battered spirit.' You see, the American films had got me so that I really forgot that I *was* in Africa. All the same, it didn't hurt less – any."

Do Professors Smoke Dagga?

At Naudé brought the actual cutting from the newspaper with him. He passed the news item over to Gysbert van Tonder, who proceeded to read it out to us – reading slowly, as he explained, so that we shouldn't miss any of it. When he came to a long word, Gysbert even took the trouble to spell it out for us, to make *quite* sure that we grasped it all right, he said. And each time after he had got through a piece of spelling, like that, he paused a few moments so as to allow young Vermaak, the schoolmaster, to step in and pronounce the word.

We found out, however, that the extreme care that Gysbert van Tonder exercised in his reading – claiming that he was doing it that way because we were just ignorant farmers that he didn't want to take out of their depth, too much – was not as helpful as it should have been. Especially when he came to a particularly long word which he didn't even try to spell, but just mumbled over it.

After that, having twice failed to take the jump at quite a short word, Gysbert van Tonder suddenly thrust the cutting into the schoolmaster's hand and asked him to finish reading it. *He* had done his best with us, Gysbert said. It was too thankless a job, trying to get an understanding of fine print into the heads of people who weren't scholars, he said.

It turned out, however, that that newspaper report was, in spite of its brevity, not without a certain measure of interest.

It had to do with a student of psychology who smoked dagga – purely as an experiment, of course, just so that he could see what it was like, so as to help him in his studies.

"In his studies of what?" Jurie Steyn demanded. "That's what I keep saying about the so-called educated people we get today. I mean, when a Kalahari Bushman comes to my back door, and I can see from his eyes – with his pupils big and round, and with no whites showing, hardly – well, you all know how a Bushman looks when he's been smoking a good bit of dagga. Laughing a lot about nothing. A hollow sort of laugh."

We said yes, we knew.

"Well, how often haven't I said that about educated white people today?" Jurie Steyn asked, sounding quite aggressive. Actually, Jurie Steyn had said nothing about educated white people, so far. Nothing we could make head or tail of, that was. But we knew how he felt about young Vermaak, the schoolteacher. And we also understood why, on that point, he could not perhaps always express himself as clearly as he might have liked.

"That's the next thing, I suppose, that is going to happen right here in my post office," Jurie Steyn went on. "A Bushman coming in with a bow and arrows and an ostrich egg with a hole in it under his arm, and so full of dagga that he laughs right out when I tell him that from next year the Ngami Bushman will have to pay hut tax, just like he's a Koranna. You know that dagga laugh. But the Bushman will say that why he is so full of dagga is because he's a student of psychology, and he's smoking it as an experiment, to help him through his second-year course."

"Third year," young Vermaak announced, decisively, shutting his lips in a straight line. "You only have dagga in third-year psychology."

Jurie Steyn shot a triumphant look at us with his right eye. His left eye was closed in a significant sort of way, the lid fluttering ever so lightly. There seemed something queer about it, somehow – the school-master with his lips shut and Jurie Steyn with one eye closed.

"It's all right," young Vermaak proceeded. "I saw Jurie Steyn wink-ing. But I didn't mean it that way. I meant that it's only in the third year that we really study the effect on the central nervous system of narcotic drugs like the barbiturates, or heroin, or opium, or – or – dagga, even."

"They say that dagga is habit-forming," Chris Welman declared, sententiously. "Not that I have ever thought to have seen you under the *influence* of it, Meneer Vermaak. The direct influence, that is –"

Young Vermaak said that he had never smoked dagga in his life. Nor opium, he said. He had studied the effect of a variety of drugs only in theory. The professor at the university had dictated certain notes and the students had taken the notes down.

Thereupon Gysbert van Tonder said that that explained a lot. He had often, in the joke column of the *Kerkbode,* read jokes about absent-minded professors, he said. He now understood what it was that *made* professors so absent-minded, he said. It was a pity, really, he said, because we all knew that they did have intellects, and all that. But, of course, professors said pretty silly things, too, sometimes. The schoolmaster had no doubt come across instances of that, while he was a student.

"Yes, indeed," young Vermaak acknowledged. "When I think of all the tripe I've had to listen to in the ethics class from old Van –"

"Habit-forming," Jurie Steyn interjected, swiftly. "That's what they all say about it, and I suppose it's true. Afterwards these professors get like that, they can't just take it or leave it. It *gets* them. Then they talk what Meneer Vermaak calls tripe."

The schoolmaster looked surprised. "*What* gets them?" he asked, stiffly.

And he turned really acid when At Naudé and Chris Welman both tried to explain, speaking at the same time. And he was positively scornful when Gysbert van Tonder asked if professors smoked berg-dagga or just the ordinary sort with red bearded ears.

There was silence after that. Quite a profound sort of silence, too.

"Look here," the schoolmaster said, after a while. "I know you all like a bit of fun – and so do I too, for that matter, ha, ha."

We agreed with him. Ha, ha, we said, also.

"But this talk about professors and dagga, well, it's so *silly*," the schoolmaster went on. "For one thing, professors are people with learning and knowledge. If ever you have called at a professor's house round about exam time – in the hope that over the tea table he might let slip something about what one of the questions is going to be – why, you'll understand, then, that a professor is a responsible sort of citizen. As a matter of fact, when I went to visit a professor once, around exam time, I came away with the absolute certainty that the professor didn't even *know*, then, what questions he was going to ask. What's more, after the second cup of tea, I felt that he didn't know the answers, either."

Jurie Steyn said, then, that he would like to see them dump a university professor in the middle of the Kalahari desert, with his wife and children, and leave that university professor to fend for himself, with just a hollow reed to suck water through the shell of an ostrich egg. He would *like* to see it, Jurie Steyn added. And we felt that he really would. Jurie Steyn started getting almost sentimental after that, about the hardships of the life of the Kalahari Bushman – which was something very unusual for Jurie Steyn, seeing that we all knew how Jurie felt about Bushmen.

And it was then that the schoolmaster came to the conclusion that we were having fun at his expense. He left shortly afterwards.

"Ha, ha," young Vermaak said, as he took up his hat. "I suppose I can stand a joke as well as anybody else. Ha, ha – ha, ha, ha!"

"Just as I said," Jurie Steyn remarked, winking again after the school-master had gone. "Hollow laughter . . . I forgot to look if there was any white in his eyes."

Art Criticism

"It must be years ago since I first saw this picture hanging on your wall," Gysbert van Tonder said to Jurie Steyn, at the same time jerking his thumb over his shoulder at a painting of a farmhouse. "And there has always seemed to be something lopsided about it, somehow."

"If you think that my wife's great-uncle, Koos Schoeman, was lopsided –" Jurie Steyn began, when Gysbert van Tonder made haste to explain that he didn't mean that picture at all, but the one next to it, the one with the garden wall.

"We all admire your wife's great-uncle," Gysbert van Tonder continued, "and we venerate his memory. Koos Schoeman was as fine a burgher as ever wore a bandolier across his shoulders, and you've got no call to think I mean *him*. I'm not so stupid that I can't tell the difference between your wife's great-uncle's face and the side of a wall. Why, you can see by his portrait that he was a good-looking man. The kind of looks that they thought were good looks in those days, I mean."

"It's not the fault of the great-uncle of Jurie Steyn's wife that fashions in men's looks have changed since his time," Chris Welman declared, sententiously. "The next generation or so would find quite a lot to laugh at in a photograph of Gysbert van Tonder, say."

"Even if the fashions didn't change, they would still have a lot to laugh at," Jurie Steyn said. It was clear that Jurie Steyn was in an unpleasant mood.

At Naudé brought back the subject to where it had started from.

"I've also been a bit puzzled by that painting before today," he said. "I can't make out if the artist painted the front side or the back – it's the painting of the farmhouse I'm talking about, Jurie," he added hurriedly.

It seemed to make it worse, somehow, that At Naudé had to explain that.

"That door that's half open, now," At continued. "Well, it's not a

151

proper top-and-bottom door, but a door in one piece. Now, with that door open, you wouldn't have that pig eating a piece of potato, there, next to the bucket. The pig would be in the dining room, eating the blancmange off the sideboard."

At Naudé made that remark with a certain amount of pride – to show how familiar he was with the interior of the up-to-date kind of farmhouse that had doors all in one piece.

"And the pig, at the same time that he was eating the blancmange, would be scratching himself against a cupboard with glass in front and cups and crossed foreign flags *and* plates inside," Chris Welman announced, determined not to be outdone when it came to knowing what it was like in a voorkamer where there was nothing for you to knock your pipe out against. It seemed that the picture on Jurie Steyn's wall was of *that* kind of farmhouse.

"And there's a brass clock on the wall, and it doesn't go," Gysbert van Tonder announced, triumphantly, "but they say, in that farmhouse, that the clock was in a ship that fought in a sea battle two hundred years ago. Their navy, you know."

We nodded solemnly. And we had to admit that the painting of the farmhouse on Jurie Steyn's wall did seem a little like the kind of farmhouse that we had been talking about. The kind of farm on which the farmer carried out all the instructions issued by the Department of Agriculture's experts in booklet form – and then came knocking at the door of the first Marico Boer to ask what he should do about wire-worm. In the end, of course, that kind of farmer would know better than to open the pamphlets from the Department of Agriculture, even, when they came by post. Or, if he did open them, he would yawn as he slipped the broken nail of his forefinger underneath the paper wrapping.

Jurie Steyn said that that painting was made in his father's time by a Swede or a Pole or a Turk – he forgot which now. And the artist just painted it out of his head, Jurie Steyn said. He walked about from place to place with his brushes and canvas and when he came to a suitable spot he would set up his easel and paint pictures out of his head.

"My father asked him why he didn't paint the scene in front of him," Jurie Steyn added, "but the artist said that he had never got that far, in his artistic studies. Not that he hadn't tried, he said. But each time he tried to paint a piece of Marico bush like it was, what would come out would look just like a neat row of pine trees – from which he could see that he was painting from memory. It was all out of his head."

"Seems there must have been something wrong with his head," Gysbert van Tonder remarked. "Not that this isn't a good painting, mind you, as far as I am able to tell."

So Jurie Steyn said, no, his head was all right.

"My father said that he had never come across anybody with so quick a mind as that artist," Jurie said, "when my father hinted that the milkshed could do with a coat of whitewash. Before my father had got to mentioning the two trestles that he could put a plank over, to stand on, the artist had already packed up and was on his way through the poort, walking at a good pace. Other farmers in this area also had occasion to notice what a quick mind the artist had."

"What has struck me about this painting," Johnny Coen said, "is also about how that front door is open. It's like somebody has just come walking out of that door. Several times I have thought of it, and quite recently, too. So it's queer that Gysbert van Tonder should have started talking about that same thing. The feeling it gives me is that somebody has just come walking out of that door and has this very moment turned down that path, there. And that's why you can't see the person. I suppose it's something that the artist remembered long ago."

Chris Welman said he imagined that it must be the artist himself who had just come walking out of the door. "After they told him that the fowl-runs needed doing up, no doubt," Chris Welman continued. "That's why you can't see him by the footpath, there. He got out so quick."

But Johnny Coen could not agree. There must have been a deeper reason for the artist remembering, long afterwards and in a foreign country, just that house and that door. Some reason that had to do with longing, Johnny Coen suggested, and with regret, too, maybe.

"It couldn't be that he left that house just because he had been told that the ceiling needed fixing up," Johnny Coen said. "Because then he would have been able to paint pictures of farmhouses from outside Cape Town to the Limpopo, with an open door that he had come out of quick. No, that house there must have been an inspiration to him. He must have known that house very well. And I have heard them say that great sorrow is also an inspiration to an artist. And that is the feeling I have about that painting – that it has to do with some great sorrow in the artist's life."

Thereupon Gysbert van Tonder said that why the artist remembered that farmhouse with so much sorrow was perhaps because the farmer not only asked him to whitewash the kitchen but also to pump water for the cattle out of the borehole.

We none of us laughed at Gysbert van Tonder's words. We just felt that he didn't have the soul to understand a fine painting. And we were glad that we weren't like him.

Johnny Coen sensed that he had us interested.

"I believe," Johnny Coen said, then, folding his arms across his chest, "that the person that has just come out of that door is a *girl*. It's a girl that the artist was in love with. And if he's still alive – old and bent and walking out of a farmhouse where something had to be done to the pantry – then I know that he's still in love with that girl. And she has just come tripping out of that house, on her way to meet her lover – who is not the artist, of course. That is why he can never forget that open door."

Several of us got up to look more closely at the painting, then. There was something that appealed to us, somehow, in the thought that it was a picture that had to do with a sweet, sad love-story of long ago.

"And maybe that's why he didn't ever paint Marico farmhouses," At Naudé suggested. "Perhaps he couldn't get the right feeling for them. But all the same I think he could have made it clearer. He could actually have painted the girl coming out of the door, to keep her appointment with her secret lover. Unless he thought that maybe she also, in years to come, wouldn't look quite so – attractive – sort of – well, you know what we've been saying. About fashions in looks changing, and all that."

We guessed, from his remark, that At Naudé's eyes had wandered to the portrait of the burgher with the bandolier.

Jurie Steyn came from behind his post office counter and studied the painting of the farmhouse carefully.

"Maybe it *has* to do with a love-story of long ago," Jurie Steyn said at length. "Only, I don't think any girl came walking out of that door. I think that door was opened to let somebody in. With the woman's husband away at the market, as likely as not. I wouldn't be surprised if it's the artist himself who has just gone sneaking in there. That's why he can't forget about it, ever. Him with his long hair and his bright tie, the . . . the . . ."

IV

Flirting on the plots, Koksoord. 25 December 1962

PART OF A STORY

It was arising out of the impending return to the Marico of Petrus Gerber's daughter, Pauline, that At Naudé made the remark he did.

Pauline Gerber was expected back that day by the Bushveld lorry from Bekkersdal. She had been away for almost a year, having gone to a young ladies' college in the Cape in order to study free-hand drawing and how to talk Afrikaans with an English accent.

"When we sit here in Jurie Steyn's voorkamer," At Naudé said, "it's nearly always just men. And in consequence we don't talk scandal, like what happens when it's a lot of women that get together."

So Gysbert van Tonder said that perhaps we should not blame the women for it too much. We men, he said, were fortunate in that we had all sorts of interests that women didn't have, with the result that we could devote our time to better purpose than indulging in idle – and, frequently, malicious – gossip. We should be grateful that we were men, he said, and therefore free from those weaknesses of womankind that were responsible for their going in for thoughtless tittle-tattle.

"Chin-wagging," Chris Welman summed up chivalrously, clarifying his meaning by working his lower jaw up and down very fast, to the accompaniment of sundry high-pitched vocalisations allegedly illustrative of the inflections and cadences of feminine speech.

It was at that moment that Jurie Steyn's wife came in from the kitchen with our coffee.

"You men!" Jurie Steyn's wife exclaimed, staring at Chris Welman with her eyes wide. "Big strong men! And not one of you can jump up to help poor Chris Welman when he's sitting here with what looks like the heaves. How long have you had it, Chris? Drink this coffee down and see if it helps . . . Yes, I suppose you men have all been so busy scandal-mongering, as usual, that not one of you even *noticed* how ill poor Chris Welman has been taken. With the heaves."

We could see that Chris Welman was proud and flattered at this un-expected solicitude on the part of Jurie Steyn's wife. Indeed, he looked quite hurt, as though we had really misused him. And when he handed the empty coffee-cup back to Jurie Steyn's wife he thanked her in low and fervent tones like the way an invalid talks who has been habitually ill-treated and finds succour just when he has about given up all hope.

"I feel like a different man," Chris Welman assured Jurie Steyn's wife.

She patted him gently on the side of his head and recommended him to cheer up.

"A different *man*," Chris Welman repeated, eyeing the company in the voorkamer in a way that would have been aloof if it wasn't that he also tried to look injured, sort of, at the same time.

Gysbert van Tonder shook his head solemnly at Chris Welman after Jurie Steyn's wife had gone back to the kitchen.

"Well, of all the –" Gysbert van Tonder began, choking, "of all the –"

But Oupa Bekker held up his hand, then. It would appear that, in spite of his deafness, Oupa Bekker had followed most of our conversation, and what he hadn't heard clearly he had filled in with the knowledge of human nature that he had acquired during the many decades in which he had knocked about on this planet. Or so he claimed, any-way.

"There were bits of talk here in the post office this afternoon," Oupa Bekker said, "that I did not hear quite as unmistakably as I would have wished. Like what Chris Welman spoke just before Jurie Steyn's wife came in. Chris Welman's mouth went open and shut too quick for me to hear anything."

We winked at each other, then. For we knew that Chris Welman hadn't *said* anything. He had just been making silly shrill noises. So that showed us how deaf Oupa Bekker really was. The fact that Oupa Bekker thought he could distinguish words in that comical jargon, imitative of female conversation, that Chris Welman had produced from the top of his throat. Well, that did give you a laugh – that Oupa Bekker was so deaf.

We just about shook, then, the way we winked at each other, and nudged.

"All the same," Gysbert van Tonder went on, after a pause, "it beats me that Chris Welman can be so *low*. I can't use any other word. I mean, here were we all saying one kind of thing, and just because a woman comes in and takes a bit of notice of him, why – a man like that would sell his own grandmother. Grand*father*, I should rather say, perhaps. Where's his sense of loyalty to his own sex?"

"It's not true that men stick together," Oupa Bekker interjected. "We all know it's supposed to be that when a woman treats a man badly, then other men sympathise with that man and side with him. To his face they do, yes. But the moment he's walked out – to the bar – it's not *his* face they think of, at all. It's the face of the girl that treated him so badly that they think of – the girl that they shook their heads about while holding sympathetic conversation with him. And when they think of that girl they straighten their ties – if they are wearing ties, that is."

For the first time we noticed that, contrary to established practice, Oupa Bekker was that afternoon wearing a tie. It was a stringy and faded affair, of a shade that might, a generation earlier, have been a kind of maroon. And such as his tie was, he began, with an almost unconscious gesture, to straighten it.

Several of us in Jurie Steyn's voorkamer commenced – equally unconsciously – to pattern after Oupa Bekker. Thus we made the singular discovery that, through some strange coincidence, quite a few of us were that afternoon wearing ties – threadbare and bedraggled things in most cases, maybe, but, nevertheless, ties. It was almost as though we were not in Jurie Steyn's post office at all, but in Zeerust for the Nagmaal.

And it was arising out of the impending return to the Marico of Petrus Gerber's daughter, Pauline, that At Naudé made yet a further remark: "Funny thing that Johnny Coen isn't here, isn't it?" At Naudé said. "I mean, it's a funny thing. The lorry arriving today with the post and all, that is."

But Chris Welman said that At Naudé must not jump to conclusions. Of course, we all knew that there had been talk about Johnny Coen and Pauline Gerber before she had left for the ladies' college in the Cape. We knew that he had seen a lot of her at one time, him riding through the poort to the Gerber farm, wearing a shop suit and with striped socks pulled over the bottoms of his trouser-legs. And then his visits had ceased.

"They say that was when Pauline Gerber got hold of the plan of going to that school," Chris Welman added. "But all the same, we don't know if she really was his girl. It's only what we heard. That she started getting ideas, I mean, and said that Johnny Coen wasn't good enough for her. Mind you, she always was *pretty*, all right."

And we said, yes, Pauline Gerber always was pretty, all right.

We also said that she wasn't the first girl, either, who had at one time or another made it clear to Johnny Coen that she didn't want him calling around, anymore. The trouble with Johnny Coen, we said, was that he was too slow, for a young man. And we straightened our ties when we said it.

Well, with one thing and another, it was almost leering, the way we got afterwards, talking about Johnny Coen and saying to each other that we wondered what on earth got into his mind to make him think that he even stood a chance with Pauline Gerber. Because we all liked Johnny Coen, we spoke about him in the friendliest sort of spirit, too. There was none of that sly back-biting that we knew perfectly well women participated in when they got together. On the contrary, we all said that Johnny Coen had some very fine points indeed. And it was because we liked him so much that we said it was a pity that he should have gone and wasted his time in the way he did, running after Pauline Gerber, who couldn't possibly be expected to see anything at all in that type of admirer, we said. We were not surprised at her having sent Johnny Coen about his business, we said. We said that though we *liked* him, personally.

"In spite of her youth, you could always see that she is a knowledge-able young person," Oupa Bekker said. "What would naturally appeal to Pauline would be the more mature sort of man. The kind of man who has seen a thing or two of the world. Like who has held high office in the old Stellaland Republic, say, before it was all ruined through –"

"I wouldn't say quite so far back as the Stellaland Republic," Gysbert van Tonder interrupted Oupa Bekker. "But certainly a man who could talk about the big lung sickness that broke out in –"

Several of us interrupted Gysbert van Tonder, then, and there were a good few adjustments made to ties, and not an inconsiderable number of day-dreams about how Pauline Gerber would look today, when there was a sudden screeching of brakes and the Bekkersdal lorry drew up at the front door.

Jurie Steyn's wife got there first. Before any of us men had even seen Pauline Gerber, Jurie Steyn's wife was already talking to her. And as friendly as anything. Jurie Steyn's wife must have slipped out through the kitchen door to get there first.

"It's so nice to see you back again, Pauline," we heard Jurie Steyn's wife say. "What a pity your lovely hat got knocked all sideways in that lorry, though. And all that red on your mouth – oh, I'm sorry, I see now – I thought you had got bumped there, too, by the lorry. It's so *nice* you're back, Pauline."

Friendly as anything, Jurie Steyn's wife sounded.

HOME FROM FINISHING-SCHOOL

We knew, from having heard Jurie Steyn's wife talking to her, that Pauline Gerber was out there, alighting from the lorry. We men, sitting in the voorkamer, would have liked to go out and bid Pauline welcome home to the Marico. But we were restrained by a feeling of shyness. For, as Gysbert van Tonder said, she had just come back from that finishing-school where she had been learning English manners and free-hand drawing, and it would not be becoming for us to go and push ourselves forward, there at the lorry, in just our rough farm clothes, and not able to play the piano.

At Naudé, tiptoeing up to the window, did, however, venture to raise a corner of the chintz curtain. We had always known that Pauline Gerber was pretty, of course. And from the low whistle that At Naudé gave now, we were able to gather that concentration on the schedule of studies at the young ladies' academy had not spoilt her looks.

"Well, of all the pie-faced –" At Naudé said suddenly, with a pronounced sneer, "the *pie*-faced – well, I give up. Drivelling old woman, I should say."

At Naudé made further remarks that did not seem to fit in with the meaning of that first whistle. Could it be, we wondered, that on closer inspection of Pauline, the money spent by her father on her higher education would appear to have been the price of so many head of cattle down the drain?

Already Oupa Bekker was weighing in with a historically authentic account of the ruin that got visited on the Van der Sandt family through the attendance of some of its junior members at the Volksgimnasium. The Molopo Van der Sandts, Oupa Bekker added.

"It's that lorry-driver's assistant," At Naudé explained. "He comes and plonks himself down right in front of her, and stands there by the radiator, talking to her as free and easy as you like. So all I can see right now is a bit of feather on her hat. He's talking, standing on one leg. Anybody would think *he's* just come out of college, where they teach you flower arrangements and higher –"

"Higher sums," Gysbert van Tonder interjected, remembering something of his own primary school curriculum and attaching to it imagined academic elevations, "and higher spelling and higher recitation and higher –"

"And now he's shifted onto his other leg," At Naudé continued. "And now he's talking . . . Ha, ha, ha. No, that really was funny. Ha, ha, ha. He was changing legs again. And he has just leant his one hand – as airy as you please – right on the radiator. Ha, ha, ha. He's lifting both his legs quite a bit off the ground, now, the way he's jumping. You can imagine how hot the radiator must be of a Government lorry that's come without a stop, except Post Bag Helbult, all the way from Bekkersdal, uphill."

Thereupon we all said ha, ha.

In the same moment At Naudé dropped the corner of the chintz curtain quickly and returned to his riempies chair. A little later two large but nonetheless trim-looking suitcases came in through the half-open door. The lorry-driver's assistant came in with them. It was our turn to whistle, then – even though, unlike At Naudé, we had not yet seen Pauline. We whistled because it was the first time we had ever seen the lorry-driver's assistant so polite to a passenger. When it came to *not* being polite to a passenger, we knew that the lorry-driver's assistant was a lot worse even than the lorry-driver himself. This was easy enough to understand, of course, seeing that the lorry-driver's assistant was trying to get promotion, and he had already learnt that the only way to get anywhere in the service was by being insulting enough to passengers.

But when Pauline Gerber came into the voorkamer we could see why the lorry-driver's assistant didn't care then about all the chances of promotion that he was sacrificing through carrying in a passenger's luggage. He could make up for it later on by losing a milk-can in a donga, maybe. Or by throwing a lighted cigarette-end among a Mtosa passenger's blankets, perhaps.

The point is that Pauline Gerber wasn't merely pretty. She brought into Jurie Steyn's voorkamer more than just good looks. And more than you could learn at just a finishing-school, for that matter. As Gysbert van Tonder said about it afterwards, Pauline Gerber's coming into the voorkamer was like the middle part of a song of which he had forgotten the words but that he could play the tune of with a comb and tissue paper. And Oupa Bekker said – also afterwards – that, far from the middle, or any other part of Pauline's entrance being forgotten, it was like something that would be ever remembered. In story and in song, Oupa Bekker added.

Anyway, there it was. The suitcases came in first, with the lorry-driver's assistant walking a little behind the handle of one of the suitcases, going a bit gingerly on that side, as though the heated radiator of the lorry hadn't done his palm much good. Then came Pauline Gerber, with Jurie Steyn's wife following in the rear.

"Not there!" Jurie Steyn's wife called out as the lorry-driver's assistant made ready to swing the suitcases onto the post office counter, nearly knocking over the brass scale and the pen-and-ink stand.

"But I can't put them on the floor," the lorry-driver's assistant mumbled, dropping the suitcases on the floor, all the same. "Wet cow-dung."

The post office floor had recently been smeared.

The sound that Jurie Steyn's wife made sounded a lot like a snort.

"Ho," Jurie Steyn's wife said, "and since when isn't cow-dung good enough for you, mister? Something seems to have turned your head, all right. Maybe you can tell us what kind of dung is good enough for you? Come on, speak up. Elephant, maybe, or – or –"

The lorry-driver's assistant looked embarrassed.

"Trouble is, I burnt myself on that verdomde radiator," he announced, studying the inside of his hand. "It's all blisters."

Jurie Steyn's wife sniffed elegantly.

In doing so she inhaled some of the aroma from the newly smeared floor that had blended – a trifle incongruously, perhaps – with the perfume that Pauline Gerber had bought at the Cape. That much came out in her next remark.

"Something has turned your head, all right," Jurie Steyn's wife said to the lorry-driver's assistant, "something that has made you turn up your nose at my floor. The same thing that made you stand there all simpering in front of the lorry, I'm sure. And that's how you got burnt. Now, if my floor isn't good enough for those two suitcases, then what you could do, see, is to sit down on that bench, there, and hold the two suitcases in your lap. Or is there something else, rather, that you would like to hold in your lap? Not that *she'd* object very much, I should imagine."

Later on, when we discussed the matter between ourselves, in private, we said, yes, we did notice how much of the conversation in the post office that afternoon seemed to have taken on something of a low tone. That was what women's influence was on company, we said. The talk in the voorkamer had never got so low, really, we said, in all the time we could recall when there were only men. Or perhaps men and just one woman, Gysbert van Tonder said. And so we said, afterwards, that, yes, it was all right when it was just men, or just men and one woman. But when it was men and there were two women, we said, then the tone of the talk got lowered in a way that we just couldn't understand. That was what we said afterwards, in private, to each other.

Pauline Gerber took no notice of the insinuations made by Jurie Steyn's wife. You could see she had been taught that it was not lady-like to show her annoyance openly. Instead, Pauline stood straight up in the middle of the voorkamer and gazed slowly about her, at the men sitting on the chairs and benches. And a look of disappointment came over her face. It was almost as though there was something about our appearance that was distressing her. But we knew it couldn't be that, of course. We realised that we were not all as handsome as Johnny Coen, for instance – who was not there, that afternoon – but we knew that as a collection of manly-looking farmers (and not sissies) we could hold our own with any bunch of men that you could pick anywhere from between the Orange River and the Caprivi Strip. Pretty though she was, Pauline Gerber must not start giving herself airs now, we thought.

Then Jurie Steyn spoke.

"Can't one of you fat loafers," Jurie Steyn shouted from behind his counter, "get up and give the young lady a seat?"

We all jumped up then, of course. Well, if that was all it was, we knew our manners, all right, even though we hadn't been to any higher ladies' college. In a moment there were half-a-dozen chairs for Pauline Gerber to pick from. And we didn't make an issue of it with Jurie Steyn, either, for what he had said about fat loafers.

Thereupon Pauline Gerber explained, in dark sweet tones, that what worried her was that nobody of her family was there to take her home. There must have been some sort of misunderstanding, she said. It was the first time she had spoken. Her words had an extraordinary effect on Jurie Steyn.

"I'll drive you home in my mule-cart," Jurie Steyn said. "My wife can look after the post office while I'm away."

We were all much impressed with the well-bred and modest fashion in which Pauline Gerber accepted Jurie's invitation.

Some time later, however, when Jurie Steyn called out from the front of the post office to say that the mules were inspanned, we wondered if that young ladies' academy in the Cape really had changed Pauline Gerber so very much. It was when Pauline walked out of the front door, with her chin still in the air. And it wasn't what she did so much as the way she did it, that made it look as though she was at heart still very much of a Marico Bushveld girl. The way she sort of half-lifted her skirts at Jurie Steyn's wife, when she went out.

Singular Events

What actually *started* the discussion in Jurie Steyn's post office that day was afterwards not very clear. For that matter, it was not too clear, either, afterwards, as to how it all ended. At Naudé did make reference, of course, to a story that he had listened in to over the wireless. But he only brought in that wireless story to illustrate something that somebody else had already said. It had to do with a ship or a boat on which there were a lot of seamen and they were drifting about for a very long time, unable to reach land, At Naudé explained. When At Naudé explained further that it was something that had happened ever so long ago, we felt that he was taking our conversation off its course, in much the same way that the seamen he spoke about had been taken off *their* course, drifting about and all like that on the ocean.

That kind of thing naturally set Oupa Bekker off talking about another ship that couldn't make port. And even before Oupa Bekker spoke we knew what was coming. It was an established fact, as far as you liked to go north of the Dwarsberge, that Oupa Bekker on his grandmother's side was directly descended from Kapitein van der Decken, jolly skipper in the service of the Dutch East India Company's merchant navy, whose square-rigged brig, a familiar sight off the southern Cape Peninsula, had with the passing years acquired the stage name of *Flying Dutchman*.

We had heard this story so often before from Oupa Bekker that Gysbert van Tonder began heading him off the moment Oupa Bekker brought up his heel to knock out his pipe against. Gysbert van Tonder was only partially successful, however. Oupa Bekker did get so far as to acquaint us once more with some of the details of his last visit to Cape Town.

"Big white sails, just like you see in pictures," Oupa Bekker concluded. "And it gave me a lot of pleasure, you understand, to be able to be there at Camps Bay and to wave at my ancestor. And when I thought of how old *he* was, I didn't feel so old anymore, somehow, myself. And on the way back to the Transvaal I told a young man in my compartment about it. The young man was a student going home for the holidays, and he had a solemn look, and he said our nation must 'Hou koers' and he seemed older, somehow, than me, or even than Kapitein van der Decken, who is my ancestor on my grandmother's side."

Seeing that, in spite of our efforts to stop him, Oupa Bekker had actually got so far, Chris Welman, winking at us, decided to humour him.

"And what did that young student say about the Dutch East Indies ship, Oupa," Chris Welman asked, "the ship that you stood on the sand and waved at?"

"Oh, you could see that that student knew a thing or two, all right," Oupa Bekker said. "The student was very fine about it. He said that the *Flying Dutchman* was a myth. *Mities*, he said it was – just like that. And so I said to him that that was just how I felt about it, too. It was a word I hadn't heard before, I told him. But that was exactly the feeling I had, standing there at Camps Bay and waving, first with my hand and then with my hat, also. I felt it was just *mities*. And I don't care who knows it, I said to the student."

Oupa Bekker went on to say that when that student alighted at his destination, which was at a siding somewhere in the Karoo, then the student looked a good few years older, even, than when he had got into the train at Stellenbosch. Older and more solemn, Oupa Bekker remarked. And he glanced over his shoulder, too, once, cautiously, as though suspicious that Oupa Bekker might decide to get off there, also.

It was Jurie Steyn who reminded us of what we had really been discussing. He reminded us in that prim and precise tone of voice that he had started adopting ever since the post office authorities had erected a strip of brass wire-netting over half the length of his counter, thereby bringing Jurie Steyn into line with the post office at Bekkersdal. And now that, for half his length, Jurie Steyn was in line with the Bekkersdal post office counter, Jurie Steyn frequently spoke in the way that the Bekkersdal postmaster spoke when he pulled down his little green curtain behind the wire-netting and told the people waiting in the queue that that section was closed until nine o'clock next morning. Of course, Jurie Steyn didn't make use of that strip of wire-netting. For one thing, he didn't have a little green curtain behind it that he could pull down. And, for another thing, even if he did have a curtain, you could always put your head round that part of the counter where there was no wire-netting, and *see* Jurie Steyn standing there.

"Anyway, what I want to know," Jurie Steyn declared, in his new voice of higher officialdom, "is how we have come to be talking about Oupa Bekker's old ghost ship. As far as I can recall –"

"It's not a ghost ship," Oupa Bekker asserted. "If you think you know better than that student –"

"Ghost ship," Jurie Steyn continued. "And what's more –"

"Student of divinity, too" – Oupa Bekker chanced his arm – "and Kapitein van der Decken was my grandmother's great –"

"Now I remember what we were talking about," Jurie Steyn announced triumphantly. "We were talking about the meat shortage in the cities and about all the different kinds of meat that's being cut into strips and hung out on a line to dry for biltong. Baboons, I remember we said. And donkeys. They say there are lots of people in the cities can't tell the difference, when it's biltong. If it's some kind of taste that they haven't had before, then they think, oh, it must be ostrich. They never think it might be donkey. Isn't that what you were telling us, At?"

But At Naudé said, no, he hadn't been discussing that side of the question at all. That was what Chris Welman had been saying, At Naudé explained. He himself had been talking, he said, about that story he had heard over the wireless about those sailors ever so long ago that were adrift for months and months in a boat miles and miles away from land. That was all he said, At Naudé made clear, at the same time expressing the hope that Jurie Steyn wasn't going to get him wrong, now.

This time Oupa Bekker did lean forward, and in such a manner that, whether he wanted to or not, Jurie Steyn had to listen to him.

"Can you tell the difference by the taste, Jurie – now, just by the taste, mind," Oupa Bekker asked, "between, say, blesbok biltong and donkey biltong? Because, if you can, *it means you have tasted donkey biltong.* Perhaps you will now tell us when, and where, you *ate* donkey biltong. You know what I mean, strips of donkey hung out on a line to dry, when there's a hot sun, with naeltjies and red pepper."

Well, that was a fair enough question. All the same, we felt that Oupa Bekker need not have been so nasty about it – particularly in his going to the extent of explaining to Jurie Steyn what biltong was, as though

Jurie Steyn didn't know. Well, we felt that Jurie would have been quite within his rights if he had said that Oupa Bekker looked pretty much like a long, unappetising strip of biltong himself, and without coriander spice in it.

But Jurie Steyn didn't say that. It was almost as though Jurie had sensed that Oupa Bekker wanted him to say that. Jurie was cunning, that way. Accordingly, "Have *you* eaten donkey biltong, Oupa?" was all that Jurie Steyn would reply, then.

Oupa Bekker paused, with his pipe in the air, looking thoughtful.

"I can't say for sure," he admitted at length. "I mean, when people hand you a strip of donkey biltong, they don't tell you it's donkey biltong, do they? Or that it's baboon biltong, either, for that matter – do they, now?"

We agreed that Oupa Bekker was right, there, of course. Not one of us could recall having had a statement of that description made to him just off-hand, sort of.

"And so there it is," Oupa Bekker announced. "I may have – I just wouldn't know. But it's silly when people try and explain to you that they can tell by the taste what sort of biltong is what. You can try and guess, of course, but as likely as not you'll be wrong."

All the same, Oupa Bekker went on, looking doubtful, he couldn't understand how all this kind of talk had come about in the first place. It seemed a bit mixed-up to him, Oupa Bekker added.

"The sailors adrift on that ship," he said. "And donkey biltong. And Van der Decken being my ancestor on my grandmother's side –"

We could see that an idea had suddenly occurred to him.

"Oh, yes," Oupa Bekker said, "I remember now. It was the biltong we had at Chief Ndlambe's kraal, when Gert Pretorius and I were the first white men to trek into these parts. And although Chief Ndlambe asked us to guess what kind of biltong it was, Gert and I just couldn't. And afterwards Gert Pretorius and I discussed the peculiar way Chief Ndlambe had laughed when we said it was a kind of taste we hadn't really come across before, we didn't think . . . Well, I know now what it is that made me think of my grandmother. Because of the strange stories we heard from the Mtosas later on about Chief Ndlambe's grandmother. About the bitter kinds of disputes she had been having with her grandson, lately, and of how she had suddenly disappeared, one day, from the tribal councils. Yes, that part of it I can see quite clearly. But what have those sailors got to do with it – drifting around for months and months on that ship At Naudé has been telling us about?"

Why, it was exactly the same thing, At Naudé said.

Those sailors, At Naudé said, had to eat.

YOUNG MAN IN LOVE

Gysbert van Tonder told us, in Jurie Steyn's voorkamer, that afternoon, that Johnny Coen would be along later. He had seen Johnny Coen, Gysbert said, by the mealie-lands, and Johnny Coen was busy scraping some of the worst turf soil off his veldskoens with a pocket knife that had only the short blade left. Johnny Coen was also making use of various wisps of yellow grass, performing wiping movements along the side of his face. Well, we all knew that if, in the middle of the ploughing season, a man took all that trouble with his personal appearance, it must be that he was thinking of going visiting.

"Of course, it doesn't necessarily mean that he's coming *here*," At Naudé observed. "I mean, if he was busy to make himself up so smart, well, it might perhaps mean that he was working up the courage to go and see *her*. You know what I mean – Johnny Coen taking all the trouble to get the turf soil off his veldskoens *and* to get the turf soil off his face.

"If he was coming just here to see us, well, he wouldn't care how much black turf there was on his face. All he would be concerned about was that he didn't leave a lot of thick mud where he walked, here, in the post office, where Jurie Steyn's wife would complain about it."

Oupa Bekker shook his head.

"We know that Johnny Coen hasn't been around to the post office here, since he heard that Pauline Gerber was coming back from finishing-school," Oupa Bekker said. "And I think we can understand why. We know the kind of talk that there was about Johnny Coen and Pauline Gerber before Pauline suddenly decided to go to that ladies' school in the Cape, after all. If you remember, we said that Johnny Coen couldn't have been much of a young man if Pauline Gerber thought that going to a ladies' academy would be more exciting. Of course, we never said any of those things in Johnny Coen's presence . . ."

Thereupon Chris Welman remarked that since Pauline Gerber's return from the ladies' school in the Cape, we hadn't seen much of Johnny Coen's presence.

It was almost as though Johnny Coen wasn't so much shy about seeing Pauline Gerber, again, as that he was shy about seeing *us*. There was a thing now, Chris Welman remarked.

Oupa Bekker banged his tamboetie walking-stick on the floor, making small holes in the floor and sending up yellow dust. For the first time we realised that he was getting annoyed.

"You won't listen to me," Oupa Bekker said. "You'll never let me finish what I was going to say. Always, you just let me get so far. Then somebody says something foolish, and so I can't get to the important thing. Now, what I want to say is that At Naudé is quite right. And Johnny Coen *is* coming here. He's coming here this afternoon because he wants to know what we think. A young man in love is like that. He wants to know what we've got to say. And all the time he will be laughing to himself, secretly, about the things we're saying. A young man in love is like that, also. And his titivating himself, with the short blade of a pocket knife and a handful of dried grass – well, you've got no idea how vain a young man in love is.

"And he's not making himself all stylish for the girl's sake but for his own sake. It's himself that he thinks is so wonderful. He knows less than anybody what she is like, the girl he is in love with. And it's only the best kind of pig's fat he'll mix with soot to shine his bought boots with. Because he's in love with the girl, he thinks *he's* something. Oh, yes, Johnny Coen will come around here this afternoon, all right. And what I want to say –"

At this point, Oupa Bekker was interrupted once more. But because it was Jurie Steyn who broke in upon his dissertation, Oupa Bekker yielded with good grace. The post office we were sitting in was, after all, Jurie Steyn's own voorkamer. There was something of the spirit of old-world courtesy in the manner of Oupa Bekker's surrender.

"—— you, then, Jurie Steyn," Oupa Bekker said. "*You* talk."

Several of us looked in the direction of the kitchen. We were relieved to see that the door was closed. That meant that Jurie Steyn's wife did not hear the low expression Oupa Bekker had used.

"What *I* would like to say," Jurie Steyn said, "is that I had the honour to drive Juffrou Pauline Gerber to her home in my mule-cart, the day she arrived here at my post office, getting off from the Government lorry and all –"

"What do you mean by 'and all'?" Gysbert van Tonder demanded.

Jurie Steyn looked around him with an air of surprise.

"But you were all here," Jurie Steyn declared. "*All* of you were here. Maybe that's what I mean by *and all*. I am sure I don't know. But you did see Pauline Gerber. You each one of you saw her. When she alighted here that day from the Zeerust lorry, on her return from the Cape finishing-school. You saw the way she walked around here in my voorkamer, picking her heels up high – and I don't blame her, her back from finishing-school and all. And her chin up in the air. And as pretty as you like. You all saw how pretty she was, now, didn't you? And the way she *smelt*. Did you smell her? You must have. It was too lovely. It just shows you the kind of perfume you can *get* in the Cape.

"And I am sure that if a church elder smelt her – even if he was an *Enkel* Gereformeerde Church elder from the furthest part of the Waterberg, I am sure that that Waterberg elder would have known that Pauline Gerber had class – just from smelling her, I mean. I am sure that that scent that Pauline bought at the Cape must have cost at least seven shillings and sixpence a bottle. Look at my wife, now, for instance. Well, I once bought my wife a bottle of perfume at the Indian store at Ramoutsa. And what I say is, you can *smell* the difference between my wife and – and Pauline Gerber."

Chris Welman, who had not spoken much so far, hastened to remark that there were other ways, too, in which you could tell the difference.

It was an innuendo that, fortunately enough, escaped general attention.

For it was Johnny Coen himself that came in at the front door of the post office at that moment. In one way, it was the Johnny Coen that we had always known. And yet, also, it wasn't him. In some subtle fashion Johnny Coen had changed. After greeting us, he went and found a place for himself on a riempies chair, sitting very upright.

He seemed from his manner to be almost unaware of our presence as he whittled a match-stick to a fine point and commenced scraping out the grime from under one of his fingernails.

Gysbert van Tonder, who always liked getting straight down to things, was the first to talk.

"Nice bit of rain you've been having out your way, Johnny," Gysbert van Tonder remarked. "Dams should be pretty full, I'd imagine."

"Oh, yes, indeed," Johnny Coen answered.

"Plenty of water in the spruit, too, I should think," Gysbert continued.

"Yes, that is very true," Johnny Coen replied.

"New grass must be coming along all right in the vlakte where you burnt," Gysbert van Tonder went on.

"Yes, very nicely," Johnny agreed.

Gysbert van Tonder grew impatient.

"What's the matter with you, man – why can't you talk?" Gysbert demanded. "You know all right what I am trying to say. Have you seen her at all since she's been back?"

"I saw her yesterday," Johnny Coen said, "on the road near their house. I had to go quite a long distance out of my way to be *passing* there, at the time."

Gysbert van Tonder made a quick calculation. "Matter of just under eleven miles out of your way, counting in the short cut through the withaaks," he announced. "Did she have much to say?"

Johnny Coen shook his head.

"Please don't ask me," he almost implored of Gysbert, "because I really can't remember. We did speak, I know. But after she had gone there was nothing we said that I could recall. It was all so different, after we had met, and we had spoken there by the road, and she had gone on back home again. It was all so different after she had gone. I wish I *could* remember what we said. What I said must have all sounded very foolish to her, I am sure."

Gysbert van Tonder was not going to allow Johnny Coen to get by so easily.

"Well, how did she *look*?" Gysbert asked.

"That was what I also tried to remember, afterwards," Johnny Coen declared. "How she looked. What she did. All that. But I just couldn't remember. After she had gone it was all like it had been a dream, and there was nothing that I could remember for sure. She was picking yellow flowers there by the side of the road, she was, to stick in her hair. Or she was carrying a sack of firewood over her back for the kitchen fire, she was. And it would have been just the same *thing*, the way I felt. But I don't know. All I was able afterwards –"

"That was what I was trying to explain to them, Johnny," Oupa

Bekker interjected, "but they never let me finish anything I start to say. They always –"

"Afterwards," Johnny Coen repeated, "after she had gone, that is, there was a kind of sweetness in the air. It was almost *hanging* in the air, sort of. Once I even thought that it might be a kind of scent, like what some women put on their clothes when they go to Nagmaal. But, of course, I knew that it couldn't be *that*. I mean, I knew Pauline wouldn't wear scent, I mean. She's not that kind."

"What I wanted to say earlier on, when you all interrupted me," Oupa Bekker declared, then, with an air of triumph, "is that a young man in love *is* like that."

Dreams of Rain

Now that the rains had come, everything in the Groot Marico was, of course, different. It wasn't the kind of rain that starts off with swallows flying in low circles over the dam and ends abruptly just after you have got the tin bath in position in the bedroom, under the leaky place in the thatch.

On the contrary, it was the kind of rain that, beginning before daybreak, goes on, hour after hour, soaking into the Transvaal veld that doesn't seem to know how to take it, quite. Having, through long practice, got used to a condition of drought, it is only in the nature of things that the Transvaal veld should be somewhat suspicious, at the start, of all this silver balm descending out of the skies. It is only reasonable that the Transvaal veld should say, "Huh."

This is only the beginning, of course. For after it has been raining steadily for half a day, with more to come, the Transvaal veld starts giving itself no end of airs. It even begins to fancy that it's the Western Province, the Transvaal veld does – just as though there aren't anti-passaat winds and longitudinal geographical escarpments and things. Quite insufferable, the Transvaal veld gets.

The rain that had commenced a long while before dawn kept pattering on the leaf of moepel and maroela and wilde mispel. As one rainy hour succeeded the next, the farmers of the Groot Marico – who, through their proximity to the veld, shared its natural pessimism – gradually came to accept it as a fact that a drought of long standing was now, at last, broken.

More than one farmer, standing in the kitchen with his second cup of coffee in his hand and looking through the window at the wet daybreak, would employ some artless device in order to reassure himself that he wasn't dreaming . . . He had been caught just that way before.

"After all," as Gysbert van Tonder said in Jurie Steyn's post office

177

that same afternoon, "what else do we dream about, mostly, during a big drought?"

As if to make sure, almost, we all of us glanced in the direction of the window. And what we saw through the panes was all right. Over the outside world there was still hung a shifting curtain of grey and white filaments. Even better proof that it really was rain, right enough, and not just a dream, was provided by the state that Jurie Steyn's post office counter was in. An appliance that consisted of a chair and an enamel basin had evidently been erected too late, and there was a suggestion of inadequacy in the absorptive resources of some spread-out newspaper and a khaki blanket. Briefly, with the rain coming in through the roof, Jurie Steyn's counter was in a mess.

"All the same," Oupa Bekker remarked, looking at the chipped areas of the enamel basin with something that came close to disrespect, "I have had rain-dreams just about as real as that. In times of long drought, mind you. The kind of drought you used to get in the old days. And we would just bear up under it, too. And there would be no newspapers to write about it in big headlines. Newspapers –"

It seemed that at that moment Jurie Steyn shared Oupa Bekker's contempt for the popular press. At all events, Jurie crumpled a number of wet sheets into a soggy ball and proceeded to replace them with fresh newspapers, the while he swore to himself in undertones.

"Well, if you must know," Chris Welman remarked, "I had exactly that same feeling, this morning. When I woke up with the rain on the roof, and I looked out into the dark and the candle shone on a puddle right at my back door – well, it was exactly like the kind of dream I have often had. I have often dreamt exactly that, and then I have woken up in the morning to see another sun pulling himself right for another scorcher – so I would again all day pump water at the borehole.

"And I've noticed that the longer a drought lasts, the more flesh and blood, sort of, a dream about rain seems to become. Why, there was one night, in a time of big drought, when I dreamt I was driving down the Government Road in my mule-cart and it was raining – I say, *that* was a cunning dream, for you, now. In my dream I started doubting if it was really raining. I *dreamt* that I said to myself, 'Well, I suppose this is just a dream.'

"And then, do you know what? In the next moment the whole Government Road was full of Mshangaans on bicycles riding back from the town to their kraal, so that they could get back home to plough while the ground was still wet. When I woke up next morning, the ground was as hard as ever, with another day of drought getting ready to bake it harder still. But how do you like that for a dream, hey? Filling the whole Government Road with Mshangaans on pushbikes just to deceive me."

We agreed with Chris Welman that it was a sad story that he had just told us. And we several of us mentioned other examples of vivid dreams we had had of rain in seasons of drought. And we acknowledged that, the more severe the drought was, the more genuine and *luminous* seemed those visions of rain that came and mocked us in the night. Came unasked, too, we said, and mocked us.

"Anyway, it's not a dream for Jurie Steyn, that it's raining now," Gysbert van Tonder remarked, eyeing Jurie's struggles with a damp stock of two-penny stamps, "although I don't say that it's not a *nightmare*, for Jurie. How does he think he'll ever get those sheets of stamps dry again? My, aren't they big, though? Must be hundreds on one sheet, and all purple. Ripe, they look to me, too, sort of. And wet. Reminds me of parstyd on a wine farm in Constantia . . . I say, Jurie, if you lay those sheets of stamps on the floor like that, on top of each other, they'll all stick together, man. Or do you *want* them all stuck together? You should rather separate them and hang them along the wall. Make the wall look pretty, too."

It was a sensible suggestion that Gysbert van Tonder had made, and Jurie Steyn proceeded to carry it out. But, as is always the case with good advice, Jurie Steyn was not properly grateful. First he asked Gysbert if Gysbert thought that *he* was perhaps the duly appointed postmaster for this part of the Dwarsberge section of the Groot Marico. And then, when he had had about half of one wall covered with sheets of stamps hanging on drawing-pins, Jurie said that *he* had thought of it first.

You could see that Jurie Steyn felt really proud of himself, afterwards, when all the wet sheets of postage stamps were pinned to the wall to dry. And it looked nice, too, all the greens and blues and purples and reds. Jurie stepped back to admire his handiwork.

"Pity I haven't got any more shilling revenues," he said. "A row of them on the left, there, would make it look real smart. I wouldn't mind if the Postmaster-General came walking in here, now. No, or the new Minister of Posts *and* Telegraphs, either."

A wistful look came into Jurie Steyn's eyes as he went on gazing at the wall.

"The Postmaster-General might perhaps even have some shilling revenue stamps with him," Jurie said.

But At Naudé, who had a wireless and also read the newspapers, and was thus well up in affairs of the day, said that that sort of highly placed personage would not be coming to Jurie Steyn's post office now.

"Not now," At Naudé repeated, with a good deal of emphasis. "You see that this is a nation-wide rain – 'n landreën – and anybody as eminent as the new Minister of Posts and Telegraphs would naturally be on his way back to his farm, as quick as he can get, to plough –"

Because of Chris Welman's laughter, then, we were unable to hear the rest of At Naudé's remarks. And suddenly, one by one, it struck us, also, as to why Chris Welman was laughing. Chris Welman was thinking of his dream, we realised – his dream of the Mshangaans on their bicycles riding home as fast as they could go. And it *did* seem funny, somehow, the picture of the Minister of Posts and Telegraphs, with his head down over the handlebars, pedalling down the Government Road, ahead of those Mshangaans.

We were all laughing when the door of the voorkamer was pushed open. But it wasn't the Postmaster-General who entered, bringing in with him a flurry of rain. At the same time, we would not have been very much surprised if it *had* been the Postmaster-General. Queer things like that do happen, when you're laughing. Or when there's a big rain after a long drought.

As it turned out, however, the new arrival was only the young Johnny Coen. And he looked very miserable. It was easy to see that his courtship of Pauline Gerber was not proceeding at all smoothly. If only he would listen to the advice of men of more understanding – even though they might be a bit older than he was, maybe – he wouldn't make such a fool of himself, we felt. And the advice we had to offer him was that, seeing that she was just back from finishing-school, Pauline Gerber wouldn't be in the least interested in Johnny Coen's type. Not while there was *our* sort of man around, sitting here in the Groot Marico. Sitting on a riempies bench and chairs in Jurie Steyn's voorkamer at that moment.

"Don't you think my wall looks – er – clever," Jurie Steyn asked of Johnny Coen, pausing for the right word, "with all those different coloured stamps?"

"Yes," Johnny Coen responded, dully. He was obviously not interested. Those stamps might all just have been of one grey hue, as far as he was concerned. It was obvious that Pauline Gerber had treated him very badly. Laughed at him, we knew. With a few high notes in her laughter, too, we hoped.

"You look so dismal, Johnny," Gysbert van Tonder remarked. "Hasn't it been raining out your way?"

Chris Welman chuckled.

"Perhaps it wasn't real rain, but he just dreamt it," Chris Welman called out. "Like what we've been saying about dreams."

Thereupon Gysbert van Tonder proceeded to acquaint Johnny Coen, at considerable length, with the purport of our conversation of that afternoon.

At the end of it, Johnny Coen folded his arms and sighed deeply.

"Dreams?" he asked in a soft voice. "Dreams? That's what you've been talking about, isn't it? Well, let me tell you about a dream I had . . . No, there were no Mshangaans with pushbikes in it . . . A dream that has come to nought. Let me tell you –"

It was at that moment that the motor-lorry from Bekkersdal arrived. Not in a cloud of dust, this time, and the rain had kept the radiator cool.

We hustled around for our mail and milk-cans. We had no time to listen to stories about dreams. It was real rain that had come. Tomorrow at dawn we would be on the lands, ploughing.

Ill-informed Criticism

It was some visitor from foreign parts who, just before leaving, made certain remarks to newspaper reporters about what he thought the Transvaal platteland was like. At Naudé retailed some of those remarks to us. Primitive was one of the words that visitor had used about us, At Naudé said. And medieval, the visitor remarked. And also he had said work-shy.

Listening to all that from At Naudé in Jurie Steyn's voorkamer, that afternoon, we were, naturally enough, pained.

"Medieval?" Oupa Bekker snorted. "Well, I don't know what that word means, not having heard it more than twice or so before in my whole life, unless it was said, maybe, by somebody talking fast, so that I couldn't catch it. No, I don't know what that word *means*. But taken along with those other things that get said about us, from time to time, I should imagine that medieval is just about the worst of the lot."

Oupa Bekker said the word over to himself several times. Medieval – middeleeus. You could see there was something in the sound of it that, in spite of himself, Oupa Bekker liked.

"Now, just imagine a man like that visitor," Oupa Bekker continued. "He couldn't even have seen the country, properly –"

"He said he had seen enough," At Naudé interjected.

"– and then he says these things about us," Oupa Bekker went on, "and then he gets out – quick. He's away in an aeroplane before anybody can prove to him that we're not medieval. That's one way, now, where I don't hold with progress.

"For instance, in the old days, if a visitor, passing through Derdepoort, say, made a remark like that about the platteland, why, we would have caught up with him before he had got to the Molopo. And we would have *proved* to him, right there by the camel-thorns with a sjambok, how mistaken he was in saying that we were savage and unpolished and – and backward – and things like that. I can't call them all to mind, right now."

Gysbert van Tonder suggested a few words to help Oupa Bekker out. And then we all remembered one or two extra words that had also been said about us at various times. It was with a sense of pride, almost, at the end, that we realised how many words there were like that that had been said about us, by visitors from foreign parts.

But it was evident that Oupa Bekker's thoughts were still on that traveller who was now thousands of miles away, riding in an aeroplane through the sky.

"Even if they had just the train to Ottoshoop, still," Oupa Bekker declared, sounding wistful, "we would yet have been able to point out to that visitor where he went wrong. We would have been able to point it out to him with a short handkarwats on the station platform."

Anyway, what At Naudé had repeated to us from the newspaper report did awaken our interest. Chris Welman turned to the young schoolmaster.

"What does it mean, now, Meneer Vermaak, middeleeus?" Chris Welman asked. "I suppose that visitor means we's just a lot of stinking —— s, his saying we're medieval? Or a lot of pot-bellied —— s, hey, with our feet sticking out sideways, like a muscovy duck's? Is medieval as low a word as all that?"

Thereupon Jurie Steyn said that Chris Welman had no occasion to use such expressions, especially as his wife was in the kitchen, and might hear. Moreover, Chris Welman could speak for himself. Chris Welman could be as medieval as he liked, Jurie Steyn said. *He* didn't care. But he himself didn't want to be included in being called a stinking ——, thanks. He wondered where Chris Welman learnt such awful language.

"It's all right, Jurie, your wife isn't in the kitchen," Chris Welman was able to explain. "She's on the roof. I saw her when I came along. Just listen, you can hear her hammering there, now. When I came along she was sawing."

"Must be trying to fix that chimney, I suppose," Jurie Steyn observed. "It's been all over to one side since that big wind we had."

We all sat forward and Oupa Bekker put his hand up to his ear, when the schoolmaster, having cleared his throat, explained that medieval had to do in the first place with the feudal system. Chris Welman looked startled. He thought he knew all the low words there were, Chris Welman said. And what he didn't know himself he had learnt the time, long ago, when he had been a white labourer in Johannesburg digging foundations. But the word *feudal* was a new one on him. He hoped the schoolmaster wouldn't let it slip out by accident in the schoolroom, one day, in front of the children, when he lost his temper about something, Chris Welman said.

But the schoolmaster went on to explain further. And it was a long sort of explanation. And it didn't seem to lead anywhere. It seemed like it had to do with history, and in the end we were several of us yawning. There was no point to it.

From what the schoolmaster was saying, Oupa Bekker commented, it would appear that the word feudal had to do with some kind of government. And so he didn't see where the schoolmaster's explanations fitted in, at all. For that matter, he didn't accept that that kind of government was much of an improvement on what we had right here in the Groot Marico.

"Most of those things you're talking about we've already *got*," Oupa Bekker said. "So what's the argument?"

"It seems to me that it's some more of that progress talk," Gysbert van Tonder announced.

"Well, we don't want any more of their progress, medieval or any other kind. They can go and have all the progress they want somewhere else, if they like. But they can't come and have it on my front stoep, they feudal well can't. And as for that visitor saying we're *work-shy* – well, does he know what work is, at all, I wonder? Him sitting in that aeroplane, all snooty."

For a good while after that we each of us started wondering the same thing, each of us wondering, in turn, if the visitor had ever pumped water for the cattle in the hot sun. Or if the visitor had ever chased a pig to put in a crate, in the hot sun, for several hours, with the visitor's family and the Mtosa farmhands falling over each other, all the time, and the boss-boy going to the police afterwards – the boss-boy claiming that the visitor had kicked him on the ear on purpose when the pig jumped out of the crate again.

Or if the visitor had ever got a letter from the storekeeper at Ramoutsa about what he would do unless the visitor made a big payment in three days, in the hot sun.

We all spoke about some time or other that we had worked.

The longest story of all was Chris Welman's. He had to take so long over it, not because he was working so much, but because it was the time he was in Johannesburg, digging foundations, and he had to tell us a lot of things about what Johannesburg was like, in those old days. There was a lot of labour trouble at that time on the Rand, Chris Welman said. And almost every other day they were having a general strike. He wasn't quite sure what it was all about, Chris said, but he wouldn't say it didn't suit him. It just meant that every so often he would have to put down his spade and pick and go home.

And they had a woman Labour leader that they called Miss Florence Desborough, Chris Welman said. He had never seen her, but he would have liked to, he said.

Not that she would ever have taken any notice of his sort, he knew. But he pictured what she was like from her name. And he thought of her as pretty, and having a soft, refined voice, and with an ostrich feather in her hat, and having high-up shoulders, like they wore in those days. He got all that just out of the sound of her name, he said – Miss Florence Desborough.

And then one day there was again a general strike that he and his mates, standing digging in the trench, didn't know about. How they got informed, Chris Welman said, was when one of those old-fashioned taxis that they had in those days drove up to where they were working, and a woman came dashing up to them out of the taxi, swinging a pick-handle, that was tied to her wrist with a piece of string. She was screaming, too, Chris Welman said. And he himself didn't stop running for about six blocks. Anyway, he himself was a bit disappointed, afterwards, when he learnt that that woman was Miss Florence Desborough, and that she had the nickname of Pickhandle Flo.

Jurie Steyn's wife, coming in at that moment with our coffee, didn't sound very different from Miss Florence Desborough, we thought. Moreover, Jurie Steyn's wife had a black smudge on her forehead from the chimney.

"What do you call yourselves?" she asked indignantly. "Of all the lazy, good-for-nothing loafers – talk, talk, is all you do. Here have I had to get onto the roof myself with a hammer. And a saw. And a pick. Who's ever heard of a white woman having to swing a pick?"

Jurie Steyn's wife said a lot more. We did not answer her.

185

"One thing, at least," Oupa Bekker chuckled, after Jurie Steyn's wife had gone out again, "one thing at least that she didn't say is that we're middeleeus."

TOYS IN THE SHOP WINDOW

"You ought to see David Policansky's store," the lorry-driver's assistant said. "My, but it does look lovely. All done up for Christmas. It's worth going all the way to Bekkersdal just to see it. And the toys in the window – you've got no idea. There's a mirror with a little ship on it, and cottonwool over it for clouds, and little trees at the side of it, so the mirror looks just like it's water. And there's a toy Chinaman that goes up and down on a ladder with baskets over his shoulder on a stick when you wind him up –"

Jurie Steyn interrupted the lorry-driver's assistant to say that he was sure to go and drive all those miles and miles to Bekkersdal, just to go and look at the toys in Policansky's window. Catch *him*, going all that way to stare at a wound-up Chinaman going up and down on a ladder with baskets, Jurie Steyn said.

Thereupon, speaking earnestly to him because this was no time for foolishness, Gysbert van Tonder said to the lorry-driver's assistant that he hoped he hadn't been talking about those same toys at every Bushveld farmhouse and post office that the lorry had stopped at on the way north from Bekkersdal. Because if he *had*, why, the children would make their parents' lives impossible between now and Christmas. He himself had several children that were still of school-going age, Gysbert van Tonder said. And so he knew.

The lorry-driver's assistant looked embarrassed.

"Well, I did talk a little," he admitted. "But I didn't say too much, I don't think. Except maybe at Post Bag Laatgevonden. Yes, now I come to think of it, I did, perhaps, say one or two things I shouldn't have, at Post Bag Laatgevonden. You see, the driver had trouble with a sparking plug, there, and so in between handing the driver a spanner or a file, maybe, I *might* have said a few things more than just about the ship and the Chinaman.

"Yes, now I come to think of it, I did, at Post Bag Laatgevonden, make some mention of the train that goes underneath tunnels and then waits at a siding for the signal to go up before it goes rushing on again through the vlakte, past railwaymen's cottages and windmills and Mtosa huts, and then it gets switched onto another line – but I'm sorry, kêrels.

"Yes, I'm really sorry. I know, now, that I talked too much, there. But Laatgevonden was the only place where I mentioned the train. At the other Post Bags where we stopped we didn't stop long enough – having just to hand over the mailbag and unload the milk-cans – and so I didn't say anything at those places about the train. You see, that train in Policansky's window goes such a long distance, round and round and round, and taking up water supplies, too, at one spot, that you can't talk about it, unless you've got a long *time* to talk – as I did have at Post Bag Laatgevonden, where the lorry-driver was trying to fix a sparking plug, and shouting that I was handing him the wrong tools as often as not."

In making that remark, the lorry-driver's assistant grinned.

"All the same," he added, "you've got no idea what that train is like. It's so real that you almost expect to see a gang of plate-layers running away and the passengers throwing empty bottles at them out of the windows."

We could see from this that there must have been a good deal of realism about the clockwork railway in Policansky's store. We could also see in which way the lorry-driver's assistant and his friends amused themselves, whenever they went on a train ride from Ottoshoop.

Meanwhile, Johnny Coen, who had once worked on the South African Railways, was asking the lorry-driver's assistant if the toy train in Policansky's window was one of the new kind of toy train, such as he had heard about. Did it have bogie wheels, he asked. And did it have a miniature injector steam pipe. But when he asked if it also had miniature superheater flue tubes, the lorry-driver's assistant said that was something Johnny Coen should perhaps rather go and ask David Policansky. He himself only thought that it looked like a train. And it looked a lot like a train, to him, the lorry-driver's assistant said. But maybe there were parts missing. He wouldn't be able to tell. It *went* all right, though, he added.

The lorry-driver's assistant was in the middle of telling us about something else that Policansky was arranging to have in the toy department of his store, for Christmas, when the lorry-driver called through the door and asked did the assistant think they could waste all day at a third-rate Dwarsberg post office where the coffee they got was nearly all roast kremetart root.

By the time Jurie Steyn walked round from behind his counter to the front door, the lorry was already driving off, so that most of the long and suitable reply that Jurie Steyn gave was lost on the driver.

Before that, with his foot on the clutch, the lorry-driver had been able to explain that his main grievance wasn't the coffee, which he was not by law compelled to drink. But he did have to handle Jurie Steyn's mailbag, the lorry-driver said. And although he was pressing down the accelerator at the time, we could still hear clearly what it was that the lorry-driver took exception to about Jurie Steyn's mailbag.

By the time Jurie Steyn had finished talking to the driver the lorry was already halfway through the poort.

"What do you think of that for cheek?" Jurie Steyn asked of us, on his way back to the counter. "He's just a paid servant of the Government, and he talks to me like I'm a Mtosa. I mean, he's no different from me, that lorry-driver isn't. I mean, I am after all the postmaster for this part of the Dwarsberge. I also get paid to serve the public. And that lorry-driver talks to me just like I talk to any Mtosa that comes in here to buy stamps."

We felt it was a pity that this unhappy note should have crept into what had until then been quite a pleasant summer afternoon's talk. What made it all the more regrettable, we felt, was because it was only another few weeks to Christmas. The way Jurie Steyn and the lorry-driver spoke to each other didn't fit in with the friendly spirit of Christmas, we felt. Nor did it fit in, either, with the even more friendly spirit that there should be at the New Year.

"And did you hear what he said about my mailbag?" Jurie Steyn demanded, indignantly. We confessed that we had. Indeed, we would have to have been more deaf yet than Oupa Bekker if we had missed any of the lorry-driver's remarks about the mailbag. Even though the engine of the lorry was running at the time, we could hear every word he said. The driver spoke so clearly. And what made what he said even more distinct was that kind of hurt tone in his voice. When a lorry-driver talks like he's injured, why, you can hear him from a long way off.

"What he said about my fowls," Jurie Steyn burst out. "That's what

I can't get over. When he spoke about the mailbag that my fowls had – had been on."

Well, Jurie Steyn was expressing it more politely than the lorry-driver had done, we thought. "And that he said afterwards that he had to handle that mailbag," Jurie Steyn continued.

Several of us spluttered, then, remembering the *way* in which the lorry-driver had said it.

"And that he declared they were a lot of speckled, mongrel, dispirited Hottentot hoenders," Jurie Steyn finished up, "with sickly, hanging-down combs. Well, that *got* me all right. There isn't a hen or a rooster on my farm that isn't a pure-bred Buff Orpington. Look at that hen pecking there, next to At Naudé's foot, now. Could you *call* it a speckled –"

Words failed Jurie Steyn, and he stopped talking.

Nevertheless, we all felt that it was unfortunate that Jurie Steyn should have had that misunderstanding with the lorry-driver. Because, what the lorry-driver's assistant had told us about the toy train in Policansky's window, at Bekkersdal, was something quite interesting. And we would have liked to talk about it some more. We felt that, in spite of Bekkersdal being so many miles away, it might perhaps be worthwhile to take our children to go and have a look at that shop window, all the same. It would be instructive for the children, we felt. But as a result of what had happened since, we weren't quite in the mood for that anymore.

It was only Gysbert van Tonder who did not seem to have his feelings completely quenched.

"When that young lorry-driver's assistant spoke about the toy train in Policansky's window," Gysbert van Tonder remarked, "well, you know how it is, a toy train, with tunnels and all. I thought right away how my children would enjoy it. I even thought of driving over to Bekkersdal in my mule-cart next week, taking Oupa Bekker with me. And then we could come back and tell my children all about it, I thought. We could also tell the children all about that Chinaman that climbs up and down a ladder with baskets. We could get Policansky to wind up that Chinaman several times, I thought, so that we could explain exactly to the children how it works.

"But I haven't got quite that feeling for it, anymore, if you know how it is. So my children will have to go without. And it would have been such fun for them, having me and Oupa Bekker telling them all about what makes that train work. What does make it work, I wonder? It might help them with their exams, to know."

But it was then that Chris Welman remembered what the lorry-driver's assistant was saying just before the lorry-driver shouted to him to get going. And it was as though that cloud that had come over us had never been.

For David Policansky had said that he was going to get a Father Christmas at his store again, this year. He said he had to have a Father Christmas. The toy trade was no good without a Father Christmas with a red cap and overcoat and white whiskers shaking hands with the children in the toy department, Policansky said. And we laughed and said that we would have thought that the toy trade was no good *with* a Father Christmas. And we also said that we hoped, for his own sake, that this year Policansky wouldn't get old Doors Perske to be Father Christmas, again, the same as he did last year.

We went on discussing last year's Father Christmas at Policansky's store for quite a long time.

As far as looks went, Doors Perske should have made a very good Santa Claus. He was fat and he had a red face. The circumstance of his face being on some occasions more red than on others would as likely as not escape the innocent observation of childhood.

But where Doors Perske went wrong was in his being essentially an odd-job man. For years he had contrived to exist in the small town of Bekkersdal by getting a contract to erect a sty, or to chop wood, or to dig a well. And that was how he had learnt to sub.

And so, when he was Santa Claus in Policansky's store, Doors Perske would every so often go and get a small advance against his pay from the bookkeeper. After a bit, the sight of Santa Claus entering the local public bar for a quick one no longer excited comment. The bartender no longer thought it funny to ask if he'd come down the chimney. No scoffing customers asked anymore could he go and hold his reindeer.

In Policansky's store, too, everything was, at first, all right. If, in shaking hands with Doors Perske, a small child detected his beery breath, the small child would not think much of it. Since he had a father – or, maybe, a stepfather – of his own, the small child would not see anything incongruous in Father Christmas having had a few.

One day Doors Perske's wife had come charging into the toy department, swearing at Father Christmas and loudly accusing him of subbing on his wages, on the sly. And Doors Perske had called his wife an old ——, and had ungraciously clouted her one on the ear before bundling her out of the store. But even that incident did not have a disillusioning effect on the minds of David Policansky's juvenile clientele.

For the altercation had taken place at the counter where there were prams and dolls'-houses and little crockery sets, and the children thronging that part of the shop were familiar with domestic scenes of the sort they had just witnessed. All they thought was that Father Christmas had just had a fight with Mother Christmas.

But it was the day before Christmas Eve that Doors Perske got the sack. He had just come back from the bar, again. And the first thing he had to do was to stumble over the shilling dips. Then, to save himself, he grabbed at an assortment of glassware stacked halfway up to the ceiling. This was foolish – as he realised next moment. The glassware offered him no sort of purchase at all. All that happened was that the whole shop shook when it fell. The next thing that went was the counter with the toy soldiers. And there didn't seem anything very martial in the way the little leaden soldiers – no longer in their neat toy-rows – were scattered around, lying in heaps and with pieces broken off them: it looked too much like the real thing. Grim, it looked.

When Policansky came rushing in, it was to find Doors Perske sitting in a wash-tub, with a teddy-bear in his arms. His red cap had come off and his Father Christmas beard was halfway round his neck. And from the position of his beard the children in the shop knew that he wasn't Father Christmas but just a dressed-up drunk.

"I couldn't get a proper grip on those glasses," Doors Perske explained. "That's how I fell."

Policansky got a proper grip on Santa Claus, all right. And he ran him out of his shop and when he got to the pavement he kicked Father Christmas, and told him not to come back again.

"Go on, there *isn't* any Father Christmas," Doors Perske jeered, suddenly recovering himself, when he got to the corner. "It's just a lie that you make up for kids."

David Policansky's face twisted into a half-smile. "I wish I could believe you," he said, surveying the wreckage of his shop through the door. "I wish I could believe there *wasn't* a Father Christmas."

. . . At this Time of Year

It was always about now, Jurie Steyn said, with the year drawing to an end, that he got all sorts of queer feelings. He didn't know how to say them, quite. But one feeling he did get, and that he had no difficulty in explaining, he said, was a homesickness to be back again in the Western Province where he had spent his early childhood.

Jurie Steyn heaved a medium-length sigh, then, thinking back on the years when he was young.

"Not that I haven't got a deep love for the Transvaal," Jurie Steyn added, in case we should get him wrong. "I am, after all, a Transvaler –"

And so we said, yes, it was quite all right. We understood his feelings for the old Cape Colony. He needn't explain, we said.

"And because I've said that I passed my young years in the Cape," Jurie Steyn went on, the suggestion of a combative look coming into his eye, "that doesn't mean to say that I am old, today."

We hastened to reassure him on that point, too – but not very convincingly, it seemed. Gysbert van Tonder even coughed.

"I know what you mean, Jurie," young Johnny Coen said, quickly, hastening to forestall any unpleasantness that might ensue on Jurie Steyn demanding of Gysbert van Tonder what he meant by clearing his throat, that way. "It's the place where you were born and bred and can't ever forget. I was born in the Marico Bushveld, and you've got no idea how homesick I got the time I was working on the railway at Ottoshoop.

"But, of course, Ottoshoop is at least ninety miles from here – further even, if you don't go the road through Sephton's Nek. So I know how you feel, Jurie. No matter how kind people are to you, even, if they're not your own people you do get very lonely, sometimes. Oh, yes, I went through all that at Ottoshoop."

Johnny Coen went on to describe a wedding reception that he had attended at Ottoshoop while he was an exile in those parts.

"They had spread white tablecloths over long tables on the front stoep," Johnny Coen said. "And there was a man at the party who did balancing tricks with a chair and a wine-glass. And I got more and more sad. The only time I laughed a little was when the loose seat dropped out of the chair and caught the man on the back of his neck when he was at the same time throwing up two guavas and a fork."

Johnny Coen went on to say that, as it turned out, his neighbour at table was also a foreigner.

"How I knew," Johnny Coen said, "was when that man spoke to me. And he said I was looking pretty miserable. And he asked was it that I was in love with the bride, perhaps, and that another man had taken her away from me. And I said, no, I was from the Dwarsberge part of the Marico, and I felt most homesick for the Groot Marico when the people around me were happy, I said. And that was how I got talking to that Englishman sitting next to me at the table. And when somebody in the voorkamer starting playing 'Home Sweet Home' on the harmonium we were both of us crying onto the tablecloth. And I never used to think that an Englishman had any feelings, until then.

"Another thing I found out afterwards that I had in common with the Englishman was that he didn't like that man with the balancing tricks, either."

Thereupon Jurie Steyn said that he, too, wouldn't like it very much if somebody were to start playing "Home Sweet Home" on a harmonium at this time of year. Of course, he knew it best as a German song, Jurie Steyn said, and it was called "Heimat Süsse Heimat". But the tune was the same. He had heard the German missionaries at Kroondal sing it quite often. And they would cry onto the thick slices of that kind of red sausage that they had on their plates, Jurie said.

"Take the Cape at this time of year, now," Jurie Steyn said, "in the summer."

So we said, very well, we would take the Cape, then, if he put it like that.

"Well, when it gets towards about now, towards about Christmas time and the end of the year," Jurie Steyn proceeded, "why, I just can't help it. I think of a little Boland dorp with white houses and water furrows at the side of the streets and oak-trees. Not that I haven't got all the time in the world for moepel or a maroela or a kremetart or any other kind of Bushveld tree. For instance, I have often walked to the end of my farm by the poort, just to go and look at the withaaks there. No, it isn't that. After all, an oak isn't a proper South African tree, even, but just imported.

"All the same, when it gets towards Christmas, the thought of those oak-trees in the Cape comes into my mind just all of a sudden, sort of. And I get the feeling of how much nobler a kind of person I was in those days than what I am today. I think of how much more upright I was in my youth."

Thereupon Gysbert van Tonder said, yes, that he could well believe.

We knew that Gysbert van Tonder – who was Jurie Steyn's neighbour – was hinting about the last bit of neighbourly unpleasantness they had, which had to do with the impounding of a number of stray oxen. And we didn't want to have *that* long argument all over again. Especially not with the Christmas season drawing near, and all.

It was quite a good thing, therefore, that Oupa Bekker should have started talking then about a quite ordinary camel-thorn tree that grew on one side of Bekkersdal when it was first laid out as a dorp.

"It was because of what Jurie Steyn said about oaks that made me think of it," Oupa Bekker said. "I was there when Bekkersdal was proclaimed as a township, and the bush was cleared away and the surveyor measured out the streets and divided up the erfs. And the Kommandant-General and the Dominee had words about whether the plein in the middle of the dorp should be for the Dopper Church, with a pastorie next to it, or for the Dopper Church, with a house for the Kommandant-General's son-in-law next to it, a site to be chosen for the pastorie that would be within easy walking distance for the Dominee."

Oupa Bekker said that in the end the Dominee decided that he wouldn't mind walking a little distance. Oupa Bekker said he had no doubt that what made the Dominee come to that decision was because the Dominee did not wish to make the Kommandant-General unhappy.

For it was well known throughout the Transvaal that few things made the Kommandant-General so unhappy as when he had to take firm steps against anybody who opposed him. And Oupa Bekker said it was also known that on occasion the Kommandant-General had taken steps that you might call even unusually firm against a person who stood in his way.

"And so the Dominee agreed, in the end," Oupa Bekker continued, "that a short brisk walk from his pastorie to the church, of a Sunday morning before the sermon, would be healthy for him. And so a house for the Kommandant-General was built on the measured-out erf on the plein next to the church. But all that happened – oh, so many years ago."

Oupa Bekker's sigh would have been even more prolonged than Jurie Steyn's had been. Only, because of his advanced years, Oupa Bekker didn't have the breath for it.

"All the same, that was a funny thing," Chris Welman commented, "for the old days, that is. And so I suppose that's the reason why –"

Oupa Bekker nodded.

For we knew where the pastorie was, today, in Bekkersdal. And we knew that the present-day minister, Dominee Welthagen, had to walk a fairish distance to the church, of a Sunday, just as his predecessor of three-quarters of a century ago had to do. But that first Dominee would no doubt have been able to take short cuts, since at that time Bekkersdal would not have been as built up as it was today.

"And that erf that was measured out for the Kommandant-General's son-in-law –" Chris Welman started to remark.

"Yes, that's the reason for all that trouble there, now," Oupa Bekker said. "But the old people always knew that the Kommandant-General's son-in-law was a bit thoughtless. All those empty bottles that used to lie in his back yard, for instance. And that back yard isn't any more tidy today. Not with all those empty jam tins and all that garbage and all those empty fruit boxes lying in it. Why, that back yard looks worse than ever, now that it has been taken over for an Indian store. And right next to the Dopper Church, and all. No wonder there's that trouble about it in Bekkersdal, now."

So we said, it was very sinful of the first Indian – who was the grandfather of the present Indian – to have gone and bought that erf right next to the Dopper Church to go and open an Indian store on.

There should really have been a pastorie there, we said.

"Bit of a pity the Kommandant-General's son drank so much," Johnny Coen observed.

In the discussion that followed about what a scandal it was that there should be an Indian store next to the Dopper Church in Bekkersdal, Oupa Bekker was able only in an edgeways fashion to tell us about the camel-thorn tree that grew at the edge of the Bekkersdal township. And we were not able to pay much attention to Oupa Bekker's story, then. Whereas it was quite a pretty story.

It appears that the streets of the newly laid dorp were planted with jacarandas – an imported tree then coming into fashion. And at the end of one street, in exact line with the jacarandas, and at the same distance from its nearest jacaranda neighbour as the jacarandas were set apart from each other, there grew that indigenous old African camel-thorn tree.

And although the street ended just before it came to him, the old camel-thorn tree really imagined that he was part of that jacaranda avenue. And he was as pleased as anything about it. And he started putting on airs, there, just as though he was also an imported tree, and not just an old camel-thorn that the veld was full of. And even though the municipality didn't water him, like they watered the jacaranda, the camel-thorn remained as cheerful as ever. He knew he didn't *need* watering.

Anyway, the point of Oupa Bekker's story had to do with the first summer that the jacarandas in Bekkersdal came to flowering. And one night there was a terrible wind from the Kalahari, so that in the morning the sidewalks were thickly strewn with purple flowers, and there were more jacaranda blooms stuck on the thorns of the old camel-thorn tree than any jacaranda still had on its branches, then. And the purple blossoms lay thick about the lower part of the gnarled trunk of the camel-thorn. It was his hour, and so you couldn't tell him from an imported tree.

We didn't hear very much of what Oupa Bekker had to say, however. We were too busy thinking out the right words for a strong letter we were drafting to our Member of Parliament. It had to do with the Indian Problem.

But it was after the railway lorry from Bekkersdal had drawn up at the front door that Gysbert van Tonder really let himself go on the Indian Problem. It was when Gysbert found out that the roll of barbed wire he had ordered wasn't on the lorry.

"It's the fault of the Indian storekeeper's assistant," the lorry-driver explained – although he used a different word in referring to the young Indian who was helping the old Indian in the Bekkersdal store. "I could see that the young Indian assistant wasn't himself. The shop was all done out with Christmas stockings, and things. And that old gramophone they've got at the back of the shop was playing 'Home Sweet Home'. And that young Indian assistant was busy crying onto the counter.

"Saying that at this time of the year he always got homesick for Natal, the Indian assistant said. Well, that beats me, all right. How anybody can ever feel homesick for Natal, I just don't know."

New-Year Glad Rags

"Uren, dagen, maanden, jaren,
Vliegen als een schaduw heen."

The partition had been removed between the two classrooms. Ink stains and the marks left behind by water that had leaked through the thatched roof in the last rains were now covered up with a coating of whitewash. All the blemishes on the schoolroom walls of that year and of former years were hidden away.

For the more unhappy evidences of a year of educational activity within those walls the virginal film of unslaked lime served as both a mask and an immaculate cerement.

Dominee Welthagen had come over specially from Bekkersdal to hold an end-of-year service in that little Bushveld schoolhouse that had for a night been changed over into a place of worship.

Many of the desks were of the old-fashioned kind, seating a good number of pupils in a row and with the front parts detachable, so that their temporary conversion into pews had not presented much difficulty. There was that other, more modern kind of desk, however, with an iron framework, that obstinately continued to look like nothing else but standard Transvaal Education Department equipment, no matter what you did to it.

Nor did the blackboard standing on its easel in the corner take kindly to ecclesiastical disguise. Since this was a Calvinist service – and that sixteenth-century reformer's views on idolatry were well known – you couldn't go and hang an icon, say, in front of the blackboard.

Maybe, if it had been a church service that Dominee Welthagen had come to conduct at some other time, the elders and deacons would not have been so energetic in altering the appearance of the schoolroom. But there seemed to be something about devotions arranged for

199

the end of the year that called for a certain measure of stage-setting.

After all, during the last few days of December one does, at times, become a prey to inner questionings. And it is only someone who is without human weaknesses of his own who will view with a cynical eye the earnest efforts of a deacon engaged in making a school cupboard look like an altar from the front. What is that thing inside the deacon – the cynic would ask – that the said deacon is trying to cloak? The answer, alas, is "Many things." For there never has been a church deacon that did not have his share of frailties.

The young schoolmaster was, strangely enough, very helpful.

It wasn't often that the schoolroom was used for a church service. And, generally speaking, a schoolmaster was not too keen on that sort of thing. In the first place, the church authorities would obtain permission direct from the Education Department head office in Pretoria to hold their service in the schoolroom, the schoolmaster's share in the formalities being limited to handing over the key of the building when an elder presented himself at the front door with a letter and a couple of Mtosa women carrying buckets of whitewash.

For the schoolmaster there was a certain amount of indignity in this situation.

All he would be able to say, reaching for his hat, was, "Well, I hope you won't slop all that stuff over my register again. Last year the inspector asked if there had been pigs at it."

Or the schoolmaster would say, unsmilingly locking some small change away in his desk, "Very well, you can take over. I've counted all the rulers and exercise books in the cupboard, there."

It wasn't that the schoolmaster was indifferent to the blessings that got conferred on the Groot Marico north of the Dwarsberge through these religious exercises. Indeed, when he thought of some of the church ouderlings he knew, he could only wonder where they would be, were it not for the benefits derived from divine intercession. Every schoolmaster who had ever taught in the Marico knew that church services held in the schoolroom did a lot of *good*.

But the trouble is that we all have our little human vanities. And the schoolmaster likes to think that in his schoolhouse he's a king. And so when a deacon, who is just an ordinary farmer, and with some of his children at that school, perhaps, turns up with a letter signed by somebody that's higher than a school inspector, even, why, it stands to reason that that schoolmaster won't feel too bucked about it. Especially if the deacon has got a kind of a sneer on his face in the act of taking over.

But with the schoolmaster, young Vermaak, it was quite different, this year, Jurie Steyn's brother-in-law said so himself. And Jurie Steyn's brother-in-law was the deacon (an ouderling not being available at the moment, because of the ploughing) who had gone to young Vermaak with a letter signed by a high authority, requesting the use of the school-house for the Almighty. We knew from that that the letter must have had a pretty high-up signature.

And Jurie Steyn's brother-in-law, the deacon, said that young Vermaak was ever so polite and friendly about it. It took away a good deal of his pleasure, at first, the deacon said. He had hoped to come into the classroom and to find the schoolmaster correcting a lot of examination papers, or filling in reports, and that the schoolmaster would have been very sarcastic about having to leave, the deacon said. He was looking forward to the schoolmaster walking out of the schoolroom in a nasty temper and asking when was he expected to do his work. And so, when the schoolmaster was, instead, helpful, he almost wished he hadn't come along with that letter, the deacon said.

The deacon went on to explain that he made the Mtosas that he had brought with him lift the schoolmaster's table off the platform that it stood on, in front of the class. And young Vermaak didn't say a word. He even went to the assistance of one of the Mtosas who, forgetting for a moment that he was on a platform, stepped backwards off the edge of it, landing with his back part in a bucket of whitewash. The school-master assisted the Mtosa with his boot, the deacon said, adding that he could not have done it more neatly himself, seeing that the Mtosa was sitting *in* the bucket of whitewash, and therefore not leaving much space, really, for getting properly assisted.

The schoolmaster went up a lot in his estimation, the deacon said, when he saw the quick way in which the schoolmaster helped that Mtosa to rise.

"And then I made the Mtosas stand the platform on its edge against the wall," the deacon added. "And they did that, one of them still limping a little from the way the schoolmaster had helped him. And then I said I would cover the platform with those sheets of black drawing paper that had pictures of mealies and maps of rivers on them. I said I would turn those drawings round and pin them onto the platform stood on its edge, and so it would look more like a preekstoel, the place where Dominee Welthagen was to stand.

"Those drawings had been made by young Vermaak himself, and they were stuck all round the walls. And I said it just for a joke, of course, in order to make him wild. And do you know what he did? He went and fetched a little packet of drawing-pins, so as to help us with that, also."

We were most surprised to hear that from the deacon. We were, after all, religious people ourselves. But we knew that there were limits. And we feared that if the schoolmaster got so religious, then it must be that there was something on his mind.

Then we remembered that we hadn't seen young Vermaak at Jurie Steyn's post office for quite a few months. Maybe, that was worrying him, we thought – the fact that during all that time he hadn't come to visit us. But we also realised that, seeing it was drawing towards the end of the year, he would be too busy, setting examination papers and correcting them, and fixing things so that his favourite pupil would come first again.

Not that we bore him any ill-will, on that account, of course. It was many years since any one of us had last been at school. And we were glad to think that we had been mellowed by the years, so that we no longer retained our childhood prejudices. We thought of a teacher's pet only as a snivelling rat that wipes his nose on his sleeve, but we had no evil feelings about him.

> "Snelt dan, jaren, snelt vrij henen
> . Met uw blijdskap en verdriet –"

It was beautiful the way we sang the words of the next verse of Hymn 160 in the schoolroom that had been converted into a house of worship, we all of us singing together.

This was a Reformed Church service. But that did not prevent quite a number of us, who were Doppers, from attending. Moveover, we who were Doppers were not allowed by our Enkel Gereformeerde Kerk to sing hymns; we were only permitted to sing psalms. And yet there was something about Dominee Welthagen's Reformed Church service that night that we couldn't resist.

And so in the end it was actually us Doppers who, strictly speaking, were not *allowed* to sing a hymn, even, that showed those Reformers how a hymn should be *sung*. But if only Dominee Welthagen had announced a psalm, instead! If only Dominee Welthagen had said "the congregation will now sing 'Kom laat ons zamen Israel's Heer'" – why, you would have heard us as far as Vleisfontein, and it would have been only Dopper voices that you would have heard, and Dominee Welthagen's own Reform congregation would have been nowhere.

There was Jurie Steyn, there, wearing his new suit that he had bought on mail order, just sending his measurements. There was Oupa Bekker, with a collar that, if it was perhaps not quite so white, anymore, as the predikant's, was certainly a good deal taller and stiffer. There was Gysbert van Tonder in a suit of formal cut, with a slit up the back of the jacket that was fashionable when Gysbert van Tonder first trekked into the Marico as a comparatively young man.

At Naudé was wearing his Sunday best, also a three-piece, that, whatever its original colour, was now, except for a few undecided areas, an almost uniform green. Young Vermaak, the schoolmaster, looked dignified in navy serge. In that light you could hardly see the places where his landlady's daughter had cleaned the jacket with paraffin.

So much for the men in their New Year apparel.

The women's dresses were, mostly, new. There was consequently little that, to the male gaze, would enable one frock to be distinguished from another. With the women themselves, of course, it was different. They had a lot to whisper, behind hymn-books, about skirt lengths and waistlines and hats – that was, if you could call a thing a hat that seemed to be a piece of cardboard with a blue handkerchief stuck on it with a brass safety pin.

But there were other words and other images, also, that some of the women, whispering behind hymn-books, used in describing Pauline Gerber's hat. But afterwards they didn't talk about her hat so much . . .

"Welzalig hij, die op U bouwt,
Geheel zijn lot aan U vertrouwt –"

We sang at the end of the service, all of us standing up.

And it was only after the church was out that we started talking about Pauline Gerber, whom we hadn't seen much of since the time she had come back, so smart and all, from finishing-school. We said that she was looking as smart as ever, now, no matter what you thought of her hat. We also started saying things about young Vermaak, the schoolmaster, then. We spoke of his singular behaviour in going away straight after the service, instead of staying to talk, first to one little group and then to another, in the way that we all did.

But mostly we spoke of Pauline Gerber. For by that time even the men, who were naturally not as observant in such matters as were the women, had noticed that, while Pauline Gerber's striped frock was no doubt styled to accord with the latest fashion, there was something in the actual fit of her dress that was obedient to a much older decree. It was well that her dress hung down wide like that, we said. It also struck us that, like young Vermaak, Pauline Gerber, too, had not stayed around outside the schoolhouse, to talk.

V

At the Mamba Klub's New Year's eve dance of the Dwarsberg Boerevereniging's Boeresport.
31 December 1965

Go-slow Strike

When At Naudé, who reads the newspapers, came into the post office he was wearing a wide grin.

"Ha, ha," he said to Jurie Steyn, who was leaning forward with his elbows on the counter. "Don't tell me, Jurie. I know why you're standing like that. You're on a go-slow strike. Ha, ha."

Jurie Steyn gazed at At Naudé uncomprehendingly.

"The newspapers say that it's not an official go-slow strike," At Naudé went on, laughing some more, "but, of course, you've joined it, haven't you, Jurie? We all know you started before the others. Years before, I should say. I mean, ever since this post office has been opened here –"

"Go-slow strike?" Jurie Steyn enquired blankly. "First I've heard of it. What do they want a thing like that in the post office for? Especially when I'm having all this trouble already with the new mealie-planter."

In a few words At Naudé acquainted Jurie Steyn with the latest news, which had to do with the go-slow strike that the post office employees were staging.

Jurie Steyn was indignant. "Well, if that's what the Postmaster-General wants me to start doing now, on top of everything else," Jurie Steyn said, "then I say he can keep his job. Let the Postmaster-General come over here and look at my new mealie-planter with the green paint on it. If he still wants a go-slow strike after that I'll tell him he can go and sit down outside and have it on his own. My wife can take him out coffee."

Thereupon At Naudé explained to Jurie Steyn that a go-slow strike was not an additional duty imposed on a Bushveld postmaster by the Postmaster-General. Indeed, as far as he knew, the Postmaster-General was not even in favour of the go-slow strike that the post office employees were taking part in. For that matter, he doubted if the Minister of

Posts and Telegraphs himself was terrifically keen about it, At Naudé said.

Before Jurie Steyn could take it all in, however, Gysbert van Tonder was saying that he had also bought one of those new mealie-planters. In consequence, we all started talking animatedly, several of us talking at the same time.

More than one farmer from the far side of the Dwarsberge had purchased one of those new mealie-planters after having had it demonstrated in front of the hardware store, the demonstration consisting of the shop assistant filling the seed-hopper with mealies and the farmer pulling the mealie-planter up and down on the stoep so that he could see how it worked, the mealies falling out just the right distance from each other with the way the wheels turned; and the farmer enjoying himself.

"Up and down, up and down I went on Policansky's stoep," Gysbert van Tonder said. "I promised David Policansky that I would be careful and not knock any of the new green paint off his mealie-planter. But he said just go ahead. Just make myself at home, he said. He would send somebody along later on to sweep up the mealies I had sown on his stoep, he said. I was not to worry at all.

"Well, I went on until about midday, and by that time I was perspiring quite a lot, because that mealie-planter gets quite heavy to pull, after a while, and the stoep of the hardware store was inches deep in mealies, the way I had been sowing them.

"And then, when it was about midday, to judge by the sun, a whistle blew somewhere – at the sawmill, I think – and Policansky came out of his store and said he thought that I could knock off now for lunch. Everybody was knocking off for lunch, now, Policansky said."

Chris Welman was able to confirm Gysbert van Tonder's remarks in a considerable measure.

"I just about laughed my head off, too," Chris Welman said, "on Policansky's stoep. How that mealie-planter could drop seeds at any distance you wanted – because you can adjust it, too, you know."

So we all said, yes, we knew you could adjust a mealie-planter. That was when the trouble started. If it didn't start even before then, At Naudé commented, sombrely.

"That's just the point," Chris Welman continued. "The mealie-planter doesn't seem to work so well on the lands, behind a plough, going over kweekgras sods and pieces of turned-up ant-hill, as it does on the smooth stoep of Policansky's hardware store. It doesn't work nearly so well, I mean. With its new green paint and all, what does a mealie-planter do, as likely as not?"

Meanwhile, Jurie Steyn had put a further question to At Naudé.

"Are you sure you read it right, At?" Jurie asked. "What it said in the newspapers, that is? Not that I want to be unfriendly, or anything, but you know you have, before today, told us something that wasn't so. Did it say all that about the go-slow strike? You know, you have been wrong once or twice –"

"Once," At Naudé admitted. "I know you're thinking of the time when I came and told you about the money for the Kunswedstryd that got stolen, that I had read about in the Bekkersdal newspaper. But then it came out afterwards that it was a mistake the printer had made in the newspaper."

Several of us spoke up for At Naudé, then. Because we remembered the circumstances. And so it wasn't At Naudé's fault at all for having given us incorrect information. It was just what he had read, about the Kunswedstryd funds getting embezzled. But Dominee Welthagen wrote to the newspaper about it, and what Dominee Welthagen wrote was so strong, we said that even a lawyer couldn't have done it better. And he got an answer right away from the editor. And the editor was very nice about it, the way he explained that it was all a mistake made by the printer. We all said afterwards that the editor of the newspaper couldn't have acted more handsome than he did, how he put all the blame on the printer.

And we said that it would be a good idea if, before he just wrote a thing, a printer went and made sure of his facts first.

And what made the whole thing still more peculiar was that there actually *wasn't* any money for the Kunswedstryd, that year.

"Yes, that mealie-planter, green paint and all, wasn't nearly as clever on the underneath side of my turf-lands," Gysbert van Tonder said. "I'll go so far as to say that for that kind of soil the old-fashioned way of getting a Mtosa to walk behind the plough and stick each mealie-seed in with his finger is even better. Yes, I really think that when it comes to the stickier sort of black turf, then a mealie-planter is less educated than a Mtosa."

We felt that was a sweeping statement. Gysbert van Tonder sensed our thoughts.

"I know it doesn't *sound* right what I've just said," Gysbert continued, "but I'm only talking about turf-soil, mind. I know that a mealie-planter with its shining wheels *looks* much more clever than a Mtosa just arrived for work in the morning from his hut. And I won't say that a mealie-planter hasn't perhaps got more human feelings, also, than a Mtosa. I'm not arguing about that, see?"

What Gysbert van Tonder insisted on, however, was that on turf-soil you had to hand it to a Mtosa for education.

"What's more, a Mtosa doesn't need to paint himself all green," Gysbert van Tonder added, as though that clinched the case. "All a Mtosa puts on himself, at a Ndlolo dance, say, is perhaps a little white and blue."

"But does it mean I've got to work slower, right here in my voorkamer?" Jurie Steyn asked of At Naudé while the rest of the conversation was going on.

"Yes, that's the idea," At Naudé replied. "You've got to work only half as fast. It's for more pay."

Jurie Steyn's eyes gleamed.

"More pay, hey?" he repeated. "Well, there's a thing for you, now. You'd imagine you'd get less pay for working only half as fast, wouldn't you? But I suppose it all goes to show. You got to know these things."

At Naudé nodded.

"Yes, it's no good being ignorant, like what Gysbert van Tonder says that mealie-planter is – more ignorant than a Mtosa even, Jurie," At Naudé acknowledged. "You've got to know what's going on. The newspaper I got this morning says just why those unofficial leaders of the post office workers decided to take this kind of action."

Jurie Steyn said that was a good one, too, if you liked.

"Calling it *action*," Jurie Steyn said. "When what they mean is *less* action. When they mean that I've got to do just half as much action, here in my voorkamer, that is. They should call it *un*-action, rather, I'm thinking."

Gysbert van Tonder's voice sounded very loud, all of a sudden.

"– a whole piece with no mealies at all," Gysbert van Tonder was saying. "And then a short stretch with every single seed in the hopper planted into it. And so planted that you can't get the mealies out again, unless you go down on your hands and knees and scrape."

Thereupon Chris Welman said that they should have a machine for doing that, also.

"A machine for scraping out the seeds that have been sown in the wrong place," Chris Welman said. "The mealie un-planter you could call it, I suppose. That would be a funny thing, now, wouldn't it? Useful, though."

But Jurie Steyn said that it was no more funny than what At Naudé had just told him. It was, indeed, similar.

Then, when the lorry-driver's assistant came in with the mailbags, Jurie Steyn attended to him with an air of studied leisureliness. And Jurie Steyn opened only one mailbag.

"The rest of your letters, kêrels," he said, indicating the second mailbag, which he had placed under the counter, "I'll let you have tomorrow. I get more pay if I do it like that."

Nor did the latest intelligence, as supplied by the lorry-driver's assistant – to the effect that the go-slow strike had been called off – make any impression on Jurie Steyn. Half-speed and more pay was quite good enough for him, he said. He asked for nothing better. He could keep it up longer even than the Minister of Posts and Telegraphs could, Jurie Steyn reckoned.

Black Magic

Naturally, we in the Marico are not superstitious. We do not believe in absurdities like sorcery and witchcraft, and all that. We accept a thing as a truth only after we have had proper evidence in support of it.

That is where we white people are different from the Mtosas, who will listen to anything that a witch-doctor tells them, no matter if it is a witch-doctor who is out of training, even, and has got to think first before he talks.

Whereas, a white Marico farmer would naturally laugh at information supplied to him by a witch-doctor, unless the witch-doctor could bring actual *proof* of what he was saying.

That was why Gysbert van Tonder was highly amused when a witch-doctor came round to his back door at the New Year and said that he had thrown the bones and had read in the bones something that was of great importance for Gysbert van Tonder.

The witch-doctor wore a flannel night-shirt with the skins of pole-cats sewn on it that seemed to need proper curing as much as the flannel night-shirt did. He carried his little bag of dolosse in one hand, and in his other hand he held a tattered umbrella.

And he wore spectacles. Taken all round, he was as proper looking a witch-doctor as you would see anywhere between the Dwarsberge and the Limpopo. What was more, he *smelt* like a good witch-doctor. Gysbert van Tonder noticed that part about the witch-doctor the moment he opened his back door to that knock that came at the New Year.

Well, Gysbert van Tonder is, of course, as far from superstitious as any man you can think of. But, as he admitted afterwards – talking about it in Jurie Steyn's voorkamer – when he smelt that witch-doctor at fairly close quarters, Gysbert van Tonder was to a quite considerable degree overawed. It was only when the witch-doctor started talking, however, that a broad smile came over Gysbert van Tonder's face.

212

For the witch-doctor said that he had thrown the bones in his hut on the previous night, and there had been a message about Gysbert van Tonder in the bones. Thereupon (having first requested the witch-doctor to stand a little to leeward side of him) Gysbert van Tonder assured the witch-doctor in as affable a way as you liked that he now realised that what the witch-doctor had come round for was a New Year present. There was consequently no need for the witch-doctor to have introduced make-believe – talking about having thrown the bones, and all that.

Gysbert van Tonder explained that to the witch-doctor in Sechuana, Gysbert concluding his remarks with a quick downward movement of his left eyelid, a form of communication whose significance, while it embraced, was not exclusively confined to, the language of the Bechuanas.

And because he was in a generous mood, this being the New Year and all, Gysbert van Tonder said to the witch-doctor that he could help himself to as much as he liked of the insides of a goat that Gysbert had but recently slaughtered, the said insides lying out there on a heap next to the stables.

Of course, Gysbert van Tonder would have been kind like that to a witch-doctor in any case, the New Year or not. Even though you are not superstitious, it is always as well to keep on the right side of a witch-doctor. You never know.

So you can imagine how surprised Gysbert van Tonder was when the witch-doctor did not appear at all grateful. With a wave of the umbrella that he had in one hand, the witch-doctor explained that he hadn't called round just for a dinner. He didn't wish to take up much of Baas van Tonder's time, the witch-doctor said, because he knew what a busy man Baas Gysbert was.

And what disconcerted Gysbert van Tonder somewhat was that, when the witch-doctor made that remark, he saw fit to imitate Gysbert van Tonder's bit of pantomime of earlier on . . . The witch-doctor's left eyelid fluttered swiftly down onto the top part of his wrinkled cheek.

Gysbert – as he said to us afterwards – would in the ordinary course of things have kicked the witch-doctor for that. Or for less than that, even. What restrained him, Gysbert van Tonder said, was that it was still the season of goodwill – even though it was a few days late, perhaps – and the fact that he didn't like getting too near the witch-doctor, in spite of the wind blowing in the other direction.

It was then that the witch-doctor informed Gysbert van Tonder about what he had seen on the previous night, when he had thrown the dolosse in his hut, the moon being at the half.

"The way the bones fell, Baas Gysbert," the witch-doctor said, "I could see a ghost talking to Baas Gysbert. I think the ghost was Baas Gysbert's grandfather or Baas Gysbert's great-grandfather, even. He was very old. And I knew by the ghost's feet that he was of Baas Gysbert's family. The ghost had the same kind of feet as what Baas Gysbert has got – big and with the same kind of flatness. Has Baas Gysbert got a grandfather or a great-grandfather, perhaps, that is today a ghost?"

Gysbert van Tonder started getting annoyed. His eyes travelled to his veldskoens, which he contemplated thoughtfully for a few moments.

"You got pretty big feet yourself," Gysbert remarked to the witch-doctor, then. "Flat, too. About as flat as any feet I've ever seen. Anyway, how can you tell all that rubbish from just throwing a sackful of bones? If it wasn't that it's New Year, and it's therefore a sin to do it, I'd set my dogs onto you. I've got an old Boer bulldog that's chased just about everything in his time. He'd be glad of the chance of chasing a witch-doctor, also, while he's still got proper teeth. Even if my feet are maybe a little what you call flat, you got no right to come and talk to me like that at the back door of my own farm."

The witch-doctor said then that he was sorry, and that he didn't mean it that way at all. It was only that the elderly ghost with – with that kind of feet – was explaining where the money was hidden. And so he thought it was his duty to come and tell Gysbert van Tonder about it. The witch-doctor was still going on, apologising some more, when it suddenly dawned on Gysbert what he had been saying.

"Money?" Gysbert van Tonder ejaculated. "What's that you've been saying about money? Look, never mind about the insides of that goat. I'll give you a piece of the goat itself. It's more than I and my family can eat, and goat doesn't keep too well in this weather. But what's that you've been saying about money?"

"It's about where the money is hidden –" the witch-doctor repeated. Then he stopped suddenly and took a step backwards. The Boer bull-dog that Gysbert van Tonder had been talking about had come sidling up from behind the water-tank and was sniffing at the witch-doctor's polecat skins.

It was evident, from the way he was growling, that the Boer bulldog was displeased about something. Gysbert van Tonder acted quickly. The

Boer bulldog streaked off in the direction of a clump of camel-thorns, yelping. The witch-doctor wiped some stray beads of sweat from his forehead.

"Au," the witch-doctor said. The witch-doctor was glad that he was not being chased. There was something about the easy loping gait of the Boer bulldog that you could not but admire.

"You dirty, lazy brute!" Gysbert van Tonder shouted out after the retreating bulldog. Then, turning to the witch-doctor, he said: "I got him a good one, didn't I? I'm glad I stopped him before he could bite a piece out of you. He frightened you a bit, though, I'm sure."

Suddenly an idea occurred to Gysbert van Tonder.

"I'll tell you what, seeing it's the New Year, and all," Gysbert said – and before he realised what he was doing, his left eyelid again came down in a swift wink – "what would put you right would be a little – you know, just a little –"

"Yes, thank you very much, my baas," the witch-doctor said. "Yes, please, just a little."

And this time, when the witch-doctor winked, Gysbert van Tonder was not so very annoyed, somehow.

After the witch-doctor had downed at a single gulp what was in the pannikin that Gysbert van Tonder had fetched for him out of the black jar in the kitchen, the two men stood looking at each other for some moments, in silence. Gysbert van Tonder didn't quite know how to reopen the subject.

"What – what the ghost was saying, now –" Gysbert began, and coughed.

He found himself restrained by an unwonted sense of the fastidious. It was strange how squeamish they had become in their conversational intercourse, the white man and the Bechuana witch-doctor. It was as though the unseen powers that institute African taboos had already got to work, prohibiting the free use of certain consecrated words.

First, the witch-doctor couldn't talk about feet – especially if those feet were big and flat – without Gysbert van Tonder getting hot under the collar. Then, as though by common accord, both Gysbert van Tonder and the witch-doctor refrained from mentioning that what the witch-doctor had drunk out of the pannikin was apricot brandy – and, what was more, good apricot brandy.

And now, finally, Gysbert van Tonder couldn't bring himself to talk about money, just straight out. It is well to keep away from the black arts. They get you enthralled before you know where you are.

Gysbert van Tonder coughed again. "The ghost with the big – I mean, that rather old sort of ghost," Gysbert van Tonder started again. "That ghost, you know, that you were talking about. He mentioned something that was hidden somewhere, I think you said . . ."

"Oh, yes, the money, Baas Gysbert," the witch-doctor said, his face lighting up with intelligence and apricot brandy. "Oh, yes, the money that is buried here on Baas Gysbert's farm."

So much Gysbert van Tonder enlarged on to us about his first meeting with the witch-doctor at the New Year. There were certain things, too, that he left out, but that we, sitting in Jurie Steyn's voorkamer, could guess.

Gysbert told us that he had already dug in several places, and pretty deep, too, sometimes.

Mostly, it was at the foot of trees. But there were other places, too, where he had dug. Like right under the bakoond at the side of his house. That was a pretty deep hole, Gysbert van Tonder commented, and because of the crack that came into the bakoond through that, the bakoond was not so good for baking bread in, anymore, although it might perhaps still do for the more ordinary sort of cooking.

"But surely you didn't go just by what the witch-doctor *said*," At Naudé enquired. "I mean, you must have asked him for *proof*. How do you know that he wasn't just telling a lot of lies?"

But Gysbert van Tonder had a proper answer to that. He said that At Naudé must not think that he was just an ignorant Mtosa. He interrogated the witch-doctor all right, Gysbert said, but the witch-doctor was able to *prove* that the bones he had in his sack were the very same bones that he threw in his hut that night he threw the bones. What was more, the witch-doctor said he could still go and point out in his hut to Gysbert van Tonder the exact place where he was *sitting* on the floor of his hut, that time.

We agreed that that was convincing enough.

"I've given the witch-doctor a few goats, since then," Gysbert van Tonder said, after a pause. "Live ones, I mean, that he can take back home with him, when he leaves. And you know, I sometimes almost wish that he *would* go. I have dug so many holes, already . . . I don't know. It sometimes looks like just a waste of time to me."

Thereupon Chris Welman asked what the trouble was. Why couldn't the witch-doctor just take Gysbert to the right place – that was, if there *was* a right place, Chris Welman wanted to know.

"That's it," Gysbert van Tonder said, "that's the whole difficulty. The witch-doctor says that the ghost didn't talk very distinctly. And that was another thing that made me believe that the witch-doctor was telling the truth. After all, a ghost *wouldn't* talk too distinctly. But there was another reason, also, why I believed the witch-doctor."

And we knew what that reason was, of course. And we knew that Gysbert van Tonder would never mention it. Because that would inevitably call to mind the unhappy nom-de-guerre of Doors Kalkoenvoet that, because of his slab-like pedal extremities, Gysbert van Tonder's grandfather had borne with him to the grave.

We knew that what Gysbert van Tonder would never admit to us was that why he had listened to the witch-doctor in the first place was because the witch-doctor had been so crudely accurate in describing the kind of feet that Gysbert van Tonder and his forebears on the Van Tonder side had.

"I know the witch-doctor is doing his best, of course," Gysbert van Tonder resumed. "But I'll tell you how I felt the other night. It was the night when I got out of bed to fetch an eiderdown out of the loft for him, because he was complaining of the cold. I felt that I should rather have kicked the witch-doctor, that day, than my Boer bull."

After Gysbert van Tonder had left we said, discussing the matter among ourselves, that black magic, as practised by Bechuana witch-doctors, was indeed an awful thing.

"As far as I can see," Jurie Steyn observed, "Gysbert van Tonder guessed right the first time. All the witch-doctor came round for was a New Year present. And it seems he got it, all right."

Oupa Bekker sniffed.

"Giving him a goat, too," Oupa Bekker said. "Well, it looks to me that, whoever the goat is, in all this, it's not the witch-doctor that's the goat."

And we said, no, it did not seem as though it was the witch-doctor, in all this, that resembled the well-known quadruped, allied to the sheep.

Laugh, Clown, Laugh

"It's the clown," Johnny Coen said, starting to laugh all over again. "The tall clown in the fancy dress – yellow and blue and the smart way of walking. I could go to the circus and see it all through again, just to laugh at that clown. He kept a straight face even when they chucked the bucket of water over him. It was a real scream to see his new clothes getting all soaked . . . oh, *soaked*. And he went on standing there in the middle of the ring as solemn as you like, not being able to make out where the water came from, even."

Johnny Coen laughed as though he was seeing all that happening again, right in front of his eyes, and for the first time.

But Oupa Bekker said that what he liked best at the circus were the elephants. The way they stood on their hind legs and the way they walked on bottles, Oupa Bekker said, balancing themselves to music.

"It's years ago since I was last able to balance *myself* to music," Oupa Bekker continued, "leave alone walk on bottles."

"Or stand on your hind legs," Jurie Steyn commented – not loud enough for Oupa Bekker to hear, though.

In the old days there wasn't any such thing in the Transvaal, Oupa Bekker went on, as walking on bottles. Even though the whole of the Marico up to the Limpopo was elephant country in those days, Oupa Bekker said – and, in consequence, he prided himself on knowing something of the habits of elephants – he would never have imagined their walking on bottles.

If an elephant had seen a bottle in his path he would simply have walked over it. To him an elephant in those days was just an elephant, Oupa Bekker said.

And the same thing applied to lions, when the Groot Marico was lion country, Oupa Bekker added. To him a lion was just a *lion*, and not a bookish person that – that, well, we all saw what those lions *did* at

218

the circus, didn't we, now? There was more than one white man in this part of the Marico that wasn't nearly as well educated as some of those circus lions, Oupa Bekker said.

Of course, he acknowledged that not every white person in this part of the Marico had had those same opportunities of schooling as the lions had.

Then At Naudé said that what he just couldn't get over, at the circus at Bekkersdal, were the trained zebras.

"And to think that this was also zebra country," At Naudé remarked. "But I would never have imagined a zebra wearing a red ostrich feather on his head, just like he's a Koranna Bushman. Or a zebra, while galloping down to the waterhole, first stopping to write something on a blackboard with chalk."

We spoke also about other animals that we had seen at the circus, and we said that the Groot Marico had at one time been that kind of animal's country, too. And all the time we had never known what those animals were really like. That sort of thing made you think, we said.

When Jurie Steyn was talking about the mule we had seen at the circus, that could jump six feet, and Jurie was saying that the Groot Marico was also mule country, Gysbert van Tonder suddenly gave a short laugh.

"And the clowns, that Johnny Coen was mentioning," Gysbert van Tonder said. "Well, it seems to me that for a pretty long while the Marico has been good clown country. And still is."

That was something that made you think, too, didn't it? – Gysbert van Tonder asked.

We were more than a little surprised, at a remark like that coming from Gysbert van Tonder. And several of us told him that we thought he should be the last person to talk. We proceeded to give Gysbert van Tonder some sound reasons, too, as to why we believed he should be the last person to talk. And some of the reasons we gave him had to do with things that hadn't happened so long ago, either.

This discussion would probably have gone on for quite a while, with each of us being able to think up a fresh reason every few minutes, when Chris Welman started talking about the fine insouciance with which the red-coated ringmaster cracked his whip.

The ringmaster didn't look very particular as to whether it was the gaily caparisoned horse he hit, or the blonde equestrienne hanging head

THE COMPLETE VOORKAMER STORIES

downwards from the saddle, her golden locks trailing in the sawdust –
so it seemed to Chris Welman, anyway.

"She didn't once stop smiling, either," Chris Welman said, "all the
time the music played."

From the way Chris Welman spoke, it was apparent that, in the
sounds discoursed by the circus band, his ear detected no harsh dissonances. Nor to his eye did the set smile of the equestrienne convey any
suggestion of artifice. It was, however, significant, that in his unconscious mind he had, indeed, established a link between those two circus
reciprocals – the music's blare and the set smile.

"After the circus was over and I had got back home, I was still thinking of her a long time," Chris Welman said. "I thought of her a good
way into the night. I thought of her with the electric light on her hair,
hanging down on the ground, and her spitting out the sawdust every
time that it came into her mouth from the way she was riding, hanging
down."

It was obvious that Chris Welman had occupied a ringside seat.

"But mostly I thought of her, about what she was doing after the
show was over," Chris Welman said. "I pictured her there under that
tent, locked up alone in her cage. It must be an unnatural sort of life, I
thought, for a girl." And he winked.

We were able to put Chris Welman right on that point, however.

It wasn't that we had any sort of inside knowledge of circus life, of
course, but we just went by common sense. It was only the more wild
kind of performers in a circus that got locked in cages, we said. The
tamer ones just got knee-haltered, we said, or tied to stakes with riems.
So he was quite wrong in thinking of the blonde equestrienne as having
to be locked in a cage after the show was over, we told Chris Welman.
Likely as not they even let her go loose, we said. And we also winked.

Thereupon At Naudé said that that was the trouble.

And after we had pondered At Naudé's remark carefully, we realised that there was much truth in it.

A pretty girl, we said, if she was wild enough, was a lot more dangerous than any kind of lion. And no matter how fiercely the lion might
roar, either, we said. Because all a pretty girl needed to do was to lower
her eyelashes in a particular way, we said. And for that she did not have
to be an equestrienne or an equilibriste or anything else, we added.

It was only natural, after that, that the talk should turn on the subject of pretty girls in general. And it was still more natural that, before we knew where we were, we should be discussing Pauline Gerber.

What made it somewhat difficult for us to talk as freely as we would have liked about what we had been hearing of Pauline Gerber lately, was the fact that Johnny Coen was there, sitting in Jurie Steyn's voorkamer.

And we knew full well how Johnny Coen had felt about Pauline Gerber, both before she went to the finishing-school in the Cape, and after she came back from the finishing-school.

As it happened, however, Johnny Coen helped us out, to some extent, and perhaps without knowing it, even.

Gysbert van Tonder had just made the admission that, insofar as he was able to judge, Pauline Gerber was not only just the prettiest girl in this part of the Marico Bushveld, but also the most attractive. "If you know what I mean by *attractive*," Gysbert van Tonder had added. "Otherwise I could tell you –"

That was when Johnny Coen had interrupted Gysbert van Tonder.

"No, no, you don't need to tell us," Johnny Coen said, hastily, "not in words, and all that. And not when it's – when it's Pauline Gerber, I should say. You've told us things like that before today. About what you find attractive in girls, that is. And so if you perhaps don't say it all over again, we won't feel that we have missed anything. Because you've said it all *before*, that is."

After a few moments' reflection, Gysbert van Tonder conceded Johnny Coen's point. He had spoken on that subject quite a good bit, he acknowledged, but there was still just this one thing he wanted to say –

"Not now, please," Johnny Coen interjected. And he spoke so sharply, and with such unwonted heat, that Gysbert van Tonder shut up, looking slightly puzzled, all the same.

"I was only going to *say* –" Gysbert van Tonder concluded in an aggrieved tone, and left it at that. For if Johnny Coen was going to act funny, and so on, well, it was not a matter for him, Gysbert van Tonder, to have to go out of his way to help Johnny right.

"Well, I've only seen Pauline Gerber a few times, since she's been back from finishing-school," Johnny Coen said. And from the way he said 'few' we knew that he wanted us to think that it meant more than, say, exactly twice.

But, of course, we weren't really interested in the number of times that Johnny Coen had seen Pauline Gerber of late. What we were anxious to learn was how often the young schoolmaster, Vermaak, had been seeing her. For it was in relation to young Vermaak, and not to Johnny Coen, that a certain amount of talk was going on about Pauline Gerber.

"Well, the few times that I have seen her," Johnny Coen went on, "it was a bit difficult for me to know what to think, exactly. The first time I saw her the schoolmaster had just left. And the second time – I mean, *on another occasion* when I saw her at her house, she was sort of expecting Meneer Vermaak to come round. But what I want to say is that what Chris Welman said about the circus girl – why, that is exactly what I *feel* about Pauline Gerber. About how pretty she is, and all that. And what makes it still more queer is that she talks about herself like Chris Welman talks about the girl that rides in the circus.

"She feels she's shut up in a *cage*, Pauline Gerber says. To have to live here in the Bushveld, with everybody so narrow-minded, Pauline Gerber said, is like being shut up in a cage."

Johnny Coen went on at considerable length, after that, acquainting us with the true nature of the sentiments he entertained for Pauline Gerber. But we were not interested. We did not in any way doubt the purity or the sincerity of his feelings. Only, we were not concerned with all that. What we really wanted to know was what was going on between Pauline Gerber and the young schoolmaster. And it was apparent that Johnny Coen couldn't tell us more than what we already knew. It was a pity that Johnny Coen should be struck with such blindness, though, we thought. It would be better if the scales were to drop from Johnny Coen's eyes, we felt.

It was Oupa Bekker who brought the talk back to a discussion of the circus – which was, after all, where we had started from.

"Walking *on* bottles," Oupa Bekker was saying. "Well, that's a new one on me. And I've known the Marico when it was elephant country. Unless, maybe, it was giraffe country. And what a giraffe would look like, standing on his hind legs, I just can't think of, right away."

That was what gave Johnny Coen his chance to get back to the clowns, once more.

"The one clown poured water from a step-ladder out of a bucket onto that other clown that I was telling you about," Johnny Coen said. "And I just about laughed my head off, each time, to see how that other clown got soaked. And they had natives to come running in from the back entrance with more buckets of water. And it all went over that clown. I enjoyed it more than I enjoyed the Chinese acrobat, even, who jumped through two wheels with knives in them. And all the time that clown didn't know what was happening. Every time I saw a native come running in with another bucket of water, why, I just about *died*, laughing."

We gazed at Johnny Coen pretty steadily, as he spoke. And we thought of what was going on between Pauline Gerber and young Vermaak, the schoolmaster. And all the time Johnny Coen went on feeling the way he did about Pauline. And we wondered if Gysbert van Tonder had been so far wrong, when he said that this was clown country.

The tears started coming into Johnny Coen's eyes, eventually, the way he was laughing about that clown.

ANXIOUS TO HEAR

Not that young Vermaak, the schoolmaster, was not talking with his usual confidence, and all that, sitting in Jurie Steyn's voorkamer. And as always, he was pretty sure of his facts. Moreover, the subject we were discussing – namely, the visit to the Marico of Dr Lesnitzky, the archaeologist – was just in the young schoolmaster's line.

And yet if you knew him at all well, through having met him at intervals over a considerable period, you could not but detect that young Vermaak was not entirely at his ease, even when he spoke most learnedly.

And we noticed that when Oupa Bekker asked him a question about Pauline Gerber – Oupa Bekker making the enquiry in what you might call a quite pointed way – the constraint in the schoolmaster's manner showed no visible diminution. It got worse, if anything. In fact, quite a lot worse.

So much so, indeed, that Gysbert van Tonder, speaking in a chummy, man-to-man fashion, advised him to cheer up. The schoolmaster bridled. And not unnaturally. You couldn't help it, but there always would be something brutal, sort of, in the sound of Gysbert van Tonder instructing anybody to cheer up.

"I don't know what you're getting at," young Vermaak informed Gysbert, speaking to him coldly, as though he was a Standard Three pupil that had got a simple fraction sum wrong, "I'm only discussing the fossilised footprints of the Jurassic period that Dr Lesnitzky has discovered in the bed of the Molopo. What you mean by saying that I should cheer up about it, I just don't understand. They aren't *my* footprints –"

The schoolmaster glanced around the voorkamer, as though expecting us to laugh. It was evident that he had made what he thought was a clever remark, and that he expected us all to laugh, whereby Gysbert van Tonder would be shown up as somebody very ignorant. As it happened, however, we didn't laugh. There had been quite a lot of talk about Pauline Gerber and the schoolmaster, here in the Groot Marico. And it wasn't the kind of talk that you could just dismiss with a laugh. Especially if there was any truth in what the women thought they had observed about Pauline Gerber, the time they saw her at the church service held in the schoolhouse at the end of the year.

For that reason, we were prepared to believe quite a few things about the schoolmaster. If there was one thing that we had reason to suspect him for – why, there could just as well be another reason. It was not unlikely that Dr Lesnitzky had found out something else about young Vermaak.

"In the Jurassic *slime*," the teacher continued, trying to make it sound still funnier.

Yes, that was about right, we thought. If Jurassic was like *that*, well we were less provoked to laughter than ever. Maybe Dr Lesnitzky had got hold of something, we thought, if he was making remarks like that about the schoolmaster.

"Mind you, it's not that I *blame* you for anything," Gysbert van Tonder declared, sententiously. "You'll find that nobody here *will* blame you for anything. Not as long as you do the right thing, that is. I mean, we are all men. We all know how a young fellow can get – can get tempted and all that. But we expect you to act square. As for what that Professor Lesnitzky says about you and the Jurassic slime – well *that* you can forget about. You can take it from me that nobody in the Groot Marico will ever hold that against you. It's the sort of thing that could happen to anybody, I should imagine. That part of it you can just forget about."

The past was nothing, Gysbert van Tonder said. It was *now* that mattered.

This time it was Gysbert van Tonder's turn to look around him, his eyes travelling from face to face. And each one that Gysbert van Tonder looked at nodded his head in agreement, each of us sitting there in Jurie Steyn's post office.

"Yes, old chap," At Naudé said to young Vermaak, talking to him comfortingly, "don't you take any notice of Dr Lesnitzky. He's a foreigner, in any case. I mean, what does he really know, what's going on in the Groot Marico? Let him say anything he likes about you and the Jurassic slime you've been talking about. That's something he'll have to prove in court. And you can take my word for it that we're with you.

225

We'll stand by you, and we'll make that Dr Lesnitzky look silly. It's only that other thing, you know –"

The schoolmaster brushed aside At Naudé's remarks with a gesture. And he spoke to At Naudé in a much haughtier way than he had done to Gysbert van Tonder. Never mind Standard Three, he addressed At Naudé as though At Naudé had just that morning come to school for the first time, and At Naudé didn't know a thing, and he was snivelling there, thinking of the place at the spruit where he made clay oxen with the Mtosa piccanins. The schoolmaster spoke to At Naudé as though At Naudé had all those feelings that a Bushveld youngster has when he comes to school the first day.

"Do you know what the Jurassic slime is?" the schoolmaster demanded of At Naudé.

"No," At Naudé replied, "but I've a pretty good idea. And all I can say is that that Dr Lesnitzky needn't talk. He's got a good bit of it on himself, too, if you ask me. I wouldn't be surprised if some of his own footprints are there, also, and not just yours. He looks that sort –"

Well, that was when the schoolmaster was able to give a short laugh, in which there was no mirth – and in which there was no implied invitation for anybody else to join in, either. It was the kind of laugh that a person has on his own, and is glad to have it that way.

And when he started talking, the schoolmaster was really able to spread himself. Several of us felt that it was a mistake to have given him that opening. For there was no doubt that this was exactly up young Vermaak's street, and so he just let himself go.

He told us things about geology that we had never known existed, until then. And he said that the footprints Dr Lesnitzky had discovered in the bed of the Molopo River were so ancient that it was quite ridiculous even to try and work out *how* old. Hundreds of thousands of years, the schoolmaster said. Millions of years, even.

And while they did not look unlike human footprints, except that they were maybe on the small side, no human being could have made them, since they were stretched too far apart for any human to have walked or even run like that.

"The Jurassic is only a geological formation," young Vermaak went on. "It is quite ridiculous to suggest the idea that there is anything *unpleasant* about it. It comes in between the Cretaceous and Triassic groups and includes the Oolite and the Lias. It is a formation rich in fauna."

Young Vermaak went on at great length. And he spoke almost with his old self-assurance. It was as though he felt that, on the dry bed of the old Molopo, he was on safe ground.

There were no quicksands, there, that he could get trapped in. While he stayed on the Jurassic side of the Molopo's dried-up bed he was beyond the reach of any present-day criticism that we could level at him, sitting there in Jurie Steyn's voorkamer. Even the Cretaceous was millions of years before Jurie Steyn's voorkamer, the schoolmaster explained.

"Abounding in echnidons," young Vermaak was saying.

Well, when it was that sort of talk, the ordinary Bushveld farmer was just nowhere. And we realised that. We had no hold on him. The schoolmaster could go on talking until the lorry from Bekkersdal came, and after that, as long as his information on the Triassic lasted out. And from the Triassic he would be able to switch to something else, no doubt.

We had no means of making contact with a man, sitting on a riempiestoel millions of years away, and taking it easy. If it came to the worst, the schoolmaster would also be able to cite those mineralogy tables, that he knew by heart.

And we were satisfied that it made him happy to do that, too – seeing how seldom we gave him the opportunity for it.

But it was when Oupa Bekker cleared his throat, and a far-off light came into Oupa Bekker's eye, that we knew that young Vermaak would not have it all his own way, anymore, for much longer. That light in Oupa Bekker's eye spoke, somehow, of battle – a battle in some forgotten war, long past, that Oupa Bekker had taken part in when he was still young.

When Oupa Bekker cleared his throat, we suddenly felt that the schoolmaster was only talking about things that were very old. But we felt in that moment that Oupa Bekker *was* really old.

"Those footprints in the Molopo," Oupa Bekker said. "Well, I've seen them. Only, that isn't the Molopo, of course. It's only an arm of the Molopo. If your Dr Lesnitzky doesn't know that, you can tell it to him from me. The Molopo itself flows on past Tweedepoort. And I've never known a time when there wasn't water in that part of the Molopo that you're talking about – in the arm there hasn't been water in living memory."

When Oupa Bekker said 'living memory' it seemed to be something that went back so far – further than the Jurassic, even, somehow – that more than one of us felt a little uncomfortable. Chris Welman coughed, too, then.

"Now, this Jurassic, that you're talking about," Oupa Bekker asked the schoolmaster. "Has it got anything to do with Jurie Steyn? I'm only asking, of course. You see, I don't know much about what has been happening in these parts, lately. Things up to the war with Sekukuni I can remember very well.

"It's only things that happened later, like Jameson's Raid, for instance, that I don't remember so clearly. Today I can't remember anymore the name of the Mshangaan woman that Jameson borrowed the white apron from that he held up, at Doornkop. But is this Jurassic that you're talking about called after Jurie Steyn?"

Jurie Steyn leant forward over his post office counter, for a moment, looking hopeful. You could sense what Jurie Steyn was feeling, too. It was as though, for a brief spell, Jurie Steyn was wondering whether, after all, he had perhaps not lived in vain. With the schoolmaster's next words, however, Jurie Steyn resigned himself to an acceptance of the common fate of all of us mere mortals.

"What do they want to call *anything* after Jurie Steyn for?" young Vermaak asked. For the schoolmaster had just been talking geology. Consequently, his concern for the factual overrode those human considerations that find their expressions in diplomatic utterance.

"I mean, it would be silly, wouldn't it," young Vermaak went on, "to go and give Jurie Steyn's name to some part of the science that deals with the condition and structure of the earth. Think of how absurd it would be to call one of the geological strata –"

Since he had no pretensions to being anything more than human, Jurie Steyn could stand only so much. All right, the Jurassic system wasn't called after him. Good, he accepted that. For that matter, he had never really expected anything else. He knew only too well – and from his own experience, what was more – how blind the world could be when it came to according a person the just due for his merits.

Jurie Steyn knew all that. It was like the time the Government auditor came from Pretoria and said that Jurie Steyn's post office accounts were all mucked up, and the Government auditor just wouldn't listen to all that Jurie Steyn had to tell him about the Mtosas dressed in old blankets that came to buy stamps and about the trouble he was having in the milking shed with his new separator. Jurie Steyn *knew* that the world was like that.

But for that young schoolmaster to come and sneer at him now, Jurie Steyn thought, and all for nothing. Well, the cheek of it. In any case, he wouldn't be in the schoolmaster's boots for anything. Surely, the schoolmaster must know that Pauline Gerber had a father who in single combat with a berg luiperd (and with only two dogs to help him) twisted that berg luiperd's left foot off. And Pauline Gerber also had an elder brother who had once bitten – But no, Jurie Steyn would rather not think of that. All he felt was that he wouldn't for anything be in young Vermaak's shoes. Not with the relatives Pauline Gerber had, that was.

And here was the schoolmaster talking in a sneering way about the impossibility of geological science having named something or other after him, Jurie Steyn. Maybe geological science *had* already named that thing after him, Jurie Steyn thought, and he hadn't come to hear of it, yet, seeing how slow news from the outside world was in reaching the Marico Bushveld.

Jurie Steyn leaned further than ever over his post office counter, then.

"Whatever Oupa Bekker is going to say," Jurie Steyn announced, "I'm certain he's *right*."

"Of course, I'm right," Oupa Bekker declared, sure of himself but at the same time trying not to look self-satisfied. "I tell you, I've seen those footprints. And Jurassic my foot . . . I was almost going to say my footprints. Seeing that Gysbert van Tonder thought it was the schoolmaster's footprints. But how old did you say they were, Meneer Vermaak?"

The schoolmaster told him. Jurassic, the schoolmaster said. Hundreds of thousands and millions of years. What you could practically call Mesozoic, the schoolmaster said, rolling the word appreciatively over his tongue. And the distance that those footprints were apart. It was obviously before man. Some being akin to man, maybe. They had a lot in common with a human being's footprints, all right. And the Jurassic was also rich in ammonites and cycads.

Oupa Bekker gave a short laugh, this time, that no one joined in.

"I never saw who made those footprints," Oupa Bekker said. "But I saw them. And I recognised them right away as Bushman footprints. And if you want to call a Bushman a human being, well, that's up to you, of course. I'm not saying anything. And why they are still there, in the arm of the Molopo, those footprints, is because there hasn't been any rain, there, for over a hundred years. No real rain, that is.

"And why those footprints are so far apart is because that was just the time when the percussion cap came in, to take the place of the flint-lock that the old Boers used in their voorlaaiers. And with the percussion cap in, and all, it was only natural that the Bushman would *have* to take longer strides. I mean, much longer strides than when it was just an old flintlock that he was trying to get away from. Has your Dr Lesnitzky ever thought of that one?"

And so Oupa Bekker put young Vermaak in his place, all right, Jurassic or no Jurassic. As we knew that Oupa Bekker would, of course, the moment we saw how his eye glittered. We were all very pleased to see the schoolmaster brought back to earth – and back to the present – out of his millions of years ago. *Now* let young Vermaak try and explain away a few immediate things, we said to ourselves. Let him try and explain about Pauline Gerber, for one thing. We were willing – and even anxious – to hear.

That was when Jurie Steyn's wife came in from the kitchen with our coffee. And to our surprise she was most kind to young Vermaak. It was something we couldn't understand, somehow. The way she told him not to worry, when she handed him his coffee. It was as though she knew all about Pauline Gerber, and forgave him for it. It was as though she forgave him much . . .

The way Jurie Steyn's wife spoke to young Vermaak, you would almost think that it was *he* that was in trouble.

DAY OF WRATH

It was what At Naudé had read in the newspapers.

Somewhere in an overseas country the people in that part had come together in a barn to wait for the end of the world, which a holy woman had gone out of her way to prophesy for them would be quite soon.

"They stopped work and sold their land for – well, I don't quite remember, now, how much they *got* for it, a morgen," At Naudé said. "But it was quite cheap. And so they just sat in the barn, waiting for the Day of Judgment."

Then Gysbert van Tonder said he wondered what those lands were like that the holy woman's followers had sold. Maybe it was just brak soil, and with ganna bushes. Well, that sort of ground you could *keep*, Gysbert van Tonder said. He had had experience of just that kind of lands. And what about turf-soil, now, he asked – the sticky kind? There was a thing for you, too, he observed.

Thereupon Chris Welman said that if those people sitting in that overseas barn, there, wanted land so cheap that it was almost *nothing* a morgen – certainly not more than ten pounds a morgen, with two boreholes thrown in – then he himself was just the right man for them to come and talk to. Did the newspaper give the address of that barn, perhaps?

In the slight altercation that ensued between Gysbert van Tonder and Chris Welman (Gysbert van Tonder contending that he had thought of it first and that Chris Welman had no right to come and intrude, talking about ten pounds a morgen for a piece of koppie that you couldn't keep a goat alive on, not unless you fed the goat an old hat or a piece of shirt, every so often), At Naudé was able to explain, several times, that they had missed the whole point of what he was talking about. It wasn't the price of ground a morgen that the newspaper story dealt with so much as the preparations that those people were making for the Day of Judgment.

"The End of the *World*," At Naudé stated majestically. "Die laaste der *dagen*."

He knew it would sound more solemn if he said it in Bible Neder-lands instead of just in Afrikaans.

But by that time Chris Welman was saying to Gysbert van Tonder that Gysbert was pretty much like a goat himself, the way he had come butting in, and Gysbert van Tonder was saying that the way Chris Welman's trousers looked from the back, it would appear as though Chris had already been feeding part of his trousers to the goats.

"Anyway, where's your shirt buttons?" Chris Welman asked of Gys-bert van Tonder, sarcastically. "I suppose the ostriches ate them?"

We felt that this was an unfortunate quarrel, between Gysbert van Tonder and Chris Welman. We sensed that it was the kind of argument that wouldn't get either of them anywhere. Moreover, when it came to a matter of dress – or, rather, to a question of tabulating things that weren't there – why, we knew that we were none of us immune from thoughtless criticism.

The jagged missiles that Gysbert van Tonder and Chris Welman were hurling at each other on the score of the respective shortcomings in their personal attire – well, a rusty old piece of that kind of weapon could wound any one of us, sitting in Jurie Steyn's voorkamer. And even if it wasn't aimed at you, and even if it got you only glancingly, it could make you feel bruised, all the same. More than one of us shifted uncom-fortably on his riempies chair, then.

But it was when Chris Welman was talking about when Gysbert van Tonder had had a haircut last that Oupa Bekker took a firm hand in the proceedings.

We were more than a little surprised that, in spite of his deafness, Oupa Bekker should have followed the argument so well. We had no-ticed that about Oupa Bekker before, however – that he didn't really miss much about what was going on: not when he was personally af-fected, that was.

"At Naudé has been talking about Judgment *Day*," Oupa Bekker said severely, at the same time moving his good veldskoen forward, so as partly to hide the place in his other veldskoen that was patched with a piece of rubber tubing. "And on the Day of Judgment we will none of us be judged by the *clothes* we're wearing, at the time. We'll be judged by just what we are."

From the way Oupa Bekker said it, it sounded that that would be bad enough.

So Chris Welman said that he certainly hoped, for Gysbert van Tonder's own sake, that on the Last Day Gysbert would not be judged by the kind of clothes he was wearing. If Gysbert's clothes already looked like that now, Chris Welman said, he would rather not *think* how they would look on the Last Day. He just couldn't imagine anything more sinful, Chris Welman added. Not just off-hand he couldn't, Chris Welman said.

Before Gysbert van Tonder could think of a suitable answer, Oupa Bekker went on to say that what really was sinful was the way Chris Welman had talked of wanting to sell his ground – asking ten pounds a morgen for it – to those people in a foreign country who didn't know any better.

"Religious people," Oupa Bekker said. "Sitting there in a barn because their prophetess woman had told them that it was the End of the World. And Protestant people, too, by the sound of it."

We agreed with Oupa Bekker that they *were* Protestants, by the sound of it.

"And just because Chris Welman wants to trek to Rhodesia, as we all know," Oupa Bekker announced, finally, "he doesn't ask even if they're Catholics, first, before he thinks of selling his farm to them, which we know *isn't* worth ten pounds a morgen, just because he wants to go to Rhodesia."

Chris Welman could only say that for those people to have his farm was better than their sitting in a barn, anyway. Whereupon Gysbert van Tonder said that he wasn't so sure.

Gysbert van Tonder also said that if Chris Welman got ten pounds a morgen for his farm, then it *would* be the end of the world.

Oupa Bekker agreed with Gysbert van Tonder. Oupa Bekker said that he knew Chris Welman's farm in the old days, when it was just concession ground. And he wouldn't be sure if he didn't even *prefer* that ground like it was in the old days, before Chris Welman had made what he called improvements on it, Oupa Bekker added.

It seemed queer that Oupa Bekker should be so very much against Chris Welman. But it was only when Oupa Bekker spoke again that we understood something of the reason for it. And we also realised in a deeper manner the truth of what we had in the course of time come to understand about Oupa Bekker's deafness: that Oupa Bekker was hardly at all deaf when there was talk going on in which he was personally affected.

"Take my own little place, now," Oupa Bekker said. "There it lies, on both sides of Pappegaai Poort. *There's* a bit of ground for you, now. For somebody that wants to make a new start, and that isn't afraid of a bit of hard work. Catholic *or* Protestant, *there's* now a –"

But Oupa Bekker didn't get any further. For by that time we were all laughing.

"Well, I only hope that on the Last Day I'm not found on *your* farm, Oupa Bekker," Chris Welman said. "Not when it comes to being judged, that is. And no matter what sort of clothes I had on, either. Even if I was wearing my black Nagmaal manel, I wouldn't fancy my chances much, if I was found walking on Judgment Day on any part of your farm. Not with all that kakiebos and those erosion sloots, I wouldn't."

All the same, it was strange to think that Oupa Bekker, at his age, should also be toying with the idea of trekking to Rhodesia. Otherwise he would never want to sell his farm. It must be that Oupa Bekker had also heard about how much you could make out of tobacco, in Rhodesia. Perhaps he had also heard about how glad the Rhodesian Government was to have Afrikaners trekking in there, so much so that they were asking questions about it in the Rhodesian Legislative Assembly almost every week.

It was only after At Naudé had spoken for some time again, trying to give us a clear picture of that prophetess woman and her followers waiting in the barn in their foreign language for the Last Day, that we began to understand properly what it *meant*.

And we started to think of Gabriel's trumpet, then. And of the book in the tenth chapter of Revelations that St. John wrote. And of the millions of people, the dead and the living, that would gather at the foot of Mount Zion. And of the vials of wrath. And the fall of Babylon. And the beast with seven heads.

There were things you could not reflect on just lightly.

"I wonder why they were so quick to listen to their prophet woman, the people in that foreign part," Jurie Steyn commented at length, scratching his head at the same time. "I mean, there must have been a reason why they heeded her words and sold up so quick. After all, there was nothing that she could prophesy to them that could be half as bad as what you can read for yourself in the last few pages of the Good Book. Things like the passing of the first world in pools of fire. I have read it more than once, for myself, in a time of drought. And it has brought me a good deal of comfort, too, in a time of drought."

Well, we were in entire agreement with Jurie Steyn, there. When there had been no rain in the Marico for three years, we said, and the last water in the borehole was drying up – if you could even call it water, with all that brack in it – well, it was comforting, we acknowledged, to sit on one's front stoep and to read of the Day of Wrath and of the second seal being opened.

It made you feel quite happy, then, we said, to think of all the awful things that were going to happen to the world; and to think that it was all just around the corner, too, from the way the holy St. John spoke.

We were suddenly able to understand something of what must have been going on in the minds of those foreign people, who listened to their prophetess woman. Seeing that we were farmers ourselves, we understood.

"I think I see what you're getting at, Jurie," At Naudé remarked, after a while. "You get a bellyful of it, sometimes, don't you? After all, even if there isn't a drought, you do suddenly find, when you take a look over your farm, including the improvements you've made on it –"

"Especially the improvements," Chris Welman interjected bitterly, "no matter what Oupa Bekker says about them –"

"Anyway, you do get the feeling," At Naudé continued, "Revelations or no Revelations – that you've just had a bellyful."

Until that moment we had not understood, properly, why it was that there was so much solace to be found in the last twenty chapters of the Good Book, ending up with "der volken daarin brengen."

If it was the End of the World, then, at least, the End of the World would be a change. And the lure of selling up and going to Rhodesia did not have much to do with tobacco-planting, but it was a thing as old as Africa.

"It's funny, now, about Policansky," Gysbert van Tonder remarked. "But the last time I saw David Policansky, he told me he was looking for a buyer for his store. He wanted to trek out somewhere, right away from Bekkersdal, he said. And you know what – from the way that

David Policansky spoke, it sounded almost as though he had also been reading the New Testament, for drawing comfort. He wasn't talking much different from what we're talking now. He would sell out quite cheap, he said, too."

LANGUAGE OF FLOWERS

"No, I don't think that's right," Gysbert van Tonder declared, gazing with marked disfavour at the bowl of nasturtiums in Jurie Steyn's voorkamer. "Now it's roses. Next it will be violets, then – then –" Gysbert van Tonder hesitated. He had come to the end of his list of the names of flowers.

"Hollyhocks," At Naudé said, helping him out, "geraniums, fuchsias, katjiepierings, daisies –"

"Yes, all that sort of thing," Gysbert van Tonder acknowledged. "But how's it you can say them straight off, like that?" Gysbert van Tonder's tone was suspicious.

"Well, some of those flower names I knew myself, in any case," At Naudé confessed, modestly. "Others I have heard from time to time over the wireless – you know, those weekly talks by the man who calls himself Neef Marius. He talks to you about how to be happy in your little front garden and about how to do greenhouse work. Not that I know what greenhouse work is, by the way."

We said we didn't know, either.

"Greenhouse work or any other sort of *work*," Jurie Steyn's wife said, then, coming in with the coffee and trying to be funny.

"And if your own little front garden isn't big enough for flowers or for greenhouse work," At Naudé went on, ignoring Jurie Steyn's wife so pointedly that it was almost as though she wasn't in the voorkamer at all, "then this Neef Marius explains to you about what to grow in hanging baskets on your stoep, or in pots on your window-sill."

We said that was a lot of nonsense. It might be all right for people living in cities, we said, who didn't know any better, and who didn't care what they listened to, sitting back in their city chairs.

But the moment a city person got up out of his chair and rested his cigar on the edge of a saucer on a tall stand, like you saw in the bioscopes, we said, and he started putting a seed or two in a hanging basket or in a graceful pot, half full of mellow loam, in a sheltered, sunny corner, like Neef Marius told him to do – that was when the city person's troubles would start, we said.

But we also said that a city person – from what we knew of a city person – would be far too shrewd ever to act on what Neef Marius recommended. A city person would have too acute a judgment ever to get up out of his armchair, once he was properly settled in it, we said. Least of all would he get up to go and pinch off the side-shoots of a chrysanthemum growing in a pot.

And we had had so much to say that Jurie Steyn's wife had gone back into the kitchen again before we noticed that At Naudé was sitting there – if not in a city armchair then at least on a riempiesbank, next to Oupa Bekker – with his pipe in one hand and with no cup of coffee in the other hand. Jurie Steyn's wife must have overlooked At Naudé, somehow, by mistake.

Oupa Bekker was the first to mention it.

"That's what I always say – women," Oupa Bekker remarked. "Now, even if you don't agree with what a woman says or what a woman does, that's nothing, as long as you're polite about it, man. You've got to be smooth and well-bred and – and refined.

"Now, why Jurie Steyn's wife didn't give you coffee was because you treated her as though she didn't exist, at all – and just on account of her having said that thing about work. I don't say she's right, of course. I mean, perhaps you could do a little more work than you do: perhaps you can't. Myself, I don't believe that in this part of Africa a white man was meant to do much work. Otherwise he wouldn't get pains from it here, and here – and –"

Oupa Bekker stood up to indicate as far as he was able – his right arm being a bit stiff – the different places in his anatomy where the white man in Africa got pains through pursuing a certain operose course directed towards a specific end.

"And what about stitch, now?" Chris Welman asked. "That's what a white man in this part of Africa gets, too, a good deal of, from work. Mostly, I get it here, sort of." His hand traversed a surface about a foot and a half square, on his left side. "Stitch," Chris Welman ended up. "From kaffir work."

But Oupa Bekker maintained that that was not the point.

238

"Why Jurie Steyn's wife didn't bring you any coffee . . ." Oupa Bekker went on, to At Naudé. ". . . Look, perhaps I can give you a little of my coffee. I can pour it into my saucer for you. Here, just a minute, I'll just pour it –"

But At Naudé said that he didn't want any of Oupa Bekker's coffee. Not after Oupa Bekker had already drunk on it, At Naudé said.

This time it was Oupa Bekker's turn to be disconcerted.

"Well, of all the low, cheap, yellow –" words failed Oupa Bekker, then.

At Naudé proceeded to make full use of the advantage which he had gained thus temporarily.

"Actually, I shouldn't have come into this, at all," At Naudé protested. "It was Gysbert van Tonder that started this whole trouble. I didn't say a thing, first. It was Gysbert van Tonder that said he didn't hold with those flowers in that vase, there. He called them roses, I think. Well, that just shows how ignorant he is.

"I only know about flowers from what Neef Marius says in his weekly talks. And Neef Marius can't show us the flowers he's holding in his hand: not over the wireless, he can't. But in spite of what Oupa Bekker says about me, I'm not so unrefined that I don't know that it's not roses in that vase, whatever *else* it is –"

"Nasturtiums," Jurie Steyn announced. "That's what my wife calls them."

"Well, all right, then," At Naudé said. "I won't argue. If that's what your wife and Neef Marius say those flowers are, then that's good enough for me. I never once said that I didn't approve of having flowers in a vase in the voorkamer. It was Gysbert van Tonder that started all that. And then – and then Jurie Steyn's wife goes and picks on *me*. Why didn't she rather walk out back to the kitchen and forget to give Gysbert van Tonder any coffee?"

Gysbert van Tonder raised and lowered his eyelids once or twice in what he intended to be an arch fashion. He also stroked his beard in what he wished us to regard as a knowing way.

"Women," Gysbert van Tonder announced, coming as near to blushing as it was possible for him. "They are funny little creatures, women. You never know where you are with them, really, do you now? I mean, women either like a man, or they don't like him. Isn't that so? I mean, you can't *reason* with them about it. With some of us men – why, it's like a sort of curse, almost – the way these little women take to us. Just going on nothing more than looks."

It just about made us feel ill, the way Gysbert van Tonder was simpering, and over nothing at all. We were glad when Chris Welman took him up pretty sharply.

"Looks," Chris Welman repeated sarcastically. "Anyway, that's one way how you're lucky, Gysbert. What you said about good looks being a curse. Well, that's at least one way that your life isn't blasted. I'm not talking about dishonesty and – and *stealing* – and things like that, now, that get a man into trouble.

"Where you stand as far as that sort of thing goes, well, it's not for me to judge. That's for the police – the mounted police in uniform and the detectives in plain clothes – to make up their minds about. And it's for the Attorney-General to say whether it is a summary trial or whether you go before the high court. But when it comes to looks, well, you can take it from me that you've got nothing to worry about."

We admired the way that Chris Welman spoke. We also doubted whether Chris Welman would have known so much about legal procedure if it wasn't that Chris Welman had a son who had been in reform school.

More than one of us thought of that old Afrikaans maxim, then, which says that an apple doesn't fall too far away from the tree. And we also thought, then, hearing Chris Welman talk, that an apple-tree doesn't stand too far away from where the apple falls, either.

But Chris Welman's remarks took the bounce out of Gysbert van Tonder, all right. It was like an apple falling – plonk – into a stretch of wet mud, without any sort of elasticity at all.

"What I was trying to explain about those flowers, there," Gysbert van Tonder said, pointing an outsized forefinger with a broken nail at the bowl of nasturtiums, "is that no good can come to the Marico – the Groot Marico, that is, the part of the Marico this side of the Dwarsberge – through having our women starting growing flowers here. I've had the same trouble about it with my wife, before today. And it was incidentally also after she had listened in to Neef Marius talking over the wireless about being happy in your own little front garden.

"All I was trying to say is that there is nothing wrong with flowers in their right place. Like the purple Ceylon oleander, now. That's the only kind of flower I know. And I know it because there is no part of the

Western Transvaal where I haven't seen that flower growing in grave-yards over tombstones. And that's how I came to know the name of that flower. Because I asked. And that's why I'll say nothing against the purple Ceylon oleander. Because it looks very pretty, in its right place, especially if the tombstone is worn a little bit, with the years and the rains, so that you can't read too clearly about how high-minded and full of good deeds the person was, lying under the tombstone."

Gysbert van Tonder went on to say, in a sentimental voice, that he desired nothing more than just that for himself, one day. He asked for nothing more than a weather-worn slab of white marble or even blue leiklip, he said, with purple Ceylon oleander clambering over it, and with just a simple inscription, giving only his Christian and surnames, and a verse from his favourite psalm, perhaps, and the dates of his birth and death, and not more than a dozen words, or so, to say how beloved he was by everybody in the Bushveld, white as well as coloured.

That was all he asked to have put on his tombstone, some day, Gysbert van Tonder said. He wanted nothing bombastic, but just the bare essentials. He wished it to be said of him only that he was generally admired, in his lifetime, in the Groot Marico. He didn't want any fulsome praise lavished on him after his death, because what good could that do you?

Chris Welman stared at Gysbert van Tonder as though he was spellbound.

"Well, of all the –" Chris Welman started to say, and then stopped.

That was when At Naudé got in.

"Well, in that case it mightn't be so bad, perhaps," At Naudé said, "having a nice thick growth of purple oleander of Ceylon around the place. The thicker the better. So that people can't read *anything* through the leaves of the oleander, even. It wouldn't matter, then, how plain it was what you had on your tombstone, as long as you had enough oleander in front of it. And it wouldn't matter so much about the flowers, either, as long as there's enough stems and leaves."

It took Gysbert van Tonder quite a little while to understand what At Naudé was getting at, and by that time the conversation had already taken quite a different turn. For Chris Welman had said that he agreed fully with what Gysbert van Tonder had been trying to say, in the first place, about flowers.

"After all, the Groot Marico is a man's country," Chris Welman said.

"And we've got no time for nonsense. This is a cattle world. The Bushveld isn't suited even for mealies. It's all very well saying that a Marico farmer can lay out a vegetable garden to grow carrots in, underneath his dam, like what that Neef Marius says, but who wants to eat carrots, anyway?"

No, we agreed with Chris Welman, we none of us wanted to eat carrots. Or turnips, either, we said. Or rhubarb.

We said straight out that this was a man's country, and a cattle world – red Afrikander cattle, particularly – and once you started sowing vegetables you wouldn't know where you'd be. The next thing, it would be roses, we said, and after that, after that –

"Hollyhocks," At Naudé helped us out, "geraniums, fuchsias, sweetpeas –"

All that sort of thing, we said. It wasn't that we went with Gysbert van Tonder all the way, we said, his wanting those ridiculous things about himself carved on his tombstone, and all. But we agreed that he did talk a certain amount of sense.

"You'll be sorry, yet, when you read all that on my tombstone," Gysbert van Tonder interjected.

We ignored him, however. Nor did we take much notice of Oupa Bekker when he started talking again about refinement and highly cultivated manners being qualities that appealed to women. Oupa Bekker was a nice one to talk, we thought. We would like to know just how much in the way of highly cultivated manners Oupa Bekker had, that was all.

We recognised, however, that this new fad of flower-growing, which had of a sudden begun to captivate our womenfolk, could not do the Groot Marico much good, in the end. It would yet undermine the Marico as a man's country and a cattle world, we felt.

It was then that Jurie Steyn's wife came in from the kitchen, bearing a single cup of coffee on a tray.

"I am sorry I was so unfriendly to you, At," Jurie Steyn's wife said. "But you know, you looked right past me, as though I wasn't here at all, just because I made a joke. Why can't you be like Oupa Bekker, now? He's always so polite."

Oupa Bekker smiled fatuously.

And Gysbert van Tonder got back to where he had started from. An oversized forefinger pointed again at the offending nasturtiums in the vase.

"Oh, that was after I had heard Neef Marius over the wireless, once or twice," Jurie Steyn's wife explained, "telling us women to grow flowers. Neef Marius's voice – well, when he speaks – you don't know how a woman *feels* about a voice like that. It's *like* flowers."

"More like fruit, Neef Marius's voice sounds like," At Naudé commented after Jurie Steyn's wife had gone out. "Squashy fruit."

Divinity Student

"For the way you're feeling now," Jurie Steyn said to At Naudé, "if you want my advice, I'd say you should go somewhere where you can get away from civilisation, for a bit. Nerves, that's what you've got. Why don't you go on a fishing trip to the Molopo for a week? You know – get right away from things."

Chris Welman had another suggestion to make.

"If you want my advice," Chris Welman said to At Naudé, "you'd go and camp for a while at the Bechuanaland end of the Dwarsberge. That's almost on the edge of the Kalahari. You've got no idea how desolate that part is. It's a howling wilderness, all right.

"You've got to be there only a day or two, and you'll forget that there ever was such a thing as civilisation. You could even take Gysbert van Tonder along with you. That should help your state of mind a lot. With Gysbert around, the lower end of the Dwarsberge would look absolutely barbaric. Gysbert has got that effect even on a city, I mean."

Somehow, Gysbert van Tonder did not seem quite as pleased as he might have been at the subtle flattery conveyed in Chris Welman's speech.

"You go and –" Gysbert van Tonder started ungraciously. Then he bethought himself.

"Ah, well," Gysbert van Tonder ended up. "I suppose one can have too much of civilisation. And I am quite willing to believe that that is At Naudé's trouble – his listening in to the wireless and reading the newspapers every day. His brain has got too active. But you can be glad that that is a kind of sickness that you will never suffer from, Chris Welman."

Gysbert van Tonder seemed very pleased with himself, the way he made that remark.

Strangely enough, the friendly controversy in which Gysbert van

Tonder and Chris Welman saw fit to indulge did not tend to allay any of the restlessness with which At Naudé's spirit was charged.

For At Naudé acted in what we could not help feeling was a quite singular fashion. First he half rose to his feet, emitting a long moan. Then he suddenly slumped back again into his riempies chair, at the same time smacking the open palm of his right hand in a despairing manner against his forehead. His visage was noticeably contorted.

"All the same old childishness," At Naudé exclaimed, "that's supposed to be clever or that's supposed to be funny. I can't stand it anymore, this heavy what's assumed to be Marico *fun*. If it's not Jurie Steyn doing it, it's Chris Welman. Or it's Gysbert van Tonder. And if it's not Jurie Steyn's wife, it's Oupa Bekker or it's *me*. And if it's not me, it's – oh, I tell you it's driving me mad. And when I switch on the wireless it's the same thing. It's either the Free State Monday Jokers or it's the Tuesday Choir of Comical Ouderlings or it's the Wednesday Half-Laughs with the Upington District and Schweizer-Reneke/Kaokoveld Trek-Boers.

"And then, when I try to escape from all that, and I come here to Jurie Steyn's post office to fetch my letters, what do I hear but somebody saying, 'That's a good one, ha, ha, ha'?"

It was clear to us that At Naudé was in a bad way. Gysbert van Tonder opened his mouth to say something, but Oupa Bekker nudged him to silence. We all felt that an unreasoned remark, at that moment, could have a very adverse effect on At Naudé. And we also knew that it would be no unique thing for Gysbert van Tonder to *make* an unreasoned remark. It was best that At Naudé should be allowed to talk himself out, we felt.

Some time in the future, making use of diplomatic skill, we would be able to point out to him, talking as man to man, the dangers to which he exposed himself, sitting day after day in his voorhuis alone, reading the newspapers and listening in to wireless programmes. If At Naudé went on like that much longer, he would become somebody learned before he knew where he was.

And where would At Naudé be then, in this part of the Groot Marico, if he had learning? Just nowhere, we felt.

"Another idea," Gysbert van Tonder suggested, "would be for you to go and pitch a tent alongside the Crocodile River. It's quiet enough there. At least one of the banks is quiet, the one where there isn't much grass on. No, on second thoughts, I don't think you should go there.

Because you might just by mistake pick the wrong bank – the one that the Crocodile River gets its name from. You'd be surprised how busy things can be on that side, in the season."

So Oupa Bekker said that if it was civilisation that At Naudé wanted to get away from, well, there was Durban. He had been to Durban only once, Oupa Bekker said, but it was enough. It was quite a story, too, how he got to Durban, in the first place, Oupa Bekker added. But Durban was quite a good place to go to, if you were sick of civilisation.

"The same old thing," At Naudé remarked to Oupa Bekker. "And I know exactly what you're going to say, too. It was in the old days. And you went there by mule-cart. Or you were a transport driver, and you went there by ox-wagon. And on the way back you gave a young student of divinity a lift as far as Kimberley.

"And years later you saw the young student of divinity's photograph in a newspaper. And he was a bit older then, but not much, for the years had treated him kindly. And then you realised, for the first time, that the young divinity student with the handsome side-whiskers that you had given a lift to from Durban was Solly Joel. I don't know how often I haven't heard that kind of story."

When we spoke about it afterwards, we said among ourselves that the expression on At Naudé's face was quite fiendish.

"And if it wasn't Solly Joel," At Naudé continued, "it was some other Rand millionaire. And if it wasn't a student of theology or a Sunday school superintendent – but, no, it *had* to be. It couldn't be anything else. Without that, you old-timers wouldn't think there was any point to your stories.

"I mean, I've never heard of any of you transport drivers giving a lift as far as Johannesburg to an Australian doing the three-card trick. But you must have, otherwise, how could they have got there? No, it's either Solly Joel, or Wolf Joel or Lionel Phillips or Sammy Marks – and they were doing nothing all the time but thumbing lifts on ox-wagons between Durban and the Rand.

"When did the Rand mining magnates find time to float their companies, then? Or time to have a bath in champagne – like we know they did? I tell you, it's more than a year, now, that I've been listening to every wireless programme that's got somebody talking about life in South Africa in the old days. And you'd be surprised how many of them are transport drivers.

"It must have been a very healthy life, I should think, driving a heavily loaded ox-wagon from the coast to the Transvaal, before there was a railway. And sometimes, when one of these old transport drivers says that what he was bringing up from Durban was a big consignment of dynamite – and the announcer starts asking him questions over the wireless – I begin to hope.

"But it turns out, in the end, that it really was a healthy life. They had no trouble with the heavy load of dynamite to speak of.

"But there was a religious-looking young man with handsome side-whiskers that the transport driver had given a lift to. And that young man became the chairman of a mine that ends with the word *Deep*. And a Johannesburg suburb is today called after him. And that whole load of dynamite, from the coast to the Rand, didn't as much as singe the young theologian's side-whiskers. You see, it's not that I don't like Oupa Bekker. My trouble is just that I've heard him before, and so often.

"There isn't a day passes but I hear something like 'Uit die Ou Dae' over the wireless. Or 'Toeka se Tyd', or 'So Het die Ou Mense Gelewe', or 'Ja-nee'.

"And I get sick of it. I just can't help it, but I do. And then . . . when I come here and sit down in Jurie Steyn's post office, and I hear Oupa Bekker talk of the old days, and I realise that he didn't have any trouble with cases and *cases* of dynamite, either (I mean, otherwise he wouldn't be here), well, it isn't that I wish Oupa Bekker any harm, you understand.

"But I've heard everything he's got to say. Every time Oupa Bekker speaks it sounds to me as though he is being introduced by a wireless announcer, and as though there is somebody playing the piano for background effects. I mean, Oupa Bekker isn't *real* to me, anymore.

"Even the way he spits behind his chair – well, it looks to me like a *put on* sort of spit, if you know what I mean. I don't feel that Oupa Bekker is spitting just because he's got to."

We looked at At Naudé in amazement. It was clear that he was in a pretty bad way. There was no telling how far this sort of thing could go. We felt that we wanted to help him, if we could. The next thing he would do, he would start crying, and right here in front of us. And all because of his nerves. We had seen just that same thing happen before, with a stranger from the city.

The stranger had been with us for quite a while, and was really trying to understand us, and the things going on in our minds. And he was

taking notes, even. And then one day – just like that – he started crying. We felt that At Naudé was going the same way, through too much
civilisation that he was getting over the wireless and from reading newspapers.

It came as a relief to us – for At Naudé's sake – to hear Oupa Bekker's
voice once more.

"The last time I went to Durban wasn't in the old days, but two years
ago," Oupa Bekker said. "And why I said that it was like a story was
because I went there by train. I had never before in my life travelled so
far by train. And that was a wonderful thing for me. Because I would
never have believed, otherwise, that you could journey so far by train.
We didn't once have to get out and walk. Or change to a post-cart. Or
mount a horse ready-saddled that would take us along a bridle-path
over the worst part of the rante –"

"Then it couldn't have been in the Union," Chris Welman shouted
out, trying to be *really* funny. "You couldn't have been travelling on the
S. A. R."

We were pleased that Oupa Bekker ignored Chris Welman.

"No trouble over the whole journey," Oupa Bekker continued. "It
was only when I got off at the station and a Zulu came and pulled my
portmanteau out of my hands. But I had never in my life seen a Zulu
like that. He had bull's horns on his head and sea-shells on his feet. That
was just how my grandfather had told me that the Zulus were dressed
at Vechtkop."

We laughed at that, of course. After all, those of us who had been to
Durban knew that about the Durban rickshaw-pullers – the way they
dressed up to look ferocious. But all they did was to transport you and
your luggage to a hotel.

"That sort of talk," At Naudé began, his lip curling, "and I suppose
when you got to the hotel –"

"That's why I say that Durban is so uncivilised," Oupa Bekker explained. "Because it was only when we got to the hotel that the rickshaw-puller started apologising for all the boot-polish brown that was
coming off his chin. He was working his way through college, he told
me. He said it was steadier work than looking after babies or mowing
lawns, the sea-shells on him rattling as he spoke. He was a divinity student, the rickshaw-puller said."

SLEEPY AFTERNOON

The heat on that midsummer afternoon was overpowering.
Alida, the native girl working in the kitchen, had several times at Jurie Steyn's exhortation entered the voorkamer and hit at the flies with a sizeable twig plucked from a maroela tree. The leaves on the twig were heavy with summer.

"Chase them outside," Jurie Steyn said to the native girl. "As far outside as you like . . . No, no, Alida, that's not the way to drive a fly – swishing sideways, like that. They only go and hide in the rafters, then. Chase them right out to the manure heap where that arsenic fly-trap is."

We recognised that that was the last place where those flies would go, of course. If it was this new kind of DDT, the flies, recovering from their first astonishment, would come back two or three generations later for more, perhaps. But there was a finality about arsenic. That was why the flies kept away from the fly-trap.

Jurie Steyn would have expostulated with the kitchen maid in even sterner tones. Only, the heat of the afternoon was making him feel sleepy.

It was consequently left to Gysbert van Tonder to tell Alida what he really *thought*. That was when, in obedience to Jurie Steyn's injunction, she started performing an oscillating motion with the maroela twig, which made the leaves thrash around in a quite smart fashion, face-high. To a person sitting on a riempies chair, say, the leaves of the maroela twig would come just about face-high, then, that was.

Several of us felt that it wasn't altogether nice the words Gysbert van Tonder saw fit to use in reprimanding Alida, who was, after all, only an ignorant Bechuana servant woman.

Some of the words were what Gysbert van Tonder employed when he stooped down to retrieve his pipe from where it had landed on the floor. The rest of the words were what Gysbert van Tonder said when he discovered the size of the hole that the roll-tobacco embers from his pipe had burnt in his trouser leg.

"Hitting a white man's pipe out of his mouth with that huge branch," Gysbert van Tonder announced to us after the native girl had gone back into the kitchen, slamming the door shut behind her. "I'm sure she did it on purpose. No respect for a white person, anymore. It's these liberal politicians. Next thing is –"

"And look at my ear," Chris Welman said, interrupting him. "But *look* at it – what are you kêrels laughing at? . . . Well, I understand now what At Naudé meant last time when he spoke about how you all carry on here, in Jurie Steyn's voorkamer, laughing at nothing and getting the Marico District a bad name, because of it . . . All right, say I *have* got big ears. But that's not the point.

"What I want to say is, just take a look at how Alida hit me with the stick part of that maroela branch on my ear. I would like to know what would have been left of my ear, if it wasn't that I was thoughtful enough to be sitting here in the voorkamer with my hat on, at the time. Just supposing I had taken my hat off –"

To our surprise, the person that showed the least sympathy for Chris Welman was Gysbert van Tonder himself. There was a thing for you now, all right. We would have imagined that, because he had suffered the same kind of misfortune, Gysbert van Tonder would be the first to stand up for Chris Welman, and to say it was a disgrace to the Marico that Jurie Steyn should have so depraved a Bechuana as Alida working in his kitchen.

Instead, Gysbert van Tonder actually slapped his leg, once or twice, laughing. Even though we could see that that action occasioned Gysbert van Tonder a certain measure of discomfort – each time he hit himself on the blistered part of his leg, from where the lighted shreds of Piet Retief roll-tobacco had fallen – that seemed to make no difference to the way Gysbert van Tonder was laughing.

But human nature is that way, of course.

Moreover, it was a particularly hot afternoon.

"I can't see how it helped you very much," Gysbert van Tonder remarked to Chris Welman, his fellow victim, at the end, "that you had your hat on. Seeing that you wear your ears *outside* of your hat, pressed down flat by the brim. Or did you perhaps not know that? What I want to say is that it couldn't have helped much, your having your hat on when Alida hit."

Gysbert van Tonder seemed to be making use of a good deal of unnecessary repetition. No doubt, the languor of the hot afternoon had a lot to do with it.

"Flies," Oupa Bekker was saying. "Zizz-zz, like that. You know, I can go on watching a fly for hours. Or if it's not a fly, it's an ant. Or else, perhaps, a dung-beetle, if there is one around. But all the same, I think a fly is the most instructive to watch. Only, it's got to be on a hot afternoon, like this, naturally. And then you've got to lie on a bed, flat on your back for it."

Then At Naudé said, yes, that part, of course, you had to have. And then you had to lie so flat that you could feel the bed for the whole length of your spine, every inch. And it had to be an afternoon when you knew you should be out on the lands. It was on such an afternoon that you could really appreciate a fly properly, watching that fly fly around, At Naudé said.

On an afternoon when you knew you had to be out on the lands, instead, supervising that there was enough seed in the hopper of the mealie-planter.

"And the things I've seen about flies in my time," Oupa Bekker continued. "When I've been lying on my back in the bedroom in the ploughing season *or* on a harvesting afternoon. That photograph of the first Molopo church council, now, where I'm sitting only two away from the dominee in the middle . . .

"I would have been sitting right next to the dominee, seeing I was senior diaken, if only Rooi Visagie hadn't come and plonked himself in between us, Rooi Visagie keeping the dominee's mind occupied with questions he was asking him about St. Peter's witness in the holy Formulier of the Communion.

"And if it wasn't that we realised full well it couldn't be, it would almost have looked as though the dominee didn't *know* the answer, the way he was scratching his head, right up to the time when the photographer said would we please look straight at the camera, and not smile, seeing that he only had one plate. That was in the old days, of course."

So Chris Welman said that he accepted it, that it was in the old days. He said that he also accepted that it might have been a very warm day, also, just like now. But that was no excuse for Oupa Bekker to wander so far away from what he had started off with.

Not that he himself cared very much, really, Chris Welman added.

It was, after all, a sleepy sort of afternoon, and it was not unpleasant to think of that other afternoon, long ago, when a photograph was being taken of the members of the Molopo church council, in the same kind of hot sun.

Although it might have been better, perhaps, for everybody (Chris Welman added, quickly) if a cloud had come across the sky in a sudden manner, just about when the photographer was putting his head under the black cloth.

But what was it Oupa Bekker was saying about that fly? – Chris Welman asked.

"Insulting," Oupa Bekker said. "There's one fly I've seen walk round and round on that photograph with its gold frame, and with no respect for its being the church council, that you would notice. Then he goes and stands right on the dominee's white tie and he turns his head sideways, studying it.

"He hasn't seen a tie like that in his life, of course, and so he doesn't know any better than to stare. When he gets tired of just staring he wipes his feet a few times on the dominee's tie and moves across to Rooi Visagie. What he looks at most is the mended place in Rooi Visagie's manel that comes out very clearly on the photograph. And he gets very superior about it, too. You've got no idea – fluttering his wings all sniffy. He's got no mended places in *his* manel, the fly thinks.

"I can't say I don't feel pleased about that bit, mind you, seeing that if it wasn't for Rooi Visagie's dishonesty, it would have been me sitting there next to the dominee, and not Rooi Visagie. But maybe next time there's a church council photograph taken it will be put right . . . Anyway, the next one the fly comes to is me.

"What I think he admires about me most is the way I wore my moustache in those days. He stands on one leg to admire it properly. It's queer to think that a simple-hearted creature like a fly should yet have so much judgment – and –"

Several of us shook our heads sadly, then.

It was, indeed, a depressing reflection, to think that old age, combined with the heat, could make Oupa Bekker go so foolish in his mind. We got the uncomfortable feeling that we might perhaps go that way ourselves, some day. We could not expect our mental powers always to be as keen as what they were now.

We sat for a while in silence. The flies came out from their temporary places of refuge in the rafters and buzzed about our heads. Zizzzimm, the flies went. So they buzzed about the portrait of the Molopo church council in the gold frame, in Oupa Bekker's bedroom. So they had buzzed long ago around the photographer's camera on a day of sunshine that would come again no more.

The lorry from Bekkersdal was late, that afternoon.

And the silence that had descended on us persisted until the lorry-driver's assistant came in at the front door. With the heat, he looked limp and wilted. He seemed very different from his usual spruce self.

On his job, the lorry-driver's assistant prided himself on how nattily he always turned out. For there were unofficial stops along the way where he would alight for coffee, to the irritation of passengers on the Government lorry who paid for their seats.

What annoyed the passengers more than anything else was the long time that the lorry-driver's assistant would spend in taking his coffee from the hands of the farmer's daughter on the other side of the barbed-wire fence, at each of those unofficial stops.

And the silly way he would pretend to catch her hand, each time he passed back the empty cup.

You would be pretty fed-up, too, if you had a ticket to be on that lorry, and the farmer's daughter acted as though you didn't exist at all.

But when he came into Jurie Steyn's voorkamer on that afternoon, you would never have thought that when he left Bekkersdal the lorry-driver's assistant's trousers were ironed as flat as a piece of Free State veld. Instead, he looked quite dishevelled. We attributed it to the heat.

It was only when the lorry-driver's assistant passed his hand over his forehead and said how awful something or other was, that we noticed his extreme pallor.

"They carried him out there right in front of us, at Schuilpan," the lorry-driver's assistant said. "The police and the doctor. One of the policemen just yawned and said it was a sleepy afternoon. They reckon it's suicide. He took arsenic that you use in fly-traps, they say, because he was going to be arrested for embezzling funds. Such a respected member of the community he was, too, Oom Rooi Visagie."

We looked at Oupa Bekker. Oupa Bekker seemed to take it even worse than the lorry-driver's assistant had done. If he was glad that he would now be able to move up one place nearer the dominee next time there was a photograph, Oupa Bekker didn't show it.

"Here, you have my coffee," Chris Welman said to the lorry-driver's assistant. "It will help to pull you right."

But even after he had drunk the coffee, the lorry-driver's assistant still looked sick. And from force of habit, when he handed back the cup to Chris Welman, he tried, playfully, to catch Chris Welman's hand. We could see the lorry-driver's assistant was in a pretty bad way, all right.

That was when Alida came out of the kitchen, once more, with a twig plucked from a maroela. The leaves on the twig that she waved about were heavy with summer.

"What the –" Gysbert van Tonder began shakily, stooping down for the second time that afternoon to pick up his pipe. "What the –" Gysbert van Tonder started again, brushing frantically at the live tobacco embers on his knees.

ALARM CLOCK

"A new kind of alarm clock," At Naudé was saying about what he had read in the paper. "Of course, it still wakes you with that old clatter-clatter noise like hitting on tin. But where it is different is that it starts playing a soothing little tune straight afterwards that makes you feel all right again.

"So you don't feel so bad, thinking you've got to get up, now. Maybe you hum a few notes of that tune to yourself, too, as you reach under the bed for your trousers. Hey, tiddly hum tum you sing perhaps, even, as you rise to face another day. With a song in your heart, instead of swearing."

We looked at each other with a certain measure of surprise, then. Not that it wasn't interesting enough, what At Naudé had to tell us about the new kind of alarm clock. But what was more interesting was to learn what he did with his trousers when he went to bed at night.

That just showed you what primitive habits a man could acquire, living like At Naudé. For we knew how much time At Naudé spent every day in listening in to the wireless and reading the newspapers.

And we also knew that no good could come of it, a man cutting himself off from the world like that.

"I wonder what they will invent next," At Naudé went on, unaware of the mild stir he had caused.

It was Jurie Steyn who pulled him up.

"Perhaps they'll invent a better place for a man to put his trousers at night than under the bed," Jurie Steyn said. "I don't say that for getting up in the morning, it's not handy, of course –"

The subtle irony in Jurie Steyn's words was lost on At Naudé.

"That's what I say," At Naudé went on. "What's the sense of hanging up your trousers in a kiaat gentleman's wardrobe like they advertise in the newspapers, when you want your trousers, first thing in the morning? I mean, I'm just a plain farmer. I'm no kiaat gentleman."

"No, or an imbuia gentleman," Jurie Steyn said, to make it clear that he, too, was not unfamiliar with the contents of a certain class of full-page newspaper advertisement.

"Or a solid polished walnut gentleman, either," Jurie Steyn added. "I mean we can see all that about you by just looking at your trousers. But why don't you hang them over a chair in front of your bed, instead? Instead of sticking them *under* the bed, that is."

There was also a four-foot convertible gentleman's wardrobe in teak or oak, Jurie Steyn added, for good measure. But what a four-foot convertible gentleman was, he would sooner not think, Jurie said. It must be quite about the newest sort of invention that there was, he reckoned.

At Naudé acknowledged that he had never really thought of hanging his trousers over a chair, until then. That just proved again what kind of ideas you could get hold of by just *thinking*, he said.

"Take that new alarm clock, now," At Naudé went on, "playing um-tiddly-um-tum first thing in the morning. Well, the man who thought that out must have done nothing for a whole month but sit down and think. Sitting down just in one place, too, I should imagine."

A pensive light came into At Naudé's eyes, then. He looked just about as thoughtful as the man thinking about the alarm clock.

"Nothing to do but sit on his – on his –" At Naudé said, wistfully, "and with somebody to bring him in coffee, every so often."

It was clear that At Naudé was reflecting on the awe-inspiring contribution that he himself could make to world progress by way of mechanical invention, given suitable conditions to invent *in*.

"If necessary, I would be prepared to spend even longer than a month over something that I was inventing," At Naudé went on, after a pause. "So as to get it just proper, for the world. There's no sense in rushing things. Once you're sitting down to it."

"Like that electric separator that David Policansky demonstrated in his store," Chris Welman said. "Now, if I had a cream separator like that . . . Why, all you do is you sit back and watch the Mtosas pour the milk in on top and at the bottom it comes out cream in one can and skim milk for the pigs in the other can, and there's no handle to turn. And *fast*. Why, it's a pleasure to be able to sit back and watch the Mtosas getting all out of breath, through rushing around with the cans and buckets, trying to keep up. Trying to keep up with the separator *and* the pigs. For that alone it's worth it, to see how the Mtosas get kept on the hop.

"That is what I mean by saying that I would also like to think out an invention some day that will be of benefit to my fellow man. Of course, I don't *know* anything more about inventing than what – what a Chinaman does."

From the furrows in Jurie Steyn's forehead, it appeared that he had been wrestling with a problem.

"It's like this," Jurie Steyn said, eventually. "According to what At Naudé and Chris Welman have been saying, an inventor sits down for a good while and thinks, somebody bringing him in coffee every so often. And what the inventor thinks out, at the end of that time, is as likely as not something that enables you and me also to sit down on our back parts, somebody bringing us in coffee every so often.

"I mean, that's what he's supposed to invent. But as far as I can see, what's wrong with an invention is that it doesn't work out that way. It's the people that start using the invention that have got to get going – and a lot quicker, too, than before."

He hoped we would not take it amiss, Jurie Steyn said, but it was indeed a truth that those of us present in his voorkamer at that very moment spent quite a good while, each week, in just sitting, and with his wife bringing us in coffee.

But it wasn't like that through anything anybody had invented, he said. It was only, of course, because we had to come there for our letters.

"But one day somebody is going to invent a way to make it easier for Marico farmers to collect their mail and milk-cans, every week," Jurie Steyn declared in sombre tones. "And that will make a big difference. It will be less talk and more jumping around for you kêrels.

"There will be less of this um-diddly-um-tum," Jurie Steyn said, as an afterthought.

In the meantime the schoolteacher, young Vermaak, had been carrying on a conversation with Chris Welman. It was apparent that the schoolmaster had taken exception to Chris Welman's statement, earlier on, about a Chinaman. With Jurie Steyn talking at the same time, the schoolmaster's words were audible only in snatches:

". . . and the art of printing – what do you think of that?" young Vermaak was saying to Chris Welman . . . "yes, and gunpowder . . .

the mariner's compass, with north and south marked on it . . . you ask what's the good of that?

"Do *you* know north from south? . . . no, Nietverdiend is west, man . . . no, man, that's Portuguese territory . . . the bold sons of the Celestial Empire crossing the . . . yes, in their junks, long before Vasco da Gama . . . discovering South Africa . . . what's that? Well, why shouldn't they have been hanged? . . . longer than from here to Cape Town via Bloemfontein and over worse parts than the Hex River. How do you mean, we should also have a wall like that, to keep the Syrians out? . . . bamboo . . ."

When young Vermaak finished speaking, Chris Welman said that he handed it to that Chinaman all right, that had thought out gunpowder. He only hoped that that Chinaman wasn't sitting *on* a barrel of gunpowder all the time he was doing his thinking, with somebody bringing him coffee every so often, ha-ha.

Anyway, the white man in this country would just have been nowhere if it wasn't for gunpowder, Chris Welman explained. He himself still had some loopers that his great-grandfather had fired through a muzzle-loader at Danskraal.

"And if you saw the size of those loopers," Chris Welman said, "well, I'm sure you'd get quite a different kind of respect for a Chinaman."

It was only when the schoolmaster got onto the subject of Confucius and Taoism that Chris Welman grew impatient.

"What did they want all that for?" Chris Welman asked of the schoolmaster, "after they had got gunpowder that could shoot loopers that big?"

For once the schoolmaster, talking then about the pagoda at Foochow, was unable to think of an answer.

"That alarm clock that At Naudé read about in the papers," Oupa Bekker announced, suddenly. "A new invention, my foot. I remember that there was the same kind of alarm clock that came from overseas and that we had here in this country at the time of the Stellaland Republic.

"Not that many people bought that kind of alarm clock, of course. It wasn't that we thought there was anything wrong with it *as* an alarm clock. Only, we just didn't want to be wakened up too early. Not in the Stellaland Republic, we didn't."

Oupa Bekker described that old alarm clock. We were surprised to find that it was not so different from the newest kind of alarm clock that At Naudé had just been reading about.

"It didn't make that clatter-clatter sort of noise at all," Oupa Bekker said. "Instead, it just played the first part of what the foreign jeweller that sold it said was the Fire Brigade song. It was the Fire Brigade song from – No, I don't remember now where it was *from*. From some place overseas, I should imagine.

"But it was awful enough. There was no um-tiddy-um-tum non-sense about it. It went something like this: K-wêêê-te-te-tah *wah rê* – It was almost like it was words. The Fire Brigade song, it was called."

The schoolmaster listened intently.

Then he asked Oupa Bekker to sing that bit again, a little more in tune, if possible. Oupa Bekker did his best. We could see that from how he threw his head back, and from the stiff way he held his shoulders. But if Oupa Bekker had sung his worst, he could not have produced any-thing more direful in the way of sound. But the schoolmaster looked, strangely enough, pleased.

"Te-rêêê ta-ta-rê," the schoolmaster joined in enthusiastically, fling-ing an arm into the air. "That's not the Fire Brigade song. It's the Fire Song. It's from the Valkyries. Te-têê –"

Gysbert van Tonder said that, wherever that song was *from*, he had rather that they had kept it there.

Oupa Bekker looked pretty foolish, however, having called that song by its wrong name. The schoolmaster had shown Oupa Bekker up, all right, for not having much culture.

"When I said it was the Fire Brigade song," Oupa Bekker apologised, lamely, "I didn't mean so much that it's the song that the new Zeerust fire brigade *sings*. I meant that it's more, sort of, the kind of things a person whose house is alight would *shout*, sort of, to get the fire brigade along, if you know what I mean."

"Tê-tê te-rê –" the schoolmaster went on singing.

Johnny Coen came to Oupa Bekker's rescue.

"You know, Oupa," Johnny Coen said, "I know just how you feel. If they had an alarm clock like what you and Meneer Vermaak have just been singing, then I would say, far rather give me the simple old clatter-clatter tin alarm clock. Because you at least know where you are with it. You know it isn't going to soothe you with Fire Brigade music afterwards.

"If they must have this new kind of alarm clock that At Naudé has been talking about, then they should make it play the tune first, to wake you up with a jerk, and only after that the alarm should come along with its old clatter-clatter, to make you feel that everything is still all right. I mean, after the Fire Brigade song, you *need* the clatter-clatter of just an alarm clock to make you feel restful, again."

"All the same," Oupa Bekker declared, reminiscently, "the old alarm clock that played what Meneer Vermaak says is the Fire Song . . . well, you only had to *hear* it, to know what I mean. Why, it could wake up a bywoner in time for the milking, two mornings out of three –"

"In that case, it should have been able," Johnny Coen interjected quickly, with a laugh, "to wake the –"

So Oupa Bekker said, yes, it could. Playing tê-re-re-rêê, like that. Nine times out of ten that alarm clock *could*. Unless it was somebody that died of snakebite, Oupa Bekker said.

Circumstantial Evidence

One story we heard was that Pauline Gerber's eldest brother, Dons, spoke to young Vermaak, the schoolmaster, on the platform at Zeerust station. According to this story, the schoolmaster was just getting ready to board the train, and Dons Gerber had a single-barrelled shotgun in the bend of his arm when he spoke to the schoolmaster.

According to the second story we heard, young Vermaak was sitting in the classroom, after school, correcting exercise books, and it was Pauline Gerber's youngest brother, Floris, who addressed him, Floris oiling the mechanism of a Mott-Mauser at the time.

It was difficult to know what to believe, exactly. Each story was so well authenticated. The circumstances relating to Dons and the railway platform embraced the language that the train-guard used when he had to stop the train, after having blown the whistle, so that the schoolmaster could get his suitcases out of the compartment again.

"It's how a ticket examiner spoke to me, once," Gysbert van Tonder observed, "when I was travelling on a mail-train to De Aar. I may say that I didn't have a ticket at the time that the ticket examiner addressed me."

If they weren't exactly *like*, Gysbert van Tonder added, the ticket examiner's words still bore a family resemblance to the expressions employed by the Zeerust train-guard in advising the schoolmaster to make up his mind.

Thereupon At Naudé was also able to recall a less happy travel experience of his own, that had to do with his ejecting an empty half-jack of brandy from a train window at Rysmierbult. He never knew where that empty half-jack *got* the ganger, exactly, At Naudé said, but he could still remember how the ganger who happened to be on the line at the time complained about it for the full twenty minutes that the train halted at Rysmierbult.

"By the time-table, the train should have stopped there only ten minutes," At Naudé proceeded, "but I think that why there was that long wait that day was because the engine-driver got a respect for the ganger's language, after listening to it for a bit, and so he felt he wanted to give him a bit of a show. I won't say that the ganger didn't take full advantage of the extra ten minutes that the engine-driver allowed him, either. All the same, I still wonder, today, where that bottle did hit the ganger."

On the other hand, the other story, which had to do with Pauline Gerber's youngest brother, Floris, seemed to be quite as well appointed in respect of circumstantial detail.

For the railway platform's strident bustle you had only to substitute the scholarly calm of the Drogedal schoolroom with its thatched roof and whitewashed walls, the pupils, their textbooks cast aside, having long since departed, on foot or by school donkey-cart.

The only sounds in that peaceful classroom, with the day drawing to its close, were the even scratchings of the schoolmaster's red ink pen in double-ruled exercise books supplied by the Transvaal Education Department.

At intervals, the schoolmaster's pen would *slash*, somewhat, and there would be a measure of unsteadiness about the schoolmaster's breathing. But those were matters readily to be understood. Mistakes in composition and sums. But, I mean, infamous mistakes.

And then, very suddenly, there was obtruded the click-click sound of the bolt mechanism of a Mauser being operated. It was a situation not wanting in drama. After all, we all know why a Mauser has got to be oiled so often. Its magazine system lacks the smoothness of the Lee Enfield.

You can't fire an old Mott-Mauser as fast as a Lee Enfield, maybe. But over 800 yards, aimed at a person running, it's more accurate.

Nevertheless, Jurie Steyn said that it seemed rather a silly thing for Pauline Gerber's youngest brother, Floris, to have done – going along oiling his gun there in the classroom.

"Why couldn't he have done all that at home?" Jurie Steyn wanted to know. "He must have been a bit soft in the head, if you ask me. Perhaps he still is."

But Chris Welman said he did not think that Jurie Steyn was well advised in making that particular kind of remark. Not where Pauline

Gerber's youngest brother was concerned, Chris Welman said. Or her eldest brother, either. Or even any of her in-between brothers.

Perhaps it would have been best if Jurie Steyn had merely said that Pauline Gerber's youngest brother had been a bit playful, walking into the classroom with a gun *and* an oil-can, and if Jurie Steyn had then just left it at that. Perhaps that was all Jurie Steyn *wanted* to imply, Chris Welman suggested, his voice sounding very gentle, all at once.

Jurie Steyn bridled.

"If you think I'm scared of the Gerbers, old Petrus Gerber or any one of his sons, or the whole lot of them together, even," Jurie Steyn announced, "then you don't know me, that's all. A lot of loud-mouthed braggarts, that's all they are. Bullies, too, if you ask me. Cowards, that's what."

But Gysbert van Tonder reminded Jurie Steyn that on the railway platform Pauline Gerber's eldest brother, Dons, had said hardly a word. It was the train-guard that did all the talking. It was the train-guard that you could say was perhaps loud-mouthed, Gysbert van Tonder said. Telling young Vermaak to hustle with his trunks, and what to do with his umbrella.

Similarly, in the classroom of the Drogedal school, Chris Welman interjected, Pauline Gerber's youngest brother, Floris, had said nothing at all.

"As far as we *know*, Floris Gerber didn't talk," Chris Welman said. "Of course, I don't suppose he had any need to talk, exactly. Working on the bolt of the Mott-Mauser was taking up all his attention, I suppose, and if he spoke he might have spilt some of the oil over the school-books."

It was clear, however, that Chris Welman had got Jurie Steyn going. Maybe even Chris Welman himself, when he had in a spirit of Bushveld perversity hinted to Jurie Steyn not to speak out of his turn where the men of the Gerber family were involved – maybe even Chris Welman had not counted on so complete a success for his stratagem.

"The more I think of this whole business," Jurie Steyn declared, "the more my heart warms to young Vermaak. The way that young school-teacher has been treated here, in the Groot Marico, just because he's a stranger. All I can say is that it's unchristian."

There was something for you, now.

It took our breath away. We tried to remember over how long a while

Jurie Steyn had regularly gone out of his way to make the schoolmaster feel small. And just because, as we all knew, Jurie Steyn's wife had a soft spot for the schoolmaster.

And yet a few simple words spoken by Chris Welman (Chris Welman having done nothing more than to impugn Jurie Steyn's physical fortitude when faced by the Gerber brothers) could have the effect of changing Jurie Steyn's outlook in a single moment.

Here was Jurie Steyn actually declaring, for all of us to hear, that he was siding with the schoolmaster. *That* gave you some idea as to how scared Jurie Steyn must be of the Gerber brothers, all right. His next remark bore it out even more clearly.

"I only wish I had Dons Gerber and Floris Gerber right here in front of me now," Jurie Steyn announced, sticking out his chest. "I'd let them know where they got off, all right. But, of course, they never come round here. They pretend it's because Post Office Welgevonden is nearer, for them. But I know that's not the only reason.

"I know it's because the postmaster at Welgevonden is too soft. He allows himself to be put upon, by bullies."

We felt that, after those remarks of Jurie Steyn's, there was very little that we ourselves could say. We had no more to say than what Dons Gerber had had to say on the Zeerust railway platform. We could express our thoughts in less words than what Floris Gerber had employed in the classroom at Drogedal.

That was when Johnny Coen started taking a hand in the conversation.

"Doesn't it strike you, at all," Johnny Coen asked, "that it can't both be true, these two different stories about how the schoolmaster came in the end to ask Pauline Gerber to marry him? Don't you think it's possible that perhaps *both* those stories are lies, I mean."

We were very shocked to hear Johnny Coen using language like that.

Naturally enough, we were quite willing to make many sorts of allowances for Johnny Coen. For one thing, we knew perfectly well how Johnny Coen had been feeling about Pauline Gerber. We realised, also, that he had entertained those sentiments about Pauline Gerber long before she had ever set eyes on young Vermaak, the schoolmaster.

But we also knew that Pauline Gerber had been to finishing-school, in the meanwhile, and so it was only reasonable that things should no longer be the same between Pauline Gerber and Johnny Coen, after she came back to the Marico. For, if she did feel the same way about Johnny Coen, it would mean that all the money that her father had spent on her at finishing-school at the Cape had been wasted.

Johnny Coen appeared to sense the constraint in Jurie Steyn's voorkamer then, following on the statement he had just made and that showed a good deal of faulty reasoning.

"I don't mean to say that you're all of you just a lot of —— liars," Johnny Coen said, giving utterance to a couple of words that the train-guard had also found useful on Zeerust station. "I don't mean that at all."

So Gysbert van Tonder said to Johnny Coen that we were grateful to him for that, he was sure.

"It's not that," Johnny Coen persisted, half-ashamed of himself for having put it so impolitely. "But what I mean is, if young Vermaak was on the Zeerust railway station, with Dons Gerber there with him, then who was sitting in the classroom marking copy-books in red ink, when Floris Gerber was there?

"I mean, they couldn't both of those things be true, could they, now? The next thing you'd be saying is that it was Floris Gerber sitting at the table marking the Standard Five spelling mistakes in red ink. That would be a muck-up, *wouldn't* it?"

The thought of that provoked Johnny Coen to laughter. We smiled indulgently. Only Oupa Bekker seemed to think that Johnny Coen did have something there. He himself didn't believe either of these stories about how young Vermaak came to ask Pauline Gerber for her hand, Oupa Bekker said.

"Jolliest passengers we've had in a good while," the lorry-driver's assistant remarked, walking into the voorkamer with the mailbags. "Laughing all the way up from Bekkersdal."

So Chris Welman said that he supposed it was more of those native convicts that were coming to work at Derdepoort.

"But what they've got to laugh about I don't know," Chris Welman continued. "And yet that's what I always think, when I see those native convicts sitting in the lorry in their striped jerseys – laughing their heads off about something. And the warder with them looking so miserable, you feel you want to go and ask can't you do something for him."

"No, not convicts, this time," the lorry-driver's assistant said. "Only Pauline Gerber and her brothers, Dons and Floris and – I forget the names of the other two –"

"Out there in the lorry?" Jurie Steyn enquired, looking not too comfortable, suddenly.

"No, they got off at Welgevonden," the lorry-driver said. "And, of course, young Vermaak was with them, too. You know, he's engaged to Pauline. They went to Bekkersdal to celebrate."

The lorry-driver looked surprised at the question Gysbert van Tonder put to him.

"How did the schoolmaster propose to Pauline Gerber?" the lorry-driver repeated. "Well, what do we all do? He rode over to the farm, one afternoon, and asked her father, of course. And Oom Petrus Gerber shook him by the hand and said he wanted a young man to help look after the farm – as though he didn't have enough already, with all those sons he's got. But why did you ask?"

Thereupon Gysbert van Tonder said, no, it was nothing. It was just something Jurie Steyn had been mentioning, Gysbert van Tonder said.

LITERARY GIANTS

"But is little Frikkie Oosthuizen really so clever at saying recitations, Meneer Vermaak?" Gysbert van Tonder asked of the schoolmaster, arising out of what the schoolmaster had been saying.

So Meneer Vermaak said, yes, indeed. That was the reason why he had asked little Frikkie to come round to the post office some time in the afternoon, after he had finished his homework, so that he could recite to us.

"You did *what*?" Jurie Steyn demanded, his voice going very high. "Did I really hear you say –"

When the schoolmaster assured Jurie Steyn that there was no need for him to get alarmed, since it wouldn't take very long, Jurie Steyn got more excited than ever. Not in his voorkamer and not in the Government's own post office, he wouldn't allow it.

Not over his dead body that stinking little Frikkie Oosthuizen with his freckles and spectacles wasn't going to say recitations here, Jurie Steyn declared. And not over the Postmaster-General's dead body either. We could see that Jurie Steyn was really frightened. Otherwise he wouldn't have invoked all the forces of officialdom to his aid, like that, against little Frikkie Oosthuizen, who was in Standard Three.

"Nor over the dead body of the Minister of Posts and Telegraphs himself, what's more," Jurie Steyn finished up, triumphantly.

The schoolmaster shook his head, then, as well he might. It was not pleasant to think of the Dwarsberg area of the Groot Marico District strewn with dead bodies.

"I know what you all think," the schoolmaster said, after a pause. "You think it's all favouritism, don't you? You think that why I – why I talk like this about Frikkie Oosthuizen is because he's the schoolmaster's pet. Let's be straight about it, I mean."

Meneer Vermaak looked slowly round the voorkamer.

Chris Welman accepted his challenge.

"Well," Chris Welman said, "when my youngest child comes home and tells me that little Frikkie got ten out of ten, again . . . well, I don't say anything. I went to school myself, as far as Standard Three. How I got so far, staying in school until I was eleven, was because there was four years of drought, so that I wasn't needed at home to help with the farming. I mean, there just wasn't any farming – not with four years of drought.

"The only farm work there was, over that time, was filling in drought relief compensation forms. And that was where I was able to help, seeing that I was so well educated. Each year, when I passed into a higher standard, I could help better with the forms. I felt almost sorry, at the end of the fourth year when the rains came and I had to leave school and help with the ploughing, instead. Not that I wasn't pretty well educated at the end of that fourth year, mind you. By that time I had learnt to fill in the compensation forms for a whole lot of losses we hadn't suffered."

Thereupon At Naudé remarked that it was a pity that Chris Welman's education got interrupted, like that.

"If you had to go on staying at school, like that, year after year, because there wasn't rain," At Naudé said, "then you would almost be a professor, by now. Think of that – Professor Chris Welman. Doesn't it make you laugh right out? And you could go on filling in the losses forms, year after year. And, you wouldn't go to gaol for it, either, like what happened to Doors Prinsloo. They would say that it was just because you were an absent-minded professor."

It was when Jurie Steyn took some pains to point out to us that this sort of talk was getting us away from the subject of schoolteachers' pets, that Chris Welman remembered what it was that he had wanted to say. Why Chris Welman pulled himself together so quickly was because Jurie Steyn made use of a low word that Dominee Welthagen had employed once, in reply to a question put to him about the proselytising activities of the Catholic bishop at Vleisfontein, Dominee Welthagen thinking, at the time, that he was talking under his breath and not loud enough for any member of the congregation to hear.

"So that when my youngest little boy comes home and tells me more things about the teacher's favourite, how the teacher's favourite got full marks again," Chris Welman said, "then I don't tell my youngest son what I really think. I don't want to put him against the schoolteacher more than what he already is. But I remember my own education. And then I think to myself, well, I wouldn't like to be that snivelling little brat that is the schoolmaster's favourite. Not on an afternoon when school is over, I wouldn't, and some manly youngster that has stood it just so long starts laying into the teacher's pet behind a clump of withaaks, I wouldn't.

"That's about as far as I've learnt with my education. Maybe if it wasn't for the four years of drought in the Groot Marico I wouldn't have learnt so far. But they say that education is no good unless you get it the hard way."

Young Vermaak, the schoolmaster, shook his head once more.

"You seem to forget that I played rugby for Potchefstroom," he said. "And I still believe that if I had played for Stellenbosch instead of Potchefstroom – mind you, I am quoting the opinion of a selector who saw what I could do in the scrum – it's not my own personal views I am expressing at all –"

And we said, no, of course, we knew that the schoolmaster would never do a thing like that.

"And I am not talking about Springbok colours, either," young Vermaak went on, "but about provincial representation – you understand I am not talking about a Springbok jersey –"

Again we said that we understood only too well. Gysbert van Tonder sniffed, even, a little, when he said it.

"But anyway, that's what the selector said to me," young Vermaak continued, "after the team had been picked and I wasn't in it. He said if he had it his way . . . well, it would all have been different. He said it to me himself, in the bar of the King Edward Hotel in Potchefstroom, right after the match. He said if I had been playing for Stellenbosch, instead, and he wasn't talking about Springbok colours, at all. And he had nothing to gain by saying that to me, seeing that I was paying for the drinks in any case."

And we nodded our heads, in solemn agreement with the schoolmaster's remarks. Even though he did not tell us, in so many words, as to what exactly the selector had said. But we had a pretty good idea as to what the selector would have said – and in so many words – if the schoolmaster hadn't been paying for the drinks.

"So when you get the idea of favouritism in your minds," young

Vermaak said – although, strangely enough, we had no idea of that sort in our minds at all: actually, we thought that the selectors would have been wrong in the head if they had chosen young Vermaak for provincial honours, leave alone picking him to wear a green jersey with a gold collar – "then I can only say that I have been through all that. And if you think that little Frikkie Oosthuizen is my pet, why, it can only make me laugh."

We did all laugh, then. Or, at least, we tried to. We wanted the young schoolmaster to realise that we in the Marico Bushveld were his friends, really, in spite of what he might think of us, perhaps, on different occasions.

"When you think of little Frikkie Oosthuizen with his freckles and his round-rimmed glasses," the schoolmaster proceeded, coughing slightly at that last thought, "then how do you imagine I must think of him? I mean, all my feelings are with a boy that *is* a boy – a boy with sore toes and with a barbel in his school desk that he caught with a tamboetie rod and a bent pin by the Molopo spruit on a day when he should have been at school learning nature study."

Several of us (those of us who were interested in politics, that was) realised, then, that the schoolmaster was quite clever. For he had hit on the best way of making us take some sort of an interest in little Frikkie Oosthuizen – by saying that he had no time for him, himself. If young Vermaak's mind could have worked equally quick in the loose – at a moment when the referee had his back turned, say – then he would have taken his rugby pretty far, we thought.

"So you see how ridiculous it is to think that a little stinker," the schoolmaster said, repeating Jurie Steyn's word, "like Frikkie Oosthuizen could ever be a pet of mine – or of any schoolteacher worth his salt. If I could pick, I wouldn't pick him for my favourite. I would pick not to have him in the school at all."

And so Jurie Steyn said, yes, exactly, and he would pick not to have little Frikkie Oosthuizen in his post office, at all, leave alone having him there to recite.

But the schoolmaster said that one had to overcome one's prejudices. And what you had to give Frikkie Oosthuizen credit for was that behind his thick spectacles he had a brain for poetry – for learning poetry and understanding poetry – that many a Normal College student didn't have. It was amazing, the schoolmaster said. He would even go so far as to call it genius. It was as though, wherever he went, little Frikkie walked with the great literary figures of the world. Meneer Vermaak started mentioning some of them.

"Well, I'm glad he's got *somebody* to walk back with him from school," Gysbert van Tonder observed. "None of the other kids would ever walk with him – not with a low little sneak like that."

Thereupon Chris Welman said that those giants of letters whose names the schoolmaster had just reeled off must be pretty low sneaks themselves. Otherwise how could that dirty little Frikkie in Standard Three have anything in common with them? – Chris Welman wanted to know.

There seemed a lot of sense in what Chris Welman had just said. And the schoolmaster, after thinking it over a little, admitted as much.

"There's one long piece of recitation, for instance, that's in English, and that little Frikkie taught himself – *wonderful* brain he's got, Frikkie," the schoolmaster proceeded.

"It's all about playing the game and about a little wooden cross below the town. It's all about being upright and fearless. I don't think many of you would understand that poem. Not because it's about being upright and fearless, I mean. But because it's in English."

We assured young Vermaak that there was no need for him to have explained that part, even. It was laughable to think he could have meant the other thing, we said.

"Well, I know something about the poet who wrote that poem," the schoolmaster proceeded. "We had him in second-year B. A. And if you take that poet's life story, I mean – well, his life story wasn't anything like the poem at all . . . the fearless and upright part, that is. I'm not talking about how good he might have been at English, of course."

Then there was the life story of another poet whose verses little Frikkie Oosthuizen recited, the schoolmaster went on. And if you went by *that* poet's life story, the schoolmaster said, well, then you perhaps wouldn't go very far wrong if you spoke of him as a stinker. Even the word that Dominee Welthagen used about the proselytising Roman Catholic bishop at Vleisfontein might, strictly speaking, not be inappropriate.

"But then what do you want to bring that dirty little rat along here to come and recite for?" Gysbert van Tonder demanded. "Especially if the people whose poems he comes and says here are the same sort of heathen blackguards?"

The schoolmaster was still busy trying to explain where the world would be without them, and about how necessary it was to encourage culture, when we got the news that little Frikkie Oosthuizen would not come and recite in the post office, that afternoon, after all.

It appeared that, on the way back from school, another Standard Three youngster had lured little Frikkie behind a clump of withaaks and had given him a pretty solid doing.

Even the schoolmaster smiled when he heard that.

ALCOHOLIC REMORSE

Gysbert van Tonder said that, while he sympathised with Jurie Steyn in Jurie not feeling so well, at the same time, it was only to be expected.

Gysbert van Tonder said that in a quite pointed manner.

"You needn't talk, Gysbert," Jurie Steyn said, but not with much conviction. "You didn't do so badly yourself. In fact, most of what I can remember about last night is how every time I saw you you were pouring more mampoer into that tin mug."

So Gysbert van Tonder said that he was glad there was at least something about last night that Jurie Steyn could remember.

And the way Gysbert van Tonder said it was again very marked.

"I'm not talking so much about the earlier part of the evening," Gysbert van Tonder continued. "It's the later hours I'm thinking of, more."

Gysbert van Tonder laid just enough stress on the word 'hours' to make a peculiar kind of a look come over Jurie Steyn's face. We couldn't miss that look. There was much disquiet in it.

"Ah, well, I suppose we did all let ourselves go a little," Jurie Steyn said, trying to talk airily and finishing up with what he intended us to interpret – just going by the sound – as a few notes of light laughter.

But he stopped suddenly. We could see that the effort to emit noises of mirth was not doing his headache any good. Moreover, the condition of our own nerves was such that Jurie Steyn's simulation of merriment jangled harshly. We were glad that he cut it short.

"Of course, I didn't really want to go over in the first place," Jurie Steyn continued, after a pause. "But seeing that Oupa Bekker had made that mampoer in his own still, and he had invited us over . . . well, I felt it would not have been properly neighbourly, sort of, not to go."

"I think it would have been more neighbourly if you had stayed away," Gysbert van Tonder told him, bluntly. "Much more neighbourly.

...nd you, as I've said, I'm talking about the later part of the night, ...ore."

So Jurie Steyn confessed that it was actually that part of it that he just couldn't remember so well, no matter how hard he tried.

"Don't try," Gysbert van Tonder counselled him. "Maybe it's best for your peace of mind that you shouldn't know. Yes, I wouldn't be surprised if it's really the kindest thing in your case that you should never know. That you should go to your grave in ignorance."

Jurie Steyn said that he wished he was in his grave, then. The awful way he was feeling right at that moment, he said. And little bits that came into his mind, every so often, of what he had said in Oupa Bekker's house.

"Of what you said and *did*," Gysbert van Tonder corrected him, sternly.

Observing how bad Jurie Steyn was looking on it, Johnny Coen advised him not to take it too much to heart.

"We nearly all of us make fools of ourselves, after we've had a few," Johnny Coen said. "And it's no good saying about a person that he doesn't know where to stop. I mean, we none of us really know, do we, now? Of course, I'm not talking now about the way you were crying onto the stuffed likkewaan about the hard life you had had."

Jurie Steyn acknowledged, gloomily, that he had some sort of recollection of that part.

"No, that was all right," Johnny Coen proceeded. "And there was nothing wrong, either, when you were on the table, with that leopard skin fastened round your behind. As Oupa Bekker said, it was an old table, and that one leg had been broken before, in any case."

Jurie Steyn said that he remembered something about that, but not much. It was all kind of cloudy.

"And when you had the koedoe horns," Johnny Coen said, "well, we all realised that you weren't really able to see that there was a window there when you went butting like that with the koedoe horns."

Jurie Steyn turned bitter, then. And he said he just shouldn't have gone there, that was all. It wasn't civilised, he said, the way Oupa Bekker had got stuffed wild animals and lion skins and wild animals' horns stuck around all over his house.

With all those things in it, Oupa Bekker's house was more like a wild man's house, Jurie Steyn said.

274

"It was that, all right," At Naudé said quickly. "Last night it w
right. But you mustn't let it worry you too much, Jurie. It's like w
Johnny Coen said, that no good can come of a man taking it too muc.
to heart after he's – after he's made a pig of himself."

Jurie Steyn pointed out that Johnny Coen hadn't said all that – at
least not the pig part of it. So At Naudé said that if that thought gave Jurie Steyn any kind of satisfaction, then he was glad. It wasn't right that
a white man should lose all his feelings of self-respect, At Naudé said,
especially if it was a white man working in a Government department,
like in a post office, for instance.

And if it gave Jurie Steyn more confidence in himself to think that
Johnny Coen hadn't actually used the word pig, in talking about last
night, then it made him very happy, At Naudé said. It wasn't nice for
a man to lose all faith in himself, no matter how low he might sink in
the eyes of other people. Even though the other people were that man's
own neighbours, At Naudé added.

That started Oupa Bekker off on a dissertation to do with white
degeneracy in the Groot Marico, Oupa Bekker being able to illustrate
his remarks with authentic case histories that gave the name and age
and former occupation of a good number of white men who had come
to lose all sense of decency and shame in the Bushveld. Among these
abandoned wretches the name of one, Sass Koggel, featured prominently.

Oupa Bekker conveyed the depth of Sass Koggel's ultimate degrada-
tion in simple but graphic terms.

"Sass Koggel came to live, in the end," Oupa Bekker said, "in scum
and spit."

There seemed to be something about the Groot Marico, Oupa Bekker
declared, that made people go that way.

Strangely enough, Oupa Bekker's talk seemed to have just the opposite effect on Jurie Steyn from what we would have thought. Jurie Steyn
appeared to be getting cheered up a good deal. Indeed, the longer Oupa
Bekker's list of depraved local white men became, the more Jurie Steyn
seemed to brighten up under it. Then we learnt the reason.

"Anyway, Oupa Bekker," Jurie Steyn said after a while, "I know I'm
low. Even before you and the rest of you kêrels here came round this
afternoon and told me, I knew all that. Just from the bits that I could
remember about last night, I've been feeling what sort of a scum of the

I am – what sort of a low thing in human shape . . . What's that
re saying, Gysbert?"

"I said it's a pity you didn't find it out sooner," Gysbert van Tonder
repeated unabashed, taking advantage of Jurie Steyn's sudden and un-
expected access of modesty.

"Maybe," Jurie Steyn answered, and without heat, "but it was only
when Oupa Bekker started talking about other miserable wretches that
have been right here, in the Marico, that I didn't feel so bad anymore,
about it. I thought, well, perhaps I am just some kind of dregs, but I'm
not alone in being that. There have been others as low.

"And quite a good part of the population, too, to judge by Oupa
Bekker's list. And if they didn't mind being as bad and disgraceful as it
is possible for any human being to get, why should I want to think I'm
any better? Or why would I want Gysbert van Tonder, for instance, to
think I'm any better?"

But Gysbert van Tonder said that he didn't think Jurie Steyn was any
better than Sass Koggel. He never *had* thought so, Gysbert added.

"You've got no idea how Oupa Bekker's talk has relieved my mind,"
Jurie Steyn went on, beginning to sound almost like himself, again.
"I woke up this morning with the most terrible dronk verdriet. There
didn't seem to be any place for me in the whole world. I felt so disgust-
ing – dragged by my feet through the mud. I felt there was no place for
me anywhere among human beings.

"And now Oupa Bekker has mentioned all those other degraded
people who have lived in the Groot Marico at some time or other, and
that I feel I've got a place with. I'm not alone. I've got company. That's
the thing."

Turning to Oupa Bekker, Jurie Steyn asked: "That Sass Koggel that
you've been talking about, Oupa, he was a human being, at least, wasn't
he?"

Oupa Bekker reflected earnestly.

"Well, yes, I suppose so. Sort of," Oupa Bekker conceded at length.

"And so what was he was living in?" Jurie Steyn enquired. "What
you said, in scum and –"

"In scum," Oupa Bekker stated positively, "and spit."

"But then, I suppose he could have got out of it, too, some time, if he
wanted to?" Jurie Steyn asked.

Oupa Bekker shook his head.

"Not Sass," Oupa Bekker announced in a tone of finality, "not ⸺ Koggel."

"And did he mind about it much?" Jurie Steyn asked.

"Not," Oupa Bekker said, "Sass."

So Jurie Steyn said that that was all he wanted to know. And he wasn't going to care, either, he said, himself.

The real thing that had worried him about last night, Jurie Steyn continued – and he had been afraid to make mention of it, even, until now – were the awful dreams he had afterwards. They were the most terrible nightmares. He doubted if even Sass Koggel, at his worst, could have had nightmares like that, after drinking mampoer.

And he had been told that to get nightmares like that, after you had been to a party, was a sure sign that your mind was beginning to give way. But he wasn't worrying about that at all, anymore, Jurie Steyn said.

"As a matter of fact, one of those nightmares was even quite funny, come to think of it," Jurie Steyn went on. "It was a nightmare about a shark. And I suppose what brought a shark into my mind was all the stuffed wild animals Oupa Bekker has got in his house. And in this nightmare it was as though I was sitting on the beach in Durban, in a café, drinking a glass of lemonade.

"I mean, that's funny enough, isn't it? I mean, the idea of *me* drinking lemonade. And then a shark came right into the café where I was sitting, and started chewing on my leg. Now, isn't that silly? I mean, you couldn't imagine a thing like that happening in Durban, of all places, could you, now?"

We all laughed, then, and said that it was absurd to think that anybody would get bitten by a shark in Durban.

"And then, of all things," Jurie Steyn went on, "what do you think happened next? It was as though the Mchopi chief came past – the Mchopi chief that lives at Tweefontein. Well, you know how things get all mixed up in a nightmare, don't you? But that's about the most mixed-up thing I can think of. The Mchopi chief coming into the tea-room in Durban. How's that for a good one? But wait a bit, you've still got to hear the rest.

"The next thing was as if the shark started chewing up the Mchopi chief's leg, starting on his ankle, instead of chewing on my leg. And the last thing I can remember was that it was as if I was that shark. Yes, *me*. Now, how's that for a pretty wild sort of a nightmare?"

so we said, yes, it was pretty wild.

We also said that was one of the things about last night that it would have been better for Jurie Steyn not to have known about. But now that he had mentioned it himself, we might as well tell him, we said.

It was after Chris Welman had taken the leopard skin away from him, that Jurie Steyn decided he was going to be a shark, we said. And it was shortly after that that the Mchopi chief from Tweefontein came into Oupa Bekker's voorkamer about some long-horned cattle he wanted to sell. And why the Mchopi chief got such a surprise was because he didn't know that the party had been going on for some time.

"But the Mchopi chief was quite all right about it afterwards," Johnny Coen explained to Jurie Steyn. "After we had given him a beaker of mampoer to drink and some axle-grease to rub on the bitten place at the back of his leg."

VI

Oom Koos Nienaber, who owned the first motor car in the Marico Bushveld, Nietver-diend. 1964

The Terror of the Molopo

Oupa Bekker was camped out near Renosterpoort with Japie Uys on an afternoon of long ago when a stranger who was tall and dark came riding up to them from out of the bush. That was how he met Hubrecht Willemse, Oupa Bekker said to us.

"I didn't know the man who dismounted there where Japie Uys and I were resting," Oupa Bekker explained. "But I knew his horse. It was one of Koos Liebenberg's prize stallions. I also knew the saddle. It belonged to Gert Pretorius. And the suit the stranger had on was Krisjan Steyn's black church clothes."

Oupa Bekker said that he identified the suit by the mended place in the knee of the trousers from where Krisjan Steyn fell on the sidewalk in front of the Zeerust bar one Nagmaal. Why Krisjan Steyn fell was because of the half-dozen steps in front of the bar that he hadn't noticed on account of the heat.

"The stranger introduced himself as Hubrecht Willemse," Oupa Bekker added, "and he said he had been round the neighbourhood a bit. Well, a good bit, he could have said, I thought, judging from his suit and horse, not to mention Gert Pretorius's saddle.

"Japie Uys and I looked at each other. And I was glad I wasn't Japie. For Japie Uys was wearing a new pair of store boots that would be just about the stranger's size."

Oupa Bekker said that Hubrecht Willemse came and sat down on a fallen tree-trunk beside Japie Uys and himself. Hubrecht Willemse took off his hat and fanned himself with it.

"And I don't know whose hat it was," Oupa Bekker said, "although it looked so old and shapeless that I wouldn't be surprised if it was Hubrecht Willemse's own hat.

"But it was when we saw how short Hubrecht Willemse's hair had been cut that Japie Uys started apologising very fast for the uncomfortable tree-stump that Hubrecht Willemse had to sit on. There was a much better trunk he knew of just down the road, Japie Uys said, and he was already half-way disappearing into a clump of withaaks after it, when Hubrecht Willemse called him back pretty sharply.

"'None of that,' Hubrecht Willemse said when Japie Uys returned, looking sheepish. 'You're going to stay right here, both of you.'"

Oupa Bekker said that although it was a hot afternoon, yet, sitting there in the bush next to Hubrecht Willemse on a fallen tree-trunk, he actually found himself shivering. He didn't feel very different from a hollowed-out tree-trunk himself, Oupa Bekker said.

Then there was a sudden, cracking sound. The white ants had been at work in the inside of that tree-trunk, and so the wood gave way in one place, with the weight of three men on it. Nevertheless, both Oupa Bekker and Japie Uys jumped.

"When we sat down again," Oupa Bekker proceeded, "Hubrecht Willemse said to us, 'You know, I'm an escaped convict.' Just like that, he said it. Of course, that information did not come as much of a surprise to Japie Uys and myself. All the same, we thought that the stranger might feel better about it if we pretended to be astonished.

"So Japie Uys said, no, he just couldn't believe it. It was just about the last thing he would have imagined, Japie Uys assured Hubrecht Willemse. And I said to him that I thought he looked more like an insurance agent.

"Then remembering about a bit of unpleasantness that there had been with an insurance agent in those parts not so long ago, I said he looked more like a Senator, perhaps."

Oupa Bekker said that his words did not please Hubrecht Willemse as much as he thought they might.

"But it was Hubrecht Willemse's next remark that made me wonder if he was quite right in the head," Oupa Bekker continued. "I started thinking that the years he had spent behind prison walls, with just rice-water and singing hymns, must have turned his mind queer. I got a chillier feeling than ever between my shoulder-blades, then, in spite of the heat."

For Hubrecht Willemse told Oupa Bekker that the reason why the men from the landdrost's office would not be able to capture him was because he had the power to render himself invisible.

"Sometimes they don't see me at all," Hubrecht Willemse said to

Oupa Bekker. "Other times they think I'm somebody else. I've noticed it all the way through these parts. That's why I am glad that I'll be crossing the border soon.

"Because it's worrying me a bit, this thing. It's a power I didn't have before. It must be something that came to me without my knowing about it, this last time I was in prison. Maybe it was something I ate."

Oupa Bekker said that he thought to himself, then, that it was not so very surprising that the landdrost's men should make mistakes about Hubrecht Willemse's identity.

"I thought, well, if I had seen him from not so very nearby," Oupa Bekker said, "and I went just by the horse he was riding, then I might easily have taken him for Koos Liebenberg. Or, again, if I had seen him just walking, with the light not too good, and going by how he was dressed, then I might have thought he was Krisjan Steyn.

"So it was not so surprising that the landdrost's men, who did not have occasion to visit the Dwarsberg side of the Groot Marico often, should get a bit mixed up, perhaps, in looking for Hubrecht Willemse. Like if he should walk into a bar, for instance, carrying Gert Pretorius's saddle under his arm, I also thought."

In the meantime, Oupa Bekker said, Japie Uys had been sitting in an absent-minded way kicking at small pieces of leiklip in front of the stump.

"That's not the way to treat store boots," Hubrecht Willemse informed Japie Uys gruffly. "I can see they're good boots — almost new, by the look of them. But they won't look like that much longer, the way you're going on. What did you say your name was? Swanepoel?"

Oupa Bekker said he wondered if the stranger had been to Welgevonden, also.

"No," Japie Uys said, "my name is Uys. Japie Uys. But I don't mind if you would prefer to call me by some other name. It doesn't make any difference to me at all, really. You can just go on calling me Swanepoel, if you want."

"Well, look here, Uys," Hubrecht Willemse said. "That's not the thing to do — kicking stones around with store boots. If you want to kick stones, take your boots off, first, and kick the stones barefoot."

But Japie Uys said that he didn't really want to kick stones. He was doing it just without thinking, Japie Uys said.

Japie Uys went on to explain that why he was wearing his new boots at all, out on the veld like that, was because they were a bit tight and he wanted to walk them in. They still hurt him in a few places, he said, still.

"Where do they hurt you?" Hubrecht Willemse demanded.

Japie Uys said, well, in his feet, mostly.

"Well, they couldn't very well hurt you in your back——, could they?" Hubrecht Willemse burst out. "What part of your feet do your boots – I mean, those boots – still pinch?"

Japie Uys told him.

Oupa Bekker said that what went on during the next hour or so was most inhuman to watch. The way Hubrecht Willemse made Japie Uys walk and stamp and prance around on the most uneven pieces of ground he could find, Japie Uys having to take particular care that the uppers of the boots did not get scratched by wag-'n-bietjie thorns, and Hubrecht Willemse calling Japie Potgieter, all the time.

"Afterwards, when Hubrecht Willemse rode off, wearing Japie Uys's boots and leaving his own worn veldskoens behind," Oupa Bekker said, "Japie Uys, with his exhaustion and sore feet, was about the most suffering-looking white man I had ever seen.

"And the awful time he had gone through made him do quite a strange thing. For the moment Hubrecht Willemse had galloped out of sight Japie Uys rose up and took a flying kick, with his bare foot, at a piece of leiklip."

Japie Uys collapsed forward onto his face, then, Oupa Bekker said, and he didn't move again until about sunset. And what Japie Uys said about Hubrecht Willemse, then, Oupa Bekker added, was most unchristian.

It was next day, Oupa Bekker said, that he saw for himself something of that mysterious power that Hubrecht Willemse spoke about having, whereby Hubrecht Willemse could become invisible or could appear to be somebody quite different.

"We were again sitting on that tree-stump," Oupa Bekker said, "Japie Uys having his feet wrapped in pieces of sacking that we had in the mule-cart. And Japie Uys was talking a good deal about Hubrecht Willemse, mostly about what he would like to do to him."

A horseman again drew up in front of them, Oupa Bekker said, and came and joined them on the tree-stump. But this time they recognised the visitor. It was the veldkornet, who had been sent from the landdrost's office on the escaped convict's trail.

"Japie Uys and I were both very glad to see the veldkornet," Oupa Bekker said, "and the veldkornet was able to tell us a lot about Hubrecht Willemse, whom he described as a dangerous character. But we knew that much without the veldkornet telling us. 'Whatever he wants he just takes, and he doesn't care how,' the veldkornet said. That, too, we knew."

The veldkornet went on to say that in the records of the landdrost's office Hubrecht Willemse was known as the Terror of the Molopo.

"What, has he been there as well?" Japie Uys said.

"No," the veldkornet replied, "but that's where he's headed for. And if he's not going to be a holy terror there, in the Molopo, then I don't know. But it's outside our district, and the quicker he gets there, the better we'll all like it, I can tell you."

Oupa Bekker said that he thought that was a very peculiar way for a veldkornet to talk. Never mind about wanting to call Hubrecht Willemse the Terror of the Molopo, Oupa Bekker thought, why, he was enough of a Terror of the Marico. Oupa Bekker tried to suggest something along those lines to the veldkornet.

"Well, if he gets into the Molopo, then it's *their* look-out," was all the veldkornet would say.

The veldkornet wasn't even much interested, Oupa Bekker said, in the veldskoens that Hubrecht Willemse had left behind, and to which Japie Uys directed the veldkornet's attention, saying that if the veldkornet smelt them, it might help to put him on the trail of the escaped convict.

"But the veldkornet said that wouldn't help much," Oupa Bekker went on. "When once Hubrecht Willemse had got across the Molopo, it wasn't so very far from there to the Bechuanaland border. Yes, he wouldn't be at all surprised if Hubrecht Willemse was almost out of the Transvaal by now."

Oupa Bekker said that, in spite of his feet, Japie Uys laughed, then. You couldn't get to the Bechuanaland border that way, Japie Uys said. Not at that time of the year, you couldn't. The only way was through the Renosterpoort. And from where he was sitting on the stump, Japie Uys pointed out the Renosterpoort to the veldkornet.

"That scoundrel Willemse will have to come right back here, again, along that same road," Japie Uys said, gleefully. "He'll have to. There's no other way. And that's when you'll get him. The blisters and skinned places on my feet don't feel quite so sore, now. What's more, Hubrecht Willemse will be coming past here again, quite soon."

Just then another cracking sound came from the hollowed-out tree-trunk. This time it was the veldkornet that jumped up suddenly, Oupa Bekker said.

"And later on that same afternoon it was proved to us that Hubrecht Willemse did have those ghostly powers that he claimed," Oupa Bekker added. "For Hubrecht Willemse came back again along that road, as Japie Uys had said he would. And from a long way off we pointed him out to the veldkornet. But the veldkornet just couldn't see him at all.

"And when, afterwards, Hubrecht Willemse got so near that the veldkornet just had to see him, the veldkornet said that it didn't look like Hubrecht Willemse to him in the least.

"It looked more like a Senator he knew, the veldkornet remarked when Hubrecht Willemse had gone past, and the sound of galloping hooves was dying in the distance."

Border Bad Man

Gysbert van Tonder was talking about the new young mounted policeman who went galloping past while he and Frits Nienaber were
outspanned alongside of the Government Road, a few days before. It
was partly at the off-mule's suggestion that they had outspanned at
about that spot.

"The off-mule stood right up on his hind legs," Gysbert van Tonder
said, "to show us how tired he was. We knew that the next thing the
off-mule would do, on account of his being fatigued, would be to drag
the mule-cart off the road and right up the side of the koppie, and with
nobody to help him, either. For the steeper a koppie is, the better that
mule likes to drag a cart up over it, when he's real tired."

And it was while Gysbert van Tonder and Frits Nienaber were outspanned by the side of the road that the new policeman on border patrol went past.

"He didn't even notice us," Gysbert van Tonder said. "We could see
that that new policeman was in a hurry to get somewhere. He didn't
even see the mule, I don't think. Of course, he's new –"

Then Oupa Bekker mentioned another occasion on which a border
patrolman came and assumed duty in the Marico for the first time.

"Of course, I am talking of very long ago, now," Oupa Bekker said,
"and the patrolman's name was Duvenhage, and we could see that they
had explained to him in Pretoria that his most important work would
be to put down the awful cattle-smuggling that was going on here, in
those days."

"Oh, yes, in those days, of course," Gysbert van Tonder said, quickly.

Jurie Steyn took Gysbert van Tonder up at once.

"What do you mean by saying 'in those days', like that?" Jurie Steyn
asked. "What about that bunch of cattle with wide horns and that are
all colours that you've got in the camp by the kloof, there, right now? I

suppose you'll tell us next that you bought them on the Johannesburg market. And how's it Frits Nienaber has about the same-looking collection of beasts on *his* side of the kloof? One thing I must say, is that the two of you seem to have divided up pretty equally. You seem to have been honest there, anyhow."

"And I expect that's why you keep that herd in the kloof," Chris Welman observed to Gysbert van Tonder sarcastically, "it's because they are a sort of cows and oxen that don't like to have people come prying into their affairs."

"Especially when they've still got Bechuanaland Protectorate clay between their hooves," Jurie Steyn remarked. "Turf-clay."

So Gysbert van Tonder said that they would have to prove it. And so Jurie Steyn told us what he would have done if he had been a border patrol policeman instead of a postmaster.

And then Gysbert said that if Jurie Steyn sorted out hoofprints in the dust like he sorted letters in his post office then you could bring Bechuanaland cattle across the Convention line in broad daylight.

Thereupon Oupa Bekker said what a queer thing it was that there should be so much jealousy among Marico farmers.

"I mean there isn't one of us wouldn't smuggle in a few head of cattle if he got a chance," Oupa Bekker said, "and yet when you hear of our neighbour doing it – and you yourself didn't do it, that time – and you picture to yourself a herd of all sorts of cattle crowded against the barbed-wire fence on one side of your neighbour's farm and sniffing the wind from the Protectorate, and lowing, why, you get pretty mad about it. It's almost like you're also pawing the polgras with your hooves, sniffing the wind that blows from Bechuanaland."

We could not but admit that there was much truth in Oupa Bekker's words. At the same time – as Chris Welman pointed out, then – there was such a thing as overdoing this cattle-smuggling business. And it was people that overdid it that gave all Marico farmers a bad name, he said.

Gysbert van Tonder sniffed. It was a different type of sniff from the kind Oupa Bekker had been talking about.

"A bad name," Gysbert van Tonder said, his lip curling, "well, there are some people sitting here in this voorkamer now that would give any district that they stayed in a bad name, just by living in it. If they lived in the Cape Peninsula, it would get a bad name. And you can't tell me there's any cattle-smuggling going on in the Cape Peninsula. Unless you can smuggle in cattle off ships."

Gysbert van Tonder grew thoughtful after that last remark. It was as though he was considering the possibilities.

"But there was a thing, now," Oupa Bekker said, getting back to the subject of Patrolman Duvenhage, of the old days, "I mean, the Justice Department sending a man who had been on the Illicit Diamond staff at Kimberley to come and keep watch on the Transvaal border. I suppose the Transvaal Government thought that a man who had had a job like that in the Cape must know a thing or two. They didn't want somebody just raw, I suppose.

"Well, I'll say this much for Duvenhage. There wasn't much smuggling being carried on by Marico farmers during the time he was a patrolman. Only, he didn't stay here very long after there was that trouble about the railway consignment notes."

Chris Welman said that, although he knew it had all happened very long ago, he did have some sort of recollection of it. It was like something he had been told in his childhood.

"Wasn't Duvenhage the patrolman that was caught smuggling quite a big herd of cattle across the border?" Chris Welman asked. "With his police-boys helping him? I seem to remember something about it. The police-boys were singing Bechuana cattle-songs, the white policeman joining in."

"Yes, the same," Oupa Bekker replied. "And I still remember my first meeting with him. He asked me *where was their hangout*. And when I said I didn't know what he meant, he said the cattle-smuggling kings. The heads in the game, he explained. He wanted to know where they sat talking and drinking."

Oupa Bekker said that he could see from that that Patrolman Duvenhage's training on the Illicit Diamond staff in Kimberley had been of such a nature as to leave him somewhat out of touch with conditions in the Groot Marico Bushveld.

"I mean, I couldn't go and tell him that there wasn't such a thing as a gang of foreign cattle-smugglers working in these parts," Oupa Bekker said. "After all, we all know that if there is such a thing as a few head of cattle being brought across the line on a night when there isn't much of a moon, well, then we know it can be almost any Marico farmer trying to do a bit of good for himself.

"And we know that there is no particular place where that Marico farmer will go and sit and drink and talk about it, afterwards.

"The only place where a Marico farmer might have a drink would be in the Zeerust bar at Nagmaal. And then he would only talk about the crops, or about the Dominee's sermon, or about how he's got the laziest bywoner on this side of the Dwarsberge, and that that bywoner has got the impudence to be making eyes at his daughter."

Oupa Bekker went on to explain the details of a piece of strategy that he and his partner, Japie Krige, had thought up to get Patrolman Duvenhage out of the way on a night when they were going to smuggle cattle into the Transvaal.

"I wrote a note to Japie Krige," Oupa Bekker said, "and in the note I told Japie Krige exactly where he had to be at Derdepoort, at midnight, with the wire-cutters.

"And Japie Krige helped me to write the letter. And we laughed quite a lot. We laughed especially at that bit in the letter where I said how careful Japie Krige had to be of that new patrolman, Duvenhage, because he was such a fine asset to the force and had eyes like a hawk.

"We were laughing to think of how proud Duvenhage would be of himself when he read that letter. Then we explained to a Mchopi messenger how he must walk past the police station in a suspicious way, so that Patrolman Duvenhage would be sure to arrest him, and find the letter on him."

In the meantime, Oupa Bekker said, he would be sitting quietly at home, and his partner, Japie Krige, would be driving cattle towards the boundary fence, and at the right moment a Bechuana would come and call him, and in the starlight they would cut the barbed wires of the fence and bring the cattle across.

And during all that while Patrolman Duvenhage would be lying on the veld miles away, at Derdepoort, next to a swamp. And why Patrolman Duvenhage would be thinking all the time of his bed at the police station, while he was lying by the swamp, was not because of the pillow on the bed, but because the bed had a mosquito net round it.

"But that evening," Oupa Bekker said, "when it was not a Bechuana from Japie Krige that came to my door, but Patrolman Duvenhage, then I knew that there was something wrong."

All the same, Oupa Bekker said, he could tell by Patrolman Duvenhage's manner that he had not come to arrest him.

"Duvenhage walked straight into my voorkamer and didn't even take his helmet off," Oupa Bekker said. "And when my little yellow brak pup snapped at him, Patrolman Duvenhage landed out one with his boot that sent the yellow brak pup flying through the door and then it travelled about a hundred yards up the road before it turned round to let out a yelp. I could tell from those signs that Patrolman Duvenhage didn't have a case against me."

So Gysbert van Tonder said, yes, he knew. It was when a border patrolman came to your house and was polite, that you had to watch out. It was when a patrolman patted your youngest son on the head, and asked him what class he was in – professing surprise that he should be so far advanced with his education – that the next thing the patrolman would say to you was to get your jacket.

Oupa Bekker said that Patrolman Duvenhage had come pretty straight to the point.

"After that Mchopi messenger had crawled about four times through the same stretch of thorns behind the police station," Patrolman Duvenhage said to Oupa Bekker, "I decided to give him a break. So I went up to him and kicked him twice, and told him to hand over the letter. Because I knew that was what he wanted. I mean, it's an old stunt on the diamond fields."

Oupa Bekker said he could see, from that, that there was an unkind streak in Patrolman Duvenhage. Thinking it was funny to let that Mchopi go on crawling through the thorns all that time, when he could have gone and dealt with him right away.

But it was when Patrolman Duvenhage started talking about how much there would be in it for himself, that an unhappy note crept back into the conversation, Oupa Bekker said. For Patrolman Duvenhage spoke very emphatically about what he called a rake-off, a word Oupa Bekker had not heard of, until then.

"When Japie Krige arrived about midnight with the herd of smuggled cattle, the drovers singing their chorus of a Bechuana cattle-song," Oupa Bekker went on, "Japie Krige came into my voorkamer prepared to be very indignant because I had not assisted him at the fence.

"But when he saw who it was, sitting opposite me at the table, Japie Krige turned very white. And I have never seen a man hide a pair of wire-cutters behind his back quicker than what Japie Krige did then.

But Patrolman Duvenhage did not even bother to look up from the figures that he was working out on a piece of paper.

"But one thing I will say is that Japie Krige and I never brought any more cattle over the line while Duvenhage was the patrolman. We just couldn't, I mean. Patrolman Duvenhage's percentage of rake-off, that he worked out for us on paper, was too high. In the end, the only man left in the business *was* Patrolman Duvenhage. I often wonder how it was that he came to lose his job in Kimberley, though."

In the silence that followed, Jurie Steyn seemed to be doing a bit of quick thinking.

"What you said at the start," Jurie Steyn said to Gysbert van Tonder, "about you and Frits Nienaber there by the roadside, last week, and this new policeman riding past, and him not seeing you. Maybe it was that you didn't want him to see you, I'm thinking. I suppose you were hiding in the bush, you and Frits Nienaber."

Gysbert van Tonder asked Jurie Steyn what gave him that idea.

"The Bechuana cattle in your camp by the kloof," Jurie replied. "And this new policeman riding so fast. And I can guess where he was going to, as well – yes, to Derdepoort. All the same, I'd like to know what you said about him in the letter to Frits Nienaber that the policeman took off your messenger."

"I wrote in the letter," Gysbert van Tonder declared solemnly, "that Frits Nienaber must be on his guard, because the new policeman was a fine asset to the force and had eyes like a hawk. And to think that he rode right past us, on his way to Derdepoort, and didn't even see the off-mule."

KITH AND KIN

One of the passengers to alight from the Government lorry at Jurie Steyn's post office that afternoon was At Naudé, who had gone to the Cape for the funeral of his uncle Ockert Sybrand Naudé, who was reputed to be very rich.

One circumstance that made his neighbours take it for granted that Ockert Sybrand was in a prosperous way was that he never smoked a cigarette unless you offered him one.

Similarly, he would never have a drink in a bar unless it was stood him. For that reason (human nature being what it is) more than one Western Province farmer felt honoured at being allowed to buy Ockert Sybrand a drink or to give him a cigarette.

Another sign that At Naudé's uncle bore about him of unusual affluence was that he had only two shirts and one pair of trousers. He had a jacket, too, but he was very modest about it. He didn't *count* it as a jacket anymore, hardly, Ockert Sybrand used to say – not since the time when a goat ate up so much of the back part of it, on the occasion on which he had hung the jacket on the line for the wind to blow out some of the mould.

"But in this area of the Western Province you don't *need* a lot of clothes," Ockert Sybrand used to explain. "I mean, as long as it's a clean piece of shirt showing under the missing part of my jacket at the back, well, then my jacket is still good enough for wearing at Nagmaal."

If a man could talk in that way, in the Cape Western Province, then there was no need for you to go and interview the bank manager to find out what his financial standing was. You just knew, out of Ockert Sybrand's own mouth, that he must be well away.

When At Naudé, alighting from the Government lorry, stepped into Jurie Steyn's voorkamer there was a healthy glow on his face. The trip to the Cape seemed to have done him good.

"Did it – did it pass off – properly?" Jurie Steyn asked when At Naudé had sat down. Jurie Steyn got just that exact tone in his voice that one uses for obsequies and bereavements. "The – the rites?"

Plegtigheid, was the word Jurie Steyn used, and when he said it there was that in his voice that made it seem, for the moment, as though Jurie Steyn was wearing a black jacket of formal cut and with the stiff edges of a white collar pressing into his chin. You couldn't help thinking, in contrast, of the deceased's own Nagmaal jacket, with important parts missing, on account of that goat. It was an unhappy picture.

"There wasn't any funeral," At Naudé declared, looking down at the floor.

If he was standing at his uncle Ockert Sybrand's graveside, and was talking, then, At Naudé could not have sounded more solemn.

"He pulled through, after all," At Naudé added.

At Naudé spoke of his uncle's recovery with an air of dejected finality that one reserves for conversing about the dead.

"Oh, he got well, did he, At? Your uncle is all right now, hey?" Jurie Steyn asked.

And this time, in Jurie Steyn's speech there was genuine condolence. There was none of that affectation of sympathy that you've got to wear a black jacket with the lapels ironed smooth on a kitchen table for. Jurie Steyn extended to At Naudé the heartfelt sympathy of one man in shirtsleeves to another.

"Isn't it a bastard?" Jurie said, simply.

At Naudé cheered up quite a lot, then. A good deal of that healthy glow – that we had noticed on him when he stepped off the lorry and that seemed to fade afterwards – came back into his face.

"Well, when I heard that my uncle Ockert Sybrand was pretty sick," At Naudé explained, "I of course went down to the Cape to see. I mean, seeing that he never got married, it was only right that somebody of his family should be there at the last. Or even a bit before the last."

Even a good bit before the last, Chris Welman agreed, nodding his head.

"In case my dying uncle got swindled," At Naudé went on. "Him being so old and all, and never having been married. If my uncle Ockert Sybrand died with a next of kin sitting leaning right over him, with his hand up to his ear to catch his last words, well, my uncle would know right away then that there was nobody around to swindle him."

But At Naudé said that when he got to that farm in the Western Cape Province with the old oak-trees bending over the road to the house and with the white curved gables and the squirrels and with the benches on the long stoep, he received a nasty surprise. He had already decided where to have one of those benches shifted so that you got more sun in the forenoon when you drank your coffee, with your feet raised, At Naudé said, when that surprise came to him.

"For when I got to the front door, who should open it for me but my second cousin, Seraphima, with three of her younger children with dirty faces hanging onto her dress?" At Naudé said. "And Seraphima asked me what I wanted. Well, I could see from that that my uncle was sick, all right. Real sick, I mean."

At Naudé said that, on the way to the dwelling house, he had already gathered that Ockert Sybrand was far from well. He gathered that much from the hushed way in which the Cape Coloured farm-workers comported themselves, At Naudé said, sitting in little groups under the old oak-trees playing cards.

"That was a sure sign to me that the master was ill," At Naudé said. "For otherwise they would be cheerily working in the lands with spades and hoes. But now they just didn't have the heart for it. All they could bring themselves to do was to sit in the shade and play cards for money.

"One of the coloured farm-workers was so moved that he was even playing a little tune on a guitar, standing up against a tree. He was playing 'Hier Kom die Alabama'. He was doing it just because the master was sick, of course. And I had the feeling, somehow, that if my uncle *saw* him at it, my uncle Ockert Sybrand would have got still a lot more sick."

Anyway, At Naudé said that, in reply to his second cousin Seraphima's question, he asked her, in turn, what it was that *she* wanted. And she said that, with Ockert Sybrand dying, it was only right that, in his last hour, he should have his next of kin around him, sitting over him and listening to what he had to say about who was to get what.

"Of course, my cousin Seraphima always had such an uneducated way of talking," At Naudé said. "And, I thought, yes, with her whole family around to listen, there wouldn't be much that they would miss, about who was to get what. It seemed that it was going to be a pretty awful sort of death-bed that my uncle was going to have, with such a lot of vultures around him, some with dirty faces, too.

"So I said I was surprised that she hadn't brought her husband, Agie, along as well, Agie being a shift boss on the mines and well out of the way, then, as I thought. About a thousand miles by rail, I thought, and the better part of a mile by that hoist thing that they have over a mine shaft.

"'Agie,' my cousin Seraphima said to me, 'is here, too.'"

So At Naudé said that he thought that, well, that was that. And it was without much enthusiasm that he walked into his uncle Ockert Sybrand's bedroom. And when he saw that his uncle wasn't lying flat down but was sitting up against some pillows, he felt less perky than ever, At Naudé said.

"I talked to my uncle a little and I offered him a cigarette, which," At Naudé went on, "he took. And my uncle said that, seeing there were only a few left in the packet, he might as well keep the packet.

"There was no doubt that my uncle was sick. But I felt, then, that he wasn't so sick that he wouldn't be able to pull himself round. From the firm way he took the cigarettes off me, I felt that he would still be wearing that awful jacket to Nagmaal."

But that part of his visit to his uncle's farm over which he would draw a veil, At Naudé said, was his meeting with his second cousin Seraphima's husband, Agie, the shift boss on a Johannesburg mine.

"I had several times asked one or other of the coloured farm-workers if they had seen another white baas around the place, somewhere," At Naudé said. "But they were too concerned about their master's illness to be able to answer me. All they said was 'Straight flush' or 'Full house' or 'Jy moet straight deal' to each other."

Nor would he like to repeat the reply he got, At Naudé said, from a couple of coloured workers who, when he approached them with his question, were, at the time, in the shade of a very old oak-tree, fighting with knives.

"It was only towards evening," At Naudé said, "that I was able to find an elderly coloured farm-worker who could conduct me to where my second cousin Seraphima's husband, Agie, was. The elderly coloured farm-worker put the finger of one hand against the left side of his nose. We went down by a lot of old stone steps. But I hardly recognised my second cousin Seraphima's husband, Agie.

"He was standing with his legs apart and he looked almost as bad as my uncle Ockert Sybrand, then. You have got no idea how changed he was from when I had seen him last. At first I thought it must be my cousin Seraphima. Then I thought it must be the mines. But it was only when Agie spoke that I realised that it was neither.

"'There's,' Agie said, stretching his legs still further apart and waving a tin pannikin at me, 'barrels of that stuff here.'"

At Naudé said that he would rather not recount the more unhappy features of his visit to that Western Province farm. What made it worse, At Naudé said, was that they were having their annual wine festival at the town some little distance away. And Agie insisted on At Naudé accompanying him into town on a good number of occasions.

"They had girls in the street, laughing," At Naudé said. "And they had wagons with grapes and people with big paper heads. And there was a merry-go-round and a thing that went round and up and sideways that they called the Octopus.

"And young fellows and the girls that a little while before had been laughing in the street went for rides on those things. But they didn't seem to laugh in the same way when they gòt off them again. Not when they got off the Octopus, they didn't."

But all this talk of At Naudé's did not seem to be leading anywhere. We were consequently glad when Chris Welman brought him back to the point.

"Your uncle Sybrand, now," Chris Welman asked. "Did he get quite well again?"

"Quite well?" At Naudé repeated. "Why, that was the whole trouble. He got so well that we just couldn't keep him off the Octopus. It got so bad, him and that Octopus – him wanting to go for rides, all the time – that life wasn't worth living anymore, afterwards, for me and Agie. And my uncle Ockert Sybrand was with that Octopus like he was with cigarettes. We had to pay for him, every time – me and Agie."

Nevertheless Jurie Steyn said that, taken all in all, he didn't think At Naudé had done so badly. Jurie Steyn said that in a significant way. For it was after At Naudé had spoken of his meeting with Agie in the wine cellar, that we had all of us started putting two and two together about that healthy glow on At Naudé's face.

"Did you bring any of it with you?" Chris Welman asked.

"Yes," At Naudé said, somewhat lamely. "A few bottles in my suitcase."

"Then why didn't you say so sooner?" Jurie Steyn asked. "Instead of wasting our time with that Octopus talk."

We all started feeling kith and kin of one another, then, with At Naudé opening the suitcase.

Rolled Gold

It was about the first time young Vermaak had come to visit us in Jurie Steyn's post office since his marriage to Pauline Gerber. We could see, in several ways, the difference it had already made to the schoolmaster to be married to the daughter of a wealthy Bushveld farmer like old Gerber.

For one thing, young Vermaak was now smoking expensive cigarettes out of a cigarette case made of a yellowish metal that he passed round to us so that we could each help ourselves to a cigarette and at the same time see the big curved lines of his initials engraved on the lid.

We knew that the schoolmaster's initials had certainly not been by any means so important before he had married Pauline Gerber.

"If I had a cigarette case like that," Gysbert van Tonder said to young Vermaak, in handing it back to him, "I wouldn't have the letters of my Christian name and my surname cut into it so big and so fat. And so *deep*. I mean, think of how much gold gets scooped off it, that way. It's a wonder the Zeerust watchmaker that did the job didn't write his own name on it as well, and his address, so that he could prune off a whole lot more gold for himself. Just lopping it off in chunks like that, I mean."

Young Vermaak gazed at Gysbert van Tonder with a thin smile.

If the jeweller's graver had been set as shallow there would have been no mark at all made on the cigarette-case lid.

"It wasn't a Zeerust watchmaker," young Vermaak announced. "My monogram was engraved by a Johannesburg firm.

"I don't know whether I should not give up teaching for a while," he said. "I would like to improve my mind so that I can fit in better in the world of intellect and culture. I want to have breadth to my mind and outlook. I have been reading a book in which are described those cramping influences that fetter the spirit like a vinculum. A vinculum is the Latin word for a chain."

299

Gysbert van Tonder said that if that was all that was worrying the schoolmaster, then he was certainly in the right place, now, at Welgevonden, for being able to enlarge his knowledge of the world. Oom Petrus Gerber, young Vermaak's father-in-law, Gysbert van Tonder said, was easily the most broad-minded man in this part of the Marico.

"I mean, just take the way Oom Petrus Gerber made all his money," Gysbert van Tonder proceeded. "Well, if that's not broad-minded, then I don't know. I mean, the Bechuanas as far as Malopolole know how broad-minded Oom Petrus Gerber is to this day about what brand marks there are on the cattle that he brings back to the Transvaal. That is why the Bechuanas have given him the name of Ra-Sakeng. It means 'He-Who-Walks-Too-Near-the-Cattle-Kraal'. And if Oom Petrus can teach you a few things in that line, then maybe you will get just as broadminded. Only, I think your father-in-law will tell you that the police pay more attention today than they did in the old days to a Bechuana's complaint about missing cattle.

"So you should perhaps not start getting too broad-minded, straight away. Otherwise you'll find your wrists fastened together with a – what was that foreign word you said?"

"Vinculum," interjected At Naudé, who was quick at picking up languages.

After an interval of silence, the schoolmaster, having first self-consciously cleared his throat, proceeded to deal with the matters on which we could sense he had really come to enlighten us.

"I have booked for a number of the Grand Operas in Johannesburg," he said. "I feel that will open up a new world of culture to me. Vision is what I'll get, I think."

We could see, from the way Gysbert van Tonder opened his mouth, that Gysbert was going to ask if that was a new word for time.

"It's some of the true glory of European culture coming here to South Africa," young Vermaak went on quickly, before Gysbert van Tonder could make any more disguised reference to the penalties for cattle-theft.

"And I think I'll be a better schoolteacher and more of a credit to the Education Department for having gone. You've got to wear an evening dress-suit with tails."

That was how you had to go to the Grand Opera in Johannesburg today, the schoolmaster added. And that was what gave Chris Welman, who had once worked on the mines, *his* chance to be sarcastic.

"I suppose you've also got to carry the right sort of dinner-pail," Chris Welman said, thinking of the times when he had been wont to present himself for the night-shift at No. 3 shaft (and of how his colleagues would laugh at an underground man who wasn't de règle, but had his sandwiches wrapped in an odd piece of newspaper). "And I suppose you've also got to wear at the opera the right kind of bicycle clips with your evening dress-suit pants."

Nevertheless – no matter what we might have pretended to the contrary – the fact was that we stood in a good deal of awe of what young Vermaak had said about the culture of Europe.

It was in recognition of this that Jurie Steyn, as though doffing his hat to the traditions of old cities, enquired of the schoolmaster, reluctantly, as to what an opera was, exactly.

So young Vermaak got his chance to spread himself, after all.

"An opera," he said, "is a play, just like *Vertrapte Harte* or *Die Dominee se Verlossing* or *Liefde op die Ashoop*. It's like any play they have in the hall next to the flour-mill at Bekkersdal, except that it's all songs and music.

"When the warder tells the condemned man that that noise of falling bricks is the hangman's footsteps on the stairs, the warder *sings* it. And when the condemned man gets a sack pulled over his head before being hanged – like in the play *Frikkie se Laaste Ongeluk* – then the condemned man comes to the front of the stage and sings his last words.

"But what it sounds like, coming through a black sack, and all, I wouldn't know. I've just learnt about operà from reading books about it. That is why I would like to see how it is actually done on the stage."

Gysbert van Tonder looked pleased with himself, suddenly. It seemed as though he had not been too far wrong, in having warned the schoolmaster of the dangers that lay in being too broad-minded.

"You don't only get those vinculum things on your feet, from having your ideas go too wide," Gysbert van Tonder assured young Vermaak, solemnly. "There's that sack over your head, also. It's how one thing just sort of leads to another."

The schoolmaster flared up, then. He said he hadn't come to Jurie Steyn's post office to be insulted. And here was Gysbert van Tonder talking about him as though he were already a cattle-smuggler and a cattle-thief – and worse. A lot worse, the schoolmaster added – thinking, no doubt, of that sack.

Thereupon At Naudé advised young Vermaak to ignore Gysbert van Tonder. *He* needn't talk, was the way At Naudé phrased it. In any case, At Naudé said, we were all eager to learn more about opera, and if people in operas got vinculums put on them, also, well, he was sure it was for more high-minded things than just cattle-smuggling and stock-theft.

But the schoolmaster said that, strangely enough, from what he had read in his book, there was one opera that *was* just like that, more or less.

The cattle part, he said, came in in the scene that was called "Exterior of the Bull-fighting Arena". And he said that when that opera was first produced in Paris or Munich or Rome or Sweden, or somewhere – (he forgot *where*, exactly, now, but it was some foreign place . . . Moscow, likely) – then when the curtain went up on the "Exterior of the Bull-fighting Arena" scene, the audience all applauded when they heard a bellowing, because they expected that a real live bull would come prancing onto the stage right up to the footlights.

But the audience were very disappointed when they found that it was just the Basso-Profondo at the back of the stage practising some notes, arpeggios, the schoolmaster called them.

"And it's queer," young Vermaak went on, "but there actually is a scene in that opera, too, that is called 'Mountain Retreat of the Smugglers'. Only, there is a beautiful girl in that Mountain Retreat, and she is concerned only with the pleasure and the passion of the passing moment."

Well, that was something like, Chris Welman said.

Several of us sat up very straight on our riempies chairs, then, to hear more. That was something quite new to us. It looked as though those Europeans had something, after all.

"She makes them aware of her charms," young Vermaak went on.

Yes, quite, we thought.

It was certainly something that had never come the way of a Bushveld farmer on a cloudy night when he had cut some strands of barbed wire to let a herd of cattle into the Transvaal.

We doubted whether anything like that had ever happened even to Oom Petrus Gerber himself, although everybody *knew* how lucky he was in such matters. In matters relating to cattle-smuggling, that was.

"This opera is full of colour and movement," the schoolmaster went on.

And we thought, yes, we could believe that. We could also understand young Vermaak having booked seats, then, even though it was all just music and singing.

"Then a gentle peasant girl arrives with a message for the officer who is now a smuggler," the schoolmaster proceeded.

Well, we didn't really care *what* he was – whether he was an officer or anything else – before he became a smuggler. Nor were we much interested to hear about that devout peasant girl, either. It was that other one that the schoolmaster couldn't tell us enough about.

"It's a very moving song that the smuggler who was once an officer sings," young Vermaak continued. "I am looking forward to hearing it. He sings it by a hole in the wall. It's through reading the message that that simple-minded girl brings him."

The schoolmaster spoke a good deal more about opera, after that. But somehow, it never sounded quite the same again as when he first started.

Even what he said about the lovely Rhine-maiden with the lily in her hair didn't come up to the level of that other one.

All the same, as the schoolmaster went on speaking, our attitude towards him began to change, in a singular way, with the result that we started feeling more human about him, and it seemed that there was something in what he called European culture, after all.

The result was that he afterwards set our feelings at rest with quite simple words.

"I am going to the opera in Johannesburg with my own money," the schoolmaster said, "that I have saved up. I know I sort of tried to lie to you at the start.

"But I don't want you to think I've changed just because I've now got a rich father-in-law. I wouldn't take his money, even if –"

"Even if he offered you some," Gysbert van Tonder said, trying to sound sardonic.

Young Vermaak smiled.

"Yes," he said, "even if he offered me some – which he hasn't. And this cigarette case of mine is only rolled gold. What's more, it *was* engraved by a Zeerust watchmaker. What Joburg engraver can make scrolls and flourishes like that today, I mean? Here, take a look."

303

HOME TOWN

O upa Bekker told us about how he had once gone back – very many years later – to revisit a village where he had lived as a child. Jurie Steyn asked him how many years, but he did not answer. He pretended to be too deaf to hear Jurie Steyn's question.

That was a peculiarity of Oupa Bekker's. He not infrequently, by implication, made claims to great age. But he never allowed himself to be pinned down into stating how old he actually was in terms of years. It seemed that he wanted to give himself a certain measure of room for manoeuvering in, on that score.

Nor did Oupa Bekker acquaint us with the name of the little place that he went back to have a look at after an interval of many years. But that did not matter. Since, for each of us, they were the remembered scenes of our own childhood, that Oupa Bekker spoke about.

"Of course, there was a railway station, now, which there of course hadn't been before," Oupa Bekker said.

"Yes, and tarred streets and a filling station with petrol pumps," Chris Welman said.

"And a fish and chips shop and a milk bar with high stools," Gysbert van Tonder said.

"And where there had been an old garden wall of red brick with honeysuckle growing over it –" Jurie Steyn began.

"No, not honeysuckle," Chris Welman interrupted him, "but a creeper with those broad leaves and blue flowers. I forget what it's called, now."

"And the wall isn't red brick," Gysbert van Tonder said, "but a whitewashed earth wall."

They were in general agreement, however, that whatever building had been erected on the site of that old garden wall must be something pretty awful, anyway.

Oupa Bekker took our remarks in bad part.

"Who's telling this – me or the lot of you?" he asked.

Then he went on to say that from the station there was a bit of a rise before you got to the village itself.

"And so you decided to walk," Jurie Steyn said, "so you could enjoy each moment of it, recalling how you had run over the veld there as a carefree boy."

"Yes," Oupa Bekker snapped. "That's what I did do. I did walk. But the way you're carrying on I'm sorry now I didn't take a taxi, instead."

That shut Jurie Steyn up for a while. And so Oupa Bekker told us how, having deposited his suitcase in the railway cloakroom, he set off along that road, which was tarred now (as Chris Welman had said it would be), and there was a soft wind blowing that was always there, on the rise, when in the village in the hollow the air was very still.

And Oupa Bekker said that he thought what a strange thing it was that, after all those years, the same wind should still be there. You think of the wind as something that blows and is gone, Oupa Bekker said. And yet after so many long years there, on the rise, there that wind still was, and not changed in any way.

So Chris Welman said that was how it always was. When you revisited a place after a long interval, the first impression you always got was that it hadn't changed. The first building you would see, as likely as not, would be the church. And the church steeple would look just like it did when you were a child, except not so tall, anymore. Only afterwards you found out how much the place had really altered.

"And when you were a child the steeple even then needed paint on it," Gysbert van Tonder observed.

"What I *noticed*," Oupa Bekker proceeded, getting bitter at the interruptions, "what I noticed, as I walked up the rise, was that rise was not as high as it had seemed when I was a boy. Only, when I was a boy I could get up over it easier. Maybe it was the fault of the tarred road. But when Chris Welman says that the church steeple did not look so tall anymore, then he's quite wrong. Because the church steeple looked *taller*, when I got there. And the church looked three times bigger than it used to be. And it seemed to be standing right at the other end of the kerkplein from where it had stood in the old days. And why it all looked like that to me was because the church *had* been rebuilt on the other end of the plein. And it *was* three times bigger."

That should have put Chris Welman in his place. But it didn't. Instead, a twinkle came into his eye.

"Where was the bar, Oupa Bekker?" he asked. "I hope you found that, all right. I mean, they didn't go and shift the saloon bar, too, did they, where you couldn't find it?"

Oupa Bekker said he was coming to that.

First he had walked about the kerkplein a good while, searching for the site of the old church.

And then he came across a row of stones that were half-buried in the long grass, and that he knew were the foundations of the old church. He went and sat on a stone, Oupa Bekker said, and a –

"And a host of childhood memories came back to you," Jurie Steyn said.

Then Oupa Bekker got really huffy.

"Look here," Oupa Bekker said. "I only hope that the same thing happens to you, all of you, as what happened to me. I only hope that one day, when you take it into your minds to go and visit your childhood homes again, you'll also find everything as changed as what I found it, that's all. Then you won't see anything to laugh at, in it.

"And I only hope you also feel as lonely as what I felt, when I turned away from the kerkplein and walked down the main street of the village, and everywhere I saw only strange faces and strange buildings, and there was nobody I could say to – and there was nobody who was interested, even – that that was my home town. But, of course, it wasn't the place, anymore, that I had spent my childhood in. Not the way they had changed it, it wasn't."

Chris Welman started feeling sorry for Oupa Bekker then.

"Was it really as altered as all that, Oupa?" he asked.

"Altered?" Oupa Bekker repeated. "Take the hotel, now. It used to be a wood-and-iron building with a long veranda. Now it was a double-storey brick building. And where there had been a hitching-post in front of it that we children used to swing on, there was now one of those upright iron box things that have to do with electricity. Electricity – why, in the old days we had hardly even paraffin lamps."

It all sounded quite sad. But then, as Gysbert van Tonder remarked, there had to be such a thing as progress. We couldn't expect the world just to stand still for Oupa Bekker's sake, or for any one of our sakes, for that matter, either.

"I went to look for the place that we children used to call the river," Oupa Bekker went on, "and that we used to fish in, and that people used to lead water into their gardens from, and that had a bridge over it."

Well, we knew what was coming, of course. And we almost wished that Oupa Bekker wouldn't go to the length of telling us about it. Because they would have put pipes there, of course. And the stream would have been covered up. And where the bridge had been there would now be the new power station. Or the glue factory.

We would rather not think what there was on the site of the garden wall that Jurie Steyn and Chris Welman and Gysbert van Tonder had spoken about earlier.

The piece of garden wall that every person who spent his childhood in a village remembers. A red-brick and honeysuckle wall, or a white-washed wall wildly rich with convolvulus.

"After I had had dinner in the hotel," Oupa Bekker proceeded – and without his having to say so, we gathered that he did not eat much: his voice told us all that – "I went to the bioscope. I had been there earlier in the day, and it had said that there would be an afternoon show.

"It was a picture about cowboys and Indians, or about cowboys and something. Or it might not even have been cowboys. I'm not sure. Seeing that the talking was all in English, I couldn't understand very much of it.

"But there was a coach in the picture, like the Zeederberg coaches they used to have here in the old days, before they had trains, much. And there was a fat man in the picture with a black manel who had other fat men under him. And he looked important, like a raadslid that they had in that village when I was a boy. And that fat-man-with-the-manel's job seemed to be to work out for the other fat men what was the best way to rob that Zeederberg coach, every time.

"And after a while, sitting in that bioscope, I began to get quite happy again, and I didn't mind so much that my home town had changed. Because the place they had there, on the picture, where all those things were going on, was just like my village had been when I was a boy. And there was the same sort of riding on horses, that I remembered well. And the hotel in the picture had the same kind of veranda. And although I didn't actually *see* any children swinging on the hitching-post, they might have been, but the picture just didn't show it. Anyway, I

307

knew it was the same hitching-post. I mean, I would know it anywhere.

"And I was pleased to see the bridge, too. It was exactly the same bridge that we had over our stream, in the old days. And there was a young fellow who wasn't as fat as the fat-man-in-the-manel's men, and who seemed to be on the opposite side from what they were on, and got in their way, every time. And the young fellow stood on that very bridge that I remembered from my childhood. He stood on the bridge with a lovely girl in his arms. And if you had looked under the bridge I am sure there would have been the same pieces of tree-trunk washed up under the side of it.

"And afterwards, when there was shooting in the hotel, it was exactly the same paraffin lamps and candles they had there that used to be in the village hotel in the old days, before they had made it into two storeys."

Afterwards, Oupa Bekker said, when it came to the end of the picture, and that lovely girl got married to the young fellow who wasn't as fat as the man-in-the-manel's men were fat, he felt happier than he had done for a considerable while – happier than he had felt at any time since he got off the train, that morning, and saw that the road over the rise was tarred.

"Because the church they got married in was the old church just as I had known it," Oupa Bekker said. "It was like the church used to be, before they made it three times bigger and moved it to the other end of the plein."

And when he went back to the station in the evening, Oupa Bekker said, descending the rise with the light wind that he knew so well blowing about him, it was with much satisfaction that he realised how, through all those years, his home town had not changed.

"But that bioscope itself," Jurie Steyn said. "That must be quite a new thing, I should imagine. They certainly couldn't have had a bioscope in that village when you were a boy."

"No," Oupa Bekker said. "Where they built that bioscope there was, before that, when I was a boy, a stretch of garden wall with creeper over it."

not forget easily, either, was the young men in Voortrekker dress firing a volley into the air as the sun was going down.

There was not the same unanimity of feeling, however, about the President Tableau, that was put on after it had got properly dark. For one thing, we had had to wait too long round that platform that had bucksails raised on it to look like a veld tent, with flaps that two Mchopis, standing one on each side of it, had to draw apart by pulling on ropes.

For another thing, we felt that they could have got some more suitable person to act the role of the president. Not that the one that took the part wasn't *good*, we said.

After all, it wasn't every day that we got somebody so prominent on the Afrikaans stage to come and present a tableau in the Groot Marico. We were honoured, of course, and we also felt that it was a great honour that was being conferred on Hartman van Beek, he being so unrefined and all. But there were some of the more conservative farmers present who felt that it would have been better if somebody else had been chosen, even if it was somebody that maybe couldn't act so well.

Then it had taken some time to get the motor-car lamps fixed in such a way as to throw a searchlight beam on the place where the opening would come in the veld tent when, at a given signal, the Mchopis pulled on the ropes.

Members of the audience had started getting impatient.

"Maak klaar, kêrels," some of them had said. "Ons moet ry."

It was already well past milking time when the car headlights were switched on and a beam of light got trained onto the platform.

Through some slight error in the manipulation of the lamps, however, the light beam missed the flaps of the veld tent and instead illuminated, very vividly, the protuberant rump of a Mchopi, who was at that moment engaged in the act of picking up a cigarette end.

Before the error was rectified there were audible, around the platform, sundry sniggers of so homespun a character that they might almost have emanated from Hartman van Beek himself.

Nevertheless, we all agreed that what followed immediately afterwards was *good*.

When the bucksails in front of the veld tent were pulled aside, there stood revealed, in the full beam of the headlights, a frock-coated figure, broad-shouldered and robust, and wearing a top-hat and a presidential sash and side-whiskers. In the silence that followed the frock-coated figure boomed out, in a deep voice, the well-known words of the president's last message.

Well, as we acknowledged freely afterwards, she was *good*. In this role, we said, Anna Wessels-Wessels was as good as in anything she had done since the play *Dronk op haar Bruilof*. But there was something about it that wasn't just quite right, somehow. And it wasn't just because she had left a hair-slide sticking out at the side of her top-hat.

We were still talking about this – Gysbert van Tonder claiming that he had seen her powder-puff sticking out of the upper of one boot – when young Vermaak, the schoolmaster, suddenly asked a question.

"But who is this Hartman van Beek that the monument was raised to?" he asked. "I mean . . . I mean . . . I know something about his character from what the speakers at the unveiling said. But who is he? Or who was he? Or what was he?"

We looked at the schoolmaster in surprise.

Jurie Steyn was the first to speak.

"You don't know – ?" Jurie Steyn began. "You haven't heard – ?"

"No," young Vermaak said, bluntly, "I haven't."

Thereupon Chris Welman spoke.

"You," Chris Welman said, his tone sounding grieved. "You, a school-master and all and you really don't know who Hartman van Beek was? "But you were there – didn't you hear what all those speakers said? I mean, even if you hadn't heard of Bartman – I mean, Hartman van Beek before, you should have learnt then. And here you're supposed to be teaching children in a classroom."

The schoolmaster bridled.

"It's because I'm a schoolteacher," he said, "that I want to know what to teach my pupils. But at the unveiling ceremony not one of the speakers said anything about what Hartman van Beek *did*, to get that monument erected to him. All they talked was the usual son-of-the-veld claptrap that gets talked when any monument is raised in the Transvaal."

Jurie Steyn shook his head. Several of us followed his example. We shook our heads, also. We wanted to make it quite clear to the school-master that we were shocked at his ignorance.

"But there was the horse commando," Jurie Steyn said in astonish-ment. "And there was that volley that the young Voortrekker men fired.

You *heard* that, didn't you? Next thing you'll be saying is that there wasn't that tableau, even. Maybe you even think, now, that there *isn't* that monument there?"

This time it was the schoolmaster's turn to shake his head. He waited quite a while before he spoke.

"You know what," he said. "I don't think any of those speakers at the ceremony knew anything about Hartman van Beek, either.

"And why has that monument got only his name on it, and not the date of his birth and his death – if he is dead, that is? And that was why the Volksraad member didn't know, if they made a statue of him, what Hartman van Beek should be holding in his hand – if it is an olive branch he should be holding, or a bottle of dop. Or a pump thing for spraying cockroaches with."

Thereupon Johnny Coen said that the schoolmaster should be ashamed of himself for talking like that about a hero. It was bad enough, some of the remarks the speakers at the unveiling had passed about Hartman van Beek, Johnny Coen said.

But the schoolmaster said that that was the last thing he would dream of doing. All he wanted was some information about the man we had honoured by erecting a memorial to him in our midst. And nobody seemed to know anything about him.

"I mean, who was Hartman van Beek?" the schoolmaster asked again. "Was he a leader or a statesman? Was he a missionary or a great hunter or a great fighting man? Or did he save a lot of people's lives, like Wolraad Woltemade? Or was he maybe just even a writer? What *was* he?"

We said that *that*, of course, we didn't know. And did it matter, really, we asked the schoolmaster. We realised, also, that it was useless trying to argue with him.

If it wasn't enough that there were the speeches and the volleys and the horse commando *and* the tableau, then there was just nothing, we reflected, that would satisfy young Vermaak.

Coffin in the Loft

"There's nothing to be *afraid* of in a ghost," Jurie Steyn said, "so I don't know why there should be all this fuss now – people saying they won't travel by the Abjaterskop road at night."

So Gysbert van Tonder said that he had never heard of any ghost ever doing a human being harm.

"Real harm, that is," he made haste to supplement his statement.

That made Chris Welman feel that he would like to go even further. There were actually instances of ghosts being helpful to human beings, Chris Welman said. Like a ghost pointing out to a party of treasure-hunters where to dig.

Ghosts were also known to have assisted in the maintenance of law and order, putting the police onto the right track when they were investigating a crime.

"Yes, and I'd like to know where the police would *be*, if it wasn't for ghosts telling them what to do," Gysbert van Tonder declared. "And not only ghosts, but a man's own neighbour, too, sometimes. A neighbour that he trusts, what's more."

So Jurie Steyn said that Gysbert van Tonder was just being silly, now. If Gysbert van Tonder thought that it was he, Jurie Steyn, that had told Sergeant Rademeyer about those long-horned cattle in the camp by the kloof, then it was the biggest mistake Gysbert van Tonder had made in his life.

"In any case, you've got nothing to complain about," Jurie Steyn ended up. "You got them out of the way in time. All except the red heifer with the white markings on the left foreleg."

"You seem to know a lot about it," Gysbert van Tonder said, sounding suspicious again. "Anyway, the markings are on the right foreleg. You can go and tell that to your friend Sergeant Rademeyer. You can also tell him that how I got the animals away in time was because I knew he was coming. I heard it from a ghost."

It took a little while, after that, for the conversation to resume a placid tenor and by that time Oupa Bekker was telling a long story about a coffin in a loft.

The ghost that stayed in that coffin was, of course, as harmless as anything, Oupa Bekker said. It would just lift up the lid at midnight and descend from the loft, using the outside stairs and not making much noise, and it would then just haunt the neighbourhood a bit, returning to its coffin well before sunrise and then letting down the lid again – and so quietly that you could hardly hear it. That ghost wouldn't hurt a fly, Oupa Bekker added.

Thereupon Johnny Coen interrupted Oupa Bekker to remark that, while we all knew that a ghost was harmless, at the same time we were none of us anxious to encounter a ghost, if we could help it.

"I mean, no matter how quiet a ghost acts, or how friendly he is, even," Johnny Coen said, "if he comes on you from behind, suddenly, and you're alone in the bush, and it's a particularly dark night, say – well, you'd rather *not* have that ghost around.

"No matter what Oupa Bekker says about how harmless such a ghost is, or about how helpful, even. I think it makes it even worse if such a ghost tries to be helpful. I don't say I'd get frightened –"

So we all said, no, of course we wouldn't get frightened, either. It wasn't a question of fear, we said. Not that we mightn't run a little, naturally, if we were on foot, or urge the horse on, slightly, if we were on horseback.

But it wasn't fear, or anything like that, we said. It just stood to reason that it was a disagreeable experience to meet a ghost alone in the veld at night. After all, it was human nature to feel like that.

Thereupon Chris Welman mentioned something he saw just outside the Bekkersdal graveyard one night.

"It's a lonely sort of graveyard," Chris Welman explained, "and so just out of human nature I didn't worry to pick my hat up when it fell off."

Then At Naudé told us about the height of the barbed-wire fence that he had cleared at one leap near Nietverdiend, in the dark, on account of human nature and arising out of what he saw.

Before Oupa Bekker could get back to his coffin-in-the-loft story, At Naudé asked what was the strength of the report about the Abjaterskop road being haunted.

Everybody seemed to be talking about it. Not that that sort of thing made any difference to him, At Naudé said. He didn't care if the Abjater-skop road *was* haunted, seeing that he hardly ever went that way – and certainly never at night.

"Well, it seems that it was some of Gysbert van Tonder's Bechuanas who first said they saw a ghost there," Chris Welman said. "Isn't that right, Gysbert?"

"They *and* others," Gysbert van Tonder replied.

"The ghost is supposed to haunt the part of the road near the broken-down walls of the old farmhouse, that we call the murasie," Chris Welman proceeded. "That's right, hey, Gysbert?"

"That part *and* other parts," Gysbert van Tonder announced. "But mostly near the murasie."

There was something decidedly creepy in the way Gysbert van Tonder spoke, so that it came in the nature of a relief to us when Oupa Bekker returned to his coffin-ghost tale.

"What made it all seem so queer," Oupa Bekker said, "was that it was an *unused* coffin that the ghost stayed in. The coffin had been in the loft of that farmhouse for as long as almost anybody could remember."

Johnny Coen asked why they didn't go up and open the coffin and look.

Oupa Bekker gazed steadily at Johnny Coen for some moments.

"Would you have liked to have gone and looked?" Oupa Bekker asked him. "In the old days, that is?"

Johnny Coen acknowledged that he wouldn't have liked it. Either in the old days or today, he said. Certainly, on his own he would not have cared to go. It would be different, perhaps, going in the company of a few people he could rely on. Say about seven or eight people.

Oupa Bekker nodded. "That's what happened in the end," Oupa Bekker said. "The farmer got a good Malay ghost-catcher up from the Cape. And when the Malay opened the coffin in the presence of the whole family, there were the mouldering bones of a human skeleton inside."

The Malay was able to tell them, also, Oupa Bekker said, that that was the kind of ghost that could never be laid. Ordinary kinds of ghosts he could catch in a bottle of sea-water that he had brought up with him for that purpose from the Cape, but the ghost in the coffin would go on haunt-ing the place until the end of the world, becoming worse the older he got.

The police were called in, Oupa Bekker said, and they were satisfied that it was murder. A more horrible murder even than ordinary, they said, because they couldn't find any clues. And the mystery was never solved, even though the ghost gave the police what help it could.

"And the Malay was proven right," Oupa Bekker concluded. "Even after his skeleton was given a decent Christian burial, the ghost kept on haunting the house. The family trekked away, afterwards, and nobody else would live in the place, which is today a ruin. That ghost is still there, and, as the Malay prophesied, with the years he gets worse."

Gysbert van Tonder yawned.

"Ah, well, I've got to be going," he said. "Maybe it would be different if I met that ghost alone in the veld at night. But on an afternoon like this – ah, well."

He walked out of the voorkamer still yawning.

"You know," Jurie Steyn said, after Gysbert van Tonder had left, "Gysbert van Tonder seemed a bit mysterious about that ghost on the Abjaterskop road, didn't he?"

We agreed that it was so.

"Well, I can see it's something he's made up – that the road is haunted," Jurie Steyn continued. "Because, from what Sergeant Rademeyer told me, that was just the trouble he had, following Gysbert and the herd of cattle, that night. It was along the Abjaterskop road, and when they came to the part near the murasie, Rademeyer's police-boys said that they had heard that the place was haunted and they wouldn't go any further. That was how Gysbert van Tonder got away. Through having spread that ghost story."

After we had said, well, how's that for cunning, Jurie Steyn acquainted us with this further insight into the police sergeant's point of view.

"Well, I could, I expect, have gone on and followed him on my own," Sergeant Rademeyer had said. "I mean, I'm not afraid of ghosts. That would be absurd. But I could see it looked funny there, by that murasie, with those dark shadows amongst the trees. And the wind makes an awful sound about there, too. And I've got a wife and four children to think of. It's not that I was afraid –"

No, it was just human nature, we said, when Jurie Steyn repeated that part of the sergeant's statement to us.

But Oupa Bekker said that Gysbert van Tonder would find out his mistake, yet. And then Gysbert van Tonder would turn grey just in one night, Oupa Bekker said.

"Because the Abjaterskop road *is* haunted," Oupa Bekker said. "And by the worst kind of ghost that there is, too, now. The murasie there is the ruins of the old farmhouse with the loft. And what that ghost must be like today, I would much rather just not think."

DETECTIVE STORY

The radio mystery serial to which he had been listening in over a considerable period had, At Naudé informed us, now come to an end. It appeared that the dénouement was eminently satisfactory.

"I wouldn't have missed that last instalment for anything," At Naudé said. "It's so clever the way everything gets explained – you've got no idea. Right through the serial everybody thinks that the lawyer did it, because of the cigar stompie the police found in the garden. But in the end it turns out that it was a Mshangaan mine-boy who had the regular habit of smoking cigars.

"Clever, hey? What's more, nobody even knew that there was that Mshangaan mine-boy until the very last instalment. Until the last couple of minutes, almost, you can say. Another thing was that the detective was getting secret information all the time from a girl that the leader of the jewel thieves was in love with. And the detective didn't let on about that, either, right until the last instalment. What do you think of that for smart, now? Because it was *secret* information, he kept it secret from everybody."

We said we wondered what they would think of next. We also said that it sounded very mixed up and clever.

"Yes, you couldn't make head or tail out of it, really," At Naudé agreed. "And after it was over there was a bar or two of music and the man who gives the scientific talks was saying a long thing about the latest laboratory research into some stuff that sounded like erughurugh, the way he pronounced it, and –"

"Is it," Gysbert van Tonder asked, his eye lighting up, "any good to drink?"

"I don't know," At Naudé replied, "but I listened quite a long way into that talk before I realised that it wasn't part of the serial. That's how the last instalment got me, if you understand what I mean."

The schoolmaster said that, from the sound of it, he didn't judge it to be such a good detective serial. The idea of detective fiction was to give the audience an equal chance with the detective of solving the mystery, he said. The audience had to be in possession of all the facts. Whereas, if the detective kept all the clues to himself it was only natural that he should be able to solve the mystery before anybody else.

At Naudé said that would be a fine to-do.

"Why, it's only in the last instalment that the detective produces the blood-stained handkerchief with the crook's initials on it that he picked up at the scene of the crime, and that he didn't mention anything about to a soul," At Naudé said. "What did you expect him to do – tell everybody and so put the criminal on his guard?"

Yes, we were all surprised that young Vermaak, who was supposed to be educated and all, and taught school as high as Standard Four, should have so little understanding as to what a detective radio story was all about.

"It doesn't even need to be over the wireless," Jurie Steyn said to the schoolmaster. "You can just *read* that sort of thing, too, week by week."

He then proceeded to acquaint us with some of the details of a serial he had once followed in a woman's paper to which his wife had subscribed because of a weekly feature in it called "The Intimate Lives of Celebrated Women Poisoners."

He never got to the end of the serial, Jurie Steyn said, because his wife stopped taking that paper when the Women Poisoners articles finished and they ran a series, instead, that was entitled "Woman, the Ministering Angel" – the first article dealing with how to treat smallpox in your own home on veld or vlei.

"But what I remember most about that mystery serial," Jurie Steyn said, "was the unusual sort of detective they had in it. The person that questioned all the suspects and carried out the detective investigations was only doing it in a spare-time way. His real job was being the sword-swallower in a circus."

That started Chris Welman off telling us about the time a friend of his, Joggem Dieder, who was then living in the Wolmaransstad District, got a sudden thirst for adventure. And he ran away from home to join a circus. Joggem was then aged sixty-three.

"We talked a lot about it among ourselves," Chris Welman said, "and we used to make jokes about Joggem Dieder riding horses, standing on the saddle on one leg. Or we would picture him, his old limbs creaking, flying high up in the air on a swing, with a plug of chew tobacco in his cheek."

But from the few letters that Joggem Dieder wrote back, Chris Welman said, it would appear that he was happy in his new career and that he had adapted himself successfully to the wild life of the circus.

"All the same, we were a bit disappointed when the circus came to Wolmaransstad and we found that Joggem didn't take part in any of the big performances, but was only in a side-show," Chris Welman said. "In fact, we hardly recognised him when we first saw him, him all dressed up in a silk frock and a yellow wig, and a hat with flowers and a blue feather, and smiling in a silly way. And his dress was arranged so that you couldn't see his feet. And so Joggem Dieder made quite a good bearded woman. I mean, he always *had* one of the longest beards in the district."

Oupa Bekker had been waiting for some time for a chance to talk.

"The neatest bit of detective work I ever saw," Oupa Bekker said, "also had in it a circus performer. But *he* did juggling and rope tricks. Afterwards he left the circus and became a bywoner on Neels Prinsloo's farm. And when Neels Prinsloo was one morning found hanging on a tree on the way to the cattle-kraal the veldkornet that came along worked out a solution to the affair that was so well thought out that people were still talking about it for months afterwards.

"The neighbour who saw Neels Prinsloo hanging from the tree just took one look and then went and fetched other neighbours.

"The neighbours knew they hadn't to touch anything. So, when the veldkornet arrived, it was to find Neels Prinsloo still hanging from the tree and a man with a shot-gun standing guard over the bywoner, in case, with his circus training, he got out of the riems they had tied him up with. For they were convinced that the bywoner had murdered Neels Prinsloo and had then hung him from the tree to make it look like suicide.

"The veldkornet took a rapid survey of the situation. 'Unknot them both,' he ordered.

"It appeared that the rope under Neels Prinsloo's chin had been tied with a kind of slip-knot that the bywoner was known to make – something he had brought with him from the circus. Another thing was that Neels Prinsloo's feet were dangling eighteen inches above the ᴊnd and there was nothing underneath that he could have stood on.

"Even if Neels Prinsloo was a circus acrobat himself – which he was ᴊar from being, with his lumbago – he couldn't possibly have tied his neck so high up from the ground like that without help. Finally, the bywoner had frequently, and in the presence of witnesses, threatened to murder Neels Prinsloo. The bywoner's last threat had been uttered only the day before.

"But the veldkornet freed the bywoner from the net of suspicion quicker than the farmers had been able to get Neels Prinsloo down from the tree, on account of the circus knot.

"'How long has the bywoner been on this farm?' the veldkornet asked. Two years, they told him. 'Well, Neels Prinsloo was one of the most progressive farmers in these parts,' the veldkornet said. 'He no doubt learnt from the bywoner how to make that kind of knot.

"'Now, you say Neels Prinsloo had nothing to stand on when he hanged himself. What time was he found hanging?' They told him, at daybreak. 'Milking time,' the veldkornet said. 'That means that he stood on an upturned bucket and a Mchopi, passing down this footpath on his way to work, took the pail along with him, to the kraal. Eighteen inches is just the height of a milking pail. And the Mchopi wouldn't have seen Neels Prinsloo hanging from the tree, because the Mchopi would have had his eyes down on the ground, all the time, looking for dagga.

"'Now, about those threats,' the veldkornet went on. 'Has there ever been a farm in the Transvaal where a bywoner does not regularly threaten to murder the farmer he works for?'"

That was Oupa Bekker's story of the brilliant piece of real-life detective work on the part of the veldkornet. But it was a story that didn't carry conviction, somehow.

"What was more," Oupa Bekker went on, as though sensing our scepticism, "why the veldkornet was so sure of himself was because he had received a letter from Neels Prinsloo, saying he was going to hang himself, because he was sick of the Government. That was why the veldkornet got to the farm so early, before he had been sent for – because he had Neels Prinsloo's letter."

We still looked doubtful. It wasn't a story that rang true, somehow, take it how you liked. Oupa Bekker coughed.

"They also found a Mchopi who admitted picking up a bucket just there that he took to the kraal for milking," Oupa Bekker declared, stoutly. "Just like the veldkornet worked out."

Still there was silence. Then Oupa Bekker played his trump card – which had the unfortunate effect of leaving us more incredulous than ever.

"When Neels Prinsloo came round," Oupa Bekker said, "he confirmed that everything the veldkornet said was correct."

Wonder Woman of Windhoek

Oupa Bekker advised Gysbert van Tonder not to attach too much importance to the statement made to him recently by the new wonder woman at Bekkersdal.

"Especially as she only says that the Kruger millions *may* be buried on your farm," Oupa Bekker proceeded. "It would be different if she says they *are* buried there."

Gysbert van Tonder conceded Oupa Bekker's point.

"No, don't worry, Oupa," Gysbert said. "I won't dig much. I'll just scratch about a bit on the spot where the cave is, and I'll maybe turn up a few sods there by the Bushman mound. I won't anywhere go deeper than about ten foot, I mean. After all, she didn't say for *sure* the Kruger gold is on my farm."

Closing his left eye in a significant manner, Oupa Bekker recommended to Gysbert van Tonder not to give up courage too soon. And he mentioned the instance, in the very old days, of Rooi Armaans, who had also been told by a wonder woman that there might be gold on his farm.

"But after digging around a bit, Rooi Armaans gave up; he sold his farm and trekked," Oupa Bekker said. "Yet where was once Rooi Armaans's farm there is today the Simmer and Jack. Rooi Armaans had only to have gone down about another two thousand feet."

But Gysbert van Tonder – not having caught Oupa Bekker's wink – said that was a different matter. He wasn't concerned with just a gold-bearing reef thousands of feet underground and that you wouldn't recognise as gold if you saw it, likely – not even if it was loaded on cocopans. No, what he meant was a lot of buried gold, all mined and melted down into handy-sized bars. The rock stuff they could keep.

Gysbert van Tonder confessed that what made him lose heart, actually, was the number of other farmers, there, at Bekkersdal, waiting to interview the wonder woman.

"All standing around with picks and shovels," he said. "And holding onto scraps of paper with writing on them, that were supposed to be maps."

He felt quite bashful about the bit of paper he himself was holding onto, with a cross to mark what might be the Bushman mound or the cave, or perhaps just anywhere, Gysbert van Tonder said.

He added that among the persons hanging about the wonder woman's place there was also a farmer from Platrand, that he knew. And so he thought he would have a joke.

"I decided to tip that wonder woman off about something I knew about the Platrand farmer," Gysbert van Tonder said. "It was something that had happened in his courting days. If she pretended to see all that in the crystal, and told it to him bit by bit, it would make him think that she had supernatural gifts, all right. And I thought of all the fun I could have in Bekkersdal, afterwards, telling the other kêrels. Real fun, I mean."

But he never got so far, Gysbert van Tonder said, for, when he went in, the wonder woman looked him up and down a number of times in a fashion that removed whatever inclination he might have had towards indulging in anything fanciful, just then.

"If I didn't know it couldn't be," Gysbert van Tonder said, "I might even have thought that she sniffed. Then she said, 'I'll start with the past. That scar you've got, now –' So I said, for a joke, that it wasn't a scar but just how my face is. 'That scar,' the wonder woman went on, 'yes, I can see here in the crystal just how you got it. It was long ago. You were –'

"'I was climbing through a barbed-wire fence,' I said. 'I was a boy, then.'

"'You were,' the wonder woman said, 'a full-grown man, then – according to the crystal. Yes, I can see you. You're standing in a – in a pigsty – no, it's a cattle-kraal. I can't see too clearly. It must be because it's night time, that you're standing there in the cattle-kraal, and you're –'"

So Gysbert van Tonder said to the wonder woman, yes, she was quite correct. An ox came and pushed him and he fell and hurt his face. She needn't go on with that, he said. There wasn't much sense in just recalling the past, anyhow.

"But the woman shook her head, and said, no, it wasn't an ox," Gysbert van Tonder continued. "She said it was a Mchopi watchman with a stick. She said she could see me running, with the watchman after me, lifting his stick. It was too awful, she said. Well, I told her not to take any notice of lies, like that, that she saw in the crystal. Because I could prove it was a lie. And I knew who those people were, too, that started that lie about me, at the time. They were persons at Platrand who were jealous of me because I was making such a success of my farming. I didn't think much of a crystal that went in for gossip, I said to her."

The wonder woman proceeded to tell him, afterwards, that the Kruger millions he was asking about *might* be buried on his farm, Gysbert van Tonder said. But she wasn't sure.

"She seemed pretty sure of the Mchopi watchman, though," Jurie Steyn interjected. "And of the stick."

"Yes, I think *somebody* must have told her something," Gysbert van Tonder said. "Maybe it was that Platrand farmer."

"Or perhaps the Mchopi watchman, perhaps," Chris Welman suggested.

But Oupa Bekker said we could never tell. So we said, no, of course we did not doubt the wonder woman's *powers*. That we would not question, even. But we did know that there was such a thing as one man, for a joke, putting a fortune-teller up to telling another man certain things. Not that that had necessarily happened in Gysbert van Tonder's case. Indeed, the more we thought it over, the more likely it seemed, we said, that the wonder woman *had* seen all that about Gysbert van Tonder in the crystal. Seeing how we knew Gysbert, we said.

Then Oupa Bekker mentioned about the time when the Wonder Woman of Windhoek came to the Dwarsberge, and he and Japie Krige went to see her.

"And I meant to go in first and play the same kind of trick on Japie Krige," Oupa Bekker said. "There was something I knew about Japie Krige, and my plan was to tell the Wonder Woman of Windhoek about it before Japie Krige consulted her himself. Of course, this happened a good while ago. And I only got it into my head to do a thing like that because I was much younger than I am today. I mean when I look back on it now I am surprised that I could have been so thoughtless.

"The thing I knew about Japie Krige was something he had told me himself, one night when we were sitting around the camp-fire and we had spoken about the miltsiek and the rust in the corn and how the Volksraad member seemed to keep away when times were troubled.

"The talk had come back to the miltsiek again when Japie Krige spoke of the girl, Martie Fouché, that he had seen at a funeral in Zeerust and that he had never been able to forget. The talk of the miltsiek had reminded him of the funeral. Her people had trekked away after the funeral and because he was just a boy, then – well, he was shy, of course. And he only knew that the Fouchés had gone when he didn't see Martie in church again, next Sunday.

"And then, when he was old enough to do something about looking for her, the Boer War broke out. And although he had made enquiries about her, afterwards, he was satisfied, with the years, that he would not see her again. 'And yet, you know,' he said to me, 'I can still see how she knelt there, in her black dress and black kappie, by the side of the grave in the red soil, and that sad look in her eyes. And she was very lovely. Of course, I was just a boy, then.'

"So I said, yes, maybe. But he was also old enough to know better than to get ideas like that about a girl at a funeral."

Anyway, that was the story Japie Krige had told him, Oupa Bekker said, and it was the story he meant to pass on to the Wonder Woman of Windhoek on the occasion when he and Japie Krige went to consult her about where the gold was buried on the map that they had.

"Seeing that we were going to see her about the same map," Oupa Bekker said, "I was afraid that Japie Krige might make some difficulty about my going in alone. I thought he would insist on coming in with me. But, to my surprise, he seemed genuinely keen that I should go in by myself.

"And suddenly it didn't seem so funny to me, and I felt ashamed of myself for having had the idea of talking to the wonder woman about Japie Krige's passion for Martie. That was when I lifted the flap of the tent that the Wonder Woman of Windhoek sat in, with Japie waiting for me outside.

"The Wonder Woman of Windhoek was thin. She had on a black frock, because she was a widow, and she was kneeling on the ground, with a big crystal on a raised black cushion in front of her. Somehow, I was not much impressed with her as a fortune-teller.

"For one thing, she also wanted to start telling me things from the past that I had to head her off about. In fact, if I didn't know it couldn't be, I would also have started thinking that somebody had been telling her things about me. Anyway, it was not at all satisfactory.

"Even as I was already leaving she was still saying that she could see something in the crystal about a schoolmaster shaking his head about me and saying I would come to no good. But with Japie Krige, when he went in, it was different –"

Johnny Coen interrupted Oupa Bekker to say, yes, he knew what was coming.

"Why Japie Krige wanted to go in alone was because he wanted to ask the Wonder Woman of Windhoek about Martie Fouché," Johnny Coen said. "And then he found out that the wonder woman *was* Martie Fouché, come back from South West. And she was a widow, now, and so they got married. That's how all that kind of stories are, I've noticed."

Johnny Coen was partly right, Oupa Bekker said – that part about their getting married *was* correct. But the Wonder Woman of Windhoek wasn't Martie. About the rest, however, Johnny Coen was right.

"In fact, Japie Krige said to me afterwards," Oupa Bekker continued, "that he fell in love with the wonder woman the moment he saw her. 'I fell in love with the wonder woman straight away,' Japie Krige said to me. 'The way she was dressed in mourning. And with that look of sorrow in her eyes, that made her very lovely. And the way the wonder woman was kneeling on the red ground.'"

The Recluse

It was significant that when we spoke of him it was as Meneer Lemare or as Old Lemare. It wasn't merely that we didn't know his first name, but that, moreover, we didn't want to know it. And on those rare occasions when he emerged from his cottage in the leegte that was all grown about with the thorniest kind of cactus, his encounters with Marico farmers were not characterised by any noteworthy degree of cordiality.

It was like talking to a more disappointed kind of one of his own prickly-pears.

"I remember, years ago, when I came across him on the road to Ramoutsa, and I told him my name was Naudé, and I asked him how he was," At Naudé said. "He told me to voetsek."

Then Jurie Steyn mentioned the time, long before he had his post office, even, when he came across Old Lemare in the Indian store. And Old Lemare was telling the Indian to voetsek, Jurie Steyn said.

"I thought of telling Lemare that it wasn't right that a man should live all by himself, the way he was doing," Jurie Steyn proceeded. "There was something from the Good Book that I wanted to mention to him in that connection. It was from Deuteronomy IX of the Good Book. But I decided afterwards rather not to say anything to Lemare about it."

"Was he carrying that thick stick with a piece of brass fastened on the end of it?" At Naudé asked.

Yes, Jurie Steyn acknowledged, that did have something to do with his changing his mind about talking to Old Lemare about the disadvantages of a life of solitude. "And although I didn't say anything to him," Jurie Steyn added, "when I was going out of the store, he called out to me, all the same, to voetsek."

That was what happened, of course, the schoolmaster said, when one retired from society, carrying under one's arm a pick-handle loaded with brass. One's vocabulary grew limited. A few simple words sufficed for the elementary day-to-day needs of the hermitage.

"But it needn't be as simple as just to say voetsek," At Naudé remarked gruffly. "A hermit doesn't need to be as day-to-day as all that."

Johnny Coen said that it sounded as though Old Lemare must have suffered some great disillusionment, in the past. Something must have blighted his hopes, all right. The cup dashed from his lips, and so forth. And that was what had made him like that.

"Yes, you can see he's frustrated," the schoolmaster said. "It's a rather heavy stick, too, I should imagine? And the brasswork on it pretty solid?"

Jurie Steyn nodded.

"I thought so," the schoolmaster said. "He's probably an infantile romanticist and he's not making a constructive utilisation of his vital energies and reserves. And so what would do him good would be a straight talking-to in plain words –"

"Words like voetsek," At Naudé interjected, readily. "You go and talk to him like that. We'll wait for you outside. Outside that clump of prickly-pears."

The schoolmaster ignored At Naudé's pleasantry and went on to talk of the mature individual's need to meet reality objectively in every situation and of about how creative self-realisation would make Old Lemare throw away that stick, this leading to an increase in his conversational powers.

What the schoolmaster said did not make much sense, and Chris Welman – who had so far not been taking much part in our talk – several times tried to interrupt the schoolmaster with something he himself wanted to say.

"Maybe Old Lemare got that way long ago through some love affair," Johnny Coen said, eventually. "Maybe some heartless girl with a pretty face and yellow hair jilted him. There is that sort. And perhaps she had long lashes, too, that curve up at the ends."

"But I tell you, it's like this –" Chris Welman started again. Only, he didn't get any further, because Gysbert van Tonder began talking then.

And Gysbert van Tonder said that if there was a girl in it, as far as Old Lemare was concerned, then the shoe might just as well have been on the other foot. It might have been that it was Old Lemare that had jilted that girl with the fair hair and the eyelashes for a newer sweetheart, and that when he was out driving in a spider all polished up with his new fancy, what should happen but that the girl he had forsaken should appear by the side of the road and, being love-lorn, should start throwing mule-dung at them, so that his new girl's satin dress and picture hat would be all ruined and so she wouldn't speak to Lemare again, blaming *him* for it – women being known to be unreasonable in that way.

While we agreed that a tendency towards anchoretism in the individual would possibly be given stimulus by the circumstances Gysbert van Tonder had conjured up, we had no reason for supposing that that was what had happened in Old Lemare's case – especially as there was so little we knew about him, actually.

This time Chris Welman had his say.

"Lemare's name is David Goliath Ebenhaeser Philip Lemare," Chris Welman said. "He was born at Groot Drakenstein in the Cape on January 18 – I forget the year, now, but I can look it up. He is a European (white) and he has an income of £15 a month from two houses, brick, that he owns in Fordsburg. He is the head of his house, here, and Piet Sikazi (Bechuana) stands in relation of servant to him. Piet gets a wage of £1 3s. 6d. a month and an egg with his mealie-pap every Wednesday. Lemare has got seven fowls that are not inoculated against Newcastle sickness, and a pig that is. He must have read the instructions on the bottle wrong. He's also –"

"All right, Chris," Gysbert van Tonder said, "we all know you were a census enumerator. And if you think it's funny to go and tell everybody what people fill in on their census forms, then I must say that I can't see the joke in it. And I'm not thinking of myself, either. I'm not ashamed of the whole world knowing everything that's filled in on my census form. But I'm thinking of other people, that aren't as fortunate as I am myself in this way, perhaps. I am as much as anything else thinking of my neighbours, who might have things they wouldn't like known."

Jurie Steyn said then, too, in a pious tone, that he was also just thinking of the other man when he spoke about how low it was for an enumerator to go around blabbing. We all of us made remarks in similar terms, some of us getting quite heated. It was good to discover the deep sense of loyalty that the Marico farmer entertained towards his neighbour. It was something that one would hardly have suspected, ordinarily.

"It makes your blood boil to think of your private affairs being bruited about all over the place," At Naudé said. Then he added quickly, "Your neighbour's private affairs, that is."

Oupa Bekker had just begun talking about a vile census enumerator they had had in the old days – Blue Nose Theron, they called him, and also Blue Nose something else that Oupa Bekker would not like to repeat because he liked to keep the talk clean – when Johnny Coen noticed that Chris Welman was moving somewhat uncomfortably in his chair.

"It's all right, Chris," Johnny Coen said, "we're not blaming you for anything. We all know it must be a hard and thankless job, being an enumerator, and when At Naudé said just now that no decent man would take it on, he didn't mean you. He was thinking of that Blue Nose man, likely."

"But Oupa Bekker hadn't started talking about that Blue Nosed —— yet, when At Naudé said that," Chris Welman replied, sounding aggrieved. At the same time, we couldn't help feeling that the epithet Chris Welman applied to Blue Nose was a lower word even than Oupa Bekker had been thinking of.

"Anyway, somebody else can have the job of enumerator next census," Chris Welman went on, "and when it comes to my form I'll put it in a closed envelope fastened down with sealing-wax, and then I'd like to see some Blue Nose —— try and find out things about me, that's all. I say a man's private life isn't safe with these low snoopers."

Having relieved his feelings in that way seemed to put Chris Welman in a much better mood. And we were inquisitive, of course, about Old Lemare. Scandal-mongering and prying into other people's affairs were – as Jurie Steyn had pointed out – things that we left to census enumerators.

But we felt that it would be instructive for us to know a bit more about Old Lemare. Like what sort of bed did he sleep in, we would like to know. And we couldn't help thinking that his kitchen must be in too awful a state for words, with dirty plates and pots all over the floor. And we would like to know if the tenants in his Fordsburg houses paid their rent regularly. And we wondered if Old Lemare and the pig washed in the same dish.

We wouldn't have minded asking Chris Welman such questions. For the interest we took in Old Lemare was quite different from just *prying*.

"Yes," Chris Welman said, in reply to a question by Johnny Coen, "it was because of a woman that Old Lemare decided to withdraw from the world – armed: that stick weighs eighteen pounds, he says, with brass and all. Old Lemare used to be a lecturer, in the old days –"

Jurie Steyn whistled.

"Well, I hope he used more words in his lectures than what he uses today," Jurie Steyn said. "And I hope he also told his listeners more things than just telling them to get the hell out of it, like he does now."

But Chris Welman said that was just what Old Lemare had told people in his lectures – telling them that they would go to hell if they didn't lay off drink. Old Lemare was a temperance lecturer, Chris Welman said, and it seemed that temperance lectures were very popular in those days.

We all said that that was something we couldn't understand, quite. It looked as though Old Lemare was already a bit queer in the head even then, we said, thinking that people would come along and hear him talk about stopping drinking.

"He said it wasn't so much the men that came to listen to him as the women," Chris Welman explained, "and he said there was one woman, Sister Gertruida, that used to go ahead and make arrangements at the places where he was going to talk, and he had an understanding with Sister Gertruida, and he was hoping to marry her, some time, because he admired how good she was at organising committees and hiring halls.

"Then, one day, he came to Barberton to lecture and when Sister Gertruida met him at the station she said that Barberton was a mining camp and a very sinful place, and Old Lemare noticed on her breath that she had been eating peppermints – because of her cough, she said.

"And then he found out that the hall wasn't booked, because of her cough, and then by the evening he noticed that the smell of peppermint on her breath was stronger than ever, and she turned her head sideways when she spoke to him, so that the smell of peppermint shouldn't upset him, she said.

"Well, it was very sad for Old Lemare when, next thing, Sister Gertruida got a job as a barmaid, and because he couldn't get on without her, he used to go and sit in the bar drinking lemonade and Sister Gertruida would laugh at him, and say he wasn't a man at all, all the while that one of the customers, a commercial traveller, called her his baby-faced angel."

Afterwards, when he came to the bar again, Chris Welman said, to look for the commercial traveller, with that brass-shod stick, Old Lemare found that Sister Gertruida had run away with the commercial traveller – flown away, likely, seeing the name that the commercial traveller had given her. And that was the story about how Old Lemare had become a recluse.

There was an interval of silence after Chris Welman had finished talking.

"Is it – is it all true?" Jurie Steyn asked.

"True?" Chris Welman snorted. "It's as true as Oupa Bekker's lies about that Blue Nose Pete, whoever he is. Or as true as Gysbert van Tonder's rubbish about the fair-haired girl throwing manure at the couple riding in the spider. It's as true as anything I've told you about Old Lemare. You don't think I'd really be so mad as to go to his house in the middle of the cactus with a census form, do you?

"No, I just filled in his census form the best way I could by guessing everything, including his Christian names and his servant Piet, and the two houses in Fordsburg.

"I just guessed all that. And if the authorities don't like it, well, I would like to see how much would be left of the authorities if *they* went round with a census form to Old Lemare."

THE UGLY TALE OF A PRETTY WIDOW

"And he says that there are still other parts of it that are too awful ever to be told," At Naudé added.

Well, the parts that we did hear about from At Naudé seemed stark enough.

"And she seems so quiet, and, if I may say so," Jurie Steyn remarked, "pretty."

So we said that that just went to show how you never knew where you were when it was a widow.

We always thought that Klaas Senekal had done very well for himself in marrying Hendrik Borcherd's widow. Of course, Klaas Senekal had been on that farm quite a long while. But then, he was only a bywoner.

And although he had certain claims to being considered good-looking – his auburn-coloured moustache, for instance, with spikes sticking out at each side of his face – at the same time it was something of a handicap for a man to have only one leg.

Not that you would notice it much, in the ordinary way, of course, when Klaas Senekal had his wooden leg screwed on. Indeed, at the wedding reception it was observed that Klaas Senekal stood in a more steady way on just one sound leg than most of the guests did on two.

This in itself did not seem too happy a presage. It looked as though Hendrik Borcherd's widow, Petronella, was already on their wedding day bending her new husband to her will.

"Yes, I still remember how Klaas Senekal was sipping homemade ginger ale out of a small glass," Jurie Steyn recalled in reminiscent tones. "And he was saying how much he enjoyed it. And he was drinking it in small sips, like that, he said, just so that he could revel in it more. And he said that Petronella had told him that when she got married to the late Hendrik Borcherd, the late Hendrik Borcherd had drunk only cocoa, that day."

Well, we said that Klaas Senekal had been on that farm long enough, as a bywoner, to know that if Hendrik Borcherd had drunk cocoa on his wedding day, he certainly didn't touch it again afterwards.

Not from what we all knew of the late Hendrik Borcherd's habits, we said.

And we also said that that just went to show you. We could only come to the conclusion that Klaas Senekal must really be in love with Petronella.

"Well, she is pretty," Jurie Steyn said again.

But Chris Welman said that that wasn't the point. What seemed extraordinary to him was that, although he had lived there so long as a bywoner, Klaas Senekal could still allow Petronella to tell him things about how superior and all that her late husband was, even though Klaas Senekal was himself in a position to know better.

"Because he also told me, at the wedding," Chris Welman added, "that Petronella had informed him that the late Hendrik Borcherd also regularly wiped his veldskoens on some leaves before walking into the house from the lands, and that he also never sat in the voorhuis with his hat on."

Ill-mannered guffaws of a nature that would have been painful to the late Hendrik Borcherd greeted Chris Welman's statement. That was if Hendrik Borcherd had been in any way the kind of paragon that his widow held him up to be. We, however, knew otherwise about Hendrik.

This started a pretty lengthy discussion about widow women in general. We said things about widow women that we ourselves recognised as more than ordinarily profound. Above all, we stressed the need for the most extreme kind of caution to be exercised by the masculine burgher in his dealings with a widow.

"It's this comparing business, too," Chris Welman said, "that poor old Klaas Senekal must have had a gutsful of, also. Not that I've seen much of him, recently. But the few times that I did come across him the spikes of his moustache seemed a good bit wilted. It's only natural that that should happen to a man – a man with that kind of moustache, I mean – if he's got to listen regularly, day in and out, to stories of what a model his wife's first husband was. Made-up stories, too, as often as not. It's not only your moustache that suffers that way, but your laugh changes, too. I mean, when you see in a mirror how the spikes of your moustache droop, then the laugh you give is a – is a hollow sort of laugh."

Young or old, Gysbert van Tonder agreed, a widow woman was best to keep away from.

"If she was happy with her first husband," Gysbert proceeded, "there's nothing that her second husband can do that she doesn't find fault with. And if her first husband gave her a bad life, she'll take it all – and more – out of the next man she marries. She'll rule him with a rod of iron."

It wasn't quite as bad as that in Klaas Senekal's case, however, At Naudé said.

"I'm only talking about when I saw him in that cheap boarding-house in Zeerust last week," At Naudé explained, "after he had run away from the farm. That rod of iron part isn't quite true. All that Petronella used to correct him with, Klaas Senekal says, was a short sjambok. But, of course, his trouble was that he couldn't ever get out of the way as fast as he would have liked, because of his wooden leg. He says he had never really found out until then – until the time when Petronella started on him regularly with the short sjambok – what a disadvantage it was in life for a man not to be able to be swift and surefooted in his movements."

Jurie Steyn said it was difficult to think of Petronella in that way. When you pictured to yourself how, when she smiled, her lips turned up at the corners.

But Chris Welman said that maybe the only corners Klaas Senekal was concerned with were the ones he was trying to crawl into when Petronella's sjambok hand came down and she wasn't smiling.

"And when you think of her eyes," Jurie Steyn continued, ignoring Chris Welman's remarks.

That was where psychology came in, young Vermaak, the school-master, said then. He had not met the late Hendrik Borcherd himself, he said, but from the few hints we had dropped it would appear that the late Hendrik Borcherd was a completely opposite kind of character from Klaas Senekal. And if Petronella had been unhappy with Hendrik Borcherd, what had probably happened was that she had taken a vicarious revenge on Klaas Senekal.

"We've all been saying that we don't know what goes on in a widow woman's mind," young Vermaak went on, sounding solemn and learned and, at the same time, slightly diffident, as though he was consciously trying to talk with a wisdom beyond his years, "but does anyone of us really know what goes on in any woman's mind? Do we married men know very much of the inner thoughts and feelings of our own wives, for that matter?"

We acknowledged quite frankly that we didn't. What the schoolmaster said there was fair enough, we agreed. It was only when he made his next remark that we winked at one another.

"All that offers us a key to the workings of a woman's mind," young Vermaak added, "is the science of psychology."

Without knowing anything about the science of psychology, we at least had enough common sense to know when a man was deluding himself. Nevertheless, because what he had started off by saying was in itself not uninteresting, we allowed the schoolmaster to continue.

"Now, you all think that why Petronella married Klaas Senekal was because of his good looks and his handsome, spiked moustache," young Vermaak said.

Maybe not only for his looks, Chris Welman said. But his looks would have helped.

"Well, I'll tell you why she married Klaas Senekal," the schoolmaster said. "She married him for his wooden leg. That's where the study of psychology is so good in giving you an insight into human nature. Because Petronella had been dominated by her first husband, and had resented it, she wanted her second husband to be a man that she could, in turn, tyrannise. And what better man could she find for that purpose than Klaas Senekal, with his physical handicap?"

Lots better, we said, straight away.

A man didn't have to be in the last stages of rheumatics for a woman to boss him around, we said. In fact, it was usually the biggest and strongest and loudest kind of man there was that was most under his wife's thumb, we said.

What was more, if a woman was really keen on giving a man a dog's life there were other ways of doing it than with a short sjambok. Ways that made your blood boil, too, we said, when you thought some of them over carefully, afterwards. Nor was it by any means just widow women that engaged in such practices, we agreed.

All the same, the next part of At Naudé's statement did appear to lend a certain measure of colour to the schoolmaster's theory – that part having to do with the widow marrying a one-legged man.

"He said there were still other things that were too awful ever to be told," At Naudé said. "And seeing that it's between a man and his wife, I didn't, of course, ask him anything more about it. Not that I didn't keep silent for quite a while, naturally enough, so as to give him a chance to talk if he wanted to. I also hinted about how much good it does a man to unburden himself freely and fully. But out of a feeling of delicacy I didn't go beyond that – except to say that if he wanted to be snooty about it and keep it all to himself, well, he could lump it, then.

"But it was when Klaas Senekal told me of how he came to leave the farm – escaped from the farm is the only right way to say it – that I began to understand something of what he had suffered. Their marriage had got to that stage of disunion, he said, where Petronella had hidden his wooden leg. He had saved some money over the years that he had been a bywoner.

"He knotted the money in a tobacco-bag, and one day, when the Government lorry again called at the farm, and Petronella was inside the house, he hopped on one leg around the back of the lorry and clambered aboard. And he didn't come out from among the milk-cans that he was hiding behind until the lorry was half-way to the boarding-house in Zeerust. All the time he was in terror that Petronella would catch up with the lorry and pull him off it."

Well, there was a thing for you, now, we said. And we said that we could imagine that Klaas Senekal must be very bitter, sitting there in that Zeerust boarding-house with the wallpaper peeling off in patches, as At Naudé described it, and brooding on the miserable way he had been treated. It seemed a shameful end to a marriage that had started off so hopefully with the bridegroom sipping homemade ginger ale.

Only time could tell how a marriage would turn out. You couldn't go by the confetti and the angel on the wedding-cake, we said.

But At Naudé told us that, surprisingly enough, Klaas Senekal seemed quite willing to let bygones be bygones.

"He explained that he would get another job as a bywoner and make a fresh start," At Naudé said. "He was just waiting a bit before looking for work again. That was what he was doing in the room of that boarding-house – waiting. He was waiting for a court order to be served on Petronella by a mounted policeman to return his wooden leg to him."

And just to think, Jurie Steyn said, that Petronella should be so pretty and all.

Thereupon Oupa Bekker said that he had a feeling that a policeman would come into it somehow. And he was glad that the policeman was brought into it for nothing more than just to fetch back Klaas Senekal's wooden leg. For nothing worse, that was, Oupa Bekker added, sounding mysterious.

And so Jurie Steyn asked him what he meant by anything worse.

"Well, I am only guessing, of course," Oupa Bekker said. "But, if my guess is right, then I can understand why Klaas Senekal should feel that he's lucky to have got away as he did, in time. And that would explain what he meant by saying that it was something too awful ever to talk about. All the same, I would still like to know was it sheep-dip he meant or ground glass."

"She is –" Jurie Steyn started. He did not finish what he wanted to say.

EAVESDROPPER

It was only natural, since Jurie Steyn was nowhere on view in his post office that afternoon, that mention should have been made of it by the assembled farmers waiting for their mail. It was also no more than reasonable that sundry possible explanations for his absence should have been put forward by the said assembled farmers. And that the theories advanced should, in the main, have been endued with sombre tints was, under the circumstances, only to be expected.

Chris Welman's suggestion that Jurie Steyn might have been arrested was discounted by the fact that Jurie's hat and jacket were hanging on a nail above the counter. For, as Gysbert van Tonder pointed out, Jurie Steyn could not be locked up in the Bekkersdal gaol and those articles of apparel left behind, it being well known that, in an arrest, the law's production of a warrant was invariably accompanied by an injunction to the prisoner to get his hat and coat.

"Not that there's much sense in going to gaol with a hat on," Gysbert van Tonder mused. "Seeing that you've got to keep taking it off all the time. And as for a jacket – I mean, they supply you with a striped jersey to wear, instead."

Well, maybe Jurie Steyn hadn't been arrested, Chris Welman conceded – at least, perhaps not this time. But he had the feeling, Chris Welman said, that we would one day again be gathered in that same voorkamer, with Jurie Steyn not present, and that then Jurie Steyn's hat and coat *would* be missing from the nail in the wall above the counter.

"The way he throws his money about," Chris Welman went on. "It can't be just his pay as postmaster or what he makes out of his farm. Take now, when his braces broke. Instead of mending them with a piece of string like any of us would do, Jurie Steyn goes and buys a brand new pair of braces with red and white stripes –"

"Maybe it's to go with that striped jersey that Gysbert van Tonder spoke about," At Naudé interjected. "Myself, I wouldn't be surprised if Jurie Steyn gets put away for quite a long while, next time the post office auditor comes round to investigate what's going on here.

"And maybe that *has* happened – I've just thought of it now. Maybe Jurie Steyn has got to hear of it that there actually is an inspector from the G. P. O. in the neighbourhood – an inspector that's trying to find out how it is that the Posts and Telegraphs Department is losing such thousands and millions of pounds every year. And so Jurie Steyn has run away into the bush to hide. Well, I only hope, for his sake, that in the thick bush he doesn't with his striped braces get taken, from behind, for a quagga."

Another thing a post office inspector would have a lot to say about, Oupa Bekker remarked – in addition to Jurie Steyn's stealing, that was – was the dreadful way Jurie Steyn loafed.

"How can he do justice to his post office work *or* his farming?" Oupa Bekker asked. "The way he spends hours every week, standing behind his counter talking a lot of nonsense to us – we who are sitting here on important post office business, waiting for the Government lorry over long periods."

Yes, we agreed with Oupa Bekker, it would be an eye-opener, we were sure, if we were to work out how much time we had regularly to devote, on those same riempies seats, to officially waiting there like that, waiting for our mail. And to think that during all that time Jurie Steyn would just stand behind the counter and laze.

We said that we were certain the authorities wouldn't put up with some of the things taking place in the post office if they knew. In our own time, even, there had been some pretty disgraceful carryings-on in the post office, we said.

"But one thing," Johnny Coen observed, "Jurie Steyn isn't standing behind the counter now, lazing."

And so Gysbert van Tonder said that it was the first time in his recollection that Jurie Steyn wasn't.

"And wouldn't it be funny if Jurie Steyn was hiding, not in the bush, but behind the counter there?" Gysbert van Tonder continued. "That would be a joke, wouldn't it? I mean, if all the time he has been listening to what we have been saying about him, ha, ha."

We laughed very heartily at that idea, and it had of course to happen that while we were still laughing our loudest Jurie Steyn suddenly did pop up from behind the counter, striped braces and all.

We learnt afterwards that he had been squatting on the floor, there, searching through some files, when a couple of us came in. Then, when he heard his name mentioned, he decided to crouch behind the counter, to hear more of what we had to say about him.

Chris Welman, in discussing it afterwards, said that how Jurie Steyn spoke then was the most awful single-handed dressing-down he had ever listened to since he was in the Kalahari with a Hollander and their Bushman guides decamped one night, taking with them a bottle of gin that the Hollander used as medicine. The Hollander spoke of the Bushmen in much the same terms that Jurie Steyn saw fit to employ then, Chris Welman said.

Only, for the Bushmen it was less painful than it was for us, seeing that when the Hollander spoke the Bushmen didn't have to sit around on riempies chairs and listen. When he heard Jurie Steyn talk, Chris Welman said, he actually wished that he was one of those Bushmen – sitting hundreds of miles out in the desert drinking gin.

Anyway, the first of us that was able to make a reasonably coherent remark, after all that, was Oupa Bekker. And Oupa Bekker said it was well known that an eavesdropper never heard any good about himself. There was an Afrikaans proverb about it, too, even, Oupa Bekker said. It was such an old proverb that it was hardly Afrikaans, either, but more like High Dutch. (Chris Welman told us, too, afterwards, that when Oupa Bekker said those words he again thought of what had happened in the Kalahari, and then he remembered that what the Hollander spoke was also mostly High Dutch, about the Bushmen.)

The proverb about eavesdroppers rhymed, Oupa Bekker went on, and one of the words in the rhyme was so low that no respectable people used it in Afrikaans anymore but only in High Dutch.

A perturbed expression came over Jurie Steyn's face. It was not difficult to imagine that he must have worn very much that same sort of look earlier in the afternoon, when he heard from behind the counter what our real opinion of him was. It was to be hoped that, through habit, Jurie Steyn's features were not going to remain set in that mould.

"If you think that, on top of everything else you've been saying about me," Jurie Steyn burst out, "if you think that on top of everything else I'm also an eavesdropper –"

But Oupa Bekker said, no, it was different in Jurie Steyn's case.

"If you think I'm nothing more than a High Dutch word –" Jurie Steyn started again.

No, Oupa Bekker said to Jurie Steyn, reassuringly, we didn't think that of him. After all, it wasn't as though he had gone and hidden himself behind the counter on purpose.

"Although," Oupa Bekker added, shaking his head half-sorrowfully, "you *could* have come out from there quicker. Before we had said some of the things that we would rather have left unsaid, perhaps."

"*Perhaps*," Gysbert van Tonder muttered, but not loud enough for Jurie Steyn to hear.

So Jurie Steyn said that if we expected him to apologise for having listened to our disparaging statements about him, well, that would give him a laugh. He only hoped that next time he would overhear us saying even worse things about him, like that he should be sentenced by a judge of the Supreme Court to get lashes, or that he should get hanged, even. And he wouldn't apologise for it, either, no matter how low the things were that he overheard us saying about him, Jurie Steyn said.

But by that time Oupa Bekker was well under way with a story of the old days that related to an occasion when he, too, was inadvertently an audience to a duologue, his own personal appearance, mind and character serving as subject matter for the spoken piece in question. The shallow nature of the duologue could, Oupa Bekker said, best be gathered from a girl's fatuous giggles and a man's guffaws with which it was, at intervals, punctuated.

It was in the old Cape Western Province, Oupa Bekker said, and there were farmhouses with thick walls and long stoeps and curved gables. And there was a girl, Lettie, that he was in love with. And there were oak-trees and ceilings with yellow-wood beams. And there was a young fellow, Gert Viljee, that Oupa Bekker despised just on sight for his giving himself such airs because of how he could play football.

And one night there was a dance at a farmhouse that had a large, old-fashioned wagon-house at the back. And it was moonlight.

"I hadn't in so many words asked Lettie to come and meet me there, by the side of the wagon-house," Oupa Bekker said, "but when two people are in love, you don't need many words. I just clasped her hand in the voorhuis, where the dancing was. Then I winked, subtly, and jerked my thumb over my shoulder in the direction of the wagon-house, a number of times. Then I slipped out of the door and went round to the back to wait for her."

He had to wait quite a while, Oupa Bekker said. It looked as though Lettie was taking her time. But then, afterwards, he did hear footsteps. And so, in order to give her a surprise, he went and hid behind the oak-tree whose leaves cast shadows on the whitewashed wall of the wagon-house – the shadow of the oak-leaves making it look like it was a creeper, Oupa Bekker said.

The approaching footsteps sounded a bit heavy for a girl, which made Oupa Bekker wonder if Lettie had perhaps been drinking a little. But the next moment he saw that it was the footballer, Gert Viljee. It was an embarrassing moment for Oupa Bekker. He would have looked silly if he had come out of hiding, then.

"And the next thing, Lettie turned up there," Oupa Bekker said. "And then I wondered for the second time if she had not been drinking, having in that way come to mistake Gert Viljee for me. I wondered that because of how she went right up to him and let him hold her in his arms. And then I heard my name mentioned, with Lettie saying what a job she had to get rid of me all evening. 'But afterwards he held my hand and made some silly signs – to say he was going home, I think,' Lettie said. 'And about time, too.'"

They made many remarks about him that they appeared to think funny – remarks that he would not repeat now, Oupa Bekker said, for it had happened long ago, and he did not wish to show up Lettie and Gert Viljee for how empty-headed they were.

"But then Gert Viljee suddenly said there were things about me that I didn't get proper credit for," Oupa Bekker went on. "And Lettie said, yes, she for one did not agree with what people said about my singing. And Gert Viljee said he thought it was very wrong of people to say that I danced like a muscovy duck. No matter how I danced, people had no right to criticise me like that, he said.

"Well, I started getting quite a good opinion of myself again, to hear how they were standing up for me. I was particularly pleased, too, to hear Lettie say that she had only a few days before spoken severely to her father for saying that I looked like a miltsiek kwê-bird.

"But the next moment I understood why they were saying all those complimentary things about me. For, when I looked at the wall, I saw that the shadow of the oak-tree's trunk had by now reached to the edge of it, and next to it there was a good deal of my own shadow sticking out. So I realised that Lettie and Gert Viljee knew I was there.

"'And it's also not right that they should always tap their foreheads like that when they talk about him,' I heard Gert Viljee say."

The silence that ensued was of some duration.

"Well, anyway, I am pleased that there was no part of my shadow showing from behind the counter," Jurie Steyn said, eventually. "I wouldn't like to hear what you would have had to say about me if you knew I was there – *if you had started standing up for me*, I mean."

Failing Sight

We did not think that the picture in the newspaper that At Naudé passed round to us was particularly funny. After all, it wasn't the first time we had known of a Bapedi chief that had got over his troubles with a motor-car that way.

And, as Chris Welman pointed out, so many things had already been said about motor-cars, and about the things that happened to motor-cars, that that sort of picture didn't raise a laugh anymore.

"Even at the Gaborone end of the Dwarsberge, where the sand starts," Chris Welman proceeded, a perceptible disdain in his voice at the thought of there actually being so unsophisticated a region, "even there they don't think it's funny, today, when a man takes a car to the garage and they find after two days that why it won't go is because it hasn't got petrol."

"Or through the engine having got stolen out of it by some mine-boys passing through there on their way back to Rhodesia," Gysbert van Tonder supplemented, "the garage taking two days to find out that the engine wasn't there at all."

Generally speaking, yes, we were inclined to agree with Chris Welman. Jokes about a motor-car were pretty stale. There didn't seem to be much point in At Naudé having gone to the trouble of cutting that photograph out of the newspaper and passing it round to us in Jurie Steyn's voorkamer. For we all knew that sort of thing. But At Naudé insisted that we had missed the true purpose of his having brought that newspaper cutting along. Had we studied the picture carefully, he asked.

"But that's what we've been saying," Jurie Steyn, whose turn it was with the photograph, observed. "We've known of a Bapedi chief doing exactly the same thing before. And it's not so very funny, I don't think. After a person had had a lot of trouble with a motor-car I can quite imagine that he would come to believe that that was the easiest way out – removing the engine, because it's just so much unnecessary weight, and inspanning a good team of long-horned oxen to pull the motor-car, instead. There's nothing unusual about it, anymore. Another thing, I'll go so far as to say it's sensible."

While there might have been nothing very unusual about the photograph, it was certainly not customary for Jurie Steyn to acknowledge that a Bapedi chief could do anything sensible. It was the schoolmaster's turn to examine the clipping.

"It's not so much that it's an old joke, although it is that, too, of course," young Vermaak said, "but it's also an old photograph. Take that jacket, now, that that white man has got on sitting in the car next to the Bapedi chief. It's years since they stopped making jackets with that narrow kind of lapel. And look how straight up the white man is sitting. It looks as though he's very proud to be in a motor-car. Or to be having his photo taken. Or to be sitting next to a Bapedi chief.

"And the car – why, I've never seen so old-fashioned a model. And that headlight sticking out behind the ox's ear – it's the kind of lamp we used to light to go to the stable with when I was a boy. The only part of the picture that looks up-to-date is the trek-chain fastened onto the car's bumper. And as for the white man's moustache – well, there's an old model-T for you, if you like."

The schoolmaster said that, as far as he was concerned, it actually *was* a funny photograph. And it wasn't the circumstance of the motor-car being drawn by a span of oxen that made him laugh, either. The real scream was that moustache.

Studying the old photograph in his turn, Oupa Bekker said that maybe it was an old joke. But he had nothing against an old joke, himself. Indeed, some of the old jokes were the best, Oupa Bekker said. For one thing, they lasted longest.

"Only, Rabusang doesn't look like that, anymore," Oupa Bekker added, shaking his head.

"But Rabusang never did look like that," At Naudé said, laughing. "It's not Rabusang but some other Bapedi chief. All it has got printed under the photograph is 'Bapedi chief cheerful about petrol shortage.' It doesn't say which Bapedi chief."

At Naudé went on to say that it was a bit of a showing-up for Oupa Bekker, his making a mistake like that. For it was well known that Oupa

Bekker, while admitting that his hearing might not perhaps be what it once was, always claimed that his eyesight was as good as ever.

"But I've just said that he doesn't look like Rabusang," Oupa Bekker explained, getting petulant. "How do you expect me to say it any clearer than what I've just said it? I've just *said* that Rabusang doesn't look like that – not unless he's changed a good deal with the years. This Bapedi chief doesn't look like Rabusang any more than that white man there with the silly moustache looks like Rabusang. In any case, the light's not too good."

Oupa Bekker didn't say whether it was the light that he himself was sitting in at that moment, or the light in which the two occupants of the motor-car had sat years ago when the photograph was taken.

"In any case," Oupa Bekker proceeded, quickly, apparently anxious that his failing powers of vision should not be made the subject of a lengthy and detailed disquisition, "I also once travelled quite a distance in a motor-car that a Bapedi chief had taken the engine out of and that was being pulled by a long span of oxen.

"It was before daybreak. I was going by ox-wagon to Ramoutsa. We had started early and there was that thick mist that hangs over the turf-lands by the Molopo on winter mornings. The voorloper was carrying a lantern to see the road. I was walking by the side of the wagon. And it was in the light of the lantern that we saw a motor-car on the road in front of us.

"A motor-car was a new thing in those days, and so I guessed that it must be the motor-car that Chief Umsufu had bought some time ago. I was surprised that it was going so slowly, though – not even at walking pace. It must be that some part of the machinery wasn't working like it should, I thought. Or perhaps Chief Umsufu had put the brakes on, I thought, since he might prefer not to go so fast in the dark.

"Afterwards, the driver put his head out of the window. Out of curiosity to see how a motor-car went, I had by that time got almost level with the motor-car, so that Chief Umsufu and I both recognised each other by the light of the voorloper's lantern coming on behind.

"When Chief Umsufu told me I could have a lift I climbed in pretty quickly. It was the first time I had ever been in a motor-car and I didn't want to miss any of the ride. It was only afterwards, when it got properly daylight, that I could see through the mist what it was that was making the motor-car move, and I felt pretty disappointed, then, I can tell you.

But I didn't get out then, all the same. For one thing, it wouldn't be polite, I thought.

"And then, for another thing, it *was*, after all, a motor-car that I was riding in, and for years to come I would be able to talk about it, telling people about how I once went to Ramoutsa in a motor-car. And there would be no need for me to say that it was Chief Umsufu's motor-car and that it was being pulled by a team of oxen. What I might mention, perhaps, was that the motor-car was not travelling particularly fast, that time, because of the roads.

"But, in the meantime, sitting in the motor-car on that early morning and not knowing that the engine part of it was rusting by an ant-hill next to the chief's cattle-kraal, I must say that I got a lot of enjoyment out of the journey.

"I could feel by the soft cushions that it was a very good class of motor-car. And then, also, the motor-car didn't make a noise. I already knew that you could tell it was a good motor-car if the engine was silent. And I don't think there has ever been a motor-car engine as silent as Chief Umsufu's was, on that misty morning. In fact, in talking to the chief, I hardly had to raise my voice at all, to make myself heard.

"Another thing I noticed was that there seemed to be lots of cattle on the road. I saw, a good number of times, through the mist when it lifted slightly at intervals, a pair of horns or the back part of an ox. At times I also heard what I took to be cattle-drovers shouting out Sechuana words. Some time later I began to realise that it was the same words, all the time. And when day broke I saw clearly that it was also the same pairs of horns."

Gysbert van Tonder said, in a nasty way, that it would appear that already in those days Oupa Bekker's faculties had started failing.

"Either that, or –" Gysbert van Tonder said, concluding the remark with a gesture to indicate that, as likely as not, Oupa had been drinking.

"What Chief Umsufu said to me afterwards," Oupa Bekker continued, "was that it was because he believed in progress that he had bought the motor-car in the first place. But I would never believe what trouble he had with it, the chief said. And then he found out that what was wrong with an ordinary motor-car was that it didn't have enough progress.

"And so he used his brains and worked out how to remedy it. And since then he had had no trouble at all with his motor-car, he said. And he didn't have to worry anymore about what the roads were like, either. Where an ox could go, there his motor-car could go, too, now, the chief said. And also where a mule could go. You could see that he was very proud of what he had done. 'Engelsman!' the chief shouted at the oxen, 'Witvoet! Lekkerland!' at the same time bringing his foot down on some piece of machinery that, I suppose, would have made the motor-car go faster in the days when the engine was still there, before Chief Umsufu used his brains on it."

Thereupon Chris Welman said that, as he had mentioned earlier, there was nothing funny anymore in stories that had to do with motor-cars. The long story Oupa Bekker had just told proved that, Chris Welman said. Since the motor-car had come into the Transvaal, life on the platteland was no longer the same thing.

The only kind of story about the Transvaal that was worth listening to, Chris Welman said, was a story about the Transvaal before there were motor-cars, or before they had that machine on Rysmierbult station that you put pennies in for chocolates.

"Or before they had cameras," At Naudé said. Then he asked Oupa Bekker if there was already a photographer at Ramoutsa, the time he went there with Chief Umsufu's motor-car. Oupa Bekker, after reflecting for a few moments, said, yes, he thought there was.

"And did you have your photograph taken?" At Naudé asked. "Before the motor-car was outspanned, even?"

After thinking about it for a bit, Oupa Bekker said, yes, he did seem to remember something about it.

"Well, take another look at that, then," At Naudé said, passing the newspaper cutting back to Oupa Bekker. "I *said* that nobody had studied it properly. Who do you see sitting in that motor-car? Don't laugh too loudly, now."

Oupa Bekker examined the bit of newspaper carefully.

"Yes," he said, at length. "Yes, it does look something like Chief Umsufu. In fact, it is Chief Umsufu. I would recognise him from this photo anywhere. But when I said at the start that it wasn't Rabusang –"

"Nobody is talking about Rabusang," At Naudé interjected, sounding cross. "But who's that white man, sitting there large as life, next to the chief? Don't laugh, now."

Oupa Bekker looked at the picture some more. Then he handed it back to At Naudé.

"It's no good," Oupa Bekker said. "It's some white man I don't know. Some white man with a silly-looking kind of moustache. But, of course, that sort of moustache was worn quite a lot, in those days."

VII

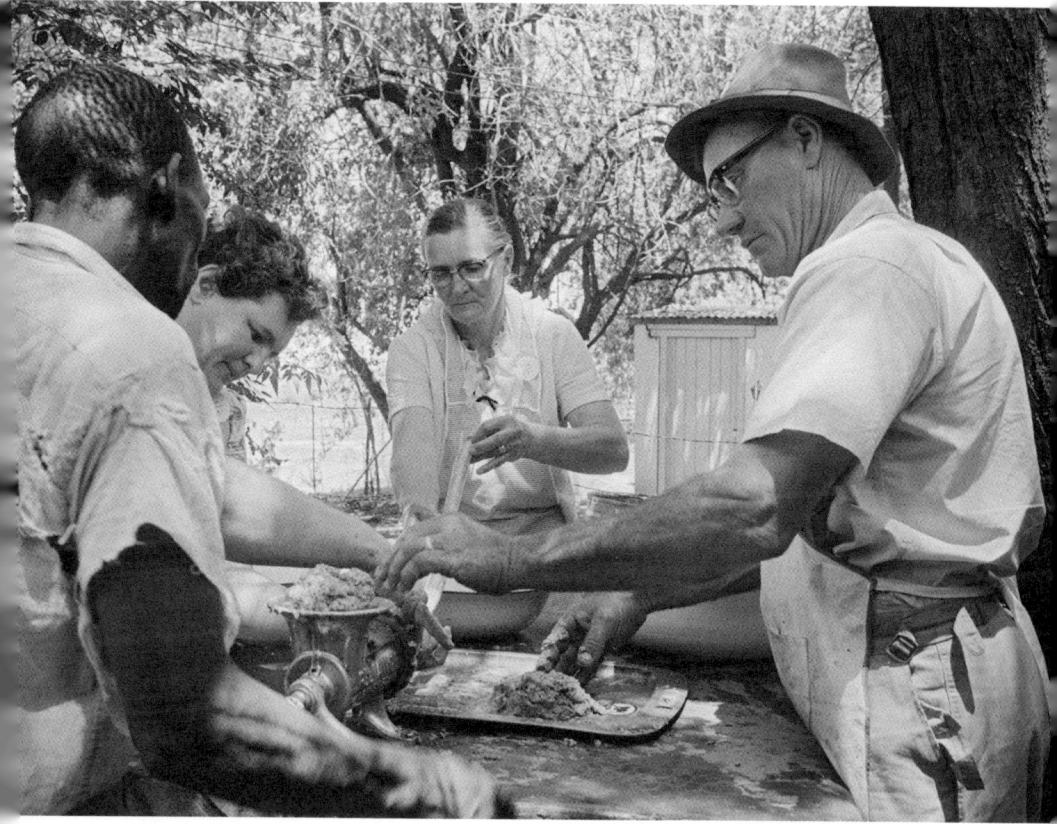

Making boerewors for the New Year festivities of the Dwarsberg Boerevereniging, Nietver-
diend. December 1965

Sixes and Sevens

"Smells good," Gysbert van Tonder observed. His manner was expectant.

"Tastes good, too," Jurie Steyn replied, with his mouth full.

Jurie Steyn was seated behind the counter. In front of him was a dish of mealie-pap and ribbok ribs that he was eating mainly with his fingers.

"Cooked it myself, too, with the wife away in Johannesburg," Jurie Steyn continued, in between taking a kick at a couple of mongrel dogs that were fighting under the counter over a bone that he had thrown on the floor.

"Sets you up, a good feed like this does," Jurie Steyn added. "I cooked it just on the ashes of a fire I made next to an ant-hill. No nonsense with a kitchen stove. I don't understand a kitchen stove."

In the main, we agreed with Jurie Steyn that we did not have much understanding of the workings of a kitchen stove, either. We would have agreed with him on anything, then.

A few minutes later Chris Welman came in.

"Smells good," Chris Welman remarked. His voice sounded hopeful.

"Cooked it myself," Jurie Steyn answered. "Just on the ashes."

Not long afterwards At Naudé came in at the front door.

"Smells good," At Naudé said, coughing in an insinuating way.

"Just on the ashes," Jurie Steyn informed him.

It was only natural, then, that we should spend some time in discussing sundry aspects of the culinary art as practised in the open. Cooking on a fire made next to an ant-hill, we said. Or made next to a boulder. Or made just next to nothing at all. And then you didn't need such a thing as a pot, either, we said, except maybe for the mealie-pap. And for that just a tin would do, also. And you needed hardly such a thing as a kettle, either, except, of course, for the coffee. And cooking out in the open we didn't need plates, at all. In fact, about all you ever used a plate for, out in the veld, was to dish the food into, that you'd cooked. And we didn't need such a thing as a knife and a fork and a spoon, either, we said, except maybe just to eat with.

About then, Oupa Bekker arrived. "Smells –" Oupa Bekker began.

"– on the ashes," Jurie Steyn declared.

From there Gysbert van Tonder started to talk about how much simpler life was on a farm than in a city; and about how much more enjoyable it was, too. You never felt that you were really alive in a city – not really living, that was. Take Johannesburg, now, Gysbert van Tonder said. It was all just big shops with plate-glass windows and bright lights and bioscopes and saloon bars with green curtains in front of them. Could you really call that living, spending your days in a place like that, Gysbert van Tonder demanded.

And so Chris Welman said, no, it was too awful to think of it, even. Especially the saloon bars with the green curtains in front of them were too awful to bear thinking of, Chris Welman added, reflectively passing the back of his hand over his mouth as he spoke.

"And you don't really need cups, either," Gysbert van Tonder remarked, reverting to his consideration of the simple delights afforded by the great outdoors, "except maybe just for drinking coffee out of."

"Or a razor, either," young Vermaak, the schoolmaster, supplemented, "except perhaps just to shave with. In fact, it seems to me that you don't need *anything* out on the veld, except just to use that thing for what it was meant for."

Naturally, young Vermaak would talk like that, we felt. Since he was a schoolmaster, it was only to be expected that he would miss some of those finer points, which you had to be born and bred on the veld to be able to understand.

"Actually, what I feel for city people," Chris Welman said, "is just pity. I mean, just think how miserable a person from the city looks, when he comes to a farm, to visit. Right here in the Marico, even, I've seen it."

"It's particularly when the farmer shows the visitor from the city over his lands," Gysbert van Tonder interjected. "And the farmer explains to the visitor where he's going to plough, next year, and where he's going to sow sugar beans. And the farmer takes the visitor right round the twenty-morgen patch where the barbed-wire fence is to come for the new camp, but where there is now just nothing but thorn-bush."

Yes, Chris Welman agreed, and at the end of it, through his having accompanied the farmer through that stretch of thorn-bush, it would appear to the visitor from the city as though the barbed wire that the farmer had been talking about was already there, in place. What would give the visitor from the city that illusion, Chris Welman said, was the way his sports blazer looked, consequent on the visitor having been through those thorns.

"What makes it even more miserable," Jurie Steyn declared, pushing aside his empty plate with a gesture expressive of contented repletion, "is when the visitor acts as though he enjoys it all. You get that sort, too. Queer idea of enjoyment, though, I must say. Give me just a plain piece of ribbok – just roasted on the ashes. That's all I ask."

Thereupon Oupa Bekker said that, speaking for himself, he wouldn't ask much more than just about that, either. With, say, perhaps just a slice of raw onion to go with it. It was funny, though, that when Jurie Steyn was out there by the fire, it didn't occur to him that he would that afternoon be having visitors in his voorkamer. Seeing that Jurie Steyn's was the only farm in those parts where you could still get an occasional ribbok in the rante, Oupa Bekker said, expressing what we all felt, there would have been no harm in his having roasted a few more pieces.

"I did," Jurie Steyn said, "roast a few more pieces. And I ate them."

Even though we had really come there just for our letters and milk-cans, At Naudé remarked, we were still, in a sense, visiting Jurie Steyn. And if he had been properly brought up, Jurie Steyn would have treated us accordingly.

Jurie Steyn puffed at his pipe with an air of deep satisfaction.

"I know you're a visitor," Jurie Steyn said to At Naudé, "but with my wife away, I can't be as polite as I would like to be. I've got nobody to look after this place. But if you'll wear your Nagmaal jacket next time you come, I'll be glad to show you all over my farm where I'm not going to plant potatoes next season. That is, among the haak-en-steek thorns."

It was clear that this was not one of Jurie Steyn's friendly days. Perhaps all that ribbok he had eaten was already beginning to disagree with him.

"All the same," Chris Welman said, after a pause, "I can't see that there's anything so very much wrong in having a bit of fun at the expense of somebody that comes from the city to visit you on your farm.

357

I don't mean anything rough, like playing tricks on a person, for instance, because he's a stranger."

So we said, no, that positively was something we could not associate ourselves with, either.

"What I mean is all right, for instance," Chris Welman continued, "is to push a small likkewaan down the back of a visitor's neck, and to pretend to him that it's a mamba. Now, there's no harm in a little joke like that, and it's usually also very amusing for the children. And what there's nothing wrong with, either, is when you're with a visitor in the bush at night and you tell him that almost anything that he sees stirring is a mamba. That's also just fun. And so is also, when he's in bed, pulling a length of hosepipe over the visitor with a piece of string, and making out to him that *that's* a mamba. You see what I mean? I don't believe in playing *pranks* on a stranger."

In his list of playful deceptions which could, with advantage, be practised on visitors from the city, Chris Welman did not betray any marked originality. Nor did he make it clear as to the stage at which a jest ceased being broadly funny and became a prank. Maybe it was the stage at which a mamba actually bit a visitor. Maybe it was that sort of thing, too, that imparted to a visitor from the city that aspect of a peculiar melancholy of which we had already made mention.

"After all, we haven't got very much that we can entertain ourselves with, here on the veld," Gysbert van Tonder agreed with Chris Welman. "And it gets so lonely here, too, sometimes, with only the bush and the koppies, that you can go just about mad, almost."

"Whereas, in a city, people have got everything," Chris Welman said. "If you want something from a shop you haven't got to drive eleven miles there. And there are the bioscopes. And all the people on the sidewalks. And the bright lights at night. And there is also –"

"Yes," Gysbert van Tonder said, "with a green curtain in front."

"Taking a visitor from the city over your farm," Jurie Steyn said, musingly. "Well, my grandfather was great on that. Right until the time of his death, my grandfather would tell this story, and laugh. What made it even funnier, as far as my grandfather was concerned, was that this visitor from the city, who wore a black frock-coat, actually was entitled to be shown all over the farm. For the visitor had come from the city with a lot of papers to buy my grandfather's farm. And my grandfather sold the farm to the visitor, my grandfather getting fifty pounds more for the farm than what he had paid for it. But, all the same, my grand-father just couldn't resist having a joke with the visitor. And because there wasn't any bush on the farm, seeing that it was a highveld farm, my grandfather got the visitor in his long frock-coat and all to climb through a barbed-wire fence, instead, quite a number of times. And why my grandfather laughed so much was because the visitor didn't know it was the same barbed-wire fence that he was climbing through, each time."

Jurie Steyn paused to pull at his pipe some more. And in between he informed us that he had also been having a little joke on us, that afternoon, seeing that we were visitors. "I've got a piece of ribbok meat wrapped up for each of you in the kitchen," he said. "I'll fetch it out for you when the lorry comes. But if you'll take my advice, you'll get your wives to cook it for you properly on the stove. It's no good roasted on the ashes. For one thing, all the gravy runs to waste. And it also *tastes* queer, cooked just on the ashes. I don't know where the old people got that idea from."

After that he started talking about his grandfather again.

"Whenever my grandfather told this story," Jurie Steyn said, "he would laugh so much that he would slap the top part of his leg, laugh-ing. But there was one side of the story of the farm that my grandfather sold for fifty pounds more than he paid for it that my grandfather never used to lay stress on, that you would notice. And I only understood that side of it properly when I went on a journey one day to the highveld to go and have a look at that old farm again. And I had great difficulty in finding it, seeing that everything about it had changed so much. They had even changed the name of the old farm. They now called it Benoni. And there was a mine head-gear where the stable had been.

"And I have often thought since then of how that visitor from the city must have laughed when he told his side of the story – how he must have slapped the top part of *his* leg, I mean, laughing.

"And it doesn't seem to me as though it's shreds of the stranger's frock-coat hanging on the barbed-wire fence. It's like it's my grand-father's own clothes hanging there, blowing in the wind."

Mental Trouble

It was bound to happen, we said, talking of At Naudé's nervous breakdown. Living by himself like that and listening in to the wireless all the time and reading the newspapers, we said, was a sure way for a man to go strange in his mind.

"Not that you can see it on him, much," Gysbert van Tonder said, "except, maybe, from that wild glare that comes into his eyes, at moments."

"One time I saw that wild glare," Chris Welman announced, "was when Gysbert van Tonder asked could he have At Naudé's wireless, now, since At Naudé would probably not be permitted to keep it in the place where he was going to be taken to. The other time was when Gysbert van Tonder was pouring himself a mug of mampoer out of the jar standing near At Naudé's bed. It was when it seemed as though Gysbert was going to empty the jar that At Naudé again got that wild look in his eye. You've got no idea how wild."

"Except that he doesn't get out of bed and that wild look," Jurie Steyn asked, "how else is he sick? Talks queer, I suppose?"

Gysbert van Tonder and Chris Welman nodded solemnly and in unison.

"That's where the rest of us Marico farmers are different," Jurie Steyn said, expressing what we were all thinking. "Look how sensibly we talk here in my voorkamer. It's through not reading newspapers and that sort of thing that keeps us healthy-minded. I suppose At Naudé thinks he's Napoleon, too, hey?"

But Gysbert van Tonder said that that was something that he couldn't swear to, really. And Chris Welman said, no, he couldn't, either – not swear to, that was.

"I mean, he didn't say straight out that he was Napoleon," Chris Welman supplemented his statement. "He didn't put his hat on sideways and hold one hand in his waistcoat and the other behind his back, like in that bioscope picture. But then, of course, At Naudé was lying in bed."

Jurie Steyn raised his eyebrows in mute enquiry.

"He didn't – ?" Jurie Steyn asked.

"No," Gysbert van Tonder admitted, determined on being truthful. "No, he didn't have his hat on in bed. I looked. Because I know that's a sign that a man isn't normal – if he wears his hat in bed, and he's not wearing his hat in bed because it's raining and the rainwater is leaking through the roof."

But Oupa Bekker said you couldn't always go by that. It wasn't always a sure sign – the Napoleon sign or the hat sign, Oupa Bekker said. Or keeping your kitchen full of scorpions as pets.

Jurie Steyn said, well, maybe Oupa Bekker was right. He wouldn't argue. Maybe a person who did things like that wasn't mad. But it was mad enough for *him*, Jurie Steyn said.

"Or bending a curtain rod into a trumpet for blowing into to chase meerkats away," Oupa Bekker continued imperturbably. "Sitting on your front stoep blowing. Or hearing voices. Or following the instructions in the Agricultural Department's booklet on how to increase your mealie production."

It was apparent that Oupa Bekker had in his time come across a pretty comprehensive assortment of Bushveld eccentricities.

"I've noticed," Oupa Bekker went on, "that if a man is queer in one way, he may be quite all right in other ways. And so it's a mistake that he's mad because, say, for instance, he – well, what was that you said At Naudé had got?"

Gysbert van Tonder explained.

"The reason At Naudé has gone to bed," Gysbert van Tonder said, "is because he says he keeps on seeing grey and black spots before his eyes the shape of aeroplanes –"

"What sort?" Johnny Coen interjected quickly. "Bombers or just passenger planes?"

They hadn't gone into it so far, Gysbert van Tonder said, in their discussions with At Naudé.

"Well, he did the right thing, anyway," Jurie Steyn said, "going to bed. Time, too, I should think. And no matter *what* kind of aeroplanes he sees. I mean, he can't get dangerous, as long as he just keeps lying in bed."

"And with his hat off," Chris Welman made haste to concur.

"As Oupa Bekker would say," Jurie Steyn remarked with a wink, "there's just nothing wrong with At Naudé, except that he just sees a lot of aeroplanes all the time, in his bedroom at Okkerneutblaar, via Sinkplaas, District Groot Marico, with the curtains drawn. Next thing he'll *give* Gysbert van Tonder that wireless set of his, simply because he won't need it anymore. He'll be able to hear all kinds of music and everything just in his room at Okkerneutblaar, and without any wireless at all. Oh, yes, you can see he's quite sane. But I only hope they move him from there pretty soon into a room that's got the walls all lined with pillows. Before he starts chopping people up, that is. I mean, seeing he's so sane."

Even though it was his own voorkamer that he was talking in, we all felt that it was not quite right that Jurie Steyn should be so heartless about At Naudé.

So we were glad when Oupa Bekker started talking again about how a man could appear to be mad in one way and yet in all other respects be completely normal. That was after Jurie Steyn had spoken of the day that At Naudé would be taken to the Weskoppies institution, outside Pretoria. And Jurie Steyn said he wondered what At Naudé would think when they passed the aerodrome and he saw real aeroplanes.

"When he sees those aeroplanes, there, taking off for Cape Town and England," Jurie Steyn said, "I suppose he'll think he's just imagining them, too. And he'll say to the male nurse in the blue uniform that he's got those spots in front of his eyes again that look like aeroplanes. And the male nurse will say, 'But, Meneer Naudé, they *are* aeroplanes.' And poor old At will think the male nurse is just saying that to humour him."

Never mind At Naudé, we thought. Jurie Steyn seemed in a pretty bad way himself, thinking out all that kind of nonsense.

But by that time Oupa Bekker had started citing the parallel instance of the mental trouble that came to Joggem Struys in the old days. What *looked* like mental trouble to outside observers, Oupa Bekker took pains to point out.

"Joggem Struys claimed he had a snake in his inside," Oupa Bekker said.

"What sort of snake, a mamba or a –" Johnny Coen began again.

"– or a rinkhals. I don't know," Oupa Bekker headed him off. "But it was a black snake that was eating out his inside, Joggem Struys said.

362

Twisting and squirming and eating. Sometimes, from his symptoms, it seemed like it might be a bakkop. Other times, again, it sounded more like a boomslang, except that a boomslang is green, whereas the snake in Joggem Struys's inside was black. Of course, it was snake country in which Joggem Struys lived, and we know that there are some pretty queer places that a snake can get into, when it's real snake country, especially in the old days –"

Thereupon Chris Welman mentioned the case of a snake that had got into the cupboard of the konsistorie where the Nagmaal wine was kept, and of the fright the dominee received when he went to that cupboard at a time when it wasn't Nagmaal. But the dominee's agitation was only equalled by the alarm awakened in an elder when *he* went to that cupboard at a time when it wasn't Nagmaal. And only afterwards it was discovered, Chris Welman said, that that snake was only a tame snake that the verger had introduced into the wine cupboard for reasons of his own.

After that, Gysbert van Tonder spoke about a quite untrained snake with a love for education that used to come and clean the blackboard for the teacher and at playtime made himself into a hoop for the children to roll around. But that snake was a bad example to the class, Gysbert van Tonder said, because of the habit he had of putting his tongue out, and forked, too, whenever he wasn't thinking. Sticking out his tongue in class was a practice that the teacher couldn't encourage and that the snake couldn't break himself of, and so he wasn't allowed to come to the school anymore, Gysbert van Tonder said.

To talk of snakes was an invitation to everybody to tell all the Bushveld lies they could think of, with the result that it was quite a while before Oupa Bekker could return to the subject of Joggem Struys and his internal complaint.

"And so it was proved from what the doctor said," Oupa Bekker ended up, having spoken at some length, "that Joggem Struys was not really so mad, after all. The symptoms of the stomach trouble that Joggem had, the doctor said, were such that could very well be described as like a black snake eating up your inside. That was what made it easy for the doctor to work out what medicines to give him. The doctor said that Joggem Struys's sickness had a long Greek name that *meant* a black snake eating up your inside."

That gave young Vermaak, the schoolmaster, his chance to show

how much he knew both about medicine and Greek. Melan, he said, was the Greek for black, and ophis was the word for a snake. What the Greek word for eating was, he did not, however, know.

Nevertheless, the schoolmaster said, one could understand, in the same way, that what At Naudé was suffering from was some form of illness that made spots come in front of his eyes. That would account for that look that Gysbert van Tonder and Chris Welman, giving a measure of rein to their imaginations, perhaps, had depicted as a wild glare.

"It is only natural, too," young Vermaak continued, "considering At Naudé's absorption in current world affairs, that he should also make use of his imagination a little and see those floating spots as aeroplanes. As jet fighters, likely as not."

Nor, the schoolmaster continued, should the significance be overlooked of that jar of mampoer that Chris Welman spoke of as being in the neighbourhood of At Naudé's bed. Within access of At Naudé's right hand when his arm was extended, the schoolmaster assumed.

"Well, that can bring spots before a person's eyes, all right," young Vermaak declared.

We nodded our heads in thoughtful agreement. Yes, we said, it could.

As it turned out – when we heard of what the doctor who attended At Naudé had to say about it – Oupa Bekker and the schoolmaster would appear to have summed up At Naudé's condition pretty correctly.

For the doctor said that after a few days of diet and medicine the spots would be gone from in front of At Naudé's eyes, and At would be about again.

And he was, too.

It was Gysbert van Tonder and Chris Welman, again, who imparted this news to us.

"He's all right now," they said.

"He's out of bed and sitting on his front stoep," they said.

"And he's got no more aeroplane spots in front of his eyes," they said.

At Naudé was very contented, sitting on his stoep. And he had bent a curtain rod into a trumpet that he was blowing into for chasing meerkats away, they said. Sitting on his front stoep blowing.

Man to Man

The young mounted policeman, Bothma, explained of course, that why he had called round at Jurie Steyn's post office, that afternoon, was just because he was on his regular rounds. He hadn't picked that afternoon, particularly, he added. And he hadn't come to Jurie Steyn's post office specially, any more than he would visit any other post office or voorkamer in that part of the Groot Marico specially, he said.

It was only that he was carrying out his duties of patrolling the area, he explained, and it just so happened that in the course of routine he was patrolling over Jurie Steyn's farm, then.

He was new to the job of being a mounted policeman, young Bothma added.

Well, we realised that much about him, of course, without his having had to say it. And because he was new to his work we made a good deal of allowance for him. But we were also pretty sure that the time would come when Mounted Constable Bothma would learn a few more things.

And he would understand then that nothing could rouse people's suspicions more than that a policeman should come round and offer all sorts of excuses for his being there.

"I just sort of make a few notes in my notebook," Bothma went on, "to say at what time, and so on, I call at each farmhouse that I do call on, patrolling, like I said."

Gysbert van Tonder yawned.

You could see, from the policeman's taking out his notebook and pencil like that, right at the beginning of his visit, and before he had sat down properly, almost, that he would yet have a long way to go and would have to traverse many a mile of made Bushveld road and bridle path, asking a multitude of questions and getting the same number of wrong answers, before his call at an isolated farmhouse would make the farmer start thinking quickly to himself.

But the way Bothma was now, the farmer wouldn't ask him had he come through the vlakte – expecting the policeman to say, untruthfully, no, he had followed the Government Road as far as the poort. The farmer's thoughts would not travel with lightning speed to his brandy still. Nor would the farmer wonder if those few head of Bechuana cattle were safe in the truck to the Johannesburg market.

All those things we could sense about Constable Bothma in Jurie Steyn's voorkamer that afternoon. It was also apparent to us that, before arriving at where we were, he had called on more than one Bushveld farmer en route. That would account for something of the diffidence in his manner. It was easy to guess that he had asked a few stock questions along the road – not that there was anything specific that he wanted to *know*, really, as he would no doubt have explained, but just because asking those questions was a part of his patrol duties – and it was only reasonable to suppose that the answers some of the Marico farmers had given him were not characterised by a noteworthy degree of artlessness.

He had doubtless discovered that while a policeman's questions might be, in terms of standing orders, stereotypes, a farmer's replies, generally speaking, weren't. Especially when that farmer's answers were being written straight into a notebook.

Nevertheless, because Bothma was, after all, a mounted policeman and in khaki uniform, with brass letters on his shoulders, we did feel a measure of constraint in his company. This circumstance of our not feeling quite at ease manifested itself in the way that most of us sat on our riempies chairs – just a little more stiffly than usual, our shoulders not quite touching the backs of the chairs. It also manifested itself in the unconventional way in which Gysbert van Tonder saw fit to sprawl in his seat, in an affectation of a mental content that would have awakened mistrustful imaginings in the breast of a policeman who had been, say, two and a half years at the game.

It was then that Chris Welman made a remark that went a good way towards relieving the tension. Afterwards, in talking it over, we had to say that we could not but admire the manner in which Chris Welman had worked out the right words to use. Not that there was anything clever in the way that Chris Welman spoke, of course.

No, we all felt that the statement Chris Welman made then was something that was easily within the capacity of any one of us to have made, if we had just sat back a little, and thought, and had then made use of the common sense that comes to anybody that has lived on a farm long enough.

"The man you should really ask questions of," Chris Welman said to Constable Bothma, "is Gysbert van Tonder. That's him there. Sitting with his legs taking up half the floor and his hands behind his head, with his elbows stretched out. Just from the way he's sitting, you can see he's the biggest cattle-smuggler in the whole of the Dwarsberg area."

Well, that gave us a good laugh, of course. We all *knew* that Gysbert van Tonder smuggled more cattle across the Konventie border than any other man in the Marico. What was more, we knew that Gysbert van Tonder's father had been regularly bringing in cattle over the line from Ramoutsa before there had ever been a proper barbed-wire fence there, even. And we also knew that, in the long years of the future, when we were all dead and gone, Gysbert van Tonder's sons would still be doing the same thing.

What was more, nothing would ever stop them, either. And not even if every policeman from Cape Town to the Limpopo knew about it. For the Bechuanas from whom he traded cattle felt friendly towards Gysbert van Tonder. And that was a sentiment they did not have for a border policeman, unreasonable though such an attitude of mind might perhaps seem. Moreover, this was an outlook on life that, to a not inconsiderable degree, Gysbert van Tonder shared with the Bechuanas.

Consequently, in having spoken the way he did, Chris Welman had cleared the air for all of us – for Gysbert van Tonder included. As a result, Gysbert van Tonder could for one thing sit more comfortably in his chair, relaxing as he sat. There was no longer any necessity for him to adopt a carefree pose which must have put quite a lot of strain on his neck and leg muscles, not even to talk of how hard it must have been for his spine to keep up that effortful bearing that was intended to suggest indifference.

Anyway, Gysbert van Tonder joined in the laughter that greeted Chris Welman's words. Constable Bothma laughed also. It was clear from that that about the first thing the sergeant at the Bekkersdal headquarters must have told young Bothma was about how he had to keep an eye on Gysbert van Tonder.

It was good to feel that there was so much tension lifted from us then, after Chris Welman had spoken, and we had all laughed, and we understood that we need not pretend to each other anymore.

"Of course, we know you haven't come here to spy on us," Jurie Steyn said to Constable Bothma, after a pause. "I mean, you've told us all that yourself. The little odds and ends of things that you put in your notebook – well, it's your job, isn't it? If you didn't write those little things in your notebook you'd get the sack, as likely as not. And if you didn't come and patrol my voorkamer, too, like you're doing now, you'd as likely as not also get the sack. And if you wrote anything in your notebook that isn't so, why, for that, of course, you would just get the sack, too."

From the way Jurie Steyn spoke, it would appear that, looked at from any angle, whatever Constable Bothma did, the one thing staring him in the face was dismissal from the police force.

"And there aren't so many things a policeman – I mean, an ex-policeman – can find to do when once he's got the sack," Jurie Steyn continued. "Because when you go and look for a job, afterwards, almost the first thing the boss will ask you is why you got the sack from the police. And no matter what your answer is, it always seems as though there is more behind it than what you say. Seeing that you are an ex-policeman applying for work the boss can never be sure about how much of what you are telling him is lies."

Johnny Coen took a hand in the conversation, then, and he said to the policeman that seeing that he and the policeman were both young, he could feel for the policeman. And he didn't want Constable Bothma to misunderstand what Jurie Steyn had just been saying, Johnny Coen went on. It was known that Jurie Steyn was like that, Johnny Coen said, but everybody knew that Jurie Steyn meant nothing by it.

It was just that we were all respectable people, respectable farmers, and so on, Johnny Coen explained, and for that reason we all got a little upset when a policeman came round, especially when the policeman pulled out a pencil and notebook. If we weren't such respectable people, respectable farmers and so on, Johnny Coen said, we wouldn't mind if even a dozen mounted policemen in uniforms came marching into our voorkamers with S. A. P. on their shoulders and with their horses waiting outside.

But it was just because we were respectable people that we got a guilty sort of a conscience when a policeman came into our house, Johnny Coen proceeded. And for that reason he wanted Constable Bothma to bear with Jurie Steyn and not to get offended at anything that Jurie Steyn said in haste.

"Oh, no," Constable Bothma said. "That is quite in order. I would not even have thought that there was anything insulting in it, in what Meneer Steyn said."

So Johnny Coen said that that was just what he meant. Any man that was not a policeman would very likely have had his pride hurt, by the way that Jurie Steyn had spoken. But he could see that it would, of course, be different with a policeman, Johnny Coen said. It wasn't that he thought a policeman didn't have *pride* –

Johnny Coen looked pretty foolish, then. For he had been trying to stand up for Constable Bothma, but had only succeeded in making Jurie Steyn's disparaging references to the police force sound a lot worse.

After that it was, of course, Oupa Bekker's turn to talk. And although Oupa Bekker's story related to some period in the past when the functions of a police constable were exercised apparently not unsuccessfully by the local veldkornet, it seemed as though the difficulties that Constable Bothma was experiencing at present had some features in common with the vicissitudes that the young veldkornet in Oupa Bekker's story went through.

"Many a man would have been satisfied with that position," Oupa Bekker was saying, "just because of the honour that went with it in those days. For one thing, even if you didn't have a uniform or an office with a telephone in it to work in, like you have today, or even a mounted policeman horse with a white star on his forehead that can keep time to the music at the Johannesburg Show – even if you had to ride just one of your own horses on a patched saddle, and you had a patch in the seat of your trousers, too, you still had a printed certificate signed by the president to say you were veldkornet, and that you could hang in a gold frame on the wall of your voorkamer."

But the glitter of rank and the nimbus of office were as nought to that young veldkornet, Oupa Bekker said. The thing that worried the young veldkornet was that, because he was charged with the maintenance of law and order in his area, he was called upon, in however delicate a manner, to act as an informer on his neighbour. The thought that, through his job, he was cut off from intimate contact with his fellow men saddened him. He liked having friends, and he found he couldn't have any, anymore – not real friends – now that he was veldkornet.

"In the end –" Oupa Bekker said.

But we had rather that Oupa Bekker had not continued to the end, which was at once stark and inexorable, pitiless and yet compelling. For the only true friend that the young veldkornet had in the end was Sass Koggel, a scoundrel the like of whom the Groot Marico District had had but few in its history. Only with Sass Koggel did the veldkornet find, in the end, that he could be as he really was.

Sass Koggel and the veldkornet took each other for what they were. Neither, in his relations with the other, had to put up any sort of pretence. They were on opposite sides of the law. The veldkornet was all out to lay Sass Koggel by the heels. Sass Koggel directed all his efforts to the end that the veldkornet should get nothing on him.

But, outside of that technicality, it would be hard to find, in the whole of the Marico, a couple of firmer friends than were those two.

It was a long story that Oupa Bekker told, and we listened to it with fluctuating degrees of attention.

But Constable Bothma and Gysbert van Tonder did not listen to Oupa Bekker at all. They were too engrossed in what each had to say to the other. And while talking to Gysbert van Tonder, the cattle-smuggler, it was only once necessary for the policeman, Constable Bothma, to open his notebook.

Constable Bothma opened his notebook at the back, somewhere, and extracted a photograph which he passed over to Gysbert van Tonder. Gysbert studied the likeness for some moments. "Takes after you, does he?" Gysbert van Tonder asked.

In his voice there was only sincerity.

FEAT OF MEMORY

"Where's that rubber stamp, now?" Jurie Steyn said, letting his eye travel the length of his post office counter. "I'm sure I had it here a few minutes ago. Right in my hand I had it."

"What's that thing you've still *got* in your hand, there, Jurie?" Chris Welman asked.

So Jurie Steyn said, well, if that didn't beat everything.

"If I didn't see it happening myself, right with my own eyes, I wouldn't believe it possible that a man could be so forgetful," Jurie Steyn said. "It's trouble does that to a person, of course, making him absent-minded like that – trouble and a high kind of official responsibility."

There were a few things that we would have all liked to have said about that, of course. We would have liked to have made mention of some of the quite unusual sorts of mistakes that happened in the post office, sometimes, with letters and parcels. And it would have given us pleasure, too, to have said that, everything considered, it was not surprising that errors of a kind we could mention crept into certain aspects of the post office's functionings.

If there were other post office servants with Jurie Steyn's high sense of official responsibility, we would have liked to have said. Instead, we let it pass. There were certain things, we knew, that Jurie Steyn did not like to be rubbed up the wrong way about.

The only one of us to make any comment at all was Gysbert van Tonder. And Gysbert contented himself with a mild statement to the effect that, with the way things were today, when you rolled up the sleeve of your right arm in order to sit down and pen a letter, you were taking your life into your own hands.

"Anyway, it said over the wireless the other night," At Naudé remarked somewhat hurriedly – in order to forestall unpleasantness, maybe – "that some of the greatest men in history have also had some of the worst memories. And it wasn't only learned men, like professors (that we all know have got very bad memories) that were like that. But also men without any kind of learning at all – men like great politicians, for instance, it said over the wireless."

And also, of the men in history with poor memories that hadn't had much learning, At Naudé continued, were some of the world's great educators. Some of the world's greatest writers of text-books for high school use, the wireless said.

So Jurie Steyn said, well, of course, he had never put forward any claims himself to having an outstanding memory. In fact, even with his job as postmaster he made mistakes, sometimes, through forgetting things, that he was sure would afford us a great deal of amusement one day when he had time to go into it all. Like he would sometimes forget for weeks on end to send a registered package on. It was really awfully funny, Jurie Steyn said.

Thereupon Gysbert van Tonder made mention of a number of great politicians that he had known in his time who suffered from extraordinary lapses of memory. There was one politician in particular, Gysbert van Tonder said, who, when he came round to the Marico before an election, knew every farmer by his first name and knew the ages of each of the farmer's children and knew where each child came in class at the end of the term.

And yet, because of that high kind of official responsibility that Jurie Steyn had mentioned, the politician's memory just *went* completely, immediately after he had been elected.

"And when I went to see him in Pretoria, he hardly knew who I was, even," Gysbert van Tonder said. "But for that I could perhaps not blame him so much, seeing that I hardly knew who he was, either, with that dark suit he was wearing, like a manel, and with a high, stick-up collar. And when I put my hand in my pocket and he saw that what I pulled out was only my tobacco pouch, a disappointed look came over his face that remained there right through all the time I had that interview with him.

"But how I saw that his memory had got really bad was when I mentioned a small favour that he had promised to do me. He had made me that promise sitting in my own voorkamer, even, drinking coffee. And yet when I spoke to him in Pretoria he had no recollection of ever having been in my voorkamer. And as for the coffee, he said he had drunk so much bad coffee in the Marico that he would actually be *glad* to forget that part."

Talking about that kind of thing (Oupa Bekker remarked at this stage), well, the man with the most extraordinary powers of memory that he had ever come across in the whole of the Lowveld was Sarel Meintjies – "Rooi" Sarel, they called him, from the colour of his hair. And there was nothing "Rooi" Sarel ever forgot, Oupa Bekker said. But just nothing.

"Except perhaps one thing, only," Oupa Bekker continued, reflectively. "Or, at least, that was how it seemed to some of us afterwards. But if people were talking, say, like the way we're talking in Jurie Steyn's voorkamer, now, 'Rooi' Sarel would remember years afterwards, even, exactly what each one said. And dates – and figures – why, you've got no idea. If you asked him, for instance, when was the big anthrax outbreak, he could tell you exactly to the year and month.

"And he could tell you in numbers what losses each farmer in the Dwarsberg area suffered, and how much each one got paid out by the Government in compensation. And he could also inform you precisely how long Japie Krige got for it, afterwards, when the Government found out just how wrong the figures were that Japie Krige had filled in in his compensation form.

"Or if you asked him how many years ago it was that the post-cart got overturned at the Molopo drift, and the driver was sacked for it, because the authorities thought he had capsized the post-cart on purpose and not just because of an illness that he was taking peach brandy for – why, then, 'Rooi' Sarel would be able to acquaint you with it to the day, and almost to the exact hour, even. And it wasn't just because it was 'Rooi' Sarel himself that was the driver of that post-cart that it was possible for him to remember so well. If it was somebody else that had been the driver of the post-cart and that was sacked for upsetting it, 'Rooi' Sarel would have had all the facts at his fingertips just the same.

"Or if you took 'Rooi' Sarel once along a road, for instance, he would never afterwards forget that road. And if you turned right off from the road and went through the veld, even, and no matter how far, it was something that made you feel you wanted to laugh your head off at it, almost, afterwards, when you found out how faithfully 'Rooi' Sarel could recall every inch of the way you took."

When Oupa Bekker paused to refill his pipe, Johnny Coen expressed the opinion that it must be of considerable advantage to a man to be blessed with gifts of an order such as Oupa Bekker credited "Rooi" Sarel with. He himself did not have a particularly retentive mind, Johnny Coen confessed, and what served to make it even worse, actually, he found, was that in recalling past circumstances and events he would as likely as not remember a lot of things also that never happened. To have that kind of a mind was, in a way, more of a handicap to a man than to have that other kind of a mind, where you simply forgot whole stretches of incidents.

More than once, Johnny Coen said, he had through this mental peculiarity of his been placed in an embarrassing situation – like seeming to remember that a girl in a blue dress and a white hat and shoes had smiled at him once when there was a Nagmaal. And then that girl's young man had come and made it clear to him, later on, about how his memory had deceived him. One reason why he agreed so readily that he had been mistaken, Johnny Coen added, was because the girl in the blue dress's young man was a weight-lifter, and had medals for it.

"It is on that account," Johnny Coen said, "that I have so much respect for that man, 'Rooi' Sarel, that Oupa Bekker has told us about. I am sure that 'Rooi' Sarel would never have made an ignorant mistake like what I made. He would have recalled right away that the weight-lifter's girl had not even looked at him. And a man like 'Rooi' Sarel, with those great gifts of his for remembering things – well, I feel he must have been very proud to have been able to make use of his gifts to help other people. I mean, not only the Marico District, but the whole country – all the nation, that is – would be benefited through having in its midst somebody with such fine powers of memory as 'Rooi' Sarel's, put to their proper use. Even if 'Rooi' Sarel did not get rewarded for it in the way he should have been, perhaps."

Oupa Bekker, having got his pipe to draw satisfactorily again – satisfactorily for himself, that was: it being a matter of lesser importance that the young schoolmaster, seated next to Oupa Bekker, had started coughing – said that he would not argue with Johnny Coen.

For it was indeed a truth that "Rooi" Sarel had been able to place his unusual talents at the disposal of the nation. And it was also true that in terms of hard cash he had not been over-generously rewarded. And yet there were those among the farmers of the Groot Marico who felt that

"Rooi" Sarel's abilities could have been more commendably employed.

"As I have said," Oupa Bekker continued, "it was 'Rooi' Sarel driving the post-cart when it capsized at the Molopo drift. And you can imagine how he must have looked when he crawled out of the water. And because all the other farmers around there had their hands full with their own troubles – since it was then right in the middle of the anthrax outbreak, and even though the Government was talking about paying the farmers compensation, it was uncertain as to how much it was going to be – nobody was able to give much thought to the misfortune that 'Rooi' Sarel was in – climbing out of the drift with the sack, and with his clothes wringing wet.

"In the end it was Japie Krige, with quite a few misfortunes of his own, at the time, that took 'Rooi' Sarel in, feeding and clothing him and giving him enough money to get to Pretoria and to keep him there until he found work again.

"And then, afterwards, as you know, there was that scandal about the compensations. It got to the ears of the authorities that some of the farmers had received money for losses they had never suffered. And that was when the police started offering rewards to people who could say – who could prove, that is, you know – who could –"

"Who could give evidence leading to the arrest and conviction of party/parties aforementioned in sub-section 2 (a)," young Vermaak the schoolmaster said, having stopped coughing by then.

"That was where 'Rooi' Sarel's great powers of memory stood him in such good stead," Oupa Bekker continued, "even though he had not stayed on Japie Krige's farm very long, and even though the reward offered by the police was not really very large.

"But there were some farmers in these parts who said that, with his remarkable memory and all, there was one thing that 'Rooi' Sarel forgot. It was a pity they said, that with so many things that he was able to remember, he should have forgotten where his loyalty lay."

Easy Circumstances

"Poverty is no crime," Chris Welman declared. He declared it loudly, a shade aggressively, at the same time pushing the toe of his broken veldskoen under his chair – a good way under. "Nor is it a matter for shame, either," he added, "to be poor."

"No, I don't care who knows that I am not particularly rich, myself," At Naudé remarked, withdrawing from general view a trouser turn-up that had been mended with string. "Of course, it's not like I've been brought up poor. When my father trekked into these parts, coming up from the Cape, he was well-to-do. I won't say diamonds, and a sitting-up chair with blue curtains that you got carried around in, and such like, as they used to have in the old days in the Cape. No doubt my *grand*father, in his time, would have been carried around in a sitting-up chair.

"But my father, when he came up from the Cape – why, we were just people in quite easy circumstances, that's all. Perhaps in the Transvaal – with the class of farmer living in the Transvaal then, I mean – we would have been thought to have been rich, even."

So Chris Welman said, yes, in the same way when *his* grandfather came up from the Cape his grandfather was reckoned to be a man of no little affluence – especially so, perhaps, in comparison with what was the financial standing of the general run of Transvaler then resident in the Transvaal. In fact, he wouldn't have been surprised if his grandfather had actually been carried up from the Cape into the Transvaal Bushveld, sitting in one of those sitting-up chairs with blue curtains.

"Yes, I can quite believe it," Gysbert van Tonder interjected in a sarcastic voice. "And it's easy to see that that's what your Nagmaal suit is patched with, too – with still a piece of that same blue curtain . . . Well, I'm not exactly penniless today, and I don't care who knows it. Also, I was brought up poor, and I'm not ashamed of that either."

So Jurie Steyn said, well, there were different ways of making money. And he wasn't sure that it would meet with everybody's approval, the way some people made their money. At the same time he couldn't but think that it was a strange thing how some people would talk about their forebears that trekked up into the Transvaal from the Cape, and about how well-to-do their forebears were, compared with the Transvalers there that lived just in reed and mud-daub houses.

After all, where did the Transvalers that lived just in reed and mud-daub houses come from, if they didn't come from the Cape? He was sure he didn't know, Jurie Steyn said.

But what he would not seek to deny about his own family when they came up from the Cape, Jurie Steyn said, was that they enjoyed a greater than ordinary measure of prosperity. Compared with most of the Transvalers, that was.

"Not that I won't admit that I'm myself a bit on the poor side, today," Jurie Steyn added, before Gysbert van Tonder could make another interjection. "And it's not that I'm ashamed of being poor, either. There's nothing about it that I've got to try and hide."

That was true enough. Shielded as his apparel was by the post office counter, there were no flaws in his garments that Jurie Steyn needed to retire from the gaze of vulgar curiosity.

"It seems to me, though," At Naudé said, "that why the people living in this part of the Transvaal in the old days – living in their hartbees houses and all, in the Bushveld – why they were, generally speaking" – he paused a moment to find the right word – "*flat*, was that they just perhaps didn't care so much in those days for riches. They were content to be poor. They knew there were more important things in life than just money."

Then Jurie Steyn said that, well, it was the same with us today, of course. We knew there were higher things than having the manager at the bank in Bekkersdal bowing and scraping to us, as though we were sheep farmers. And let a sheep farmer come and try to run sheep here among the thorn-bushes of the Dwarsberge, where it was just *made* for blue-tongue, and then see how it would be with that sheep farmer after a couple of seasons.

It just made him laugh, Jurie Steyn said, to think of that sheep farmer going to see the bank manager at Bekkersdal after that, and the sheep farmer getting treated by the bank manager like any one of us got treated.

When Jurie Steyn made that last remark Chris Welman gave a short, harsh laugh. It was clear that Chris Welman was recalling some interview of his own with the Bekkersdal bank manager.

Thereupon At Naudé said that, speaking for himself, personally, he was glad to think that he, personally, had got inside himself a good deal of that fine spirit that the old Transvalers already had inside themselves, in their wattle-and-daub and reed-and-daub houses, long before his own immediate forebears had even thought of trekking up from the Cape.

He was glad to think that he himself today had higher beliefs than just to imagine that to be rich was everything. What was more, from what he had heard over the wireless, there was no guarantee that wool prices would always remain up there in the sky, somewhere, anyway.

Chris Welman laughed again. This time it was a more human, openhearted sort of laugh.

"After all, where does it all lead to?" At Naudé continued. "All the money these sheep farmers are making, I mean. Those new lavish homes they're building with inside bathrooms that have got pipes going off right underneath the dining-room floor. And the walls painted smooth with cream paint like a looking-glass. Is that so much better than to have just a –" (his eyes swept along the walls of Jurie Steyn's voorkamer) "– just a ceiling of plastered-over Spanish reeds, with pieces of the mud coming away in places? Or uneven walls with huge brown splotches where the whitewash is peeling off in places? Or the clay marks there where the white ants went all that way up – at a time when Jurie Steyn's wife didn't have any paraffin or Cooper's dip in the house, I suppose?"

Jurie Steyn coughed uneasily. Maybe he was protected, all right, as far as his clothing below the level of the post office counter was concerned. But there was the whole of his voorkamer exposed in the nakedness of a poverty that – as we had all said in a manly way – we were none of us ashamed of. Jurie Steyn could not go and hide the walls of his voorkamer behind the counter, or thrust them out of sight under a riempiesbank, the while he declared that honest poverty was no sin, and that his people, trekking up from the Cape, had not been unacquainted with some of the hedonistic titillations imparted by creature comfort.

"The absolute filth, even," Chris Welman proceeded from where At

Naudé left off, "of living in a pigsty like this – well, we all know it's just because that sort of thing doesn't worry Jurie Steyn, at all. He's above it. What I mean is, stink, even –"

That was when Jurie Steyn indicated to Chris Welman, in somewhat strong terms, that he reckoned he had gone far enough. Not that he didn't realise, of course, Jurie Steyn said, that both Chris Welman and At Naudé, in the remarks they had made, were only seeking to compliment him on the higher kind of attitude that he had to life, which led him to scorn low gain.

But there were limits to the amount of flattery a man could put up with, Jurie Steyn said. And, in any case, Chris Welman needn't talk. Just look about how careful you had to be where you put your feet down on Chris Welman's front stoep. Half the time you didn't know if it was a front stoep or a fowl hok, Jurie Steyn said.

Before the discussion grew really acrimonious, however, Oupa Bekker had begun to relate an old Transvaal story that introduced a good many of the features we had already touched on. It was a story of a poor girl, Miemie de Jager, who lived with her parents in the Groot Marico in the kind of hartbees house that we had already been talking about.

"It was the kind of dwelling –" Oupa Bekker started.

"You don't need to say that part of it again. We already know all that," Jurie Steyn interjected. For Jurie Steyn had noticed that At Naudé was again surveying his voorkamer in a thoughtful manner.

"Very well, I'll just say then that Miemie de Jager's parents didn't stay in exactly a palace –" Oupa Bekker proceeded.

"Yes," At Naudé nodded. "I can imagine just the kind of hovel she stayed in. I must say I think I've got a pretty good idea, now. And I think the less said about it, the better."

Thereupon Jurie Steyn burst out that At Naudé should be the last person to talk. If Miemie de Jager had ever seen At Naudé's kitchen, and the kind of plates he ate out of, Jurie Steyn said, then Miemie de Jager would feel, next to it, that her parents were rich people from the Cape who had just trekked in, sitting in sitting-up chairs.

Jurie Steyn talked as though he already knew what Miemie de Jager was like. By comparison with At Naudé's kitchen, she would think that, Jurie Steyn said.

Only after Gysbert van Tonder had spoken at some length, and in a sneering way – saying that for people who weren't ashamed to be poor it was surprising how fussy some of us were – was Oupa Bekker able to get on with his story.

"Miemie de Jager," Oupa Bekker said, "lived with her parents in a – in just a plain house, that's all, that was near the first sawmill that they had in this part of the Transvaal. And one morning, when she was on her way home again from the sawmill –"

"Good Lord!" Chris Welman ejaculated suddenly. "You don't mean to say they were that poor. You don't mean she *worked* in the sawmill – those heavy thirty-foot logs – that's no work for a young girl with fair hair and dimples – sawing –"

It was apparent that Chris Welman had already formed a picture in his own mind of how Miemie de Jager looked.

But Oupa Bekker said, no, it was just Miemie de Jager's father that worked in the sawmill. Miemie went there every morning to fetch firewood in a sack.

"And then that morning, on her way home through the bluegums," Oupa Bekker continued, "she saw a young man approach along the path – a young man that she didn't know. She guessed right away that he must be a son of those new people that had bought up the sawmill and the whole property. Rich people from the Cape, they were.

"And so she let the sack of firewood fall from her shoulders quickly, and she hid the sack behind a bluegum. She didn't mind the young man seeing her walking barefooted, but she didn't want him to see her carrying that sack of wood. It went against her womanly pride. Not that she was ashamed of her parents being poor –"

No, no, we said. Poverty wasn't a crime, we said. But we *had* noticed Chris Welman hiding his broken veldskoen. And we *had* seen what At Naudé had done, furtively, almost, with his trouser turn-up, a little earlier on. So we knew just how Miemie de Jager felt about that sack, that symbolised how her parents were none too well off.

"She decided to walk straight on, and pass the young man, and then after he was out of sight she would go back and fetch the sack," Oupa Bekker said. "But after she had passed the young man – keeping her eyes down on the ground as she passed him – and she turned round to see if he was out of sight yet, she saw that he had turned round, to look back at her. And when he saw her turning round, he thought – oh well, they were both young. And so they walked slowly towards each other,

Miemie de Jager walking much more slowly than the young man, and blushing a good deal.

"And the young man said that he was going to look at the sawmill that his father had just bought. And Miemie said that she had come out for a walk through the bluegums and to pick yellow veld-flowers. And they stood talking a long while in the pathway. And afterwards the girl said she had to go home, now. And then the young man said, oh, but what about her firewood. And he asked could he carry it home for her. And she said, yes. And when she saw him lift the sack of firewood onto his broad young shoulders, she knew that she would never need to carry a sack of firewood home again."

But Jurie Steyn wanted to know how Oupa Bekker knew all that. All about what went on in Miemie de Jager's thoughts, Jurie Steyn said.

"She told me after we were married," Oupa Bekker answered. "You see, I was that young man. It was my father that had just bought that sawmill. You must understand that, when we came up from the Cape to the Transvaal, my parents were in easy circumstances."

Weather Prophet

That was after At Naudé had gone over the whole thing several times, telling us not only what he had heard over the wireless, but also what he had read in the newspapers. He made it clear to us what a weather wizard was. He also explained – although in his case not quite so clearly, perhaps – the functions and raison d'être of the meteorologist.

What made it more difficult for At Naudé was the fact that, while we already knew about weather prophecy, having met some prophets and having on occasion tried our hand at forecasting, ourselves – in the time of sowing, say – the lengthy word, meteorologist, was a new one on us.

"All the same," Jurie Steyn persisted, after At Naudé had finished with his explanations, "I still don't see why you should speak in such an off-hand way about a weather prophet, just because he can prophesy a good while beforehand what the weather is going to be – and he gets it right. It shouldn't matter that he goes by just simple things like it's the last quarter of the moon on Wednesday and the wind changed last night."

Chris Welman expressed his agreement with Jurie Steyn.

"Well, I don't pretend to be a weather prophet or anything like," Chris Welman said, "but you'll remember how only last year I was right when I said, that time, that we'd have rain in three days. And when I said it, there wasn't a cloud in the sky. But I just went by what my grandfather once said about when the wind blows from the Pilanesberg with the new moon, what to expect."

And we said, yes, you could also tell if it was going to rain by other signs. "By the way swallows fly," Johnny Coen said. "And red ants walking around after sunset," Jurie Steyn said. "And by how the smoke comes out of the chimney," Gysbert van Tonder said. "And by spiders –" Oupa Bekker began.

At Naudé looked very superior, then, and he wore a thin smile.

"But you haven't any of you perhaps got a balloon going up on an island in the sea, have you?" he asked. "Or has any of you got a whole string of weather stations right through the Union? Just one weather station, even, maybe?"

With none of us answering, At Naudé looked more satisfied than ever with himself, then.

"That's where a meteorologist is different," At Naudé announced. "A meteorologist has got all those things."

Although he realised then that he was beaten, Jurie Steyn could nevertheless not bring himself to yield straight away.

"It still doesn't make sense, quite," Jurie Steyn declared – but with less conviction than before – "that what you call a meteorologist doesn't say that next week there's going to be snow – and there *is* snow. Or that there is going to be a whirlwind – and then next week we've got no roofs left. It looks like it's only a weather prophet that comes and forecasts about that kind of thing. It looks like a meteorologist doesn't worry about it – or know of it, even."

"And does a meteorologist need to?" At Naudé asked, triumphantly. "Why should he trouble about working out when it's going to rain, say, seeing how he's got all those things for taking ground temperatures with, and for measuring the wind with, and he's got a balloon on an island in the sea? I mean, he's a scientist, a meteorologist is. You don't catch him walking outside to see what kind of smoke is coming out of his weather-station chimney. Or going by red ants – no matter how many red ants may be walking around after supper-time. Or by spiders –"

The absurdity of that last idea struck At Naudé so forcibly that he spluttered. We laughed a little ourselves, too, then. Yes, bringing in spiders seemed to be going just too far.

"After all, a meteorologist must be a man with a certain amount of learning," At Naudé finished up. "And so I don't suppose he'd be able to prophesy the weather right, even if he tried."

We could not but acknowledge, then, that what At Naudé said was indeed true. Such weather prophets as we knew to speak to were not people of great learning. And when one of ourselves, for instance, forecast correctly about did we have to put a bucksail over the wagon on the road to Bekkersdal, then we realised, also, that our way of working it out did not owe much to the letters we had been taught to write on our slates in the schoolroom. It was easy to see that a meteorologist would be far above a thing just like telling us when to put in autumn giant cauliflowers. Our Hollander schoolmaster had been just as far above it, too.

"Of course, what helps you a lot in weather prophesying," Chris Welman said, "is mealies. I mean, after you've sown a patch of mealies, and they start coming up, then you know right away there's going to be a long piece of just absolute drought. And when a mealie gets to that size – if he ever gets to that size, I mean – where a head starts forming and you've *got* to have rain, then, or you won't get a crop at all, well, then you can be sure that for a whole month there's going to be just clear blue skies, so that you sit on your front stoep for day after day, working out in one of your children's school writing-books how much you owe the Indian storekeeper at Ramoutsa.

"And when I see by my youngest son, Petrus's, quarterly report that he is good at sums, I think, yes, and I know what he's going to use all those sums for, one day, sitting on his front stoep with a pencil and a piece of paper, waiting for the rain. He'll need all the sums and more that they can teach him at school, I think to myself, then."

Thereupon Jurie Steyn, who was not unacquainted with conditions prevailing years ago in the Cape Zwartland, said that if there was anything better than a mealie for prophesying the weather with, it was just a wheat plant.

"When a wheat plant," Jurie Steyn continued, "has got to there where you say to yourself that next week you'll start reaping and so you've got to see about getting all the sickles sharpened, then it's almost as though that wheat plant is himself so educated that he can tell you not to worry about it. For there's going to be the biggest hailstorm in years – it's like it's the wheat plant himself that's telling you that: an ordinary Hard-Red wheat plant with no learning to speak of."

When it was a matter of hail, now, Oupa Bekker said, well, there was Klaas Rasmus. As a weather wizard Klaas Rasmus could have been said to specialise in hail, Oupa Bekker explained. Of course, nobody knew what methods Klaas Rasmus employed, exactly, Oupa Bekker said, although it was reasonable to suppose that it wasn't weather charts and graphs and rainfall figures and things like that. For one thing, it was unlikely that Klaas Rasmus would have known what rainfall figures were if you showed them to him, even.

"Not that he would ever have let on that he didn't know," Oupa Bekker continued. "Klaas Rasmus was not that kind of a man at all. If you had shown him the kind of rainfall figures, say, that At Naudé has been talking about, Klaas Rasmus would have nodded his head up and down solemnly quite a number of times.

"And he would have said, yes, that was just about how he would have worked it out himself, he thought, if he had had a piece of paper handy with lines drawn on it like that, and all. And then he would ask were you sure you were holding those rainfall figures the right way up, seeing that there were just one or two things there that he wasn't sure if he agreed with, quite.

"You see, that was Klaas Rasmus all over. If he understood a thing or not, it didn't make much difference to him. He would have something to say about it, all the same. But because he was so good at prophesying hail (being proved right time and again) there were a lot of little weaknesses he had that we could overlook."

Jurie Steyn said, then, that he thought he had heard that name, Klaas Rasmus, before, somewhere. Didn't he have some sort of nickname, Jurie Steyn asked.

Yes, that was quite right, Oupa Bekker said. They used to call him Klaas Baksteen, because of the size of the hailstones that used to fall each time that he prophesied hail. The hailstones would come down then the size of half-bricks.

"And I also seem to remember from something that I heard of long ago," Jurie Steyn went on, "that he – no, I can't recall it quite, now. But it was something that didn't seem to make sense, altogether, in a way."

Oupa Bekker said that he believed he knew what it was that Jurie Steyn was thinking about – something that Jurie Steyn had been told, about a happening in the Marico long ago. Before Jurie Steyn had ever heard of the Groot Marico, even, maybe. It was a long story, Oupa Bekker added, and as likely as not it was something quite different from what Jurie Steyn was thinking about.

"You see, like with all cases of real greatness," Oupa Bekker said, "there was some doubt, in some people's minds, about whether Klaas Baksteen was really as good at prophesying hail as he was held to be. There was talk that he was wrong, sometimes. And there was also talk that he would only forecast that there was going to be hail the size of half-bricks when the sky was already black and high up, and with awful white patches just above the horizon from which a child of four would know that after another half an hour there would be no harvest left that year.

"And so, one day, when he had worked out, to the hour, almost, when there was going to be a hailstorm the like of which this part of the Marico had rarely seen, and that hailstorm still a week ahead, Klaas Baksteen journeyed down to Bekkersdal so that the editor of the newspaper there could print it in his newspaper well before the hailstorm actually happened. And Klaas Baksteen put up at a hotel there, deciding to wait until his prophecy came out. And they say that everybody was very interested, of course. And quite a lot of people who didn't believe in Klaas Baksteen's powers said that that would show him up, all right, seeing that his prophecy was printed in the newspaper.

"And they say that it must have been pretty dreadful for Klaas Baksteen himself, waiting there in that hotel on the day when there was to be the hailstorm – more especially since up to quite late in the afternoon it was an absolutely cloudless sky. And Klaas Baksteen worried about it so much that afterwards he sent for a brandy, even, to try and calm himself. And afterwards he sent for another brandy. And when the waiter brought him the second brandy the sunlight shining on the glass was so bright that it blinded Klaas Baksteen, almost. That was how little chance there seemed to be of hail, then."

Oupa Bekker put a match to his pipe and puffed steadily for some moments.

"But before it was evening," he said, "there was such a hailstorm in Bekkersdal that hardly a window was left unbroken. Well, that was a proud moment for Klaas Baksteen, all right. Just with that he proved that he was the greatest hail-prophet in the world. And before the sun had quite set a man who cultivated asparagus under glass frames just outside the town came and called on Klaas Baksteen at the hotel. And you've got no idea how proud Klaas Baksteen was that that man visited him. Even though Klaas Baksteen always used to wear a moustache after that. It was a thick, curling sort of moustache that Klaas Baksteen grew to cover up the place where his front teeth used to be before the asparagus man called round to see him."

But he couldn't understand that, Jurie Steyn said. It didn't make sense to him, Jurie Steyn said, quite. Although he had heard something about it, he seemed to remember.

"Well, why Klaas Baksteen was so happy about it," Oupa Bekker said, "was because that proved how great a weather prophet he was. The man who grew asparagus under glass frames *proved* it, by cutting up so rough. It made Klaas Baksteen king of hail-prophets, that."

Lost City

"It used to be different, in the Kalahari," Chris Welman said, commenting on At Naudé's announcement of what he had heard over the wireless. "You could go for miles and miles, and it would be just desert. All you'd come across, perhaps, would be a couple of families of Bushmen, and they'd be disappearing over the horizon. Then, days later, you'd again come across a couple of families of Bushmen. And *they'd* be disappearing over the horizon.

"And you wouldn't know if it was the same couple of families of Bushmen. Or the same horizon. And you wouldn't care, either. I mean, in the Kalahari desert you wouldn't care. Maybe in other deserts it is different. I'm only talking about the Kalahari."

Yes, all you would be concerned about, in the Kalahari, Jurie Steyn said, was what the couple of families of Bushmen would be disappearing over the horizon *with*. For you might not always be able to check up quickly to find out what was missing out of your camp.

"But from what At Naudé has been telling us," Chris Welman went on, "it looks like you'd have no quiet in the Kalahari today. Or room to move. From Malopolole onwards it seems that there's just one expedition on top of another, each one searching for a lost city. And you can't slip out for a glass of pontac, even, in case when you come back somebody else has taken your place in the line."

It was apparent that Chris Welman was drawing on his memory of some past unhappy visit to Johannesburg.

"It's not hard to think of how that city got lost in the first place," Jurie Steyn observed. "It must have been that the people that built the city didn't know what a couple of families of Bushmen were like. Still, I can't believe it, somehow, quite. Not a whole city, that is. I can't somehow imagine Bushmen disappearing over the horizon with all that. For one thing, it wouldn't be any use to them. Now, if it wasn't so much a question of a whole lost city, but of some of the things that got lost *out* of the city – well, I could tell those expeditions just where to go and look."

But At Naudé said that we had perhaps misunderstood one or two of the less important details of the news he had communicated to us. There weren't quite as many expeditions as what Chris Welman seemed to think, out in the Kalahari looking for a lost city. Moreover, it wasn't a city that had got lost in the way that Jurie Steyn meant by lost. The city had just been built so many years ago that people had afterwards forgotten about it. Don't ask him how a thing like that could happen, now, At Naudé said. He admitted that he couldn't imagine it, himself.

"I mean let's not take even a city –" At Naudé started to explain.

"No, let a few Bushmen families take it," Jurie Steyn said, promptly, "with the washing hanging on the clothes-lines and all."

"Not a city, even," At Naudé continued, pointedly ignoring Jurie Steyn's second attempt that afternoon at being what he thought funny, "but if we think of quite a small town, like Bekkersdal, say . . . Not that I won't agree that we've got a wider water furrow in the main street of Bekkersdal than they've got in Zeerust, of course, but it's only that there are less people in the main street of Bekkersdal than they've got in Zeerust, if you understand what I mean . . . Well, can you imagine anybody in Bekkersdal forgetting where they built the place? After all, anybody can see for himself how silly that sounds. It's like Dominee Welthagen, just before the Nagmaal, suddenly forgetting where the church is. Or David Policansky not remembering where his shop is, just after he's done it all up for the New Year."

We acknowledged that At Naudé was right there, of course. With Dominee Welthagen we might not perhaps be too sure. For it was known that in some respects the dominee could at times be pretty absent-minded. But with David Policansky At Naudé was on safe enough ground. Especially after that big new plate-glass window that David Policansky had put in. It was not reasonable to think that he would be able to forget it. Not with what he was still likely to be owing on it, we said. You just weren't allowed to forget anything you were owing on.

"So you see how much more silly it is with a city, then," At Naudé concluded. "Thinking that people would go and build a city, and then just lose it."

Thereupon young Vermaak, the schoolmaster, said that he had learnt in history of how for many centuries people believed that there was a foreign city called Monomotapa in these parts, and that numbers of expeditions had been sent out in the past to look for it. It was even marked on maps, long ago, the schoolmaster said. But if you saw that name on a map of Africa today, he said, well, then you would know that it wasn't a very up-to-date map of Africa.

As likely as not, there would not be the town of Vanderbijl Park marked on that map, young Vermaak said, laughing. Or the town of Odendaalsrus, even. There was supposed to be a lot of gold and diamonds in that city with the foreign name, the schoolmaster added.

Well, with those remarks young Vermaak broached a subject with which we were not altogether unfamiliar. More than one of us had, before today, held in his hand a map showing as clearly as anything with a cross the exact spot where the hidden treasure would be found buried. And all we'd be likely to dig up there would be an old jam tin. The apocryphal element in African cartography was something we had had experience of.

"All I can say," Gysbert van Tonder observed at this stage, "is that I don't know so much about a lost city. But it seems to me there's going to be more than one lost expedition. Depending on how far the expeditions are going into the desert beyond Kang-Kang."

Several of us looked surprised when Gysbert van Tonder said that. Surprised and also impressed. We knew that in his time Gysbert van Tonder had penetrated pretty deeply into the Kalahari, bartering beads and brass wire for cattle. That was, of course, before the natives in those parts found that they didn't need those things, anymore, since they could buy their clothes ready-made at the Indian store at Ramoutsa. Nevertheless, we had not imagined that he had gone as far into the desert as all that.

"But is there –" Jurie Steyn enquired after a pause, "is there really a place by that name, though?"

Gysbert van Tonder smiled.

"On the map, yes," he said, "it is. On the map in my youngest son's school atlas you can read that name for yourself there, big as anything. And in the middle of the Kalahari. Well, there's something one of those expeditions can go and look for. And maybe that is their lost city. At least, it's lost enough. Because you certainly won't be able to tell it from any other spot in the Kalahari that you're standing in the middle of, watching a couple of families of Bushmen disappearing over the horizon from."

So Jurie Steyn said, yes, he reckoned that if it was a lost city that an expedition was after, why, then he reckoned that just about any part of the Kalahari would do for that. Because when the expedition came back from the Kalahari without having found anything, it would prove to the whole world just how lost that city actually was, Jurie Steyn reckoned. If that was what an expedition into the Kalahari was for, then that expedition just couldn't go wrong. In fact, the less that an expedition like that found, then, the better. Because it would show that the city had been lost without as much as a trace, even, Jurie Steyn added.

"It's a queer thing, though," the schoolmaster said, "when you come to think of it, that for so many hundreds of years, when the interior of South Africa was still unexplored, there should have been a legend of a Golden City. And people were so convinced of the existence of this city that they went searching for it. They were so sure that there was that city of gold that they even marked it on their maps. And what seems so extraordinary to me is that one day that Golden City actually would arise, and not too far away, either, from where the old geographers had centuries before indicated on their maps. It was as though they were all prophesying the rise of Johannesburg. And at most they were only a few hundred miles out."

That was something that passed his comprehension, young Vermaak said. That men should have been able to mark on a map, centuries beforehand, a city that was not there yet. That to him was one of the mysteries of Africa, the schoolmaster declared.

Thereupon Oupa Bekker said that if it was a thing like that that the schoolmaster thought wonderful, then the schoolmaster would have a lot to learn, still.

"After all, with South Africa so big," Oupa Bekker said, "they were bound to go and build cities in it, somewhere. That stands to reason. And so, for a person to go and put a mark on a map and to say that some day there is going to be a city there, or thereabouts – well, what would have been wonderful was if it *didn't* work out, some time. And to say that it's surprising how that man made that mark on the map centuries ago, even. Well, I think that only shows how bad he was at it. If Johannesburg got started soon after he had prophesied it, then there might have been something in it, then. But it seems to me that the man who made that map wasn't only a few hundred miles out, as Meneer Vermaak says, but that he was also a few hundred years out.

What's more, he also got the name wrong. Unless you also think that that name – what's it, again –"

"Monomotapa," young Vermaak announced.

"– isn't far out from sounding like Johannesburg," Oupa Bekker said.

It made him think of his grand-uncle Toons, all this, Oupa Bekker said.

Now, there was something that really did come as a surprise to us. The general feeling we had about Oupa Bekker was a feeling of immense antiquity, of green and immemorial age. In the lost olden-time cities that our talk was about we could, without thinking twice, accord to Oupa Bekker the rights of a venerable citizenship. And in that crumbled town we could conceive of Oupa Bekker as walking about in the evening, among cobwebbed monuments.

It was foolish, of course, to have ideas like that. But that was the impression, in point of appearance and personality, that Oupa Bekker did make on us. He seemed to belong with the battered although timeless antique. He occupied a place not so much among living humanity as in oral tradition.

And so when Oupa Bekker spoke of himself as having had a grand-uncle, it just about took our breath away.

"You were saying about your grand-uncle?" Jurie Steyn, who was the first to recover, remarked. From the tone in his voice, you could see that Jurie Steyn pictured Oupa Bekker's grand-uncle as a lost city in himself, with weeds clambering over his ruined walls.

"My grand-uncle Toons," Oupa Bekker continued, unaware of the stir he had caused, "also had the habit, when he first trekked into the Transvaal that was all just open veld, then, of stopping every so often and looking around him and saying that one day a great city would arise right there where he was standing, when it was now just empty veld. On his way up, when he trekked into the Northern Transvaal, he stopped to say it at where is today Potchefstroom and also at where is today Johannesburg and Pretoria. In that way you could say that he was just as good as the man that did that map. And I suppose he was, too. That is, if you don't count all those hundreds of other places where my grand-uncle Toons also stopped to say the same thing, and where there is today still just open veld."

It was Jurie Steyn who brought the conversation back to where we had started from.

"Those expeditions going to search for the lost city," he asked of At Naudé, "have they set out yet? And do you know if they are likely to pass this way, at all? Because, if it's last letters they want to send home, and so on, then my post office is as good as any. I mean, their last letters have got a good chance of getting to where they are addressed to. I don't say the expeditions have got the same chance of getting to the lost city. But instead of taking all that trouble, why don't they just drop a letter in the post to the lost city – writing to the mayor, say? Then they'll at least know if the lost city is there or not."

But At Naudé said that from what he had heard over the wireless the expeditions were on the point of leaving, or had already left, Johannesburg. And as for what Jurie Steyn had said about writing letters – well, he had the feeling that more than one letter that he had himself posted had ended up there, in that lost city.

"Johannesburg?" Oupa Bekker queried, talking as though he was emerging from a dream. "Well, I've been in Johannesburg only a few times. Like with the Show, say. And I've passed through there on the way to Cape Town. And I've always tried to pull down the curtains of the compartment I was in when we went through Johannesburg. And I have thought of the Good Book, then.

"And I have thought that if ever there was a lost city, it was Johannesburg, I have thought. *And how lost*, I have thought . . . The expedition doesn't need to leave Johannesburg, if it's a lost city it wants."

Mother-in-law

"It's not that she's here now," Jurie Steyn said. "Not actually in the house, I mean. Last time I saw her was about half an hour ago. She had her hat on."

So Chris Welman said that he could sympathise with Jurie Steyn, since having your mother-in-law coming to stay with you was about the oldest kind of trouble that there was in the world.

And he always used to think that with himself it would be different. For that reason he had been, in the past, not a little impatient when other men had spoken about how much sorrow had come into their lives from that moment when they opened the top part of the front door and there was an elderly little lady standing there with suitcases.

"Looking as though butter wouldn't melt in her mouth," Jurie Steyn declared.

It was because those married men who spoke like that didn't have proper feelings, he used to think when he was first married, Chris Welman went on. And he used to think that a man must have a very mean heart if he didn't have room in it for a frail little old lady standing at the front door with –

"Not so frail little, either," Jurie Steyn interjected. "And with her hair fastened back in a tight bun. And sniffing suspiciously if there's a smell of drink, before she's got her foot right in over the front step."

He also used to think, Chris Welman continued, that if for no other reason than just for his wife's sake a man should be able to force himself to act in a kindly way towards his mother-in-law, no matter what he thought of her privately.

If he was anything of a man at all, that was, Chris Welman used to believe. And he never saw anything funny, either, in jokes about a mother-in-law. He used to shake his head in a pitying way when a man told what was to be a comic story about a mother-in-law.

"And her saying, 'It's all right, there's nothing in that suitcase that can break,' while you're carrying it inside for her," Jurie Steyn said. "Trying to make out that it's through drink that you stumbled over a chair, when all the time it was because you were nervous."

But Chris Welman said that his own ideas underwent a considerable degree of modification as a result of his mother-in-law having come to pay them a somewhat extended visit.

"Now I come to think of it," Chris Welman remarked, "she didn't really stay very long. It only *looked* like that. And then when it came to the time when it was understood that she would be going back again, she at the last moment stretched out her stay. Once more, I must be honest and admit that she didn't stretch it out very much. And it wasn't through her own doing, either, that it happened like that. But people who knew me well, and whom I hadn't come across over that time, told me how much I had aged since they had last seen me.

"Anyway, why my mother-in-law stretched out her visit was because there was trouble with the Government lorry that she had to go back on. It took the lorry-driver and his assistant the best part of two hours to get the engine going again. And that was the length of time that my mother-in-law stretched out her visit. As I say, I don't claim it was her fault in any way. Although actually, I am not so sure, either. I mean, when I think of some of the things she did get up to –"

All the same, Chris Welman added, he even today couldn't see anything funny in mother-in-law jokes. He had noticed that that kind of joke was always told by a coarse type of person with no real feelings. Just let such a person have the experience of having his mother-in-law come and stay with him – just once, Chris Welman said – and that person would never laugh at a mother-in-law joke again. In fact, he doubted if that person would ever again in his life laugh at anything, very much.

"The worst thing," Jurie Steyn announced, "is the comparisons she makes. Not so much in words, either, perhaps, as in other ways. And by hints. How her other daughter that's married to the booking-office clerk has got coal to burn in her kitchen stove and hasn't got to go out with a Price's candles box to pick up cow-dung –"

"Not today she can't," At Naudé interjected. "Not with the coal shortage in the towns that the newspapers are full of. Today she'd be glad to have just that candles box to burn, if I know anything."

"Or the comparison she makes with her youngest son, Jebediah, who is now a deacon in the church," Jurie Steyn continued. "Well, I'm not saying anything about Jebediah, the way he is today. Because I only knew Jebediah before he was a church deacon, and that was on the diggings. Well, the diggings would hardly be a place for a church deacon to feel at home on, especially the kind of life that was led on the diggings in those days. But I'll say this much for Jebediah – that he never once let on how hard it was for him to fit into that low life, or what a nightmare it was to him. You would never imagine what a suffering it was for him to stay in that sinful place – the way he took to it, I mean.

"And I suppose Jebediah would still be there today, sitting in a saloon bar and doing his best to close his eyes to all the disgrace around him, if it wasn't that the diggers' committee afterwards called on him and ran him off the diggings. For some reason, while they were talking to him, the diggers' committee were also pouring tar on Jebediah, and they were shaking feathers onto Jebediah out of a pillow that they had brought along."

And it was that same Jebediah, Jurie Steyn said, that his mother-in-law was today holding up to him as an example. Not always in so many words, perhaps, Jurie Steyn said, but certainly by way of hint and allusion.

"And if I try ever so slightly, and without mentioning anything near the worst, even," Jurie Steyn said, "to give her a perhaps different idea of her Jebediah, then she just sits back and smiles. She acts like she feels sorry for me because she thinks I'm jealous of Jebediah. What came out of that pillow-case seemed to be muscovy duck feathers, mostly."

It was pretty much that sort of thing in his own case, Chris Welman said, that led to so radical a change being effected in his outlook.

"I don't think I would have minded so much if it was just her son that my mother-in-law said was so much better than me, the time she came to stay with us," Chris Welman said. "I think I could have stood for that. In any case, I was at school with her son, and he used to copy spelling off me in class. And that used to make me feel very proud – to see him copying. Because until then I used to think that I was the worst at spelling in the whole school."

Later on, however, the schoolmaster was to declare openly that that other pupil (that nobody knew then would one day be Chris Welman's brother-in-law) was the worst at spelling in the whole of the schoolmaster's experience.

"And no one guessed," Chris Welman said, "that why he was so bad was because he was all the time copying off me. And so you can see that, no matter what his mother might say, I could never have anything against him. But it was her late husband that she would always talk about. That and –"

"Yes," Jurie Steyn remarked. "And drink."

"Because I would take a little mampoer brandy now and again to cheer myself up," Chris Welman continued, "she would act as though I was a miserable lost drunkard that regularly beat his wife black and blue. And I used to get to feeling that way about myself, too, that I was a lost miserable drunkard –"

Gysbert van Tonder interposed, then, with the comment that as far as he could see the visit of Chris Welman's mother-in-law could only have done good. There could have been no flies on her, Gysbert van Tonder said, for her to have been able to sum up so quickly what was Chris Welman's trouble. Although she would have been pretty unobservant if she hadn't noticed – the moment she stepped in at the front door, even. And that was all the thanks she got for it – with Chris Welman talking so ungratefully about her now, and all.

He only hoped, Gysbert van Tonder said, that Chris Welman didn't forget himself so far as to beat his mother-in-law black and blue as well. All the same, he added, he could quite understand, now, why that kindly old lady's visit should have upset Chris Welman so much, seeing that she just meant everything for the best. It was through no fault of hers that Chris Welman was what he was.

"If you had taken her reproof to heart more," Gysbert van Tonder said, "you would have been a different man today. Instead of being just hardened in your awful habits and not being able to find a good word to say about your own wife's mother. And all that goes for Jurie Steyn, too."

Before the two personages so addressed could think of a suitable reply, At Naudé mentioned that he had that same afternoon seen Jurie Steyn's mother-in-law. She was walking across the veld. Walking at a good pace, At Naudé said.

"Yes, I've already told you that I saw her put her hat on and go out," Jurie Steyn said. But he added that he was not going to be foolishly hopeful about it, seeing that she hadn't taken her suitcases with her.

"About her late husband, now," Chris Welman said, reverting to the subject of his own mother-in-law. "It was when she stood looking at the front of the house that she said that was where her late husband was different, now. Her late husband would never have allowed the front of *his* house to get so dilapidated, she said. Not even when he had got so with the rheumatics that sometimes he wouldn't show his face outside of his bedroom for days on end. You see, in those days they used to call it rheumatics. Well, anyway, it was for that reason that I got out the old step-ladder and a bucket of whitewash and started on the front of the house.

"And then, of course, my mother-in-law had to come past and say that one thing about her late husband was that he would never splash the whitewash on just anyhow, but that he would apply it with even strokes of the brush and not get his face and the brush-handle and his clothes all messed up.

"And then when the string of the step-ladder broke on account of its being so old, she didn't even ask me did I get hurt falling, or could she help me get my foot out of the whitewash bucket. She just said that her late husband would never have got onto a step-ladder drunk and then have tried to murder her from there."

So Gysbert van Tonder said, well, what did Chris Welman expect? If Chris Welman got onto a step-ladder with a bucket of whitewash and he was full of mampoer, there would be almost bound to be trouble, Gysbert van Tonder said.

"I've already told you it was the string," Chris Welman answered, sounding surly. "In any case, during all the time that my mother-in-law stayed with us I never once had a drink in the house. Before my mother-in-law came I moved the brandy still out of the wagon-house and went and hid it in an old potato shed in the kloof that I didn't use anymore because it was too far out of the way. That was where I used to go when I needed a drink, then – all that far."

Gysbert van Tonder made a clicking sort of sound, to show how up-set he was at the thought that a man could be so degraded. The way he was carrying on, it looked as though it was Gysbert van Tonder and not Jurie Steyn's brother-in-law, Jebediah, that was the church deacon.

"And what I'll never forget," Chris Welman proceeded, "is that af-ternoon when my cattle-herd, 'Mbulu, came running to tell me that the old miesies had come to him in the veld and had sent him to fetch the police at Nietverdiend. But 'Mbulu didn't go for the police, of course.

He knew better than that. He came and fetched me instead. I hurried along with him and he led me straight to where my mother-in-law was standing right in front of the disused potato shed. 'It's too terrible,' she said when I arrived. 'I only hope the police get here in time. Do you know what's inside this shed? No, I'm sure you'll never guess. It's a still. It means that the Bechuanas on your farm are making brandy here in secret. If you stand here and look through this crack in the door you can *see* it's a still.'

"I pretended to look, of course, and I said, yes, she was right, and it was too terrible to think of how out of hand the Bechuanas were getting. I would talk to them about it very severely, I said, seeing that what they were doing was so low and illegal, and all. But, of course, we mustn't bring the police into it, I said. We didn't want that kind of trouble on the farm. But you've got no idea how hard it was to dissuade my mother-in-law, who had worked it out that the sergeant from Nietverdiend could get there in under an hour.

"In the end I was actually pleading with her to give those shameless Bechuanas another chance: even if (as she said) their making illicit mampoer brandy was worse than if they had still been cannibals. Afterwards she relented. But it was only after I had satisfied her that I had broken every jar in the potato shed and there was nothing left of the still but a few yards of twisted brass tubing that you could never put together again."

Chris Welman sighed. "And to think that it was one of the finest brandy stills in the whole of the Groot Marico," he said, finally.

Jurie Steyn was looking strangely agitated.

"But where did you say she was *going*," he asked of At Naudé, "walking over the veld with her hat on? I mean, what *direction* did she take? Talk quick, man."

At Naudé explained to the best of his ability.

"Oh," Jurie Steyn ejaculated. "Oh, my God!"

FIVE-POUND NOTES

"It explains in the newspaper how you can tell," At Naudé said, "the difference between a good five-pound note and these forged ones. There are a lot of forged notes in circulation, the paper says, and the police are on the point of making an arrest."

"Bad as all that, is it?" Gysbert van Tonder asked. "Because I've noticed that when the papers say that about the police, it means that unless somebody walks into the charge office to confess that he did it, the police are writing that case off as an unsolved African mystery. There's only one thing worse, and that is when it says in the papers about a dragnet, and that the police are poised ready to swoop. That means that the guilty person left the country a good while before with a lot of luggage that he didn't have when he came into the country, and with his passport in order."

Gysbert van Tonder's lip curled as he spoke. It was sad to think that an occasional misunderstanding with a mounted man on border patrol should have led to his acquiring so jaundiced a view of the activities of the forces charged with the state's internal government.

"It says how you can tell that it's not a proper five-pound note," At Naudé proceeded, "is because –"

"Yes, I know," Chris Welman interjected. "It's because the forged note is twice the size of the genuine banknote. And it's not properly printed, but is drawn just on a rough piece of brown paper with school crayons. And the lion on the back of it has got a pipe in his mouth.

"Oh, yes, and another thing – the portrait of Jan van Riebeeck is all wrong. Because Jan van Riebeeck is wearing a cap pulled down over one eye and a striped jersey with numbers on it. From that you can tell that the forger is in gaol, and he's forging five-pound notes just from memory, and he's forgotten that striped jerseys with numbers on isn't the way everybody dresses. If somebody hands you a five-pound note like that, you must just say you're sorry you haven't got change.

"Because it's quite possible that the person is entirely innocent and is giving you the note in good faith. He might have got it from somebody else, and hadn't noticed that there was anything wrong with it."

Chris Welman's broad wink passed undetected by Jurie Steyn. Chris Welman was busy pulling At Naudé's leg, and Jurie Steyn didn't know it.

"In good faith," Jurie Steyn repeated. "Why, if a man came and palmed a piece of nonsense like that off onto me, just drawn with crayons on a piece of brown paper, I'd know straight away he was a crook. Never mind the lion with the pipe or the striped jersey, even. Just because it wasn't printed I'd know it was a forgery. I'd be very suspicious of a man who came to me to change a five-pound note for him that was drawn by hand, however neatly. And I wouldn't care who that man was, either.

"Even if it was Dominee Welthagen himself that came along to me with that class of banknote, I'd start getting funny ideas about what Dominee Welthagen was doing in his spare time. No matter how reverently Dominee Welthagen might speak about accepting the lion with the pipe in his mouth in good faith, either."

Young Vermaak, the schoolmaster, said that this was giving him something to think about. It would be a new subject for a composition for the children in the higher classes. The adventures of a shilling, passing from hand to hand, was a subject he had already set several times, and the children enjoyed writing it. But one got bored with having the same thing too often.

"The adventures of a spurious banknote" would introduce a desirable element of novelty into school essays, he thought. Young Vermaak went on to say another thing that nobody in Jurie Steyn's voorkamer seemed to get the hang of, quite. He said that if the poet's purse was filled with the kind of brown-paper, crayon-executed banknotes that Chris Welman had been talking about, then he could understand what the poet meant when he said that who stole his purse stole trash.

"How you can tell," At Naudé continued patiently, "that it is a counterfeit five-pound note is not, either, because on the picture of the ship the sailors are all standing round watching the captain doing card tricks. I mean, if Chris Welman wants to say ridiculous things, well, so can I. But the point is that it is actually a very good imitation note. The only way you can tell it's a forgery is that it is better printed than the genuine note and that it's got the word 'geoutoriseerde' spelt right."

The schoolmaster looked interested.

"Well, they keep on changing Afrikaans spelling so much," he said, "that I don't know where I am, half the time, teaching it. Anyway, I'd be glad to know what is the right way to spell that word. But, unfortunately, I haven't got a five-pound note on me at the moment – and I don't suppose there's anybody here who would care to lend me one."

His tone was pensive, wistful. But he was quite right. Nobody took the hint.

"Just until the end of the month," young Vermaak said, again, but not very hopefully.

After an interval of silence, At Naudé said that even if somebody were to lend the schoolmaster a fiver – which, in his own opinion, did not seem very likely – it would still not help him with the spelling of that word. Because it was the genuine banknote that had the spelling wrong – spelling it the old way. Only the counterfeit note had the correct new spelling.

"I mean, if somebody here were to lend you a fiver," At Naudé said, trying to be funny again, since Chris Welman had started it, "I suppose it would be an honest fiver. I mean, I know that there are a lot of things that a Groot Marico cattle farmer will get up to – especially in a time of drought – but I don't think that printing counterfeit banknotes at the back of a haystack is one of them."

But Jurie Steyn said *there* was something that got him beat, now. Calling it a counterfeit note, Jurie Steyn said, just because it had better printing and spelling than a genuine note. It was one of those things that just made his head reel, Jurie Steyn added. No wonder a person sometimes felt in the world that he didn't know where he was. That was one of those things that made him feel, sometimes, that the Government was going too far. It was setting a pace that the ordinary citizen couldn't catch up with, quite.

"Saying that just because it's *better* than a real note," Jurie Steyn continued, "then for that reason it's no good. That's got me floored, all right."

A situation like that opened up possibilities on which he, personally, would rather not dwell, Jurie Steyn went on.

"By and by it will mean that if a respectably dressed stranger comes here to my post office, driving an expensive motor-car," Jurie Steyn said, "and he hands me a banknote that I can see nothing wrong with, except that it looks properly printed, then it means I'll have to notify the police at Nietverdiend. But if a Mshangaan in a blanket comes round here and he doesn't buy stamps, even, but he just wants change for a five-pound note, then I'll know it's all right, because the banknote has got bad spelling and the lion on the back is rubbed out in places, through the pipe in his mouth having been drawn wrong the first time."

Oupa Bekker nodded his head up and down, thoughtfully, a few times.

Yes, there were certain matters relative to currency as passed from person to person that did not always admit of facile comprehension, he said.

"Take the time the Stellaland Republic issued its own banknotes, now," Oupa Bekker said. "Well, of course, the Stellaland Republic didn't last very long. And it might have been different if it had gone on a while. But I am just talking about how it was when we first got our own Stellaland Republic banknotes, and of about how pleased we all were about it.

"For the trouble in that part of the country was that there were never enough gold coins to go round, properly. Even before the Stellaland Republic was set up, there was that trouble. You could notice it easily, too. Just by the patches a lot of the men citizens had on the back parts of their trousers, you could notice it.

"And so, when the Stellaland Republic started printing its own banknotes, it looked as though everything would come right, then. But the affairs of the nation did not altogether follow out the course we expected. One thing was landladies of boarding-houses, I remember. What they wanted at the end of the month, they said, was, I remember very clearly, money. I don't think I have ever in my life, either before or since, heard quite that same kind of sniff. I mean, the kind of sniff a Stellaland Republic landlady would give at the end of the month if she saw you feeling in an envelope for banknotes.

"Then there was the Indian storekeeper.

"I was with my friend, Giel Haasbroek, in the Indian store, and I'll never forget the look that came over the Indian's face when Giel Haasbroek produced a handful of Stellaland Republic banknotes to pay him with. Amongst other things, what the Indian said was that he had a living to make, just like all of us.

"'But these notes are perfectly good,' Giel Haasbroek said to the Indian. 'Look, there's the picture of the Stellaland Republic eagle across the top, here. And here, underneath, you can read for yourself the printed signatures of the President and the Minister of Finance – signed with their own hands, too.'

"I'll never forget how the Indian storekeeper winced, then, either. And the Indian said he had nothing against the eagle. He was willing to admit that it was the best kind of eagle that there was. He wouldn't argue about that. From where he came from they didn't have eagles. And if you were to show him a whole lot of eagles in a row, he didn't think he would be able to tell the one from the other, hardly, the Indian said. We must not misunderstand him on that point, the Indian took pains to make clear to us. He had no intention of hurting our feelings in any way. He would not take exception to the eagle in any shape or form.

"But when it came to the signatures of the President and the Minister of Finance, then it was quite a different matter, the Indian said. For he had both their signatures in black and white for old debts that he knew he would never be able to collect, the Indian said. And of the two, the President was worse than the Minister of Finance, even. The President had got so, the Indian said, that for months, now, on his way to work in the morning, he would walk three blocks out of his way, round the other side of the plein, just so that he didn't have to pass the Indian's store."

Oupa Bekker interrupted his story to get a match from the schoolteacher. That gave us a chance to ponder over what he had said. For they had fallen strangely on our ears, some of his words. There appeared to have been a certain starkness about the texture of life in the old days that our present-day imaginings could not too readily embrace.

"But they never caught on, really, those Stellaland Republic banknotes," Oupa Bekker continued. "Afterwards the Government withdrew the old banknotes and brought out a new issue. But even that didn't help very much, I don't think. Although I must say that the new series of banknotes looked much nicer. The new banknotes were bigger, for one thing. And they were printed in more colours than the old ones were. And they had a new kind of eagle on the top. The eagle seemed more imposing, somehow. And he also had a threatening kind of look, that you couldn't miss. It was like the Stellaland Republic *threatening* you, if you got tendered one of those notes for board and lodging, and you were hesitating about taking it.

"But, all the same, those banknotes never really seemed to circulate, very much. Maybe that Indian storekeeper was right in what he said. Perhaps after all it wasn't the eagle, so 'much, that they should have changed, as those two signatures on the lower portion of the banknote. Perhaps they should have been signed so that you couldn't read them.

"And, as I have said, the queer thing is that there was nothing *wrong* with those Stellaland Republic banknotes. They weren't counterfeit notes in any way, I mean. They were absolutely legal. The eagle and the printing were both all right – they were the smartest-looking eagle and the smartest printing that you could get in those days. And yet – there you were."

We agreed with Oupa Bekker that the problem of money was pretty mixed up, and always had been. Shortly afterwards the Government lorry arrived from Bekkersdal. The lorry-driver's assistant went up to the counter.

"Change this fiver for me, please, Jurie," he said.

This was Jurie Steyn's turn to be funny. He took full advantage of it. He turned the note over several times.

"The printing looks all right," Jurie Steyn said. "And for all I know, the spelling is also all right. And the lion hasn't got a pipe in his mouth. What kind of a fool do you think I am – handing me a note like this . . .? About the only thing it hasn't got on it is an eagle."

Since he didn't know what our talk had been about, the lorry-driver's assistant looked only mystified.

405

FORBIDDEN COUNTRY

"But surely the shortest way," At Naudé said, with reference to yet another expedition from overseas that was setting out for the Kalahari, "would be for them to go through Ramoutsa and then through the Tsifulu –"

"Not so fast," Gysbert van Tonder interrupted him. "The expedition from abroad can't go through that part of the Tsifulu just as fast as you're saying it now, At."

"Not through the Tsifulu," Chris Welman concurred.

"The Tsifulu is forbidden country," Gysbert van Tonder explained.

"Forbidden country," Chris Welman echoed.

"It's forbidden to go through there," Gysbert van Tonder repeated, in case he wasn't properly understood the first time.

"Forbidden," came from Chris Welman with the sombre inevitability of a one-man Greek chorus.

Oh, that, At Naudé said. That sort of thing just made him tired. We all knew the Tsifulu was called the Forbidden Country, At Naudé said. But it was just a name given to that part. It didn't mean anything. It was just like Gysbert van Tonder's farm being called Paradise Kloof.

He could picture the surprise of a visitor to Gysbert van Tonder's farm, At Naudé continued, that visitor going by just the name of the farm, and then that visitor suddenly seeing who it was sitting on the front stoep drinking coffee. Seeing Gysbert van Tonder sitting there, the visitor would think that he had come to the exact opposite place of paradise, At Naudé said.

But Jurie Steyn said that he was in agreement with Gysbert van Tonder and Chris Welman. As long as he had been in the Marico he had known that that section of the Tsifulu was the Forbidden Country. And that was enough for him, Jurie Steyn said. If it was, as At Naudé claimed, just a name, then why did it have that name?

"If the place is all right," Jurie Steyn added, "why don't they call it by a name like 'Potluck Corner', or something meaning 'Home from Home', say? Maybe that part of the Tsifulu isn't really forbidden, but I've never been around to look. The name is enough for me. I can take a hint as well as the next man, I suppose."

Young Vermaak, the schoolmaster, said then that he had also heard that there was that part, there, known as the Forbidden Country. He had never given it much thought, he said, but now that mention was being made of it, well, it did seem interesting to him as to how it should have got its name in the first place. Since Oupa Bekker was the oldest inhabitant of the Groot Marico, did Oupa Bekker know, perhaps?

But Oupa Bekker said, no, during all his years in those parts he had just always known of that section of the Tsifulu as being the Forbidden Country. How it got the name, he would not presume to guess, Oupa Bekker said.

"One thing, though," he added. "In the old days, when you spoke of the Forbidden Country, you would say: it with more of a respect for it in your voice, sort of. You would also, as likely as not, take your hat off, then, without thinking, even."

That made it sound yet more interesting, young Vermaak said. "But that expedition from overseas, now," he asked. "How will they be able to tell, when they come to the Tsifulu, what part of it is forbidden? Why can't they go just straight through it? I don't suppose they've got notice-boards up there to say: 'Forbidden Country – No Visitors' or 'This Area Taboo – Keep Out.' Not that it would help much, I should think, putting up notice-boards like that.

"Because, seeing what human nature is, even if the expedition had no intention of going through there, just to be told they weren't allowed in would awaken their curiosity. You can't beat just a plain word like 'Unholy' for getting you really interested. I mean, it sounds much more inviting than 'Pull in Here for a Nice Cup of Tea'."

The schoolmaster was partly right, Gysbert van Tonder said. It was indeed a truth that there were no notice-boards up. Furthermore, it was all mostly nothing more than thorn-trees and sand in that part, so that, just to look at, you would hardly even know which was the Forbidden Country area and which wasn't.

"But all the same you don't need notice-boards," Gysbert van Tonder said.

"Don't need them," came from Chris Welman by way of endorsement.

407

"When you're there you just know it," Gysbert van Tonder added. "You can feel it in your bones."

"Bones," Chris Welman echoed, his voice sepulchral. It made you think of the mortal remains of some unhappy traveller lying bleaching in the sun.

"But where Meneer Vermaak is wrong," Gysbert van Tonder said, "is in thinking that when you are there you would want to go in further, after some passing Bushman or Bechuana has told you that it's the Forbidden Country. Because that's sure to happen. At some time or other a Bushman or Bechuana is sure to come up to you to ask for tobacco. And then you are also certain to ask him which is the best way of getting to where you want to go. Because it doesn't matter if you're going by a map, and you've got a very good map. Or if the way got explained to you so clearly at the Indian store in Ramoutsa that you just can't miss it.

"For, by the time the Bushman comes up to you to ask for tobacco, you are sure to have already passed a whole line of koppies that it says nothing about on the map. You will already have come across three dry river-beds and a deep donga and a petrified forest that not a word was spoken of in the instructions you got in the Indian store at Ramoutsa. I mean, it's always like that with a road you can't miss. After the first half-hour you know you should have had more sense than to have listened to the Indian. It is also not nice for you to know that you will one day be held accountable for all the things you have thought of the man who made the map.

"So you're glad when you come across that Bushman. Or, if it's a Bechuana, you're just as glad."

Chris Welman interposed to say that the only time you were not glad was when it was a Mshangaan mine-boy, and he was riding a bicycle on his way home from the mines, and he came and asked you where he was.

What you at least felt about that Bushman, Gysbert van Tonder continued, was that he was not the dishonest kind of person who would deliberately mislead a stranger. You couldn't think of him as working behind a store counter, for one thing. Nor could you think of that Bushman as sitting down with a ruler and a pen and ink and drawing a map that would get printed to confuse the unsuspecting traveller, Gysbert van Tonder said.

"And after you've told that Bushman where you want to go, he'll point to the right or the left," Gysbert van Tonder continued. "You must turn off for half a day's journey, he'll say, before you again go on. It's also not impossible that the Bushman will point straight back, along the way you've come, and he'll make it clear to you that it doesn't matter very much whether, after that, you remember if it's the right or the left, you've got to turn to – just as long as you don't waste any time about getting straight out of where you're in.

"You'll have guessed, by that time, that where you are in is in the Forbidden Country.

"The Bushman will also most likely advise you not to waste time in cutting off some roll-tobacco to hand him. Just drop the whole roll where you are, right in the sand, he'll say, and he'll pick it up himself afterwards. He doesn't mind how much sand there is on the roll of tobacco, the Bushman will tell you, just as long as you get out of the Forbidden Country in time."

But he still didn't see why, the schoolmaster said, you had to turn back, simply on account of an ignorant Bechuana or a Bushman. No sensible person would be influenced by that sort of thing, young Vermaak said.

It wasn't the same thing, Gysbert van Tonder explained, as sitting in Jurie Steyn's post office, drinking coffee.

"It's quite different, when you're out there," Gysbert van Tonder said. "When you're in the Tsifulu. With nothing but the sun and the sand and the thorn-trees. You feel quite different about things there. And if somebody tells you, then, that that area is forbidden country, you just take one look at it, and you know that it is so. I mean, it's no good saying it here, where we're sitting, now. You've got to be there, actually in the Tsifulu, to understand it. It's – well, it's Africa, there, see?"

"Afri –" Chris Welman started to chime in, and then checked himself because it sounded foolish.

"But will anything happen to a person that goes into that part of the Tsifulu that's forbidden?" the schoolmaster asked.

"No, I don't think so," Gysbert van Tonder said. "Nothing more than would happen to him anywhere else, I suppose."

"Well, would he come back alive, for instance?" young Vermaak enquired further.

Gysbert van Tonder looked surprised.

"Alive? I don't see why not," he said. "I mean, there's nobody going to murder him there, is there? What's there about it that he shouldn't come back alive?"

It was the schoolmaster's turn to look puzzled.

"I don't get it," he said. "If there's nothing going to happen to you for going into that part of the Tsifulu – just nothing at all – then what's going to stop you from going there?"

"Because it's Forbidden Country," Gysbert van Tonder said.

"Forbidden," Chris Welman said.

Thereupon the schoolmaster asked Gysbert van Tonder and Chris Welman if they would go into the Forbidden Country, the two of them going in together, if they were in that part of the Tsifulu – seeing that nothing would happen to them for it.

"The Lord forefend," Gysbert van Tonder said, his voice sounding hollow.

"God *forbid*," Chris Welman said.

That kind of talk seeming to be getting nobody anywhere, Oupa Bekker made mention of an excursion he had once made into the Forbidden Country in the very old days.

"I was young, then, of course," Oupa Bekker said, by way of apology. "And another thing was that in those days there was a Swiss mission station in the Forbidden Country. So I thought perhaps it would not be too bad to go in there, after all. I had a whole lot of glass beads on my wagon to trade with the natives for cattle. I don't know how that story got around that natives, who are cattlemen themselves, would be so foolish as to trade off a cow or an ox for glass beads. In any case, I never found any that would. And after a chief offered me some brass wire for two of my lead oxen I knew it was no use trying anymore, either.

"I camped out for a quite a while near the Swiss mission station. And in the evenings I would go over and talk to the missionary. He was glad to see me because, since it was the Forbidden Country, there was no white person, with the exception of his wife and daughter, that he had to talk to from one year's end to the other.

"The missionary's daughter had quite a simple name – Ettie. And she had laughing eyes and dark hair. And she used to bring us in coffee while her father and I sat talking. One night when she came in she smiled at something I said. The next night when she gave me my coffee her hand brushed against mine. The night after that she was at the front gate, in the starlight. And that was the last time that I saw Ettie.

"It was on account of the missionary coming upon us unexpectedly, from behind, just as I was reaching sideways over the gate to kiss Ettie, that I didn't see her again, of course. Because he was a Swiss missionary, I don't think it meant very much to him about it's being starlight. And the next thing I learnt was that Ettie had been sent back to Switzerland for more education.

"I don't need to tell you that I felt very bad about it – and for a long time, too. Naturally, I knew that it was the Forbidden Country, there, right enough. But still I couldn't help feeling that it needn't have been quite as forbidden as all that."

At Ease on the Dung Heap

It wasn't that he didn't agree that the Government soil experts were doing useful work, Chris Welman said to At Naudé, after At Naudé had told us of a new way of planting sweet-potatoes that had been announced over the wireless in the half-hour farming talk that was called "At Ease on the Dung Heap". But a lot of the advice they gave you wasn't practical, Chris Welman maintained.

"That's right," Jurie Steyn said. "And it's on that point that I don't hold with the agricultural experts, either. I have found out, myself, that in nearly every case of new advice they give you, it means you've got to do more work. They're not practical, at all."

It was for that very reason, Jurie Steyn said, that he had long since come to disregard the so-called skilled counsel of the agricultural authorities. There was so little, in the suggestions they made, that could be usefully applied. He had also, at one time, set some store by the pamphlets issued by the department, and he had found that you could count them on the fingers of one hand, Jurie Steyn said, the practical kind of expert who would just tell you to stick the thing in the ground and leave it.

"Yes," Chris Welman said, nodding his head, "I found just that same thing. Every time I've got to hear about a new kind of farming that's supposed to have brought good results in a country like Sweden, say, I have discovered inside of a week that it's no good for South African conditions. I don't say that it mightn't work very well in, say, Sweden, of course.

"But I've found every time that to carry out that new kind of method in South Africa I've got to get up a lot earlier, every morning. A lot of these new plans they recommend just aren't suited to South African conditions, I mean. Not that I've got anything against a Belgian or that kind of foreigner, of course. But it's only that here, in the Groot Marico, well, it's different. It doesn't work out that way, here. I mean, you just take the soil here in the Marico –"

There was no need for Chris Welman to proceed any further, for even At Naudé himself, who had introduced the discussion, acknowledged that it was with several mental reservations of his own that he had passed on to us the latest sweet-potato-growing theories as expounded by the radio farming authority.

"I mean, I listened carefully," At Naudé said, "because, as you all know, I've got no prejudice against the At-Ease-on-the-Dung-Heap man. – I mean, he's much more human than the broadcaster before him, that gave the "On Your Toes at 4.15 a. m." talks. Every reasonable farmer boycotted *him* at the end, naturally, him with his liberal use of sulphur for reclaiming brak soil and painting every plant with a camel-hair brush for soft scale. He never said *who* was supposed to go round doing all that painting . . . But I don't know how long this new man is going to last, either. Of course, we all know that what he says is kindly meant.

"Still, when he mentions things like design and feature and good proportion, and he's talking about sweet-potatoes, then you know it won't be long before a few Bushveld farmers start writing in about it. Because you know that, when once he starts using words like that, there is going to be a lot of extra work sticking out for somebody. And that is where I say that the wireless is so much better than the Government experimental farm pamphlets.

"The wireless encourages the farmer to write in what he thinks about the talks. The agricultural experimental farms don't. They've learnt better. In any case by the look of it, I should say they're too busy. Making the bottom soil gradually shelve up to the sides, like they say in their pamphlets. Well, there must be somebody on a Government experimental farm doing all that, I suppose. And so he'll be too busy to answer farmers' letters. Or to show the farmers' letters to his boss, even.

"And the experimental farm man doesn't care how many complaints he gets from farmers about how unpractical his advice is, through the extra work. He just starts off again in his next pamphlet with the words: 'Proceed as follows.' I have noticed that the At-Ease-on-the-Dung-Heap man is a bit careful, there. He never says, 'Proceed,' straight out, like that. After he explains what he thinks is a good method he just tells a few jokes to make you laugh. It looks like he wants to keep his job."

There was another thing too, Gysbert van Tonder said, that the agricultural expert never seemed to pay enough attention to. All right, he didn't say that if you followed the expert's advice, whatever that advice was, that you wouldn't then be able to grow more sweet-potatoes. But even without the expert's advice you could grow all the sweet-potatoes you wanted, just sticking bits of it in the ground.

But if every farmer in the country started growing sweet-potatoes on such a scale, what were you going to do with all those sweet-potatoes in the end, Gysbert van Tonder asked. And never mind about design and good proportion and all those other things that At Naudé mentioned, Gysbert van Tonder said. He was just talking about ordinary sweet-potatoes that came up anyhow.

"Why, I can remember only a few years ago, that time of the big rains," Gysbert van Tonder said, "that I had so many sweet-potatoes, they just rotted on the market. And I couldn't sell them to the jam factory, anymore, even, either, afterwards. Even when I showed the owner of the jam factory that my sweet-potatoes didn't have soot fungus on them, he still said he couldn't use them. Not even for strawberry jam, the jam factory owner said to me. It wasn't the soot fungus, he told me, but he just didn't have any more tins. Bring him some tins, he said, and he would talk business."

That got Jurie Steyn talking about the anthrax epidemic of years ago. When a beast died, and it looked like it might be anthrax, Jurie Steyn said, they got instructions from Pretoria that the beast hadn't to be moved but that he had to be buried right on the spot where he lay, and a barbed-wire fence had to be erected round him, and a blood smear of the dead animal had to be sent inside two pieces of glass to the research laboratory. And the grass had to be burnt for twenty yards around where the ox or the cow was buried, to prevent infection.

"Well, that was in my father's time, of course," Jurie Steyn said. "And we carried out all the instructions, as best we could. I didn't have much to do with it, myself, seeing that I was still just a boy, then. All that my work was, when a beast died and it looked like anthrax, was to go round to the oldest Bechuana I could see standing in front of one of the huts on the far end of our farm.

"And I would tell him. And the old Bechuana would look thoughtful; and he would sigh and say how sorry he was to hear that my father had suffered again a loss. Au! It was bad, the anthrax, he would say, clicking his tongue. But about an hour or so later you would hardly recognise that Bechuana for the same man. The way, I mean, that he would be jumping around the dead ox that the women were cutting into pieces for roasting. He wouldn't look old at all, then, or thought-ful, the way he was leading everybody there in a beer-dance.

"And that party would go on into the morning – or, at least, until such time as there was still any ox left. And I used to eat some of it myself, too. And although I believed that I could taste the anthrax in it, on account of all that I had heard about anthrax, it nevertheless didn't – because I was young, I suppose – taste to me very awful. As a matter of fact, I wouldn't mind having some of that right now: here, as I'm stand-ing in my own post office – just so's I could have the appetite, too, to eat it as it tasted, then, when I was young.

"And another thing, too, that went with those instructions – that the remains had to be buried and that the grass had to be burnt for twenty yards around. Well, after the party was over there was just no remains left to be buried. And as for the grass, well, as likely as not a mile and more of it would have been burnt, and right into the next people's farm, even. And that would be only on account of the beer-drinking – nobody noticing that the fire that the ox was being roasted on was starting to spread."

The view that he himself must take, young Vermaak, the school-master, said, of all that Jurie Steyn had been telling us, could not be otherwise but dim. There was the department trying to help us, he said. Placing at our disposal free of charge, the schoolmaster said, the enlightenment come by through expensive scientific research, the schoolmaster said, and costly experiment, endangering lives, even, in some cases, and here were we, instead of co-operating, carrying on like a lot of bush baboons.

The schoolmaster should never have spoken like that, of course. Because it took him a long while – not counting the time occupied in straight apologies – to convince Jurie Steyn that he hadn't meant that Jurie Steyn's father was a bush baboon. It took him an almost equally long time to persuade Chris Welman that nothing could have been fur-ther from his thoughts than to have implied that Chris Welman's father was a krantz ape.

Nor did the schoolmaster seek to suggest – Gysbert van Tonder having invited the schoolmaster to come outside, at one stage – that in Gysbert van Tonder's ancestry as far back as Jan van Riebeeck there was anybody even remotely resembling a withaak gorilla.

All that he had tried to make clear, the schoolmaster said, in those words of which we had misunderstood the meaning, was that we should try to co-operate with the Government's agricultural department, when the department was only doing its best. He himself had heard a few stories of those old anthrax days, young Vermaak went on, and he honestly couldn't see that those stories reflected much credit on the farmers concerned. Like some of those things that for instance went on with the glass slides in which the farmer was supposed to put a blood smear of the ox that had died of anthrax.

"Through a misguided sense of what was funny," the schoolmaster said, "the farmer in question would as likely as not put a blood smear of his own in, in between the two glass slides. And it is also known that quite a few farmers would not take a hint from the answers they got back. They really thought that the scientists in the Government laboratory were that ignorant and couldn't distinguish between human and ox blood. They didn't know that the research workers in the laboratory were having a quiet, scientific laugh."

That just showed how cut off the schoolmaster was from realities, Jurie Steyn said, then. For the laboratory scientists *were* as ignorant as all that. It was one of the things that made most of the Marico farmers this side of the Pilanesberg lose all respect for the agricultural pamphlets. When they saw how little those scientists really knew, Jurie Steyn said.

"Take old Ockert Struwig, now," Jurie Steyn said. "Why, I remember when one of Ockert's trek-oxen died of what we all knew was the anthrax. And so, what does Ockert Struwig do, but just for a joke he sends in to the Pretoria laboratory a smear not of the trek-ox's blood but his own blood, and what is the answer he gets? This: 'A weak-minded beast like this is better dead.'

"That gave Ockert Struwig a laugh, all right, to think how wrong the research institute people were. For the joke of it was that Ockert Struwig was as alive as anything, and the trek-ox of his that had died of anthrax wasn't in any way weak-minded. I mean, you can well understand that none of us had much faith in the research science experts after that."

We were all gratified to note that the schoolmaster couldn't answer that one, at all. All the schoolmaster could do was to stare in a bewildered fashion.

"And this thing, before buying ground," Gysbert van Tonder remarked, then. "Taking samples of the soil at different places and sending it for analysis. Well, what kind of farmer is that, I'd like to know? If you can't just take it in your hand and crumble it, and know what kind of soil it is."

"Or looking how high the weeds get to, that are growing on it," Jurie Steyn said. "Seeing how *they're* liking it."

"Or going to where there's a donga, and seeing how far the soil goes down," Chris Welman said. "That tells you a few things. Where's a research chemist then?"

"Or, when nobody is watching, taking a little of it in your hand and tasting it," Oupa Bekker said. "That gives you a better idea than any, of what the soil is like. And I've still got to see an agricultural department soil expert doing that, that's all."

And he applied no more than just that simple test of tasting the ground, Oupa Bekker said, when, many years ago, he bought his present farm.

"I tasted it for quite a bit," Oupa Bekker said. "For I wanted to make really sure. I mean, I wasn't too young, even then. And so I made up my mind that the ground had to be right. Not only for tilling, but for lying in many years after I had finished tilling. I couldn't ask an Onderstepoort soil expert to do that for me."

VIII

The barn in which Herman Charles Bosman and John Callaghan taught school. The Haasbroek farm, Heimweeberg, Nietverdiend. 1964

No Spoon-feeding

"It's difficult," young Vermaak, the schoolmaster, said. "Difficult for the teacher, that is. It seems that at a particular age it's worse than at other times. The questions children ask me. The things they want to know. 'Why is . . . ?' they ask me. And 'Can a . . . ?' is another way they have of putting a question. There seems no end to the things a child wants to know at a certain age. 'If a . . . ?' is another very popular kind of enquiry. So is 'What makes . . . ?'

"And some of the things children pop out with unexpectedly. You've got no idea. Like 'Where does a . . . ?'"

Gysbert van Tonder gave a low snigger.

"Not that," the schoolmaster said, taking Gysbert van Tonder up sharply. "The schoolchild of today is quite different from what you were like, in your time. He's much more natural about everything. More healthy-minded, too, I should imagine."

Gysbert van Tonder looked somewhat perturbed. From the way the schoolmaster spoke it would appear as though he regarded Gysbert van Tonder as somebody that was at his age harbouring unwholesome thoughts. As though in Gysbert's lucubrations there lurked the mephitic, the noisome. From the way the schoolmaster's lip curled you could sense all that.

"All right," Gysbert van Tonder said, after a while, coughing awkwardly, "if you think I've got an unhealthy sickness in my brain, sort of, I won't argue about it. I only hope it's catching, that's all."

Having made that observation, Gysbert van Tonder seemed quite cheerful, again. It did not occur to him that in giving expression to so antisocial a sentiment he was merely supplying background and colour – and collateral evidence – in substantiation of the mental fault that the schoolmaster had hinted about him.

"Questions starting with 'Which . . . ?' for instance," young Vermaak continued. "Like 'Which side of the cloud is the thunder on?' Now, there's something for you to have to answer.

"I tell you, I've grown to dread it – when a child puts up his hand and he doesn't ask, quite politely, can he leave the room, please, Meneer, but he puts me a question starting with the word 'Which . . . ?' Another kind of opening sentence I'm never too happy about is 'Who was . . . ?' Or 'How far . . . ?' Or, an old favourite, 'Say now, Meneer . . .' Because, when it's 'Say now, Meneer . . .' then I don't mind telling you that it's as likely as not a question that I can't answer.

"The chances are, even, that it's a question that nobody has ever heard of before. I can't go and look up the answer in a book, even, and then come back next day and explain it all on the blackboard, as though I knew it all along, but I was just giving the class an opportunity to think it out for themselves first.

"And it's a funny thing, but the longer I keep teaching, the more I discover that the Theory of Education that I had to learn at the Teachers' College really does amount to something. When I was a student I used to sneer at a lot of the things the lecturers said. But I find that in many things they were very sound. Like one thing they used to say was: 'Don't answer a child's question immediately: give him an opportunity to try and think out the answer for himself first.'

"It means that it also gives the teacher a chance to think out the answer, first. It also gives the teacher a proper chance to look up the answer after school, in a book. It's not in the best traditions of the Theory of Education for the teacher to come out pat, just like that, with the answer, including all the exact dates, if it's a history question, or right down to the decimals, if it's a sum. The child must not be just spoon-fed. Next day the teacher can work it all out for the class, on the blackboard, in a free and easy manner, oh, airily, even if the teacher's eyes are a bit red around the rims, through having sat up late.

"More and more I am growing to realise that they knew a thing or two, the old lecturers and professors at the Teachers' College. It wasn't just pure Theory of Education they were palming off onto us and that we had to make notes about. A lot of it was what they had learnt from sound, solid practice."

Young Vermaak sat silent, then, for some moments. Before his inner vision there passed in procession the dry-as-dust lecturers at his alma mater – unimaginative exponents of a haphazard pedagogy that embraced impartially Johannes Duns Scotus, Montessori and Circular 88 (c) of the Transvaal Education Department. He realised now that one thing, at least, that they didn't have on them, lecturers and professors alike, was flies.

He was, belatedly, acquiring a respect for them. He saw, now, that they had been through the mill, all right. In the very triteness of some of their aphorisms – what they called golden rules – there was an element of the sinister that they could have come by only in the course of the bear garden rough-and-tumble that teaching in a classroom consisted of.

There was the first lecture he had listened to about the importance of maintaining discipline in the classroom. And he remembered how that lecturer had stressed the fact that discipline was the opposite of anarchy. It was the contrary state to turbulence, also, the lecturer had made clear. Discipline was also the inverse of rampaging and running amok, the lecturer had said.

It was the antithesis to pandemonium, the lecturer had made clear. Discipline was most decidedly not uproar and violent rumpus. Only after he had himself been teaching for a short while did young Vermaak begin to understand something of the years of patient suffering that imparted a measure of shrillness to the lecturer's statement, like a red ink line drawn underneath it with a ruler.

Then there was that other lecturer – dull-eyed but, on occasion, red-faced – who had struck a note that young Vermaak was subsequently to recognise as having been happier. "The best way of correcting a pupil's work," was the counsel proffered by the lecturer whose face was always markedly red round about the end of the month – the Post Office vermilion of his visage being accompanied also by a certain unsteadiness of gait, "is to correct it right in his presence. Call him up to your desk and show him where he went wrong."

Young Vermaak had since learnt that that was sound pedagogy. It meant that that was an exercise book he didn't have to take home to correct.

And the idea of not spoon-feeding a child. With his own practical classroom experience, young Vermaak could detect that there was, in the originator of that maxim relating to the science of imparting knowledge, an element of genius. Even if it was a Standard Five schoolchild asking a question as a trap, the riposte, "Now, now, you must try and work that one out for yourself," was for the schoolmaster a perfect means of escape. It was the teaching profession's sheet anchor, the custodian of the educator's dignity and reputation for scholarship. "How many l's in parallel, Meneer?" – "Try and find out for yourself, and then you come and tell *me* in the morning."

Gysbert van Tonder had, in the meantime, been thinking.

"Look," he said to young Vermaak, eventually, "did I get it right, that you said that you don't know, lots of times, what the answer is when a child asks you something?"

"Of course, yes," the schoolmaster said. "Well, I mean, just take some of the kind of questions, like –"

"You don't *know* the answer?" Gysbert van Tonder repeated. "To a simple sort of question that a *child* asks? And you supposed to be an educated man? And then you had something to say about my brain – that my brain isn't up to much."

It was Gysbert van Tonder's turn to wear a thin smile.

"Well, just take a few samples," the schoolmaster said. "Such as 'Does a luislang dream?', 'Why did my father say his hair stood on end when Oom Koos came to visit us and my father thought at first Oom Koos was a tax-collector?', 'Why doesn't the sky fall?', 'Can a fly hear?', 'Why does Meneer's cane go swish before it hits?', 'Why does a ghost go through the wall when there's the window open?' – Now, does anybody know, just straight out, the answers to questions like that? And what makes children ask questions like that?"

Gysbert van Tonder observed that young Vermaak was getting just like a schoolchild himself, asking those last few questions in the way he did.

"A child asks a thing because he wants to be informed, that's all," Gysbert van Tonder said. "It's something a child doesn't know yet, and that he would like to learn about. And so he asks his teacher. Because he doesn't *know*, he asks. But I can see, from what Meneer Vermaak has been saying, how foolish it is with this new kind of education for a child to ask his teacher about something he doesn't know. It's because he's so ignorant as not to know that his teacher hasn't got the answer that he asks. The child hasn't learnt, yet, that his teacher is a new kind of teacher who isn't supposed to know anything."

Gysbert van Tonder started off in what he intended to be a tone of gentle satire. But he got more and more worked up as he talked.

"The child doesn't know, yet, that his teacher is just a pudding-faced ass," Gysbert van Tonder remarked. That was where it was different when he went to school, Gysbert van Tonder said, when they had just the old-fashioned kind of Hollander schoolmaster that had as likely as not been a sailor in his time, and had seen a thing or two, and had no frills about him. And if he didn't quite know how to spell a word, he would at least guess. The old Hollander schoolmaster would never let on to the parents of his pupils that he could not answer even the simplest kind of questions. Nor would he so far forget himself as to suggest that a respected Marico farmer seated opposite him in a public post office had something the matter with his head.

Jurie Steyn was inclined to agree with Gysbert van Tonder.

"After all, those questions that the schoolmaster has mentioned, that he gets asked in class," Jurie Steyn said, "well, I don't pretend to be a very highly educated man, myself, although I can hold my own with the next man, I think, when it comes to book learning. But I don't think that those questions are too hard to answer, especially for a person that takes a bit of notice of what's going on around him.

"I mean, that one about the ghost, now. Why, has anybody ever heard of a ghost coming through a door – unless it's a locked door – when there's a wall for him to come through? It stands to reason that a ghost isn't going to climb through any open window when there's a two-foot-thick wall of sun-baked bricks for him to walk through, and him out to scare you all he can. It's just because he *is* a ghost that he doesn't look around for an open window to rest his knee on the ledge of before jumping in. A ghost has got more sense than that. More sense than a child that asks such a question – and more sense than a schoolteacher that doesn't know the answer, too, I'm thinking."

Or about a schoolchild's father saying that his hair stood on end when somebody called round that might have been the tax-collector from Zeerust, Chris Welman said. Well, it might almost have been his own child that asked the question, by the sound of it, Chris Welman said. And how else otherwise did the schoolmaster expect a farmer in such a situation to act up, Chris Welman wanted to know.

Apart from asking the visitor would he sit down and have a brandy – perhaps several brandies: say five or six full-strength peach brandies, before trying to talk, seeing that the visitor must have travelled a good distance for the best part of a hot day and on an empty stomach – how otherwise did the schoolmaster expect a farmer of the Groot Marico to carry on when there was a tax-collector come to see him? Did the schoolmaster think that the Marico farmer would just bring out a photograph album for the tax-collector to look through while he was sitting in the farmer's voorkamer, Chris Welman asked.

"And about the sky falling down," Chris Welman added. "Well, you do sort of wish that the sky could fall down, then, when you're in that situation. Or that the ground you're standing on could disappear from underneath your feet, then. You know that it's too much to hope for that the ground will disappear from underneath the polished-shoes feet of the tax-collector, I mean."

Between At Naudé, Gysbert van Tonder, Jurie Steyn and Chris Welman, a pretty satisfactory set of answers was found to most of the questions posed by the schoolmaster in behoof of his pupils seeking enlightenment.

Only Oupa Bekker looked, at times, doubtful. He had lived a long time in the world, Oupa Bekker said, and so, for that reason, he could not feel that young Vermaak was wrong, altogether. He had, with the years, grown more than a little sceptical of the facile exposition, Oupa Bekker gave to understand. The happy solution, the neat definition, the striking story illustrative – as he grew older, they did not, somehow, weigh with him so much, Oupa Bekker confessed.

"As often as not a thing is quite different from how it looks," was the way Oupa Bekker expressed it. "And a puzzle is a puzzle. The older I get, the more I think like that. So I wouldn't like to say that the schoolmaster has got it all back to front. There's life, now, for instance. And just look how long I've lived. And yet I feel, life . . . can anybody tell me what it's all about, anyway?"

Young Vermaak's eyes twinkled.

"Now, now, Oupa Bekker," he said. "That's something you've got to work out for yourself. You don't expect me to spoon-feed you, do you?"

Bekkersdal Centenary

We were talking about the centenary celebrations at Bekkersdal. They were doing it in real style, we said, and it gave us a deep sense of pride, in this part of the Marico, to think that our town, that we had regarded as just *being* there, kind of, should have so impressive and stirring a history, and what was more, a future resplendent with opportunity and promise.

"Well, I had never thought of Bekkersdal in quite that way before," Chris Welman said, "but when I went in week before last to have this tooth pulled out" – he inserted a couple of toil-discoloured fingers in his mouth to disclose the cavity – "I did notice a few of these centenary things they were talking about."

Chris Welman made some further remarks, but there was a certain lack of precision in his articulation through his holding his mouth open that way while he was talking. It did not contribute to a clarity of diction – Chris Welman uttering sounds with his jaws prised apart and his tongue moving up and down behind his fingers.

After Jurie Steyn had said that with Chris Welman having his mouth so wide it was like there was a draught in his post office that he hadn't noticed before, and after young Vermaak, the schoolmaster, had explained about how he had been trembling, all the time, in fear that one of Chris Welman's fingers might slip into a part of his mouth where the teeth were still all in, and so get bitten off – in his classical studies at University he had read about a boxer who, having stopped one from a Greek boxing-glove, was spitting out teeth, the schoolmaster said, and he did not feel happy at the thought of somebody spitting out fingers on the floor of Jurie Steyn's voorkamer – after all that, Chris Welman said that he had a good mind not to go on talking anymore about his impressions of the Bekkersdal 100th-year celebrations, seeing how unappreciative we were.

And as for the Greek boxing-gloves that the schoolmaster had mentioned as what he had learnt about in the classics, Chris Welman said, well, they didn't seem, by the sound of it, to be much different from the brass boxing-gloves that members of the Jeppe gang just wore over the knuckles of the right hand.

And he did not think that the Jeppe gang were students of the classics so that you would notice it, much, Chris Welman said.

Thereupon At Naudé remarked that Chris Welman having a tooth out in Bekkersdal wasn't really of historical importance. It wasn't of much significance one way or the other, he reckoned. Especially today, with the newspapers and the wireless having a lot to say about Bekkersdal's centenary.

"If it had been a Voortrekker leader that had a tooth pulled out there a hundred years ago, it would have been different, perhaps," At Naudé continued. "If it had been the Voortrekker leader Andries Loggenberg, say, and it had been the time of the trouble between the Hervormde church and the Doppers, say – well, that would have been something.

"With Andries Loggenberg having his face all bandaged up, I mean, through the way they had of pulling out a back tooth a hundred years ago, well, he just wouldn't have been able to get onto an ox-wagon, then, and make a two-hour speech straight out of the Bible about what a blot on this part of the Dwarsberge the Cape Groote Kerk was.

"All he would be able to do, with his face all swathed in cloth like that, just his eyes and a piece of beard sticking out, would be to join a little in the hymn-singing afterwards perhaps, singing a few of the easier bass notes, that would still sound all right coming from behind the folds of dressing."

All the same, At Naudé informed us, we would be surprised to know what progress had been made in Bekkersdal in recent years. We would not perhaps observe it so much ourselves, he said, just going there to buy things, or to take produce to the market or to drop in for a talk with the bank manager to find out could we draw a little against next year's substantial cheques from the creamery that we were sure to get.

Indeed, it was actually in the course of a friendly exchange of views in that manner with the bank manager – the inkpot as likely as not upsetting on his desk from the way you were banging it to show him how amicable you felt towards him – that you might be inclined to feel that Bekkersdal had a considerable amount of leeway to make up, At Naudé said.

A ten-minute conversation with the bank manager could, At Naudé proceeded, leave you quite flabbergasted at the thought that Bekkersdal was only a hundred years old. The cobwebbed absence of forward-thinking, At Naudé said, the inability to keep pace with modern development that you encountered in that office with the leather-upholstered easy-chairs that the doorman conducted you into when you had an up-to-date idea for the bank to be able to benefit itself by, was really astounding, seeing that the bank had to pay out nothing more than, immediately, a few hundred pounds in cash.

"'You've got *Founded in 1875* on the front of the bank, Mr Coetsee,' I said to the bank manager last time," At Naudé informed us, "and I said to him, 'I see the *one* is so worn, you can hardly read it anymore, through the years of wind and rain. And I think, well, you should just let it weather like that, Mr Coetsee. Because, from the ideas going on in here, it wouldn't be far wrong for this bank to *have* in front *Founded in 875*.'"

We felt that At Naudé was using rather a lot of words to tell us that he didn't get an overdraft. Well, we had more than one of us had that same difficulty. But we weren't so expansive about it. We merely said, in a few well-chosen words – short words – just what we thought of Mr Coetsee. And we said it, always, when Mr Coetsee wasn't there.

"But in other ways," At Naudé went on, when he saw that he wasn't getting any sympathy from us, "the town of Bekkersdal is advancing with rapid strides. There has been a lot over the wireless and in the newspapers about it. The newspapers have had mostly photographs and the wireless has had mostly what the Town Clerk says. Take population, now.

"Well, I read about the increase in population in the newspapers and I heard it over the wireless. Did you know that there has been an increase in the white population of Bekkersdal during the last ten years of over eighteen percent? No, I didn't, either, but there has. And there has also been an increase in the native population. But the biggest increase of all – and the Town Clerk talking over the wireless coughed a bit uncomfortably when he said it – was in the Indian population.

"And then, what do you think is Bekkersdal's income? No, I don't know the exact figures, either. But it's big, I tell you. It's big, not only for a municipality the size of Bekkersdal, but it's big also for a municipality a lot bigger. That's how everything that's going on in Bekkersdal is, it's big."

Because At Naudé was not able to quote exact figures, Chris Welman could revert to his eye-witness account of his recent visit to Bekkersdal that happened to coincide with some of the less exuberant features of the town's preparations for its centenary festival.

"I couldn't enjoy anything very much, of course," Chris Welman said, "on account of my tooth. I mean, even after it was pulled it was just as sore, almost, as if it was still in. Except that, when it was still in, I didn't have to look every twenty yards or so for a likely place, not exactly in the street and not exactly on the sidewalk either, where I could spit – seeing that my tooth went on bleeding all day.

"Well, anyway, that was one thing I found out about a town, then. How hard it is, in a town, to find a place to spit. I mean, when you're on a farm, and you've got a few thousand morgen, none of it under irrigation, you can then just spit anywhere. And it needn't be because you've had a tooth out, either. Or because of the plug of chewing to-bacco that you've got in your mouth. Or because of something you've just thought of.

"The thing is that on a farm you can just spit anywhere, and for no reason, and without thinking about it again. If you're taking a walk along the edge of your mealie-land, for instance, and there's been no rain, and you see what's coming up, on your mealie-land, and more particularly what isn't coming up – and you happen to remember that you sowed there – why, there's no place at all, then, on the edge of your mealie-land, that you aren't allowed to come to a stop and stand and spit. And you can't do that just anywhere you like to in a town.

"But what I did come across quite a lot of in Bekkersdal was how enthusiastic everybody was about the progress the place was making. Like one man said to me how his daughter had been picked to dance in the Volkspele part of the hundred-year birthday celebrations of Bek-kersdal. 'I don't mean she's *dancing*, actually,' he said to me. 'My wife and I would never allow that, of course. All my daughter does is she moves in Voortrekker costume in time to the boereorkes music – and you simply can't keep your feet still, when it's boereorkes music – and she is partnered by a young man also in Voortrekker costume, and she springs, too, naturally, when it comes to that portion of the boereorkes music, and the young man in Voortrekker costume springs, too, when it comes there, because he would look silly if he didn't just then, spring, but of course, I would never allow my daughter to *dance*.' They're holding the Volkspele on that piece of vacant ground where the next jam factory is going to be. How's that for progress, hey?"

Except for the schoolmaster, who said that it sounded a bit sticky – the jam factory part of it, he meant – we agreed that Bekkersdal was indeed making an impressive-sounding advance.

"And that old building with the thick walls and the small window-panes and the gable," Chris Welman went on, "that we called the old drostdy, standing right there in the middle of the main street – it must have been one of the first buildings they put up in Bekkersdal: I mean, it was just about stinking with age, what with those cracked tamboetie-wood ceiling beams and those ridiculous iron gates that they say came from . . . oh, I just can't remember now, but they were so heavy, you could hardly push them open – well, the old drostdy is gone, now.

"You've got no idea how different the main street looks. A man with a camera who came to photograph the old drostdy cried when he saw that it wasn't there anymore. But they told him that he didn't have to worry, because that was where the new bioscope was going up that would have electric signs at night that you could see as far as Sephton's Nek. And he could come and photograph the new bioscope in a few months' time, they said to the man with the camera who was looking around him in a lost way, crying."

Right in our own time, too, we said, and never mind about the centenary celebrations, there had been a lot of progress made in Bekkersdal. Look at the year they chopped down all those oak-trees, we said, that lined the road going to the north. At least five miles of old oak-trees they must have chopped down, we said. And, well, how was that for advance? Didn't that show that Bekkersdal was really getting some-where? On the map, wasn't Bekkersdal getting somewhere, we asked.

When people hinted, sometimes, that we weren't keeping pace with the on-coming floodtide of civilisation here in the Marico, well, there were a few things we could draw their attention to, all right. We spoke at considerable length, then, and Chris Welman was able to acquaint us with some of the details, that he had heard in the town, of the size of the sideshows that were going to be erected by the merry-go-round people who had contracted to help with the centenary celebrations.

"Is there going to be a merry-go-round?" Oupa Bekker enquired, his eyes lighting up. "Why didn't you say so before? Bekkersdal was named after my grandfather. But I didn't even think of going to the hundred-year birthday. I never thought they would have a merry-go-round, too. They're doing it grand, hey? The first merry-go-round I saw was when I was a child, and we had to go all the way to Zeerust. But you say they're really going to bring the merry-go-round to Bekkersdal? The horses going round, and brass music, and silver paper stars?"

"More than anything else, silver paper stars," Chris Welman said.

Oupa Bekker was genuinely excited.

"My! My!" he said, and again, "My! My! To think that after all these years such a thing should happen to Bekkersdal. We're all going, of course, aren't we? Bekkersdal's hundredth year's birthday. What Chris Welman says is as good as a centenary, just about. And brass music and silver paper stars."

We all said, yes, of course we would go. The only person that seemed a bit out of it was the schoolmaster.

And because what he said was what he had learnt at university, the schoolmaster's words did not make sense to us, overmuch.

"The drostdy," young Vermaak said, "gone. It's like the front teeth knocked out of Bekkersdal's main street. It's as though I've had my own front teeth knocked out by a caestus. It's like I'm myself spitting out teeth."

"Silver paper stars," Oupa Bekker said, who hadn't heard what the schoolmaster was saying, and wasn't interested, anyway.

Who would want the southern hemisphere's summer heavens, when there was the majestic firmament of a merry-go-round side-show fashioned of speckled silver paper?

Dying Race

We agreed with Gysbert van Tonder that, for ignorance, the T'hla-kewa Bushman took a lot of beating. For real ignorance, that was, of course. And then it had to be a real T'hlakewa Bushman, also. It had to be the genuine article and no nonsense. We didn't want a Flat-Face Koranna that you could see by his toenails was half Mchopi coming along and pretending to us that he was a Bushman.

Nor did we mean the high society kind of Bushman, we said, that had lived for a while at a mission station and had there learnt one or two civilised tricks. Like wearing a collar stud stuck through his ear lobe, we said. Or rubbing axle-grease in his hair in place of the gemsbok fat that he had been used to. Or painting lines in washing-blue round his eyes and from there to his ears, to look like spectacles, we said. No, we certainly did not mean a Bushman like that, that had learnt city ways.

When it came to proper ignorance, we said, it had to be a raw T'hla-kewa Bushman just out of the desert: so raw that the soles of his feet were worn through, with his walking over hard ground after being used only to the sandier parts of the desert. That was what we meant by a raw Bushman, we said – one that had his feet raw. We didn't mean the kind of Bushman that when he saw a petrol pump would go and get fuel for his lighter there.

"It's funny that you should talk like that," Gysbert van Tonder said, "but I remember a Bushman in the Kalahari once mentioning to me about what he took to be a new kind of policeman in a red uniform that he had seen, at a distance of eleven miles – the Bushman having no wish to get any nearer to a policeman than that.

"I realised afterwards that it wasn't a policeman that the Bushman had seen there but a petrol pump painted red. But the Bushman took no notice of my explanation. 'How I know he was a policeman,' the Bush-man said, 'is because he never moved more than he had to.' And so I still don't know if he was a real ignorant T'hlakewa Bushman or if he had learnt a thing or two."

It was these scientists, Jurie Steyn said, coming along into the Kalahari and studying the Bushmen and their ways and listening to what they had to say, that were giving the Bushmen wrong ideas. How a self-respecting white man, and one supposed to have a certain amount of education, too, could waste his time like that passed his understanding, Jurie Steyn said.

And he wasn't talking even about how much of the Bushman's time got wasted. For the Bushman needed every spare moment of time he had, Jurie Steyn reckoned, in order to be able to meditate properly on what kind of a lost heathen he was.

"That's the only way the Bushman will ever get right," Jurie Steyn said, "through sitting down and using his brains a bit – thinking out quietly about why he's such a bane to mankind. It's only in that way that he'll be able to change his ways a little and not get the human race such a bad name wherever he goes, just through his belonging to the human race."

But instead of that, there were these scientists actually coming along and studying the Bushman's ways, and making notes, Jurie Steyn said. What could the Bushman think other than that his manner of life was all right, and something to be proud of, even, when white men came and asked him questions about it, telling him that they were anxious to learn about his habits?

That gave the Bushman no end of a high opinion of himself – thinking that white travellers had come all that way into the desert just to look him up so that they could *learn* from him. It made the Bushman quite insufferable, Jurie Steyn contended. The Bushman stuck his chest out, and acted as though he was some sort of a professor, talking just any kind of rubbish that came into his head as though it was the most profound wisdom.

"I've known," young Vermaak the schoolmaster said, winking, "more than one university professor that was just like that."

"You'd think that a Bushman would be only too glad to keep quiet about his habits, seeing what most of his habits were," Jurie Steyn continued.

And he wasn't talking even about a Bushman's habits to do with laundry that he saw hanging on a clothes-line when there was nobody within sight. Or a Bushman's habits with a sheep that had strayed from the flock and the shepherd having his back turned for a few minutes. Or his habits with watermelons that you weren't watching. Or with a blancmange pudding when the pantry window was open.

There was the Bushman's established practice, Jurie Steyn said, of going down on all fours in front of an ant-hill that he had broken the top of off, and just licking up the ants as fast as he could go, and without washing them first. And his custom of popping a scorpion in his mouth and swallowing it down without chewing, not even thinking under what kind of a stone that scorpion might have been. And then patting his stomach afterwards.

Naturally, it gave a Bushman wrong ideas about things, Jurie Steyn said, when a well-dressed white man, instead of asking him wasn't he ashamed of himself for being so low, said that he had come to the Bushman to learn, and started making gramophone records of the things the Bushman had to say. Or a film.

"I even heard one of those records," Jurie Steyn added, "and you know what, I could hardly understand what the Bushman was saying, with all the extra clicks he put in, him thinking he's so smart, talking into a gramophone. But what I say is, if a scientist wants to study something, why can't he go and learn something high up? Like high dictation – or – or –"

"Or ethnology?" the schoolmaster suggested. "Or anthropology?"

"Yes, something high up like that," Jurie Steyn agreed. "What's he want to fool around with studying Bushmen? The scientist can take it from me that no good can come of that. Next thing, he'll also be patting his stomach after eating something that he didn't take the insides out of first."

Another thing, At Naudé said, that was causing a quite unnecessary amount of disorder in these parts, was that story that the scientists had been spreading of late about the Bushmen being a dying race. Every year their numbers were decreasing, the scientists said. Soon the Bushmen would be no more.

Gysbert van Tonder said he was glad At Naudé had mentioned that, because he was coming to it.

"As though the Bushmen haven't always been cheeky enough," Gysbert van Tonder said. "And now here's this new piece of nonsense, about the Bushman disappearing. Well, we all know, of course, that when it's with something slung over his shoulder that doesn't belong to him, then there's nobody can disappear as quick as a Bushman. I mean, when you look again, he's just vanished. And, of course, that's what happens every time with the scientist. The scientist is sitting out in the desert on a camp-stool with the recording instrument on one side of him and a bottle on the other, and the Bushman is talking.

"And when the scientist hears the machine going click-click-click quicker than what the Bushman is making clicks, he knows it's time to change the record. And, naturally, when the scientist turns round again, the Bushman isn't there anymore. And because he's absent-minded, being a scientist, he doesn't see that the bottle isn't there any-more, either. And because he doesn't notice the Bushman around, he thinks, ah, well, the Bushman must be dead. It's only a scientist that would get hold of a muddle-headed notion like that, of course. Or what do you think?"

We did not demur.

"And the advantage," Gysbert van Tonder proceeded, "that the Bushman is taking of this tomfool story that he is dying out, is just too awful. He thinks he's something precious, because he's dying. Like I said to a Bushman in the Kalahari a little while ago, no, he couldn't have any more chewing tobacco. He'd had enough for one morning, I said ... So what does this Bushman answer? 'You'll be sorry for this one day, baas,' he says. 'One day when I am not here anymore. When all that will be left of me will be a gramophone record.'"

When he did feel sick, though – really sick – Gysbert van Tonder said, was when the Bushman said it would be a happy release for him.

"I got him in the end, though," Gysbert van Tonder remarked, look-ing pleased with himself. "He was loafing on the job. So I told him to shake himself. 'Hurry up,' I said to him, 'you know you haven't got too much time.'"

We said to Gysbert van Tonder that it was easy to see that that one couldn't have been a very raw Bushman. The only part of him that might have been raw, we said, would be the inside of his hands – raw from trying to make a fire by rubbing two sticks together in front of a movie camera.

There was another side to being a film actor that was different from just getting your name in front of a bioscope in electric lights, we said. And the Bushman was beginning to find that out for himself. For one thing, he also had to start thinking out silly answers to the questions the scientist asked him. Because, unless he gave a silly answer, the scientist would think he wasn't a proper Bushman, and that would be the end of the Bushman's film and gramophone career.

"It makes you sick," Gysbert van Tonder – who was apparently not feeling quite himself that afternoon – said for the second time. "Like one Bushman that a scientist asked 'What happens when you throw a stone into the water at Lake Ngami?' . . . and the Bushman said, 'It makes brass bangles come on the water, baas.' Now, that Bushman just about choked, trying not to laugh. He knew as good as you or me that if you chuck a stone into a dam it gives off yellow ripples, with the sun shining on them.

"But the Bushman knew that, to have a film made of him as the last survivor of a primitive race, his answer had to be as absurd as possible. And you've got no idea what a fuss the scientist made of that Bushman, who was trying not to choke. The scientist said to the camera-man that they must have a close-up of the Bushman right away."

He felt like choking himself, too, Gysbert van Tonder said. With indignation.

"It made my stomach turn," he pursued in the vein of earlier on. "And so I said to them, well, if that Bushman is now becoming a film star, the next thing he'll want is to be allowed to wear a collar and tie, and to vote. And then the scientist said that he was sorry he was a bit short of film, because he would like a close-up of me, also."

But just to think, Gysbert van Tonder observed finally, that the Bushman had today already grown so ignorant that he couldn't make a fire anymore by rubbing two sticks together, but had to use matches. It might even be true, Gysbert van Tonder suggested, what the scientists said about the Bushman – that he was a member of a dying race.

But young Vermaak, the schoolmaster, advised us not to be too hasty in our conclusions. All the scientist was doing, he said, was to try and trace back the story of man to its beginnings. How man rose from savagery. How he advanced by virtue. How he started enquiring after truth. How he attempted decoration early on in his upward march. How he followed his destiny, with science and knowledge as his guides.

Maybe the Bushman was the wrong person for the scientist to come and ask these questions of, the schoolmaster said, but it was a fact that, belonging to a very primitive division of African humanity, the Bushman was a true prehistoric type. And maybe the first cave-man would also have liked to play-act before a movie camera, pretending he didn't know more than a stone axe.

"And what we've been saying about the Bushman's ignorance," the schoolmaster added, half laughing, "well, we know he's a member of a dying race. Face to face with the King of Terrors. You know what I mean – The Great Adventure, and all that. Anyway, it's queer to think that – with all his ignorance – the *Bushman will shortly know more than any of us.*"

In the Old Days

"Ah, yes, where are those days?" At Naudé said, sighful for the sweetness of long-vanished youth. It was a rhetorical question. He expected no answer.

"How do you mean, where those days are?" Jurie Steyn demanded, a shade aggressively and in a spirit of fact-finding realism. "What days do you mean, anyway? It's about the silliest thing I've ever heard anybody ask – asking what's happened to days.

"If you ask where's my roll of barbed wire that I ordered from Bekkersdal and that the lorry-driver says must have been offloaded by mistake at Welgevonden, and that Koos Nienaber at Welgevonden tells me he knows nothing about – well, that would be a sensible question to ask. Especially as Koos Nienaber was planting poles for a new cattle fence when he assured me that he hadn't even seen my roll of barbed wire. And he got quite nasty about it, too, afterwards, swearing and all. And saying it wasn't neighbourly for me to come and stand there in an unbelieving sort of way.

"Spoiling a friendship of long standing, Koos Nienaber said, just for the sake of a rusty old roll of barbed wire. And with so many kinks in it that it would snap the moment you put the pliers to it, Koos Nienaber said.

"Well, that would be sensible, now – to ask where's my barbed wire. Or to ask where is . . . well, something that you can say, oh, it's lost, or oh, it strayed down the Government Road and you've got a pretty good idea in whose kraal you'll find it, with a changed brand mark on it. But to ask where are some days: maybe they are in a crate hung under somebody else's wagon on the way to market."

Jurie Steyn guffawed. That was a good one he had just said, he felt.

"A couple of Large White days," Jurie Steyn went on, expanding

439

the metaphor, "or Berkshires, and they getting dizzy in the crate from watching the spokes of the wheels turning."

It seemed that Jurie Steyn was a bit dizzy in his mind himself, At Naudé responded, for him to talk like that. But he would pass it over, At Naudé said. He could only see now how deeply the loss of his roll of barbed wire had affected Jurie Steyn, At Naudé said.

"All I meant," At Naudé proceeded, "was about how the past is gone. The good old times, and all that. When I was young the world didn't only look different, but it also smelt different. People were nobler when I was young, and more human. The women were more beautiful than what you get them today. The men were braver; stronger and thicker. The lies they told were bigger.

"I had an uncle that was called Jors Groot-Lieg, just because of all the bare-faced untruths that he could tell. And he was proud of his nick-name. And he did his best to live up to his reputation for being the most awful liar in the district. But where would my uncle, Jors Groot-Lieg, be today? His family would be ashamed of his weakness. And they would as likely as not get the elder, when he came round, to pray for him. And my uncle would be all abashed and humble. And he would say, yes, he did perhaps exaggerate a little about the length of the python that had swallowed him when he was camping by the Molopo. The length *and* the width, he would say.

"And, with the elder looking on pleased, my uncle would also admit that the python didn't swallow the whole of him down, with just his veldskoens sticking out, like he said the first time. He remembered now that he hadn't been pulled down into the snake's inside to much below his knees, he would admit, because he could recall how he lay back and crossed his legs, the time the snake rested a little from swallowing.

"And so it is with everything, today. The world was bigger long ago; and wider and fatter; more blown out in the face, too. Look at the ambitions we used to have when we were young. Like being an engine-driver. Not only because of the speed of the engine and the hot coals and the roar, and the fire it shoots out going uphill in the night. But you also used to think that if you were an engine-driver you would be able to drive very fast round the Hex River bends and give all the grown-ups in the train a fright."

At Naudé paused to heave another sigh, filled with the wistful melancholy that clothes the past in Tyrian-dyed habiliments.

"And only the other day I asked a little boy what he was going to be when he grew up," At Naudé added. "And he said 'Prime Minister.'"

He felt sorry, then, that he had asked, At Naudé said. For when that little boy spoke there was something about him that made At Naudé feel that he would make it. Something distasteful, At Naudé seemed to imply.

"Well, it's funny, but when I was young," Chris Welman remarked, "it was my ambition to be the best mouth-organ player in the whole of the Marico. And I can still remember how excited I was the birthday when I got my first proper German mouth-organ that had a picture on the cardboard box of a man on the stage with a very curled moustache – curled up like that so it wouldn't get entangled with some of the top notes of the mouth-organ he was blowing into, I suppose. And the theatre in the picture on the box of the mouth-organ was crowded – women with jewels and men in uniforms. And one man in a uniform had a moustache that was almost as curled as the mouth-organ player's.

"And I found out afterwards that he was the German Kaiser, sitting there in the audience and his hand raised to keep time with the mouth-organ music. And that German mouth-organ was just as grand as the cardboard box it came in. And I was very pleased to have it, of course. You've got no idea how pleased. But play – no, that I couldn't do, naturally. Not *play* it, actually. I was too afraid that I might blow a wrong note on it, and what would the ladies with their jewels and the German Kaiser with his curled moustache think?

"So I just went on playing on the cheap tin mouth-organ that I had bought at the Indian store at Ramoutsa and that I had had a long time. I felt that I wasn't good enough to play on that grand German mouth-organ – not with all those stylish foreign people sitting straight up in their velvet chairs to listen. I mean, I was proud to have that German mouth-organ. But somehow, after that, I didn't believe, altogether, quite, that I would one day be the best mouth-organ player in the Groot Marico.

"And after a while I gave up trying to play any kind of mouth-organ at all. I felt there wasn't a musical career in it for me anymore. And I didn't want to be a mouth-organ player that was good enough for just playing a mouth-organ around the farm."

It was Chris Welman's turn to sigh, then, recalling his Chopin youth dreams, tricked out in romantic finery, swallowtail-coated.

"But all the same," Chris Welman proceeded, "I still think I could give it a go. Yes, even today, if I had the time for it, to practise. More than once, lately, when I was in Bekkersdal, I was on the point of walking into Policansky's and asking Solly to sell me the best German mouth-organ he'd got – telling him to take it out of the cardboard box first, and that he could *keep* the cardboard box. When it's after sunset, and the evening wind is just beginning to stir from across the vlei, and I think of other people that have got reputations for being supposed to be able to play the mouth-organ – well, you've got no idea what I feel, then . . . what I can do, yet . . . For one thing, I've got more time to practise, than I had years ago. And I've today also got more sense. Today if people say anything against my playing, well, I know how much of it is jealousy."

Chris Welman clenched his teeth. An ugly expression came over his face. He glanced from one to the other of us, looking truculent. In the role of a thwarted artist he did not appear at his best.

The first to break the somewhat uncomfortable silence that followed was At Naudé. What Chris Welman had just said, At Naudé explained – although to most of us it was not quite clear what the analogy was, if any – fitted in very exactly with his own earlier observations, about how much more worthwhile the world was when we were young. He acknowledged that he could not absolutely compare notes with Chris Welman when it came to mouth-organs, At Naudé said, since his own adolescent predilections had been for girls that had pink flowers embroidered on their blouses and for mule-carts with high-up wheels.

"But life was bigger," At Naudé said, "in the old days. It was a higher and deeper thing then, life was. Wider, too, if you know what I mean. And puffier under the eyes, also. Life in the olden times had everything."

At Naudé was just getting ready to sigh again, seeking, once more, through a breath coming up out of his lungs with shuffling step, to convey to us his feelings about the strange splendours in which the long-lost past was clad. But Jurie Steyn interrupted At Naudé before he could get the whole of that sigh out of him.

"What you said about ambition," Jurie Steyn said, in tones of a businesslike practicality. "Well, take me, now."

Jurie Steyn's voice held, suspended in its vibrations, a self-satisfaction that you couldn't miss. He looked about him – slowly and confidently. It was quite different from the way Chris Welman had looked round him.

"Not that I might not perhaps when I was young have had bigger ideas for myself than what I have actually reached to," Jurie Steyn admitted modestly. "But take just how far I've got – that I'm today postmaster, for one thing. Of course, we all know that it isn't that I started at the bottom and worked my way up. And it isn't that I've got up any higher since then, either. I mean, we all know that when the department wanted a post office for this part, all they were looking for was a voorkamer, with a roof and a farmer that could come in from his lands every now and again to look after what was going on in his voorkamer.

"I mean, they wanted an ambitious kind of farmer, of course, and not one that was so indifferent to his family's welfare that he would just stay the whole day out in the fields, working, no matter how hot, and never coming in, even for coffee.

"But to be postmaster today for this part of the Marico – well, it's something."

Jurie Steyn recognised, of course, that where he was handicapped was in not having started in the post office service right at the bottom, delivering letters door to door, for instance. That was how you reached the highest rung of the ladder, Jurie Steyn believed, this being a democratic country.

Every postman carried in his mailbag, along with letters and wrapped newspapers, a Postmaster-General's cigar – according to Jurie Steyn's reasoning. And because he himself had joined the post office service somewhere in the middle, bypassing the avenues of orthodox noviceship, it was not for his hand to grasp the more ultimate prize; not his head – a bit flat at the back – would be crowned with the chaplet that was at once simple and scentless to signify that there was nothing higher to come after that.

But as long as he got his pay regularly every month, Jurie Steyn didn't care much about the lustre of position, about ribbon or palm. He knew he hadn't started in the post office the right way.

"Seeing that I didn't begin at the bottom," Jurie Steyn said eventually, "I feel I didn't do too bad. My people were just farmers, I mean."

Jurie Steyn stopped talking. Nobody answered. He looked around him, but less confidently, this time. Indeed, in his eyes there was something of the look almost that Chris Welman had had, when he told us how good he was with a mouth-organ, and nobody properly able to appreciate the way he played.

"Just plain farming folk, that's all," Jurie Steyn repeated.

Gysbert van Tonder took him up on that.

"All right, Jurie," Gysbert van Tonder said. "We heard you the first time. But what do you want to give yourself airs about it for? Have you ever come across any kind of farming that isn't plain farming – or any farmer that isn't just a plain farmer? I've still got to hear of a farmer doing some high-toned pumpkin-weeding, say. Or a dainty bit of pouring of hog-swill into the troughs. Or getting a few refined blisters on his feet through walking behind the plough with a lot of good taste. 'Just plain farming folk . . .'"

Gysbert van Tonder paused, speechless.

It seemed that At Naudé's mind was still on the past, and that for him the past was bedizened with frills. Decked out in rich stuffs. Not wearing just ordinary khaki working-pants with a rent in the seat from where the past climbed through a barbed-wire fence. The past was dight in satins and wore wristbands.

"In the old days," At Naudé announced, "it was different. Life, in the old days –"

"Yes, I know," Gysbert van Tonder interjected. "I know all about the old days. The old days had grey mildew and slimy rot on them. People didn't know about dusting with lime sulphur."

Gysbert van Tonder guffawed. It was a laugh that, in a salon, would have caused eyebrows to lift.

Neighbourly

A fence between the Union and the Bechuanaland Protectorate, At Naudé said. According to the radio, the two Governments were already discussing it.

"I hope they put gates in the fence, though, here and there," Chris Welman said. "Otherwise how can we get to Ramoutsa siding?"

Yes, with a fence there, At Naudé agreed, goods we had ordered from Johannesburg could lie for years at the siding, and we none the wiser. "And likely as not we wouldn't even notice the difference," At Naudé added. "We'd think it was just the railways again a bit slow."

There was one queer thing about putting up a fence, Oupa Bekker said, that he himself had noticed long ago. And it was this. When you erected a fence around your farm, it never seemed to keep anybody out. All you were doing was to fence yourself in, and with barbed wire.

In the meantime Gysbert van Tonder, with his somewhat extensive cattle-smuggling interests, had been doing a spot of thinking. When he spoke it was apparent that he had been indulging in no glad, carefree reveries. His reasoning had followed a severely practical line – as straight as the five-strand course, theodolite-charted, of the fence that would provide the Union and the Bechuanaland Protectorate with official frontiers.

"There should be a proper sort of a border; that I do believe in," Gysbert van Tonder announced, piously. "It makes it a lot too hard, smuggling cattle from the Protectorate into the Transvaal, when there's no real line to smuggle them over. I'm glad the Government's doing something about it. These things have got to be correct. I've got discouraged more than once, I can tell you, asking myself, well, what's the good. You see what I mean?

"Either you're in the Marico, or you aren't. And either you're in the Protectorate or you aren't. When there's no proper border you can be standing with a herd of cattle right on the Johannesburg market and not be feeling too sure are you in the Transvaal or in Bechuanaland. Even when the auctioneer starts calling for bids, you don't quite know is the answer going to come in pound notes or in rolls of brass wire.

"You almost expect somebody to shout out, 'So many strings of beads.' So I can only say that the sooner they put up a decent kind of fence the better. The way things are, it's been going on too long. You've got to know if an ox is properly smuggled over or if it isn't. You've got to be legal."

The years he had put in at cattle-smuggling had imparted to Gysbert van Tonder's mind an unmistakably juridical slant. He liked arranging things by rule and canon, by precept and code. The next question he asked bore that out.

"In this discussion that our Government is having with the Protectorate Government," he asked, "did the broadcast say rightly what kind of fence it is that they are going to put up? Is it the steel posts with anchoring wires kind that you cut? Or will it have standards that you pull out and bend the fence down by the droppers for the cattle to walk over on bucksails? That's a thing they should get straight before anything else, I'm thinking."

The conversation at that point took, naturally enough, a technical turn. The talk had to do with strands and surveyors, and wrongly positioned beacons and surveyors and rails, and the wire snapping and cutting Koos Nienaber's chin open in rebounding, and gauges and five-barb wires, and the language Koos Nienaber used afterwards, speaking with difficulty because of all that sticking plaster on his chin.

"And so the surveyor said to me," Chris Welman was declaring about half an hour later, "that if I didn't believe him about that spruit not coming on my side of the farm, then I could check through his figures myself. There were only eight pages of figures, he said, and those very small figures on some of the pages that didn't look too clear he would go over in ink for me, he said.

"And he would also lend me a book that was just all figures that would explain to me what the figures he had written down meant. And when I said that since my grandfather's time that spruit had been used on our farm and that we used to get water there, the surveyor just smiled like he was superior to my grandfather. And he said he couldn't understand it. On the other side of the bult, in a straight line, that spruit was a long way outside of our farm.

"What that other surveyor, many years ago, was up to, he just couldn't make out, he said. With all his books of figures, he said, he just couldn't figure that one. Well, I naturally couldn't go and tell him, of course. Although it's something that we all know in the family.

"Because my grandfather had the same kind of trouble, in his time, with a surveyor more years ago than I can remember. And when my grandfather said to the surveyor, 'How do you know that the line you marked out on the other side of the bult is in a straight line from here? Can you *see* through a bult – a bult about fifty paces high and half a mile over it?' Then the surveyor had to admit, of course, that no man could see through a bult. And the land-surveyor felt very ashamed of himself, then, for being so ignorant. And he changed the plan just like my grandfather asked him to do.

"And the funny part of it is that my grandfather had no knowledge of figures. Indeed, I don't think my grandfather could even read figures. All my grandfather had, while he was talking to the land-surveyor, was a shotgun, one barrel smooth and the other choke. And the barrels were sawn off quite short. And they say that when he went away from our farm – my grandfather having proved to him just where he went wrong in his figures – he was the politest surveyor that had ever come to this part of the Dwarsberge."

There would, he said, then, unquestionably be a good deal of that same sort of element in the erection of the boundary-wire between the Bechuanaland Protectorate and the Transvaal. More than one land-surveyor would as likely as not raise his eyebrows, we said.

Or he would take a silk handkerchief out of his pocket and start dusting his theodolite, saying to himself that he shouldn't in the first place have entrusted so delicate an instrument to a raw Mchopi porter smelling of kaffir beer.

In the delimiting of the Transvaal–Bechuanaland Protectorate border we could see quite a lot of trouble sticking out for a number of people.

"I also hope," Jurie Steyn said, winking, "that when the Government sends up the poles and barbed wire for the fence to the Ramoutsa siding, there isn't going to be the usual kind of misunderstanding that happens in these parts as to whom the fencing materials are *for*. I mean, you'll have farmers suddenly very busy putting up new cattle camps, and the fence construction workers will be sitting in little groups in the veld playing draughts, seeing they've got no barbed wire and standards."

Anyway, so there was a fence going to come there, now, along the edge of the Marico, through the bush. Barbed wire. A metal thread strung along the border. Sprouting at intervals, as befitted a Bushveld tendril, thorns.

"A fence, now," Chris Welman said. "Whenever I think of a fence I also call to mind a kindly neighbour standing on the other side of it, shaking his head and smiling in a brotherly-love sort of way at what he sees going on on my side of the fence. And all the time I am just about boiling at the advice he's giving me on how to do it better.

"Like when I was building my new house, once, that was to provide shelter for my wife and children. And a neighbour came and stood on the other side of the fence, shaking his head at the sun-dried bricks in a kind-hearted manner. Turf-clay was no good for sun-dried bricks, he told me, seeing that the walls of that kind of stable would collapse with the first rains. And I didn't have the strength of mind to tell him the truth. I mean, I was too ashamed to let him know that I had really meant those bricks for my house.

"So I just built another stable, instead, which I didn't need. And it was only a long time afterwards – through a good piece of the mud that he had smeared it up with in front crumbling away – that I found out that my neighbour's own house, which he always talked in such fashionable language about, was built of nothing more than turf-clay bricks, sun-dried."

Yes, Jurie Steyn said, or when you were putting up a prieel for a grape-vine to trail over.

"And then that neighbour comes along and says, what, a shaky prieel like that – it'll never hold up a grapevine," Jurie Steyn continued. "And then you say, well, it's not *meant* for grapes, see? You're not that kind of a fool, you say. You're only making a trellis for the wife. She wants to grow a creeper with that feathery kind of leaves on it, you say.

"And then your neighbour says, well, he hopes it isn't very heavy feathers, because it won't take much weight on it to bring that whole thing down. By that time you feel about like a brown weevil crawling over one of the side-shoots of the grapevine you intended to plant there. And it's a funny thing, but you never really take to the blue flowers of the creepers that you put in there, instead."

It was significant, we said, how you would on occasion come across a stable that looked far too good for just an ordinary Bushveld farm, with squares and triangles in plaster cut out above the door of the stable. And with a stoep that, if you didn't know it was a stable, why, you could almost picture people sitting drinking coffee on it. And spidery threads of creepers twining delicately if somewhat incongruously about solid scaffoldings with tarred uprights. Looking as though why the farmer made the pergola so sturdy was that the pale gossamer blooms shouldn't just float away.

And it would all be because of the advice of a neighbour who had at one time stood on the other side of the fence, kind-hearted, but with his eyes narrowed. Almost as though he couldn't believe what he was seeing there. And his one hand would be resting easily on the wire, as if at any instant he could jump clean over and come and take what you're busy with right away from you, and show you how it should be done. His other hand would be up to his forehead so that he could see better. And he would be shaking his head in a kindly fashion in between making recommendations.

That was what a fence represented to us, we said. Young Vermaak, the schoolmaster, made a remark, then. It was the first chance that he had had, so far, to talk.

As far as he could see, the schoolmaster said, the effect it was going to have – erecting a fence between the Union and the Bechuanaland Protectorate – was that it was going to make the Union and the Protectorate really *neighbourly.*

Marico Man

We were talking about the fossil remains discovered in a gulley of the Molopo by Dr Von Below, the noted palaeontologist. Dr Von Below claimed that what he had found were the remains of the First Man. And it was going to do us on this side of the Dwarsberge a lot of good, we said, especially as Dr Von Below had paid us the compliment of giving his discovery the name of the Marico Man.

The distinguished professor had already given a talk over the wireless about the Marico Man that At Naudé had listened in to. And the schoolmaster, young Vermaak, had read an article on the Marico Man in a scientific magazine to which he subscribed.

"The professor made his find using just the simplest tools you can think of," At Naudé informed us. "Just a simple digging-stick and a plain hand-axe."

"Sounds like the professor is a bit of a Stone Age relic himself," the schoolmaster observed, "using that kind of tools." Nobody laughed.

The important thing, the schoolmaster added, when his joke hadn't gone over, was that as a result of this discovery the Marico Man would now take his place alongside of the Piltdown Man and the Neanderthal Man all over the world in scientific circles where the question as to who was the First Man on earth was being discussed. It was something of which we could be justly proud, young Vermaak said. It was an inspiring thought that the Groot Marico was the ancestral home of the human race.

"That here in the Dwarsberge the First Man, millions of years ago, lower than any savage, started painfully on his upward progress," the schoolmaster said.

But Jurie Steyn said that, speaking for himself, he wasn't too keen on that 'lower than any savage' part. Especially as the professor had decided to call his discovery the Marico Man, Jurie Steyn said, with a quick wink at Chris Welman that the schoolmaster did not intercept.

"Yes, that's true," Chris Welman said, coughing and also shutting and opening his left eye too quick for the schoolmaster to see. "I must say I don't fancy it, either – calling an ignorant creature like that the Marico Man. It's that sort of thing that gives us Marico farmers a bad name."

And we didn't want any worse name than what we already had, Chris Welman reckoned.

"And look now what it says about the professor finding the Marico Man's remains in a ditch," Jurie Steyn continued, almost spluttering at the thought of the way that he and Chris Welman were pulling young Vermaak's leg. "Right away people will start getting to think we're so low here that when a person dies his relatives don't give him a proper Christian burial but they just go and throw him away in the first ditch they see. Next thing they'll say is that the Marico Man was found buried with a clay-pot next to him. And beads."

By this time Gysbert van Tonder had also tumbled to what was going on. If it was a bit of fun at the schoolmaster's expense, he didn't mind joining in himself.

Frowning on the suggestion of Bushman obsequies in relation to the Marico Man, Gysbert van Tonder declared that he would rather just lie in the veld and get eaten up by wild animals than be buried with the Bushman religion.

"For one thing, what won't my children think of me, I mean, when we meet in the next world and it comes out that I was buried according to the Bushman religion? Or take the Pastor of the Apostolic Church, now, that I told to his face how unchristian his Nagmaal service was that I looked in through the window of his church and saw.

"I can just imagine how tight the Pastor will draw his mouth when he comes across me in the hereafter, me having been buried under a half-moon and with an ostrich egg painted blue. I'd feel that I was walking with nothing more than a stert-riem on, in the hereafter."

Not able to keep his face as straight as the Apostolic Church pastor's, Gysbert van Tonder burst out laughing. And so he pretended that he was just laughing at the incongruity of the thought of himself wearing a Bushman's wildcat-skin loincloth. "Isn't that a scream," he asked, "the thought of me wearing a stert-riem in the hiernamaals?" When nobody answered, Gysbert van Tonder's face fell.

It seemed a bad afternoon for jokes. The only people who appeared to be enjoying themselves were Jurie Steyn and Chris Welman.

They kept it up quite a while, saying silly things about how much discredit the Marico Man was going to bring on the inhabitants of the Dwarsberge area, and doing their best to sound earnest.

"People all over the world will think we don't even know enough to have an ouderling saying words at the graveside," Jurie Steyn was announcing.

"But what's all this talk of funerals and the rest?" the schoolmaster interrupted, looking perplexed. "It's not as though the Marico Man died just the other day, after a long and painful illness that he bore with a patience that was an example to the whole of the Dwarsberge. He's got nothing to do with anybody living here now. So I can't understand your talking about him almost as though you're feeling sentimental about him. After all, it's millions of years ago since the Marico Man was on the earth."

It was when Jurie Steyn, choking over his words, started to say that that was what made it all the more sad, that young Vermaak realised what Jurie Steyn and Chris Welman had been up to.

The schoolmaster thought deeply for a few minutes.

"Anyway, it's like this," he said, eventually. "We know that it can do us a lot of good, in these parts, to have the Marico Man. He's going to make our district world-famous. In radio talks and newspapers, in lectures and theses and textbooks, wherever the Neanderthal Man and the Piltdown Man get mentioned, the Marico Man will have to be spoken of, also. Now, that's something, isn't it? Quite a bit of an achievement for a South African, don't you think?"

Young Vermaak recognised, however, that a certain element of jealousy crept into these things. Even the world of science was not altogether immune from that regrettable spirit of partisanship which, in the education department, for instance, could lead to a man who had only a Third Class Teacher's Certificate getting appointed to an A-post over the head of somebody who had excellent academic qualifications, failing only in blackboard-work.

"And I still say," young Vermaak declared – speaking, as it were, in parenthesis – "that, give me a piece of chalk that *writes* and a blackboard easel that doesn't fall over backwards the moment you touch it – the department examiner hopping about directly afterwards, holding his one foot – then I still say I'm as good at blackboard-work as the next man."

We felt that it would have been in better taste, on young Vermaak's part, if he had abstained from drawing aside the veil that had, until then, screened from public gaze the circumstances attendant on his having got low marks in one of the subjects he took for his teacher's diploma.

"I am only trying to explain," he continued – closing, in a somewhat self-conscious fashion, the parenthesis – "that in the scientific world there will as likely as not be prejudice against the Marico Man. And just because he's so good, that is. They'll have spite against him just because he's so *good*. And so they won't sometimes mention his name when they ought to – like when they're mentioning the Neanderthal Man's name, say, or the Piltdown Man's name.

"He's great, I'm telling you – the Marico Man is. As a claimant for being the First Man, why, the Marico Man has got the Piltdown Man licked hollow. And as for the Neanderthal Man – I really believe that next to the Marico Man the Neanderthal Man hasn't got a leg to stand on, leave alone two legs *and* two hands to stand on, which I believe is how the Marico Man actually stood, if the truth were only known. That is how good I think the Marico Man is.

"And so you can quite understand that there would be scientists that would be jealous of the Marico Man, and they would talk slightingly of him. And as likely as not they wouldn't mention him, if they got the chance not to. Just because the Neanderthal Man is a pet of theirs. They don't like an outsider coming along competing against local talent.

"They don't like to have to accept it that their Neanderthal Man went up like a rocket but came down like a stick, the moment the Marico Man arrived on the scene – arriving on the scene walking on all fours, even, and with his mouth hanging sort of half-open in surprise. They don't want to have to hand it to the Marico Man, that's all. Just because of that awful kind of jealousy.

"There are going to be scientists that will hesitate to let on, in fashionable places, that they have even heard of the Marico Man. And all just because they think he's a bit too crude. Everybody naturally expects the First Man to have been somewhat rough. A trifle unpolished in his everyday manners, sort of. But when he's just out-and-out offensive, like it looks as though the Marico Man must have been – and he not even worrying about it, much – well, you can understand that quite a lot of scientists are going to be pretty haughty in their treatment of the Marico Man. Especially when they've got the future of their pet, the Neanderthal Man, to think of. Or their other pet, the Piltdown Man. *His* career. Next thing they know, the Piltdown Man will be out of a job. He'll be on the sidewalk, cadging sixpences for drink."

Needless to say, the way the schoolmaster put it then made it all look different. If there was going to be prejudice against the Marico Man, merely because he came from this side of the Dwarsberge, well, we wouldn't stand for it, that was all.

"I'd like to know what right they've got to despise the Marico Man," Jurie Steyn said, "just as long as he did the best he could, while he was alive. That's what I say. Just so's they can crack up one of those – what are they, again?"

"The Neanderthal Man?" the schoolmaster asked. "The Piltdown Man?"

"Yes," Jurie Steyn said, "those. A couple of foreigners – immigrants – that a Marico-born man has got to stand cheek from, when he's just as good."

The point, the schoolmaster said, about the Marico Man, was not only that he did his best, but that he achieved far more than any of his closest rivals in the competition for being acclaimed the First Man. From the shape of his skull, you could see that the Marico Man had all the opposition beaten to a frazzle in respect of weakness of brainpan.

The Marico Man was so much slower-witted than the Piltdown Man that it was pitiful. Pitiful for the Piltdown Man's chances of getting recognised as having been the First Man, that was. Nobody, no matter how primitive, had any chance of being accorded senior classification as a human being, when all the time there was the Marico Man lurking in the background. *Skulking* in the background would probably be a more accurate way of expressing it.

It was a solemn thought, the schoolmaster said, to contemplate the Marico Man as we knew him – the Marico Man supporting himself in an upright position with the help of his knuckles, his eyebrows lifted high and his jaw protruding several inches more than the Neanderthal Man's jaw. The Marico Man in that particular posture, looking at a planet. It made you think, the schoolmaster said.

Gysbert van Tonder was the first to tumble to it that in all this long thing he was saying the schoolmaster was just being sarcastic – on account of his leg having been pulled earlier on.

454

"But I still say," Gysbert van Tonder declared, doggedly. "With all this nonsense that has been talked, I still say that if that Dr Von Below knows what is good for him, he'll keep away from this part of the Dwarsberge. We won't think twice of running him out of the place. Running him *and* his precious Marico Man out of the place. And seeing which of them goes quicker. What I can't get over is the cheek of this scientist – digging up a handful of bones and calling it the Marico Man. And talking about him walking almost four-footed; and having a weak brainpan; and a jaw like a gorilla; and –"

"It's a closely reasoned treatise," the schoolmaster said. "I've read it."

"About the only insulting thing," Gysbert van Tonder observed, "that this scientist doesn't say about the Marico Man is that the Marico Man is also cross-eyed and left-handed."

This was one of those days when Oupa Bekker was somewhat more deaf than usual. He had heard and followed only part of our conversation.

"The first man in the Marico?" Oupa Bekker asked. "You mean, the first Marico white man? Well, that's Louw Combrink . . . Louw Toutjies, we used to call him in the old days. He used to walk sort of bent forward . . . Hey? What's that? . . . No, not his beard. It's the way his jaw stuck out . . . Louw Toutjies? . . . Of course, he's still alive. He's living in the mountains just other side Derdepoort . . . Scientist? Well, I'd like to see what Louw Toutjies does to a scientist that's been telling people he's dead. I'd like to *see* it, that's all."

Homecoming

We wouldn't have felt quite that way about it, of course, if it wasn't that we had seen Diederick Kleynhans growing up in front of us, as it were. And we knew, naturally enough, what it was that had spoilt him.

It was clear that Diederick Kleynhans had been undone by his own youthful vanity and by the way he had been praised for his drawings and compositions by the schoolmaster who had been schoolmaster at Drogevlei long before young Vermaak came. Anyway, that schoolmaster had left Drogevlei years ago. He was no doubt still teaching school telling some Standard Five pupil – who otherwise had no real evil in him – how well he could recite.

One could readily picture that same schoolmaster in paradise, casually sauntering up to the nearest angel standing in a row and complimenting him on his outstanding talents as a harpist. And the angel – not knowing that it was the schoolmaster himself who was just harping on his one string – would start getting ideas in his head. There was really no end to the amount of trouble in paradise that that sort of thing could cause.

And now, that schoolmaster having long since left the Marico, here was Diederick Kleynhans sitting in Jurie Steyn's post office, back from a lengthy sojourn in the city of Johannesburg, whither he had gone to engage in those studies that would enable him to make his way in the world as a commercial artist. From his talk we could understand that Diederick Kleynhans had come back embittered. From other things we saw that he had come back a failure.

Diederick Kleynhans was not a bad-looking young man. There was an honesty about his eyes that were set far apart – as was characteristic in the Kleynhans family. From his hands, too, you could sense that he had a natural candour – not only from the shape of his hands, but also the size. To have hands like the thick end of a leg of mutton was an-

other Kleynhans family trait, developed through generations of standing bent forward in Cape vineyards with a spade.

"I am an artist," Diederick Kleynhans was saying in the voorkamer.
"And so my spirit revolted at the Philistine subjects they taught me at
the commercial art school."

He spoke in a tired voice.

His soul rebelled at design, he went on. And at anatomy. Spending months and months at drawing from dead clay models and for
no reason but just so as to learn to draw it *right*. That made him want
to laugh, of course – not him, but his psyche. And portraiture, now.
Going on and on painting a face just so as to get it to look like the person you're painting. Well, his genius couldn't stand for that, naturally.
And wasting weeks and weeks learning how to mix paints – just so
the paint wouldn't all crack off the canvas again, once you'd put it on.
Well, his subliminal self could not but recoil from so low an idea of art.

While we could not understand very much about what Diederick
Kleynhans was saying, it nevertheless seemed pretty awful, the things
they had done to him at the art school. Once Chris Welman had opened
his mouth as though to ask a question. We could guess what that question was. Chris Welman would have liked Diederick Kleynhans to have
spoken in simpler language, using words we could all comprehend, in
his vituperative references to the goings-on in the place where he had
been studying. We had also heard a few things about the way artists
lived, and all that. Just because we were farmers in the Marico, it didn't
mean that a few hints and such like of what went on did not reach us
from time to time.

Why, each time a theatre company visited Bekkersdal, Dominee
Welthagen – without letting on that his sermon had any bearing on the
red and blue placards prominently displayed in the town – would talk
about wickedness and offending Adam and human frailty and lowest
dregs. But we knew he meant the theatre company, all right. And it
was sad, also, that more than one young person would, with a view
to changing his profession, go and interview the producer of the play
on the very Monday after the dominee had thundered against foibles
and shortcomings and cloven hoof and irreclaimable. Sometimes that
young person would not even wait until Monday. Sometimes that person would not be conspicuously young, either.

And we knew that an artist lived in a way that wasn't very different from how a play-actor lived. We also knew that why Chris Welman hadn't interrupted Diederick Kleynhans was because of how tired Diederick Kleynhans sounded.

It sounded as though what Diederick Kleynhans was saying consisted of nothing more than words, now. We had known our Volksraad member to talk just like that, in the past. And it was at such times that we had not fancied our Volksraad member's chance of getting re-elected, very much. The words the Volksraad member would use on such occasions would be good enough, no doubt.

Only, he wouldn't put the right sort of feeling into those words – as though he had said them too often, so that he had got a bit bored, saying them – just as though those words were making not only his audience, but also the Volksraad member himself, a bit drowsy.

"The same thing happened, afterwards, when I started working for a firm of advertisers," Diederick Kleynhans went on. "And they said I had to do a drawing of a nattily-dressed man smoking a cigar that they wanted to go into a newspaper. And then they said my drawing was no good. It wasn't the cigar they wanted to advertise, they said. It was the trousers. And, they said, what was the good of a drawing of a cigar that was so good, it looked almost as though it had been traced with tissue-paper from an overseas magazine, when the trousers seemed as though the man had slept in them in a tram shelter?"

Well, it was, of course, very hurtful to his artistic pneuma to be spoken to like that by those advertising people, and so he had to go to the library and trace a pair of smart trousers, also, out of an overseas magazine with tissue-paper. Endless trouble, they gave him.

That (even though it did not mean much to us) was still not the sort of thing we wanted to hear from Diederick Kleynhans about the life he had led, along with other artists, in Johannesburg. He had said nothing, as far as we could understand, about a den, so far. Nothing – as far as we could follow – about a couple of painted Jezebels. We started wondering if Diederick Kleynhans's real trouble wasn't, perhaps, that he hadn't got into the right sort of artistic circles. It looked like Dominee Welthagen was more enlightened that way. Gysbert van Tonder was the first to hint about it, quite openly.

"It looks to me, Diederick," Gysbert van Tonder said, "that you wasted your time not only in mixing paints, but in other ways, also. If you ask me, well, that's what I think."

Diederick Kleynhans looked somewhat surprised.

"Well, we also had to, at art school," he said, "study things like tempera and water-colour washes and –"

"That's what I mean," Gysbert van Tonder said, giving Diederick Kleynhans a man-to-man sort of look, "they never let you into the really plain part of it, did they? It was all just high-sounding things you learnt. I mean, after your studies were over for the afternoon, and you had wiped as much paint as you could get off yourself with paraffin and sand – I've also done a bit of painting around the farm; like a door or a roof, say – and after you'd put the lid back onto the tin of paint, did you then go and spend the night in some low place? In some disgraceful haunt, like what Dominee Welthagen says play-actors frequent?"

Oh, that? Diederick Kleynhans asked. Why, yes, indeed, he said, the place he went to each night, after his day's work was done, was pretty low. If any of us were to have seen it we would have been quite shocked, he felt. Like the way the ceiling was falling down in one corner, and the landlord not prepared to do anything about it. And the flies that would come in, through the municipal mule stables being just across the way.

And how he had to keep his window shut, also, he said, against the dagga-smoke that hung about the place like a mist on account of the proximity of the ricksha yard. Where he stayed was not only low, Diederick Kleynhans said, it was actually a blot on the city of Johannesburg. But that was all he could afford in the matter of rent.

"My finances were also low," he said. "At a low ebb, ha-ha."

Ha-ha, several of us said, too, then, our laughter sounding almost as tired as Diederick Kleynhans's own laughter.

But he was glad, Diederick Kleynhans proceeded, that Dominee Welthagen was exposing from the pulpit the impropriety of the way artists lived in a big city. He only hoped it would do some good. The kind of life artists led was a public scandal and of a sort that must bring a blush to the cheek of innocence.

"Oh, yes, and I almost forgot," Diederick Kleynhans added. "A lot of the floorboards were also loose."

Well, we knew, of course, that Dominee Welthagen hadn't meant about artists leading loose lives quite in that sense.

And from how he spoke was one way in which we realised that Diederick Kleynhans had come back home a failure. The other way we knew it was from how he looked and how he was dressed. For we had known many young men from this part of the Marico who had gone to the big city to seek their fortunes and, having achieved success, had returned to the Dwarsberge for a brief visit, just so as to have a bit of a look round before setting out again to make still more of a success of their lives in some great city, concrete-paved, where neon lights winked.

There was Prinsloo du Toit, for instance, with his hair slicked back with hair-cream and with the striped socks above his pointed patent-leather shoes held up by suspenders. You could actually *see* the suspenders each time Prinsloo du Toit changed his position in the riempies chair and pulled his neatly-creased trouser-legs up high.

Why, if Diederick Kleynhans wanted a model for a smart pair of trousers to draw from, there would have been Prinsloo du Toit's trousers right away. Diederick Kleynhans wouldn't have needed to go to the Public Library with a sheet of tissue-paper in his wallet and asking for an overseas magazine. And what was more, with all his success Prinsloo du Toit was amazingly modest about it all. If you asked him what he was actually *doing* in the great city, he would as likely as not just smile diffidently and puff a few more times at his cigar. It took quite a deal of straight-out questioning to get Prinsloo du Toit to confess that he had indeed in a few short years progressed as high as first-grade ganger on the railways.

Similarly, there was Frikkie Pienaar. Even if it wasn't for his talking noticeably louder than we had known him to talk in the old days, when he was still just a Marico farm-boy, there were other ways in which Frikkie Pienaar had success written all over him, on the occasion of his paying a flying visit to the Bushveld during his three weeks' leave from the Consolidated Goldfields mine where he was a rising young cocopan conductor. Just one way how you could see that Frikkie Pienaar had pulled it off was in his producing from his coat-sleeve, at intervals, a large white handkerchief with which he flicked at specks of cow-dung from the voorkamer floor that had landed on his pants.

And there were others like Prinsloo du Toit and Frikkie Pienaar. And so we knew the signs of success pretty well. And Diederick Kleynhans had none of those signs on him. For one thing, he wasn't slick and clean-shaven. Indeed, his beard was longer and more matted than almost any Bushveld farmer's you could think of. And his hair was wild: there was no hair-cream on it, smelling beautiful. And so far he was from flicking specks of cow-dung from his pants with a white handkerchief, why, he looked just about like he had no handkerchief at all – the way he would at times, while talking, pass, across the lower portion of his face, the sleeve of a corduroy jacket of a style and pattern that had long ago ceased being worn in even the more mountainous areas of the Dwarsberge.

Just from all that we could see that Diederick Kleynhans could not have made much of a success of his career as an artist. Another thing, also, was that he didn't talk loud. For we liked young men, when they came back to the Marico from the city, to talk loud. It showed they had got on.

We felt sorry for Diederick Kleynhans, of course. After all, he was no longer as young as he might be. And to think of all those years that he had wasted in the city. Good Lord, just look at Koos Pretorius. Koos Pretorius had been in the same class with Diederick Kleynhans, sitting at the same desk with him. And Koos Pretorius, just because he had had no nonsensical ideas about himself, was today a deacon. A thought like that must be pretty galling to Diederick Kleynhans, all right – the thought of what he had missed.

After a long silence, young Vermaak, the schoolmaster, spoke.

"Kleynhans . . . Diederick Kleyhans," the schoolmaster said. "It's not you that's been writing those poems in the *Tydskrif* is it? You're not *that* Diederick Kleynhans, are you?"

The note of admiration in young Vermaak's voice was unmistakable.

"Yes," Diederick Kleynhans said. "That's me, all right. You see, the schoolmaster that turned my head didn't say only that I was good at drawing. He also said I was good at writing composition. And I only hope you don't go and give any youngsters in your class silly ideas, also. That schoolmaster should have looked, not at my drawings but at my hands. And I still believe I've got as good a pair of hands for holding a plough as anybody sitting here in this voorkamer."

Diederick Kleynhans suddenly did not sound tired, anymore.

Shopkeeper in his store at Ramoutsa, Bechuanaland (Botswana). January 1966

Cemetery, Nietverdiend. December 1964

Herman Charles Bosman was born near Cape Town in 1905, but spent most of his life in the Transvaal. In 1926 he was posted as a novice teacher to a farm school in the Marico District. His spell at the school was cut short when, during a vacation to the family home in Johannesburg, he shot and killed his stepbrother. Initially sentenced to hang, his sentence was commuted to life imprisonment and he was eventually paroled in 1930, having served four years.

After a period working as a journalist in London, he returned to South Africa in 1940 and was thereafter employed on various magazines and newspapers. *Jacaranda in the Night*, a novel, and a collection of Oom Schalk Lourens stories, *Mafeking Road*, both appeared in 1947. His gaol memoir, *Cold Stone Jug*, followed in 1949. A year later he returned to the Marico, the region that had made him famous, in a series of sketches written weekly for *The Forum* under the rubric "In die Voorkamer". At the time he was a proofreader on *The Sunday Express* and working on *Willemsdorp* (published only posthumously in 1977). Bosman died in 1951.

A selection of the Voorkamer sketches first reappeared (after their initial publication in *The Forum* in 1950 and 1951) in *Jurie Steyn's Post Office* and *A Bekkersdal Marathon* (both 1971), edited by Lionel Abrahams, but the entire sequence was printed for the first time, unexpurgated and in the original order, as *Idle Talk: Voorkamer Stories I* (1999) and *Homecoming: Voorkamer Stories II* (2005), edited by Craig MacKenzie for the Anniversary Edition. The Voorkamer stories appear here in one volume – and also in their entirety and in sequence – for the first time.

Craig MacKenzie has edited 10 volumes of Bosman's stories, seven of which were part of the Anniversary Edition of Bosman's works, a project that he undertook with Stephen Gray between 1997 and 2005. He is Professor of English at the University of Johannesburg.

David Goldblatt was born in Randfontein in 1930, attended Krugersdorp High School and later studied part-time to obtain his B Com degree. At age 33 he started to work as a professional photographer. His first book was *On the Mines* (1972), with Nadine Gordimer, and was followed by *Some Afrikaners Photographed* (1975); thereafter he went on to establish himself as the pre-eminent photographer of South African people, structures and landscapes. In 1964 he went on the Bosman trail, visiting the Marico and photographing people and places Bosman knew in the 1920s, which he published as "Bosman's Bosveld" in *The S. A. Tatler* in February 1965 (reproduced in *The Illustrated Bosman*, 1985). Previously unpublished items from that collection are used here. Goldblatt's photographic images also adorn the covers of nine of the 14-volume Anniversary Edition of Herman Charles Bosman.